W9-BNM-736

Praise for *Firebrand*

"Gripping . . . alive with expertly drawn details."
—*RT Book Reviews*

"Once a year, a new novelist really blows
me away. Last year it was Suzanne Collins
with *The Hunger Games*. . . . This year
it's Gillian Philip's *Firebrand*. . . . A fantastically
violent, utterly thrilling tale . . . *Firebrand*
is one of the very best. . . . Philip's clear prose
is as fiery as whiskey. . . . The best
fantasy novel of 2010."

—*The Sunday Times* (U.K.)

"Philip has created an utterly believable other
world, where male and female are equals in arms.
It is often stark and brutal but with moments
of heartbreaking beauty."

—*The Guardian* (U.K.)

FIREBRAND

REBEL ANGELS
BOOK ONE

GILLIAN PHILIP

TOR® fantasy

A TOM DOHERTY ASSOCIATES BOOK • NEW YORK

This is a work of fiction. All of the characters, organizations, and events portrayed in this novel are either products of the author's imagination or are used fictitiously.

FIREBRAND

Copyright © 2010 by Gillian Philip

A Tor Book
Published by Tom Doherty Associates, LLC
175 Fifth Avenue
New York, NY 10010

www.tor-forge.com

Tor® is a registered trademark of Tom Doherty Associates, LLC.

ISBN 978-0-7653-6941-3

Tor books may be purchased for educational, business, or promotional use. For information on bulk purchases, please contact Macmillan Corporate and Premium Sales Department at 1-800-221-7945, extension 5442, or write specialmarkets@macmillan.com.

Originally published in Great Britain in 2010 by Strident Publishing Ltd.

First U.S. Edition: February 2013
First U.S. Mass Market Edition: October 2013

Printed in the United States of America

0 9 8 7 6 5 4 3 2 1

For Lucy and Jamie, as always
and for Cherry Allsopp, with love

THANKS

A lot of people kept me going when Seth MacGregor was being his ever-difficult self, and I'm hugely grateful to everyone who read the manuscript and gave advice—in particular to Hilary Johnson, Michael Malone, Ruth Howell and Elaine Reid. Special thanks, though, are due to Linda Gillard, who rescued me from the pit of despond (and Seth from the fire) at a bad moment.

I'm indebted to Catherine Czerkawska for help with historical research, and for her permission to use a quote from her play *The Secret Commonwealth*. David Worthington pointed me in the right direction for details of Scottish rural history.

Some very kind Gaelic speakers helped me out. However, the Sithe have been living in another world for many centuries and have played fast and loose with a beautiful language—so any inaccuracies, inconsistencies and plain old errors are entirely down to them (oh, and to me). I should add that in his lazy way, Seth tends to anglicise when he can get away with it.

I'm so grateful to the wonderful people at Tor Publishing—especially Whitney, Alexis and Amy. Thank you all so much—meeting you in Tor's New York office was like stepping over the veil (in a good direction).

Finally, as always, I thank Ian, Jamie and Lucy for their endless patient tolerance while I've been away with the faeries. I owe one of you many drinks, and the other two an awful lot of Happy Meals and cinema visits. (Within reason.) You're the tops.

This dabbling with the other world
is a perilous undertaking.
And I have risked a glamour which can
only be exorcised by fire, by cold iron.

Catherine Czerkawska
The Secret Commonwealth

FIREBRAND

The courtyard stinks of animals and muck and human waste. And wasted humans, I can't help thinking, because beneath the stench and the louring sunset sky lies the taint of death, like a stain that can't be shifted. My brother isn't the first to die here, and he won't be the last.

I rub my filthy arm across my nose, and then across my eyes because they're blurred and I can't see properly. Then I shut them altogether and curl up against the parapet. I want to be a hundred miles away, but what use would I be to Conal then? Anyway, the hideous weight of the crossbow in my arms can't be ignored. I hate crossbows, I always have: a horrible weapon, brutal and distant, and I've never liked to touch them or even look at them. It's as if I was born knowing I've an appointment with one that I'm not going to want to keep.

I sniff and rub my eyes again, wishing I could be more of a man, wishing I wasn't so afraid. I'm sixteen years old, more than old enough to kill and die, a lot older than I was when I watched my father die, hacked almost to bits and still scrabbling for a last breath. His death couldn't be avoided and neither can this one. What's the point of premature grief?

My eyes jerk open. A clattering rattle of wheels on flagstones, and I glance over my shoulder. This is a good vantage point, but I'll likely be seen as soon as I fire, and I'll have to be fast to get down the tower walls and away. I can't think about that, not now. The mob that so far has been muted, only muttering with the day's excitement, now raise their voices as one, turning as if by black magic into a single howling beast. I make myself look. And I gasp.

That isn't my brother, it can't be. That is not Cù Chaorach, Hound of the Sheep, Father of his Clann. He's never been so thin. His face is half-blackened and bloody, his hair is gone, sheared roughly off. His shirt is ripped and frayed and through the gashes in the linen I can see the bloody marks of a lash on his back.

Oh, no. *No.* The girl is with Conal. She can't be any older than me, and she's taken a few beatings too, poor cow. I've never seen such bruised terror in a human face, and she is weeping uncontrollably. Their hands are bound but Conal's shoulder is pressed hard against hers, and when they're yanked apart and thrust down from the cart, he quickly recovers his footing and presses close to her once more. There's a dark stain on her filthy grey shift: she's wet herself. And my brother, the great noble fool, is all concern for her, when she's one of them, and in slightly altered circumstances she'd have been howling at him with the rest of the mob.

He turns his face to hers, his lips move. It's all rubbish, probably. He's telling her it'll be over quickly, she needn't be scared. The liar.

Gods, Conal, you're going to want me to fire twice. Do I have time?

I can't do this alone, I was never any use without him. I can't stop myself calling out to him.

~ *Conal!*

Conal goes very still, but he doesn't look up. As he whispers to the girl once more a smile spreads across his wounded face, a smile of pure happiness.

~ *Seth!*

'Look at the warlock, he's grinning!' Something flies out of the crowd and strikes Conal's cheekbone, making him stagger. 'Happy, scum? You'll be seeing your Master soon!'

'Aye, not soon enough!' Raucous laughter. 'See if he smiles when he's burning!'

'The Satan-spawn won't smile when he's burning in Hell!'

Hatred rushes over me in such a hot violent tide I'm dizzy with it. It's the tail-end of the sixteenth century, for gods' sake: when do these people plan to evolve?

My fingers tighten on the crossbow. Then I can feel his mind inside mine, soothing, reassuring, the way it's been since I was a feral snarling infant and he tamed me.

~ *Murlainn. Little brother. Don't lose your focus!*

~ *Conal, I can't fire twice! I haven't time!*

~ *Yes, you have. Don't panic.* Turning his face briefly to the girl, Conal manages to kiss her hacked and shorn scalp before she is yanked away and hauled up onto the pile of firewood.

~ *She's nothing to us. She's one of them!*

Conal's head angles very slightly upwards, as if he'd like to look right at me and give me a real piece of his mind. I see the flicker of a smile.

~ *She has a name, Seth.*

I don't want to know. I don't want to know her damned name. I'm here for Conal.

~ *Catriona. Her name's Catriona.* His eyes almost find mine across the hazy dusk, and he half-smiles. And with that he knows I'll do it. He must have known I'd do it anyway. I'd do anything for him.

He's dragged up behind her and bound to the same stake, ropes tightened around them both. He strains his fingers enough to touch the girl's, and he's speaking to her again, but I doubt she can hear him above the noise of the baying crowd. The pale-eyed priest steps forward, robes billowing, a black crow hungry for carrion. He stays in the long shadow of the courtyard wall; I notice that. Smiling, he raises his bible.

~ *Be calm, Seth. Hands steady, both eyes open, remember.*

~ *Conal, I . . .*

~ *I love you, little brother. I'll see you again, I promise.*

Oh, no, we'll never meet again. I stare down at the priest, his ringing declamations of hatred raised above the yells of the mob. Not in that devil's heaven. It doesn't exist, and worse, there's no hell for him to go to after he's died screaming at my hands.

That's *my* promise, Cù Chaorach.

But I don't let Conal hear it. I block it coldly away, because he wouldn't approve, even now. My hands are steady now; my hatred helps a lot. I'm glad I don't have time to shoot the priest as well. A bolt to the heart would be too fast.

~ *I love you, Cù Chaorach. I'm sorry.*

~ *I'm glad you're here. Don't be sorry. Be quick.*

I roll onto my stomach. I won't be seen; I do have time. No one's looking upwards toward my hiding place, no one wants to miss a moment of the spectacle. Probably they'll take a while to realise what's happened in the confusion. I may hate crossbows but I'm good with them: he taught me himself. I can get in two shots. I can reload, fire, and still get away. *Yes.*

I level my gaze and aim. The girl first, so she'll know nothing, and so Conal will know I've done it and be pleased with me.

And then, Conal. My brother, my friend, my Captain. My father in every way that ever mattered. *Oh, please, you nonexistent gods, please give me the strength.*

Two men step from behind the priest, blazing torches held high.

That's it. I blink away the sweat and the tears and the terror. And my mind is as cold as my heart as I tighten my finger on the trigger.

PART ONE

GHOST

1

You deal with him.

That was the first and last communication my mother ever had with my father about me. My father was more surprised than angry when my mother's emissary rode through the dun gates with a sullen brat on a pony behind him and an expression of pained endurance on his face. The man had ridden three days with me and I'd made sure they were the longest three days of his life. He was so glad to see the back of me, he didn't even take bed and board from Griogair for the night; he stayed for one meal and a very stiff drink, then turned right round and rode back the way he came. I hope Lilith made it worth his while.

Even later my father was never angry about it. He wasn't involved enough for that; at most he was mildly irritated. Deep down I'm sure he wasn't convinced of my existence, that he thought I was just one more of Lilith's illusions.

My stepmother believed in me, all right. I used to

feel Leonora's cold blue gaze like frost on my skin, and if I looked up, she wouldn't look away. She was the only one who didn't. The rest of the clann averted their eyes, as if I was a colossal embarrassment. Well, that's what I was, so as soon as it became clear Griogair wasn't going to embrace me as his long-lost heir, they adopted the policy of pretending I didn't exist. The small band of children took more of an interest, the older ones freezing me out or taunting me at best, and giving me thrashings at worst. The younger ones ran from me: I made sure they did.

But my stepmother didn't bully me or fear me or ignore me. She watched me. I thought it quite likely she'd eventually kill me, but I never could read Leonora's eyes, let alone her mind. It wasn't that she felt threatened by me; she wasn't threatened by anyone. I'd watched her and my father together and I'm sure he never smiled at my mother like that, or touched her so gently, or spoke so tenderly. Certainly he never treated me that way. If he caught sight of me his brow would furrow and he'd set his teeth and look exasperated, as if I was a reminder of some great mistake, a souvenir he couldn't get rid of. Leonora? All I could ever make out in her was pity and a degree of contempt, and I hated her for it. I'd have liked to hate my father too, but I couldn't. All I ever wanted was his love, or if I couldn't have that, his notice would do.

I never had a chance.

But my mother sent me back to him anyway. She was living at court by then, an adviser to the queen: oh, her exile had brought her up in the world. From being Griogair Dubh's afterthought lover, she'd risen to be one of the most powerful courtiers in Kate NicNiven's halls. What she didn't need was a truculent attention-seeking toe-rag who was always getting into trouble, calling the captains names and the courtiers worse ones, getting thrashed on a regular basis and generally being an embarrassment. So she sent me back to Griogair.

I liked it better with my father anyway. The women of our race don't do motherhood well, it's a known fact, so I didn't really miss Lilith, not after a while. Sithe women make wonderful fighters, wise and wily counsellors. If they're healers or smiths they do it well; when they're witches they excel at witchcraft. What they do not excel at is motherhood. It's not something that happens easily, we're not a fertile race; maybe that's where those ridiculous stories come from, the ones about us being baby-stealers. Let me tell you, our women can barely tolerate their own brats, let alone someone else's. Our women don't yearn for children, because what's the point mourning for centuries over something that may never happen? Instead they harden themselves, and even if they do breed they never quite shake off that hardness. Anyway, some of them don't even take lovers, the loss of their virginity is so physically painful. Must be, to stay loverless for centuries.

Well, my mother must have got over that problem. She had plenty of lovers, though what she wanted more than anything was to be Griogair's bound lover and that was something she'd never get for all her wiles, because he'd bound himself to Leonora decades before Lilith came along. When it became clear I wasn't going to advance her cause in any way, Lilith lost interest in me altogether.

Which was fine by me. Being sent away from Kate NicNiven's labyrinthine caverns was like breathing for the first time, and there was no-one I missed from her pale and haughty court. There had been even fewer children underground than there were above it, but anyway, I needed neither friends nor mother. At my father's dun I was content to skulk in the shadows and watch; that way I could see how the fighters trained, how the children scrapped and competed, how the strange and complex hierarchies of dun life operated. There were daredevil games on horseback that I might have liked to join, and when the wild racing music played on moonlit nights I used to half-wish I could throw myself into the dance with the rest of them. But it was fine, I was fed and clothed and relatively safe, and I was learning a lot—not that anybody made me study, or even tried to make me work the fields or learn a practical skill. My education was self-inflicted and unconventional, but I knew that the lessons would come in useful for the rest of my life. The most useful of them was the one I learned first: I was responsible for myself. In life and death you're on your own, and I knew that better than any of my peers.

It seems stupid now that I looked forward so much to living with my father. I must have had some childish romantic picture in my head, me and him doing father-son things together, fighting and hunting and laughing and confiding.

But it turned out he already had a son, a perfect one, so he didn't need another.

2

I was fishing that morning. This was what I liked best about living in my father's dun: it was in the open air. I'd hated Kate's underground caverns. They were beautiful, breathtaking, but lightless. You couldn't see the sky.

At my father's dun there was sky to spare. The fortress rambled across a rocky headland, its stone walls falling sheer to the sea on its western side. It was as much a part of the land as the great grey rocks that jutted from the earth, mottled with yellow lichen, hacked and split by the weather of aeons. To the north and south were blue bays; inland was the machair, wild with flowers, and an expanse of moorland so huge it blurred to a haze at the horizon. I had no sooner seen it than I loved it and knew that I'd die here.

The sooner the better, if you asked my new clann.

I didn't care what they thought of me. Now I could run free where and when I liked; I had no boundaries, no limits. I could swim and fish and snare rabbits; I could spend the whole day taming a wounded falcon while I ate what I found or caught. It was a loveless existence, but so what? I was eight years old and I was free for the first time in my life. Nobody knew or cared what I did or where I was. It was a kind of heaven and a kind of hell, but I fixed my mind on the heaven part and it was fine, it was a good enough life for a boy who wasn't meant to be born.

On the first day of my twelfth month in the dun, my life as a ghost ended.

That summer day, the hours stretched ahead of me like a gift, sunlit and lazy. The lochan on the moor was still and steel-blue: not a good day for fishing, but I had nothing better to do with my time. Was there anything better? My ribs still hurt from my last beating, but my nose had stopped bleeding and I had the blood of my enemies on my own knuckles, their skin under my fingernails, and I'd cost one of them a tooth. My pride was intact and I knew it always would be. I was bruised and battered but the breeze was warm on my skin, the heather smelt of honey, and I was happy.

I'd been teasing that trout for almost an hour. I didn't use my mind. It's hard and boring to enter the mind of a fish, and anyway, I liked the challenge. This was a cunning old one; plenty of people had tried and failed to catch him, and I wanted to be the one to get him. I had some vague notion of presenting him to my father, seeing Griogair's eyes light up with pleasure and maybe a little respect.

So there I was, on my stomach in the scratchy heather, letting my fingertips graze the still surface of the lochan, singing softly to my trout. He was sleepy and fat among the weeds, and the water so brown and cool that I longed to curl my fingers round his sleek body, but I knew I mustn't rush it. When I let my forefinger trail a delicate line along his spine, and he didn't stir, I knew I had him. Gripping him firmly, I tossed him out of the water with a yell of triumph.

He floundered on the grey rock, looking stunned and a little betrayed. My delight faded as I stared down at his gasping, flopping body. Now he didn't look so fine.

I thought about my father again. This morning I'd seen him ride back from a dawn hunt with my half-brother, a sleek roebuck slung across their garron's back. This half-brother had returned to the dun a month earlier, from secondment to another clann seventy miles to the north, but since his arrival he'd shown no interest in me. Well, the contempt was mutual.

As they rode right past me the two of them were laughing together, easy companions, and you could see the pride burning in Griogair's eyes when he looked at Conal, the love nearly choking him. I half-wished it would. Griogair had barely registered me there, but Conal's gaze had slewed towards me, unreadable. He didn't try to get into my mind—that's how far I was beneath him—and I'd no intention of going near his, even if he'd let me. I didn't want to read his scorn and superiority, his first-born arrogance. I did notice there was only one arrow missing from his quiver. He'd got that buck first shot, and it was a beauty.

A fish? My father wasn't going to care a damn for a fish.

I picked up a stone to stun it, but once I'd hit its head I found I couldn't stop. I went on smashing the stone into the pathetic creature long after I'd put it out of its misery. There was translucent flesh all over the rock, and bits of skin and shattered pale bone. Still I went on pounding, till I began to wonder how I'd ever stop.

'Well, don't take it out on the fish.'

I leaped to my feet, the stone clutched in my fist and raised to strike.

Conal was watching me from a rock outcrop, barely six feet away, his arms resting casually on his knees. Gods, how I hated him. He was everything I wasn't. Grown-up, for a start: he had to be more than a hundred years older than me. He had his mother's dark blond hair, cut short but unruly, and Griogair's light grey eyes, dancing with laughter. He had everything of Griogair's, not least his love and trust. And all I had was Griogair's black hair, like the villain I knew I was destined to be. I decided then and there that I'd grow it long.

Conal was wearing his sword on his back, his silver-embossed sword that Griogair had had made for him, and I wondered if he'd come here to kill me. I wondered if the prospect bothered me that much, and I decided that it did. My fingers tightened on the stone. I'd damn well hurt him first.

'Go away,' I snapped.

He shrugged lightly. 'But this isn't your rock. And I like it here.'

'Don't look at me,' I snarled, raising my stone a little higher.

Sighing, he turned himself round on the boulder so that his back was to me. 'Better?'

No. Worse. I went on glaring my hatred at him. The

sword was a beautiful thing, and more than beautiful. I'd seen Conal wield it in practice, I'd seen how it sang in the air, light and fast as his thought, perfectly balanced on its tang, answering him like his own hand. My father, I knew suddenly, would never give me anything like that. It didn't matter how hard I tried, I would never be his son. Not really.

'But you're my brother,' murmured Conal.

'That means you get to lord it over me, does it?'

'No.' He glanced over his shoulder but didn't quite look at me. 'It means I'd like to know you. And it means that what I want . . . it isn't the same as what Griogair wants.'

'He wants me to go away.'

That silenced him. He didn't even bother to contradict me, because he knew it was true.

'I don't,' he said at last.

Hot tears spilled out of my eyes, and the humiliation made me loathe him even more. 'Shut up!'

'Seth . . .'

'Don't call me that!' My words got all tangled up in my tears.

'Isn't that your name?'

I sniffed violently. I wanted to hit him with the stone. I wanted to hit him like I'd hit the fish, till he didn't exist any more. Then he'd know how it felt. My face was all tears and snot, like some infant, streaked with the dried blood from my nose.

'Go ahead,' he said.

I stared at the back of his head.

'Preferably not with the rock,' he added, 'but go ahead and hit me.'

I don't know why I dropped the stone. I could just
have used it anyway, but I did drop it. Before I could
think any harder I ran at him, and struck him hard on
the side of his face. Then, like a coward, I ran away
again and crouched, ready to bolt for my life.

Slowly, a little stunned, he put his hand to his face. I
knew I'd hurt him and if he pretended I hadn't, I promised myself I'd hate him forever. But he shook his head
slightly, wincing as he touched his cheekbone.

'Strong,' he murmured. 'You're strong.'

'I hate you,' I said.

'I know. Can I turn round yet?'

'No!' I didn't want him to see the fresh tears brim-
ming in my eyes.

'Did that make you feel better?'

'Yes,' I lied.

'Good.'

I could tell he meant it. He wasn't trying to teach me
some stupid moral lesson about the futility of violence.
He actually just wanted me to feel better.

'Your mother had my mother exiled,' I spat, as much
to remind myself as him.

Shrugging very slightly, Conal half-turned. 'Well,' he
said, a smile just creasing the corner of his mouth.
'Your mother did try to poison my mother.'

I slumped down into the heather and gnawed on my
knuckle for a while. The silence between us was almost
companionable. Almost. If I hadn't been on the verge
of tears I'd have been closer to contentment then than
I'd ever been, just sitting there in his company. I had to
keep reminding myself he was Griogair's first-born,
the only one my father loved, the one who'd made me

superfluous before I was even conceived. If he tried to
tell me now he'd be my friend, I'd pick up the stone
again and kill him.

After a while he said, 'Do you know Sionnach Mac-
Neil?'

I did, but I said nothing. He was a nice enough boy,
about my age, one of the few human beings in the dun
who'd acknowledged my existence, one of the few
children who didn't torment me. If I was the kind of
child who ever needed a friend, I remember thinking
he might do.

'He knows where there's a fox den, up in the pinewood,' Conal went on. 'He'll take you up there if you
want.'

'Who says?' I snapped.

'He did.'

'All right,' I said, because I could think of no other
answer.

'So can I turn round yet?'

'All right.' Quickly I rubbed my nose on my sleeve.

So he turned and looked at me. I didn't want him to
smile at me, and he didn't. Instead he reached out a
hand to me, simple as that.

Biting my lip hard, I looked at his hand. And then I
took it, simple as *that*.

Then Conal did smile. But by then I didn't mind too
much.

So after that, I had at least one friend in the dun. Sionnach liked the things I liked, and we spent most of every day together, and being Sionnach's friend gave me

a bit more status, since his father was Griogair's second-in-command; Niall Mor MacIain was actually kinder to me than my own father. And Conal, while keeping a distance that was entirely my choice, slowly made me part of the clann; so slowly and gently, in fact, that neither I nor the clann noticed the moment when I stopped being Griogair's unwanted mistake and became one of them.

Now, when he rode into the dun with Griogair, from a hunt or a patrol or a diplomatic visit to Kate, Conal would say sharply ~ *Athair! Father!* That would be enough to make Griogair start, and look at me, and almost smile. It was all I ever got but it was more than I'd grown to expect. Conal would reach down a hand and pull me up onto his ferocious black horse—and sometimes Sionnach too—right in front of the whole clann. Then I'd just about burst with pride. I wasn't Griogair's son, not in any true sense, but look at me! Look at me, you dogs that used to sneer at me and kick me and ignore me: I'm Conal MacGregor's *brother!*

It was all I'd ever be, but by then, it was more than enough. So one night I went to bed still believing I hated him, because I'd planned always to hate him. And in the morning I woke up knowing that I loved him. If Griogair wouldn't be my father, Conal would, and I would love him till the day I died. And he hadn't even had to twist my mind.

3

By the time I was eleven, I was in love in a different way. Gradually I'd made other friends, though not many: there was Feorag, a year younger than me and my partner in crimes that Sionnach refused even to contemplate; there was Orach, a quiet golden-haired girl who shot like a dream, and who tended to follow me around though she rarely spoke. I liked her company, and I enjoyed her devotion, and a year or two later, in the cool darkness of the sea-caves beyond the bay, we stripped each other of virginity.

I've loved a few women: loved them honestly and intensely and with all my heart. Many more I've loved with my body but only half my heart. Sithe life is too long for whole-hearted love. A heart can only break so many times. I'm not saying it fails entirely: just that it mends the wrong way. It warps. It's stitched together loose and askew and it doesn't work as it should.

If I'd known that earlier, I'd have been more careful with it.

Orach was my first love, my always-occasional love, the love and comfort of half my life. She was there when other loves left, when other loves died. She was there till another came along, as unexpected and stunning as a freshwater spring in frozen tundra.

But that was my last love, and far too many centuries in my future. Back in my stupid youth, and Orach notwithstanding, my angry young heart belonged to Eili MacNeil.

She was Sionnach's twin, an imperious beautiful girl who treated me with cool kindness. She had brown eyes to drown in, and dark red hair that she cut roughly short with a dagger, and she was more of a tomboy even than the other young girls of the clann: all she lived for was swordplay, and archery, and horse races on the machair.

And Conal.

Eili followed my brother around like a puppy, and this was the degree of her obsession: the only reason she cut her hair short was to be like him. I didn't take her crush seriously, though. In a way it made me happy, because being Conal's brother, but the same age as Eili, seemed to me an irrefutable advantage. The more I saw of Eili the more I loved her, and it didn't matter to me that she was devoted to Conal. After all, so was I: we had that in common. And I looked like Conal, despite my black hair; I even fought like him, because he was teaching me swordplay whenever he could. I knew that one day she would simply stop loving him and start loving me instead, and after all, we were pure-blooded Sithe. If we didn't have all the time in the world, we had as much of it as anyone could want.

How did it never occur to me that in long, long lives, age comes to mean nothing?

But in childhood, Sionnach and Eili and I were the best of friends. Whatever other children came into our orbit, it always came down to the three of us. We fought and rode and played and hunted together, and dogged Conal's footsteps when he was around the dun, and pestered the cooks and the stablehands and the smiths till they were half-demented with us. Generally, in other words, we were children.

It was the swordsmith Raineach I'd gone to annoy, one autumn day just after I turned twelve. I liked the woman, surly as she was, and I admired the way she worked, and I was hoping that one day she'd make me the sword I wanted, so I sucked up to her relentlessly. She knew that was what I was doing, but she put up with it, because she liked me as much as I liked her. I think when Raineach was young she'd been an outcast too. We can always recognise one another. It's something feral in the eyes.

That day, as soon as I stepped from the bright morning chill into the dark wall of roaring heat that was her workshop, she raised her eyes from the half-made weapon hissing in the long water trough, gave me a nod, then jerked her head very slightly towards a corner. I thought she was palming me off on her two sons, both good company but younger than me. There was no sign of them. Instead Eili was there, intent on a small piece of silver that she was twisting with pliers. Pushing sweaty spikes of hair out of her eyes she licked her lips, fixated on the work. Raineach's three-year-old stepdaughter stood watching every move of her hands, dark eyes wide and mouth open.

Trying not to go straight to Eili's side, I folded my arms and watched the smith beat the soldered steel, the razor hard strips to the softer core.

'Another sword?' I said hopefully.

'Aye,' said Raineach darkly. 'Not for you, greenarse.' She thrust it back into the furnace.

'Who, then?'

'Not that it's any of your business.'

'No, but who?'

'Eorna.'

'Why does Eorna need another sword?' I said resentfully.

With a sigh of exasperation, she whipped the annealed metal from the furnace, then wiped sweat off her face with her bare forearm. 'Don't you keep your cloddish ears open? You know fine Alasdair Kilrevin's restless. Kate expects trouble from him, and she expects your father to put him back in his box. Happens every decade or so. Kilrevin gets bored if he can't do some killing now and again. The bastard needs to let off steam.'

'Good,' I said hopefully. 'Can I fight?'

'You, greenarse? Don't make me laugh.' She laughed anyway.

'I'm good enough.'

'You're a fumbling beginner and you're too damn short. Look at your brother. When you're as tall as he is and half as good with a sword, then you can fight.' She slammed her hammer onto the steel, fountaining white-hot sparks.

Scowling, I turned on my heel, hoping Eili hadn't overheard that. Did the sharp-tongued cow have to say it so loud? It was pretty rich coming from Raineach, who wasn't so tall herself: she was small and slender, elfin-faced, and you'd never have thought from looking at her that she had the power in her arms to forge swords.

Eili remained hunched over her workbench till I was beside her, and only then did she look up with a wry smile. Her brown eyes were sympathetic. Hell: she'd heard Raineach's snide remark. The little girl shrank back behind her, mistrustful, but Eili tutted.

'Come on. He doesn't bite, believe it or not.'

I bared my teeth and gnashed them, and the child giggled.

I stuck out my tongue, and she giggled again, and stuck hers out in return.

'So short I can't even scare a midget like you,' I said.

'Take no notice of Raineach,' said Eili softly. 'She doesn't mean it, it's the way she is.'

'Course,' I said, as if I didn't much care. 'What's that?'

In fact I could see what it was. She had twisted thick silver wire into a rope, and now she was coaxing it into a torque, the size that would fit a wrist. It was a basic piece, but she'd made it well, and she was taking enormous care to shape the curve of it just right. With tongs she softened it briefly in the small stone forge, then cooled it in a bowl and examined it critically before taking the little hammer to it once more. On the workbench lay two spherical knots of silver, ready to be soldered to the ends of the torque. Eili wasn't keen on delicate ornamental silverwork; it was weapons-smithing that interested her. This must be a special project, and she must have been working on it for a while.

She hadn't answered my question. Maybe she thought it was a stupid one. Or maybe . . .

My heart clenched with an aching hope. I didn't have any jewellery to wear, not so much as a ring, and she'd commented on that more than once. Sionnach wore a wrist torque, and I'd admired it before, in Eili's presence. Biting my lip, I decided not to ask again, but my heart slammed my ribs when I saw the ferocious care she was putting into the thing, when I remembered her kind smile and her warm eyes as she turned to me.

Perennial optimist, that was me.

4

I snapped awake to black winter stillness. I don't know what time it was: either late or incredibly early. Close by my room there were footsteps, and murmurs, but I knew they hadn't woken me. Something else had, like a claw scraping lightly down the nape of my neck, but when I slapped my hand at the spot, there was nothing there: no insect, no spider. No dream-monster even, because I knew what I'd felt was real. Instantly I felt a hungry curiosity and the kick of adrenalin.

I listened hard. Nobody had any business being awake at that hour. Yes, if they'd been giggling with drink, or high on music or love. But night walkers had no business talking that way, quiet and intent. The footsteps weren't aimless; they were heading for the lower halls of the dun and the antechamber to Griogair and Leonora's rooms. They were the light clicking steps of women, and I knew the voices well, because I'd heard them often enough for the first seven years of my life: Kate, and Lilith.

That morning our queen had ridden into the dun, the skirts of her long silk coat draped over her mare's chestnut haunches like a robe, my mother at her side, and a detachment of fighters at her back. Kate hadn't announced her arrival: she hadn't had to. Leonora had felt her coming.

I watched her arrival—and my mother's—from the parapet. I'd been half-hiding, wondering if Lilith's gaze would roam the courtyard in search of me, flicker eagerly over the faces of the clann. I shouldn't have worried: Lilith had eyes only for Griogair. They glittered, riveted on his austere beauty. Her own skin almost glowed. What a beautiful pair of lovers they must have made. But either Griogair couldn't feel her adoration, or he was ignoring it. He didn't so much as look at his old lover.

Leonora did.

My father took Kate's hand as she slipped elegantly from her horse's back, and kissed it, then pressed it to his forehead. There was respect but no humility in the gesture. He was, after all, Captain of his own dun. When Kate offered her cheek, he kissed that too, and smiled his fierce formal smile. The fierceness made it no less charming. Ah, despite my best efforts, my father still fascinated me.

It seemed to be no more than a friendly visit. I didn't think for a second I'd be invited to sit near my father at supper, and I wasn't, but as far as I could make out the conversation at the top table was casual, light and funny. The fighting cadres got along famously, as well they might; those who weren't friends or acquaintances were at least distantly related. There was rivalry concerning horses, weapon skills, speed and dogs and hawks, but it didn't even come close to blows. It felt more like a festival than diplomacy. Orach huddled into me, passing on gossip and making me laugh, and high on a party and on one another, we fought all comers among the other clann children and beat them.

Half the fighters ended up bedding each other, and across loyalties too. By sundown Conal's arm was draped round a redhead I remembered from Kate's caverns, one I used to insult before running, fast. He'd beaten her three hours earlier in a swordplay bout—oh, the heat and the sweat and the ferocity—but he'd loved the fight in her and had presented her with an elaborate silver arm ring by way of a compliment. Now, curled against him, she had a look that was half smug, half lustful.

'Griogair!' yelled one of Kate's fighters. 'Send Cù Chaorach to deal with Kilrevin next time. The brute would never show his face again.'

Griogair smiled thinly. 'Alasdair Kilrevin's mine. I need the exercise once in a while.'

Orach dug me proudly in the ribs, and the hall echoed with laughter.

'You let him off lightly,' growled a voice. 'Every time. He needs killing.'

Griogair wasn't used to being criticised about Kilrevin, and for a moment he only stared in silence at the speaker. The surly-faced lieutenant sitting in the shadows had had one too many whiskies, and Griogair obviously decided it wasn't worth a quarrel. Kate was watching the drinker too, and I could not decipher the expression on her face.

'He kills for the sake of it,' the lieutenant said. 'He kills for pleasure, and the slower the better. I saw the last settlement he routed. I was there to clear the corpses.' He took another swig of whisky. 'Give Kate his head.'

Kate laughed lightly. 'Now, what would I want with such a thing?'

Griogair's smile had grown tighter. 'Anyone can tell atrocity stories.'

'Are you saying I'm a liar?'

'Hey.' Conal's smile took in both men. 'It's late. It isn't the time for this talk.'

'It's past time for it,' snarled the drinker. 'Kilrevin's a thug and a bandit.'

'And no worse than he ever was,' shrugged Conal, running a hand through the redhead's braided hair to loosen it. 'He keeps the Lammyr at bay beyond the borders, doesn't he? You want that dirty job yourself?'

'That's enough,' said Leonora, and her cool quiet voice was enough to shut them all up. 'You were right the first time, Cù Chaorach: this isn't the time. Righil! Carraig! Broc! I thought you'd give us music, but perhaps you're too drunk?'

That was a challenge they wouldn't let go, so bleak talk of thugs and Lammyr gave way, as it should, to fiddle and bodhran. I didn't dance with Orach, though I loved the furious beat. I waited for my own moment, when the dancers tired, and the drummers eased their sweating rhythm.

The first time I sang—I think I was ten—I did it out of bloody-mindedness more than anything. Convention demanded they shut up and listen to a singer, which made a pleasant change, and I wasn't shy. But as it turned out, I could sing quite well. I didn't have a sweet or a pure voice—it hadn't broken by then, though there was already something rough-edged about it, raw and wild—but for some reason the clann liked it. From that first night and the first few notes, they let me sing. They'd say nothing afterwards, but I'd know from their fascinated eyes and their tense bodies that while I kept my song going, they were mine to entrance.

It was the same the night Kate and my mother came to the dun. As a single bow drew a long sad melody out of a single fiddle, I lifted my head in my shadowy corner and sang. And one by one, they shut up and listened.

I didn't want centre-stage; I didn't need their applause. Leaning casually in my corner, arms folded, I sang a sad and angry war-lament. Orach leaned on her fists and listened, entranced. Griogair watched me, silent. Conal smiled, one arm tightening around his redhead. When I finished my song I pushed myself away from the wall and walked back to Orach, not waiting for approval that would never come. Sure enough, the conversation swelled again almost instantly. But I'd held them all spellbound for long minutes, and I felt a violent screw-you pleasure at it, and anyway singing made me high. It always did. I knew I wouldn't sleep well.

Sure enough I lay awake for an age after the ceilidh died, my mind buzzing, wishing Orach was with me. The sleep that eventually came was light, the sound and movement of strangers more than enough to penetrate it.

I sat up, listening, frowning. My head was clear, but I was surprised anyone else's was. Clearly I'd misread something during the evening, and that irritated and intrigued me. Of course I was going to get up and investigate. Who wouldn't?

Anyone with half a brain, I suppose.

I was alone, and just as well. You can't skulk and prowl with a partner, not without getting caught. I knew this by instinct and I'd proved it to myself by taking Feorag with me once or twice, just for fun. He wasn't stupid and he wasn't clumsy; he just didn't understand the importance of not being seen. He grew bored, breathed or moved at the wrong moment, or simply didn't think it mattered a damn if some guard caught us eavesdropping. A couple of hidings later—which I blamed entirely on Feorag and not on the guards—I stopped taking him with me. I liked Feorag. It didn't mean he was stitched to my backside, and I liked my own company better. Sionnach I could have taken, because Sionnach lived in calm silence the way he lived in his clothes: the boy wasn't even capable of excessive noise. I'd have taken Sionnach with me anywhere. It was just that Sionnach would never have been stupid enough to come.

The halls and passageways were preternaturally quiet. That felt different. On any ordinary night, and especially in the wake of a party, you'd have heard people still stumbling towards bed or a lover or another drink. I certainly expected to have to dodge sentries, not to mention the filthy-tempered Fionnaghal who ran the kitchens I had to creep past. But no-one moved, no-one stirred, no-one breathed. I didn't like it. If no-one was about, what had I heard?

I felt her before I saw her, and I went still as a stone. I'd never worked out why Leonora hadn't had me killed, and I wasn't at all sure the decision was final. I wouldn't have admitted it, back when I was young, but she scared me. The funny thing was, I think I scared her too. Not in quite the same way, of course.

It struck me that I hadn't seen the old witch since she'd demanded music in the great hall. She'd slipped away, as she often did, and now here she was, walking silently away from the kitchens. What she'd be doing there, I couldn't imagine: not indulging a late night hunger, anyway. Not unless she drank the blood of foxes or bats, because all I could smell on her was night air. I could smell Outside; I could smell the moor. She'd been out of the dun, and recently, but I was damned if I could imagine how, or why, not to mention why she'd make a detour to the food stores on her way home.

At that point I almost lost my nerve and went back to my rooms, but my luck held and she didn't sense me hiding there. Preoccupied, she dusted cobweb and earth from her embroidered coat, and passing within an arm's length of my hiding place, she walked swiftly towards the passageway and the stairs that led to the west side of the dun.

Yes, of course I should have turned back then. No, of course I didn't. She was only joining the night wanderers. Of course I was going to follow. I thought, as idiots do, that I'd die if I didn't know what was going on. And I knew my curiosity was justified when she turned the corner that opened into her anteroom, and I slipped silently after her, and I saw Lilith.

For a few mad seconds I thought it would be an assassination; then I saw the others. The anteroom was vast, and more like a network of rooms, with its alcoves and recesses and aisles. Griogair stood waiting, and so did Conal: dragged prematurely away from his red-head, poor sod. Kate sat smiling at Leonora in her deceptively vacuous way, and at her side stood my mother, impassive as a carving. On the back of an oak chair Leonora's raven companion squatted—I'd better not call it a familiar—its black eyes taking in everything and everyone. Each group was focused on the other, so it was easy enough to slink into the shadows unnoticed. I'd blocked my mind as always, but it's possible more than one of them knew I was there, crouched in the darkest corner. The bird probably knew.

Conal certainly did.

'Perhaps we could make this quick, Kate dear.' Leonora gave the queen a smile that was both sweet and fantastically patronising. 'It's been a long day.'

'Leonora, of course.' Kate returned the smile, detail for detail. 'I'll keep this simple.'

Lilith couldn't resist joining in. 'We won't keep you long, Leonora. Politics can be so terribly burdensome . . .' She didn't add *at your age*, but the thought fairly reverberated off the antechamber walls.

Griogair slumped into a carved chair, silent. He didn't look at any of the women, only at Conal. Then he looked at his fingernails. And finally, the ceiling.

'We've been waiting for you, Leonora,' said Lilith. 'I hope we didn't hurry you back?'

Leonora gave absolutely nothing away. I had to admire her.

Lilith's mouth tightened with annoyance, but she pretended she hadn't been snubbed. 'Kate has a proposal.'

'We could have heard it in the hall last night, I'm

sure,' remarked Leonora. She extended her fingers to tickle her raven's throat, and it croaked fondly.

'It's rather . . . delicate,' said Kate.

With his father's gaze somewhere else, Conal took a casual step back, resting his back against a pillar. It brought me into his sight line, or it did when he turned his head a little to the left. Now he was looking straight at me. He couldn't have *seen* me, in the suffocating darkness. But he Saw me, all right.

The expression on his face made me shiver. Tentatively I lowered my block against him, and he slapped it brutally aside.

~ *Fool. Greenarse. Stay out of sight.*

~ *Sorry . . .* I began.

~ *Out of sight,* he snapped. ~ *Or die. Get your block back up.*

I did as I was told. I felt ashamed, but brittle with curiosity. I didn't dare move a muscle, not even to rub my temple where Conal's bark had given me a throbbing headache, but I wouldn't have wanted to. What, slink away now?

Griogair was frowning at his beloved firstborn again, suspicious, but the women were still circling and biting like dogfish round bloody bait.

'Kate, dear. Why should any proposal of yours need my help?'

Shrugging lightly, Kate subsided onto a chaise. 'Because I'm not strong enough, Leonora. Not without you.'

That shut Leonora up. (Which alone made my risk worthwhile.)

'Kate has an . . . *ambitious* suggestion.' Lilith's smile

landed over Leonora's shoulder: right on Griogair, in fact. 'Have two such powerful Sithe ever coexisted at once, and at the height of their skills? There has to be a purpose to it, Leonora. And you have not just your own mind's strength, but the backing of a *magnificent* dun captain.'

Lilith wasn't even pretending to smile at Leonora now. She was looking at my father as if she'd like to rip off his clothes with her teeth. As Griogair shifted slightly in his chair, I grinned to myself.

So did Lilith.

Kate was enjoying herself too, but with a sigh she combed back her hair with her fingers and got down to business. 'So. Leonora. You know the Veil is nearing the end of its life?'

That made my breath catch. *The* Veil? The *Sgath*? The strong membrane that kept our own world separate from the occult and dangerous otherworld? The only thing that stood between us and the despised creatures on its other side?

And suddenly I knew what had wakened me: a disturbance in it. That's what I'd felt, that cat-scratch on my spine. A shuddering jerk on the Veil, as if someone had tugged hard at it, tested its strength. It wasn't something I'd felt before, because who'd do such a thing? I knew it, though; I knew it by instinct.

The Veil was a thing I could feel and touch, after all. I could play with it a little, feel its fabric between my fingertips: tug it, stroke it, hold it in my fist. That was all. There seemed no purpose to that extra sense of mine: the Veil was simply something I touched each day that was something less than physical. I thought everyone could. I must have been ten or more when I realised they couldn't. I was the only one; nobody else could feel the Veil the way I could. Except, perhaps, for Leonora, but she was a witch like my mother.

As soon as I'd thought that, I had realised my talent was witchcraft. It was witches alone who could manipulate the Veil, in their small way. And where would we be if it weren't for the ones who wove the Veil in the first place? Yes, yes, I appreciated witches, we all did, but who'd want to be one? Not me.

So I tried not to feel the Veil any more. And I kept my mouth shut about the fact that I could. Nobody needed to know. It wasn't as if I could sweep the Veil aside and see the otherworld. I couldn't tear it, or repair it: no one could. I could feel it, that was all. I certainly couldn't *harm* it. The Veil didn't have a life, it just *was*, and it always would be. Existence without it was unthinkable.

But that night, when Kate announced it was dying, Conal was the only one who looked shocked. Did he ever.

'It's failing? Why, I had no idea, Kate.' Leonora's voice dripped sarcasm. 'Is there a point to this?'

Conal interrupted, voice shaking. 'What do you mean, *the end of its life?*'

Leonora flapped her fingers dismissively. 'It has centuries left, dear. Don't fret.'

'*Centuries?*' he began, then in his horror turned to Griogair. 'Centuries isn't enough!'

'Well, of course it isn't,' said his mother irritably.

Griogair was watching Conal very intently, partly I

think so that his gaze wouldn't stray to Lilith. 'Your mother will find a means of reinforcing the Veil, Cù Chaorach. Anything else is unthinkable.'

'Unthinkable? The death of an entire world? That's one way of putting it, *athair*.' Conal stared at each of them in turn. 'Perhaps we should be thinking about it?'

'Your father's told you, dear. I already am.'

I think it stung me more than it stung Conal, the way Leonora still treated him like a little boy.

'Besides,' interrupted Kate smoothly. 'There's a third way.'

Griogair looked at her askance.

Leonora said, 'Meaning?'

Kate paused for effect, bestowing her smile on each of them in turn.

'We could get rid of it.'

The silence was so complete, so oppressive, I was afraid to breathe. I only realised then how warm the night was. The candles and torches didn't gutter at all. Beyond the walls of the dun a night bird screamed, and the raven cocked its head to listen.

Kate went on smiling in her open, innocent way. Conal had gone white. Leonora and Lilith both looked at Kate, but they wore strikingly different expressions.

At last Griogair gave a brief explosive laugh. 'Don't be a fool, Kate.'

The queen's smile vanished like the moon behind a cloud. Her breathing grew rapid, her eyes cold, but she didn't reply.

'Now, why would we want to do that, Kate?' Leonora

turned to pour a whisky, and handed it to Conal. He looked as if he needed it.

Kate shrugged one elegant shoulder. 'Because it will die one day whatever we do.'

'That's not unavoidable, I think. And why would we hurry along its death?'

'Because its death can work to our advantage. Isn't that obvious?'

Conal laughed sharply. 'You're mad.'

She turned on him the same look she'd given Griogair. I don't think the woman had much of a sense of humour.

'The otherworlders are weak,' Lilith broke in. 'Compared to us, they're cripples.'

'And what a lot of those *cripples* there are,' murmured my father.

'I believe we are outnumbered by our own cattle, Griogair.'

'Lilith, what a perfect metaphor!' laughed Kate, as if they hadn't agreed on it earlier. 'They'd be as malleable as beasts. We could have unimaginable power over the full-mortals, were the worlds to fuse.'

'Fuse? They wouldn't *fuse*,' snapped Conal. The whisky glass trembled in his hand. '*This* is the world that was made separate by the foremothers. This one will *die*.'

'And so would we,' said Leonora. 'As you well know, Kate.'

I didn't see the look Kate gave Leonora then; her face was angled away from me. But I did see Leonora pale. I'd almost swear she flinched, if it was possible. But she recovered fast.

'The full-mortals have free will, just as we do,' said Conal, and took a gulp of whisky. 'They'd be free to kill us. It's their world and without the Veil we'd be at their mercy. You can't mould the mind of a people.'

'We wouldn't have to,' smiled Lilith. 'Only a few key ones.'

'Tchah. You'd need absolute unanimity among the Sithe,' said Griogair dryly. 'And when did you last hear of that?'

'She won't get unanimity, and for a good reason.' Licking her fingertips, Leonora began to extinguish the candles, and the raven flapped down to her wrist. 'If you're so keen to be loved and obeyed and worshipped by the full-mortals, Kate, why not go there? Try it for a while. See how you get along.'

'I can't do that, Leonora, as *you* very well know.' There was something vicious and resentful in Kate's tone now.

'And that's why you need to destroy the Veil, dear.' Leonora smirked. 'Isn't it?'

'And you? You'd rather wait for it to die? When our options will have narrowed to nothing? Destroy it now and *we* can rule *them*. If it lives on, even as a motheaten old shroud, we cannot begin to have the influence we need. And Cù Chaorach, you're young and strong and you shouldn't be so nervous. We've interacted with the otherworlders for as long as we've existed.'

'And always had a place to run to when they saw us clearly, saw what we were, when they grew afraid of us. When they tried to wipe us out.' Leonora's damp fingers hissed on another flame, and it died, and the blue shadows deepened at the corner of my vision. 'Your way, Kate, we'd have nowhere to run. Cù Cha-orach's right. It would be the death of our race and you know it.'

'Leonora, you're too dramatic. I wouldn't suggest this if I thought *we* would suffer.'

'*You* wouldn't suffer. Would you?'

Kate drew herself up. 'Why would I seek to destroy my own people?'

Leonora shrugged. 'Because you're bored?'

If anything passed between their minds after that, I don't know what it was. I didn't understand about the Veil, and I was desperate to ask Conal, but I was terri-fied to let down my block for fear of detection. All I wanted now was for the terrible silence to be over, for the last flames to die to cold night, for them all to leave so that I could too.

At last Kate nodded and said, 'Very well. I'm not go-ing to change your mind, am I?'

'No,' said Leonora.

'I accept that. I have to, don't I?' Kate rose and stretched sleepily. 'I can't destroy the Veil without you, Leonora. Ah, well. I still think it was a fine idea. But perhaps a little ahead of its time.'

'It isn't going to have a time, dear.'

Kate laughed a genuine laugh. 'Goodnight, Leonora.'

I let my breath out very slowly. Kate accepted an-other kiss from Griogair, and an extremely restrained one from Conal, and then she and Lilith were drifting in a cloud of scent and silk from the anteroom. When the heavy wooden door had clunked shut behind them, the raven cawed derisively and hopped back to its chair. Leonora extended her hand to Griogair, ready to turn and smile her goodnight at Conal.

'Mother,' he snarled.

Leonora turned, wide-eyed, and lifted her fingers to her perfect mouth.

'The Veil's *dying?*' he hissed. 'And you couldn't even tell me?'

'Darling. Of course it isn't dying!'

'Leonora!' barked Griogair.

'Ah. All right.' Leonora gave him a tiny sheepish smile before turning back to Conal. 'Not yet, dear. And there *will* be a way to prevent its death. I've heard, er . . . rumours. There's something that could mend the Veil, restore its strength. A talisman, a charm . . .'

'Rumours?' he snapped. 'A *prophecy*, you mean. From that barking old soothsayer again? Mother, for gods' *sake*. Blink and it'll be the seventeenth century.'

'Conal. Such a cynic! I'll find a way to preserve the Veil, and in plenty of time.'

'What? Before Kate finds a way to kill it?'

'She wouldn't dare,' said Leonora, and placed her hand in Griogair's demanding one. 'She hasn't the knowledge, any more than I do. And truly? She wouldn't dare.'

I didn't like the way she said that twice.

5

'Is my name *Greenarse?*'

I spat the words with a degree of bitterness, but only because I was afraid. What if it *was* my name and I just wasn't recognising it? If that was the name I had to take through my life, I decided I'd just kill myself now.

Conal was staring at me, his hand stilled, the comb halfway through his horse's glossy mane and caught on a tangle. There was disbelief in his eyes, but suddenly he laughed.

'You daft greenarse! Of course it isn't your name!'

His ridicule galled a little, but it was reassuring. I knew he wouldn't lie to me, and he wouldn't even laugh at me unless he absolutely couldn't help it. I said, 'So when do I get one?'

'A name?' He shrugged, and pulled the comb out of the mane. 'When it's found.'

'Why can't you find it now? Or just give me one?'

'Not how it works. You know that fine.'

'Eili and Sionnach have their names,' I muttered.

'It's all they do have. They've been *Eili* and *Sionnach* almost since they were born. You're more, um . . . complicated.'

I didn't want to be that complicated. I wanted my name.

He sighed. 'Look at it this way, you're lucky. You'll always have two names. Like me. Nobody remembers the birth names Eili and Sionnach were given.'

'Everybody else has their true names too.'

'No, they don't. Nobody knows my mother's.'

That's because she's a witch, I thought, but I didn't say it.

'I heard that, greenarse.' But he grinned. 'And Griogair didn't get his name till he was older than I am now.'

'Griogair has a name?'

'Uh-huh.'

'Is that right? Did you use it the other night, in the antechamber? Just between you and him?'

His spine stiffened, and his eyes iced over. 'I'm surprised you have the nerve to mention it, you little *greenarse*. Yes, I used his name.'

Shamed by his anger, I hesitated, but only for a moment. 'What is it?'

'Griogair's name?' Conal too paused, biting his lip as if afraid he'd gone far enough in hurting me. 'Fitheach.'

Oh. In a moment of violent, unbearable resentment, I wondered if that was why Leonora kept a pet raven: so she'd have a matching pair.

I said, 'Nobody else uses his name.'

Sighing, Conal tapped his temple. 'In here we do. We all do.'

So I was the only one in the dun who hadn't known

my own father's name. Sometimes I thought I was going to spend my whole life feeling galled. To hell with it, and to hell with the mighty Raven. It wasn't as if I loved him or anything.

I loved Conal, of course, with an unswerving loyalty, but I still envied him. I did envy him Griogair's love. I envied him Eili's hero-worship. And I envied him that horse.

I wanted the creature with a longing that was physically painful, and Conal knew it. He knew too that I knew I could never have it, and maybe he felt a little sorry for me, because once it grew used to me and I proved I could handle it, he would let me feed and groom it, though I could never ride it, not without him on its back at the same time. I knew what that horse was, I knew even before I mixed my first feed for it and saw the skinned and quartered hare laid out ready. There was no mistaking the black eyes, lightless and flat like a deadly fish. More than once, when it was impatient or irritated, I saw its gills flap out from its cheekbone to expose spongy red flesh. Unsurprisingly, the stablehands wouldn't go near it, but that was superstition; Conal was in control of it, after all. He had its bridle.

Not that having its bridle was the same as mastering it. Most days I had its bridle to clean, as Conal did the grooming, and I still wouldn't have dared ride the animal alone. I loved cleaning the bridle just as I loved honing Conal's sword, because the one was as beautiful as the other. The bridle was soft black leather, the buckles and bit solid silver, and its noseband and cheekpiece were chased with an elaborate silver inlay.

Cleaning it was a lot of work, but I guarded the chore with a snarling possessive pride. I refused to let any of the stablehands touch the thing.

Conal was watching me as he brushed his horse's glossy black flank. Snorting fondly, it swung its head round to nibble at his hair. 'Don't you ever get tired of that?' he said.

'No.' I scraped at a fold of leather with my thumbnail.

'I mean,' he said patiently, 'doing my work.'

I stiffened. I was not his skivvy, and for him to say so implied that deep down, he imagined I thought I was. Complex and tetchy, I know, but my pride was all I had.

'I'm sorry,' he said, reading my mind. 'That's not what I meant.'

I glared at him, and sighing, he laid down the brush and shoved his shirt sleeves up to his elbows. Like all the fighters, his forearms were scarred with defensive wounds, and now he scratched idly at a recent scab from a swordplay accident. His scars weren't what caught my eye, though. I couldn't tear my gaze from what glinted on his left wrist. The thing was exquisite, she'd finished and polished it beautifully. She'd made a lovely job of it.

His hands stilled as he realised. Then he tugged down his sleeve, futilely and too late, over the silver rope torque.

'Seth,' he said, and nipped his lip. 'She's thirteen years old. She's infatuated, that's all.'

I stood up, flung the bridle at him, and stormed out.

'Seth, stop!'

I walked faster.

'Seth!' There was anger in his voice, overcoming his remorse. 'You're in love with nothing but hatred!'

I half-turned only to spit on the ground. Once out of the dun gates, I ran.

I sprinted across heather and through the shining serpentine patterns of the outgoing tide. I scrambled up small rock faces and along beaten paths, the black cattle thundering panicked out of my way. I didn't stop running till I was empty of breath and all care, till I was on the crest of the rock outcrop that overlooked the bay. Lying on my stomach, the stone rough and hard beneath me, I glowered at the blue shimmering horizon and the silken curve of the sea. With a yell of frustration I punched the rock, punched it again, then ground my knuckles till I felt the broken skin tear and rip. It still didn't hurt enough, so I raised my fist high to bring it down as hard as I could.

Halfway to the rock my wrist was caught in a hard grip.

'Don't break your sword hand, you little fool.'

My blood thundered in my eardrums, and my wrist trembled in his grasp as he crouched and glared into my eyes. I couldn't tear my hand away; he was too strong, and I was too unbalanced by anger. The clash of minds was almost painful.

'Shush,' he said at last. 'Shush.'

Like he was talking to his horse, his wild mad demon-horse. And just like his horse, I found myself calming down, my heartbeat slowing, my breath easing in my aching lungs. He relaxed his grip on my hand as he examined it, then tugged a handful of moss from the boggy ground, pressing it to my bruised and skinned knuckles. It felt wet and cool, as soothing as his touch, and I shut my eyes in case I was going to cry.

'You little idiot,' he said again, more gently.

I didn't care how often he called me a fool; it was the rest of it that was like a shard of steel in my chest. Perhaps it was the truth in them, but I had no idea words could hurt just like a blade.

'Hell, Seth, I'm sorry. I'm sorry I said that, it was stupid. It's not true. You've a right to hate more than you do.'

Falling silent, he sat down beside me, and I dragged myself up to sit next to him, letting him dab my hand with the wet moss. The torque slipped up and down his wrist as he cleaned away the blood, and he watched me watching it.

'I'd give it to you,' he said at last, 'but it isn't what you want, is it?'

I shook my head.

The autumn sun was warm and I was so tired now, but it was fine, he didn't seem to expect me to speak. When he let my hand go, the silence between us was easy again. A last bee blundered in the heather, blades of grass quivered in a tiny breeze, a buzzard keened in the updraft. Drowsy, I found myself leaning against Conal's shoulder, but he didn't make the mistake of putting an arm round me, so I didn't pull away. We stared out at the shining horizon and the islands, suspended above the firth in a crystal sky.

'You're a good fighter,' he said at last, quite casually. 'You need to control yourself but you're good. You need to work on your short sword. Eorna can help you with that, and the crossbow. Oh, you put up a good mind block, by the way, but sometimes it's a little crude. Too obvious. I was terrified for you the other night. Get Eili to teach you her tricks, will you?'

I turned to stare at him, but he had lifted my hand again, and was examining it very intently. 'What's wrong with you?' I asked.

Sighing, he pressed the damp moss against my skin. It felt warm now, the same temperature as my blood.

'I have to go away, Seth.'

'*What?*'

'I have to go. Kate's called on me, she's requested me from Griogair. It's not really a request, by the way. I have to go and be one of her captains now.'

'She can't do that!' I yelled.

Conal laughed wryly. 'She can do what she likes, Seth. She's our queen.'

'Only by consent!' As if I knew anything about politics.

'She has it,' he pointed out.

'She can't do this,' I moaned again, trying desperately to think why not. 'Alasdair Kilrevin is planning raids, everybody knows it. Griogair needs you.'

'Griogair can deal with Kilrevin by himself,' said Conal. 'He always does.'

Pulling away from him, I turned to look at him properly. 'What's the witch up to?'

'That's enough.' He met my eyes. 'Forget what you saw, Seth, forget what you heard. Kate had a wild thought, and a wilder idea: monarchs do. That's why they have counsellors, to talk them back to reality. That'll be one of my own duties now. Griogair was her captain and her counsellor in his time, and now it's my turn. Don't be always angry at your rulers, Seth. There's no point. It would drive you mad.'

'Not as mad as her,' I muttered.

He hissed. 'Don't think that way, not ever. It'll be fine. And, hey!' he added cheerfully. 'You'll have Eili to yourself. She'll forget all about me.'

No, she won't, I thought. Any more than I will. 'You're proud of this, aren't you?'

'Yes, of course. I don't want to go, believe me, but I'm proud of it. It's not forever, Seth. A few years. That's all.'

Yes, and a few years was nothing to us, so why did I feel this terrible ache of abandonment and despair? Furiously I fought back tears—twelve years old and weeping, what kind of shame would that be?—and Conal at last put an arm round my shoulders and hugged me fiercely. I didn't shove him away. I could feel his mind inside mine, his strength leaking into me. I wanted it to be enough, but it wasn't.

'You said you were always going to be there for me.' I could hardly speak, and I rubbed my arm across my face.

'Seth, I will *always* be here if you really need me. Reach out with your mind if you do, and I'll hear.'

I gave him a sceptical look. 'You will?'

'We're brothers by blood, Seth, of course I will. Don't you know that?'

I just looked at him.

'No. No, you don't know anything about family, do you? Well, it's true, okay?' He raked his fingers through my tangled hair. 'Look. I have something for you.'

Leaning down, he lifted a roll of soft fabric he'd dropped in the heather, and carefully unfolded it. Inside was what looked like a bundle of leather straps, till he lifted it by a forefinger and they fell into shape: a bridle, black leather and absolutely plain, but soft and smooth and beautifully made. The bit was solid silver. I stared at it in silence.

'There's a colt at the Dubh Loch,' he said, when it became clear I wasn't going to speak. 'A blue roan, a beauty. Evil-looking beast; it killed a man the other day. It needs mastering.'

I didn't dare to think. 'But you're leaving,' I mumbled.

'But I'll help you do it when I'm home again,' he said, 'and besides, the creature isn't mine to master.' Dryly he added, 'You and that horse are made for each other.'

I reached out a trembling hand to touch the cheekpiece. It felt soft as lambskin beneath my fingertip. 'You can't give me this.' My voice felt scratchy in my throat.

'Why not?'

Because I haven't been given anything before, I wanted to say, and I don't know how to be in another person's debt. I don't know how to thank, I don't know how to be grateful. I don't know how it's done.

'You don't have to do any of that,' he said roughly. 'Just take the damn thing.'

I did. The straps slid between my fingers like thick silk; my skin tingled with the touch of it. It was new, perfect, and I realised this wasn't some leftover thing he'd kept in a kist for years. He'd commissioned the bridle: he'd told the tanner and the smith exactly what he wanted, and he'd told them to make this thing especially for me.

I stood up abruptly and ran from him, hurtling down the rock-strewn slope so carelessly I was in danger of breaking my neck. The tide was half in across the white sand but I ran through it anyway, getting soaked to my thighs.

When I reached my cramped room between the dun gate and the tannery, I slammed the door and leaned against it, breathing hard. The bridle was still clutched in my fingers, and now I laid it carefully down. Then I crawled onto my bed, pressed my face hard against the pillow and wept silently into it, for kindness and love and the loss of it all.

6

'So what happens now?' I asked Eorna. Stumbling to my feet, I dusted the sand of the arena from my clothes and limped to the fence, leaning on it while I got my breath back. My entire body ached like a giant bruise, and my head was still ringing from the blow he'd caught it with his hilt. The bastard wasn't even out of breath.

'What happens now,' he said, 'is you unwrap your blade and spend an hour sharpening it. Then you might have a chance in hell if you ever have to use it, you useless greenarse. Assuming you don't cut yourself first.'

He was unwinding the cloth from his own sword as he spoke, and I eyed the naked blade with wary respect. It had hurt more than enough getting hit with the bound-up version.

'And then,' he added, 'you get your scrawny backside back here so we can practise with short swords. Your father won't thank me if you get skewered in your first battle.'

'My father won't give a shit,' I told him.

He shrugged. No argument. 'Your brother, then. And when I say your first battle, I don't mean the next one coming. You'll only get in everybody's way. I never saw such a hopeless piece of crap in my life. What have you been doing with your time?'

I knew fine I wasn't that bad, but Eorna never smiled and he never praised me; indeed he was relentlessly obnoxious. Practically a soulmate. I liked him.

'Not what I meant, anyway,' I said. 'I mean, what happens with Kilrevin?'

Eorna's good-looking face darkened. 'Kilrevin will raid the dun lands to pick a fight, and your father will kick his impudent backside, and if Kilrevin is lucky Kate will exile him for another few years to the other-world, to live with the full-mortals. And it's *Alasdair* Kilrevin to you, greenarse. You may as well show the bastard some respect, since you'll never show him a naked blade at the rate you're going.'

I ignored that. 'What's so bad about exile? Doesn't ever seem to bother him, does it?'

Eorna shrugged. 'It's not that easy. You've never met a full-mortal, have you, short-shit? They don't get along with the likes of us. Never have. They don't get along with *different*.'

'We're not different,' I said.

'No, but they are. They can't . . .' He tapped his temple with a forefinger, lost for words to explain it. 'They can't do this.'

It took me a long moment to realise what he meant, and then I gaped at him. I remembered, now, what my mother had said: *the otherworlders are cripples.* Suddenly I knew what she was talking about.

I couldn't imagine such a disability. 'They can't?'

'No, and if you ever have to live with them, you won't let on that you can, either.' He shook his dark blond head, growling. 'It's terrible over there. They're all ruled by priests of one sort or another. Their women are downtrodden like you wouldn't believe, they put them in skirts all the time and they can't even fight, they just breed, *all* the time. Aye, and they burn them. They burn their women for wearing trews, they burn them for picking herbs. Men too, mind you. They'll burn men too if they don't like the shape of their backside.'

'You're making that up,' I told him scornfully.

'It's true, I'm telling you. They can't bind themselves to a lover, either, not of their own free will. Not at all, if they want one the same sex. Even a man and a woman need permission from priests, and then they're not allowed another lover. Not ever.'

'You're joking,' I said, my jaw wide.

'And you're a naïve greenarsed infant. Take it from me, you want to stay on the winning side here, so you never have to be exiled. Which means being fifty times better than you are right now, and that'll do no more than keep you alive. Eili MacNeil could whip you into butter, you dirty waste of space.' He was glowering at his own blade then, so he didn't see the shudder go through me at the mention of her name, the flush race into my cheekbones. 'Aren't you thirteen now? When are you planning to grow, shortarse? Same time you plan to learn to fight? Now piss off, you're wasting time. Mine and yours. Back here this afternoon, and I want to see your blade sharp enough to cut thrown silk, or I'll give you more than a hiding. Get to work.'

I didn't take Eorna that seriously. I knew I was better than he told me, knew that he knew it. He was fond of me in his own surly way, and he only wanted me to be safer, so in my arrogant youthful idiocy I decided at that moment that I'd be at the battle. Not fighting, maybe: I believed him when he said I'd get in the way. But I'd watch. I wanted to see what it was all about, I wanted to teach myself some tricks, just by observing the experts. I was tired of being called *greenarse* and *shortarse* and besides, I wanted to see my father hand the traditional whipping to Alasdair Kilrevin. I wanted to see the brute routed.

He was already burning crofts close to my father's lands, taking the cattle and slaughtering the inhabitants, and he was doing it simply to taunt Griogair. Griogair hadn't risen to it yet, but everybody knew his glacial control was close to cracking. The atmosphere in the dun was unnaturally still, febrile with bloodlust and nerves. You could feel the tense thrill of longing in the air, like a wire running through every vein and every mind. All the fighters wanted it begun, every man and woman, and there would be no real peace till it was finished.

Maybe Griogair was wound as tightly as the rest of us; maybe that would account for it. Maybe he was just looking for a distraction from the irritation that was Kilrevin, but whatever the reason, he began to appear near the arena fence while Eorna was putting me through my paces. At first he gave us little more than a passing glance; later he would wait to watch, for minutes at a time. Sometimes he said nothing at all, then snorted and walked on to more important business, but on one or two occasions he shouted something to me. Never with fondness or paternal concern, it's true, but he was at least addressing me directly. The first time it happened I came to an abrupt halt in such astonishment that I almost fell, and then Eorna finished the job for me and struck me to the ground with his staff, a blow that put an end to my training for the day. In my daze of pain I remember seeing my father spit, shake his head, and walk off towards the stables.

I thought he wouldn't bother to come back, but three days later he was leaning on the fence again, giving me a disparaging look as I ducked from Eorna's slash.

'You!' he barked.

Respectfully Eorna backed off, and I stood there and stared at my father.

'What's the armour of a Sithe?'

'S—speed,' I managed to choke.

'What is a Sithe's defence? What's your shield?'

'Speed,' I mumbled, and when he glared at me I gabbled, 'and speed.'

'Greaves? Breastplate? Helmet!'

'Speed,' I replied, my voice now high-pitched with nerves. 'Speed! Speed!'

He fell silent, giving me a long stare that held all the contempt in the world.

'So why,' he said at last, 'are you moving like a pregnant three-legged ewe?'

As he walked away I thanked the gods that I knew what greaves and breastplates and helmets were, because Eorna had lectured me on how the full-mortals fought in battle, and why the Sithe never used armour like theirs. All our defence was in our quickness, and we didn't even carry shields or targes; if we carried anything in our left hands it was only a short sword to deflect and parry. Our battles were not the grunting chop and stab of the full-mortals; they were swift deadly dances of lightning flight and slash and lunge. Our weapons were long and light and they had to be as fast as we were, or we were lost.

And so the next time I caught sight of Griogair at the arena fence, I tried to be clever, leaping high and twisting to catch the back of Eorna's skull. My tutor dodged my stroke with laughable ease and I stumbled clumsily to the ground, earning another whack so hard it left me retching into the sand.

'Left yourself exposed, you fool,' yelled Griogair. 'Feint and come at him from below.'

So when I had the chance, I did, rolling with his strike and jabbing my staff upwards. It sent Eorna grunting to his knees, voiceless with pain as he clutched his groin. He'd done it more than once to me, and I felt no remorse, only glee and a dizzying pride. I turned for Griogair's reaction, but he'd gone.

Next time, I promised myself and him. Next time you'll see it. Next time you'll smile.

But the next time I saw Griogair it was two days later, as he rode out of the dun gate at the head of thirty of his favourite fighters. He was smiling then, all right. Most of them were laughing and grinning: I remember that well. I laughed myself, dizzy with it. Kilrevin was an outlaw and a bandit and they wanted him punished, we all did, but there was nothing noble or altruistic about the song in our blood that morning. It was the thrill of killing that set our hearts racing when Griogair walked out into the courtyard that day and shouted for his horse and his sword. Even Leonora was smiling as she kissed him goodbye. And in my ignorance I was as thirsty for blood as any of them. These days I'm as familiar with a human being's innards as I am with the palm of my sword hand, but I'm not and never have been so proud of it as I was that day, a stupid know-it-all child who had never seen real blood.

What did I know?

Eili was on the dun walls, watching too, and I met her laughing gaze. She was as hungry for the fight as I was, I could tell by the wild light in her eyes. I thought of taking her with me, then decided against it. Later, I decided as I quietly blocked my mind and made my sneaky way to the deserted northern wall. Later I'd tell her all about it, I'd boast of what I'd seen, but for now I wanted to do this alone. I didn't want company, not even Eili's.

That's why my heart sank when I felt the tug of a hand on my sleeve.

I glared over my shoulder. I should have been a fraction of a moment faster. Already up on the parapet, I had one leg swung over the northern wall, ready to clamber down using the handholds I knew were there.

I didn't want to be held back because I already had a lot of catching up to do, and there was the risk my father might finish it before I'd seen any of the fun.

Orach gripped my sleeve tighter. 'Don't go,' she whispered.

'You must be joking,' I growled. 'I'm not missing this.'

'Seth, please. Please don't. I had a bad dream.'

I stared at her. There was a hint of chill in my bones because it wasn't like her, to be honest; then I decided the atmosphere of the last days and weeks must have got to her more than I'd realised. Softening, I touched her cheek, then impulsively leaned down and kissed her.

'I'll be back tonight,' I assured her. 'I'll tell you all about it. We'll go to the caves, right?'

The promise didn't bring a shy smile to her mouth the way it usually did. She only looked afraid. I felt the touch of her mind on mine, begging me.

~ *Seth. Please don't go.*

I couldn't be doing with it. Not now. Almost brutally I broke the mental contact, yanked my sleeve from her grasp, and swung over the wall.

7

I ran with the devil on my heels, but still the sky was darkening by the time I found them. My lungs ached and my limbs trembled with exhaustion, but I found them. It was the sounds I followed, of course; if I used my mind, they'd know I was there and there would be hell to pay. But the sounds of a battle are unmistakeable. Unbearable, unmissable, but unmistakeable.

Seven miles inland and further south there was a cluster of crofts that lay within my father's area of control, and Griogair owed the community protection in return for the grain and meat they sent to the dun. The cottages huddled round an ancient well that was sunk below ground level, with cropped grass sloping down to it as if the earth was trying to swallow itself. Roofed and walled in wet green stone, it had never run dry and the water was sweet without a hint of brackishness; I knew because one of the crofters had shown me it once, and given me a beakerful of the water. It had been a hot day, and I'd wandered miles, and I was nine years old and ravenous and parched. He'd laughed his head off as I glugged beaker after beaker of the water till I finally threw some back up, and grinned at him. Then he'd given me some bread and dried beef, just because I made him laugh.

I stepped over his corpse as I ducked behind his cottage. I knew it was his corpse because I recognised the face grimacing at me, and his red hair; and that head on the spike of the fence seemed to match the torso at my feet.

Laughed his head off, indeed.

And now I had a bad feeling about this. The feeling was no more than a feeling, because I still didn't dare reach out with my mind, but that was no longer about getting an earful of trouble from Sionnach's father or my own. Now I found I didn't want to give my position away because I didn't want my head on a fence spike. I looked back at the crofter's face again, knowing from his expression he hadn't died well. I suppose the other body parts scattered round the yard were his lover, but I had to count to make sure. The gods knew where her head was.

What was the point of being a wild thing if you couldn't listen to your wildest instincts? I stopped then, right in the centre of the blood-boltered yard, and listened, really listened. Dusk was well advanced now, the day only a strip of pearl above the horizon, so I could forget my eyes. I forgot my mind too, forgot my crazy fears and conjectures, and let myself smell and feel the battle. I let myself hear it, hear it properly. That wasn't hard, because it was drawing closer. But it could only be drawing nearer to here if my father was in retreat.

Now I could hear individual voices, individual screams and howls and yells among the clangour and screech of metal against metal. There were some voices I recognised, and those were the ones panicked by defeat. There were some I did not. Those were the voices raised high in vicious war cries.

I ran.

The trouble was, I didn't run far enough and I didn't run in the right direction. My instincts had had their moment, and now I lost it as panic swept over me. I ran towards a copse of windblown pines, and knew it was a death trap. I ran back the way I had come, and knew suddenly that on the open moor I'd be exposed for miles, and my enemy was on horseback. So for hideous seconds and minutes, fear turning my muscles to ice and my innards to water, I stood in the centre of the ravaged cottages and their destroyed inhabitants, and I could not move.

I don't know what made me run to the well. It was a place to be cornered and caught, but it was a place to hide too. I could feel minds hunting other minds, but I was better at blocking now. If I blocked Kilrevin's searching mind long enough, Conal would find me. Of course he would. He'd come for me. He'd said he would.

But I couldn't call out to him, even in this rout. The battle was on me, now, the noise of it numbing my ears and dazing my brain, and I didn't dare look back as I stumbled down the treacherous stone steps cut into the slope. Below, in total darkness, I could see the maw of the well, no longer welcoming but ready to swallow me whole. I was terrified of pitching forward into the black glistening water, and more terrified of not getting down there fast enough. I grabbed for the wall, scraping my palm, almost losing my balance and then sinking up to one ankle in coldness. For an instant I froze in terror, but the shouts were louder now, the clang of steel more vicious, the grunts and howls of dying men clearer. Gripping a ridge of rough stone with my fingertips, I swung myself round and backed against the unseen inner wall. I was up to my thighs in water but I didn't care that the cold bit into my flesh like the teeth of the underworld.

Men were fighting their way down the steps after me: two of them. Edging further along the wall into deeper darkness, I saw flames flicker on the black surface, but as the tiny waves I made rippled wider, the flame-light briefly sputtered and went out. I tried to breathe without a sound, but it was hard.

Then that problem was solved, because I stopped breathing. There was the hideous ring of steel, the laboured hissing breath of men intent only on killing one another. One staggered back; I heard his sword scrape on the stone close to me. The steel-clangour echoed now from the stone roof: the men were inside the well-cavern. The first one grunted as he fended off a blow, and I knew it was my father.

If it had been Conal I'd have gone to help him, I swear I would. But he wasn't Conal, and I barely knew my father, and the stark truth is, I was rigid with terror. All I did was watch as the reflected flames flared again and Alasdair Kilrevin beat my father back towards the black pool. They both looked worn down, as if this was a fight that had lasted too long, and there were no lightning moves from either of them, only a relentless bloody slash-and-parry.

Griogair was so hacked about, I was amazed he was still moving, let alone fighting, yet even at that moment I was afraid of him. A gash had been opened across his face from right temple to left jaw, and I think one of his eyes was dead. His arms and chest were ripped in great slashes as if a great cat had played with him, or a well-fed wolf. I remembered now, that was what they called Kilrevin: the Wolf, and now I knew why. Griogair's face was distorted by rage and hatred as well as the sword-slice, but even as he beat my father back, Kilrevin was smiling.

Griogair's foot caught on the last uneven step and he toppled back, and Kilrevin leaped with him, dropping his sword as my father lost his grip on his. Kilrevin closed his fingers round Griogair's throat, and shoved his mutilated face under the water.

I must have breathed, eventually, but my father didn't. He never got another chance. Kilrevin straddled his body, shoving him down as his limbs thrashed for an age, then only twitched, then grew still.

I pressed myself against the stone, motionless. I mustn't make another ripple, not while Kilrevin stood staring down thoughtfully at my father's drifting corpse. One clawing hand twitched again, so Kilrevin lifted his sword and thrust it casually into Griogair's throat, withdrew it and wiped the blade on his sleeve.

He stood very still. So did I.

He silenced his breath. I did the same.

His mind reached out. I closed my eyes for fear the light of them would be reflected in the black pool.

Then he spat, and turned, and ran back up the steps.

Trembling, I stared at my father, thinking: I'll never know him now. And I stood there thinking that, over and over again, till for all I knew hours had passed. The noise of fighting faded, and eventually so did the screams, and the darkness became complete. Only then did I get my mind back, and only then did I scream in my head like an infant for Conal.

I think my father must have called out to Conal earlier, when he realised he had somehow been deceived into his own death, because my brother came faster than I could have hoped. I'd clambered on all fours up the well steps, because I could not stay in there with Griogair, not for anything. When I looked around me in the fire-lit darkness, I sat down on grass that was saturated with blood and entrails and the gods knew what else. There were no moans or cries from the wounded because there were no wounded. Those who hadn't escaped were dead, and I tried not to think about what I'd heard as I stood frozen and shivering in the well, waiting till all the screams had died.

I sat there on the blood-sticky grass for the whole of that long cold night, till dawn broke grey and weary at the far edge of the moor and I heard Conal coming. Two of his lieutenants came with him at the gallop, but what was the big hurry? Long before they drew to a halt they must have known they were hours too late.

Slipping off their horses, they murmured together, awed by the slaughter, already planning how to deal with the corpses. In the morning they'd bring a detachment to recover them, but there were too many for proper rites just then. Niall Mor MacIain lay with his belly open from crotch to breastbone, his throat slashed and drained; I'd sat and stared at him for an age in the darkness, wondering what I could or should tell Eili and Sionnach about his end. There were limbs and heads and charred bodies strewn around the crofts, male and female fighters alike. Raineach's brother had been crucified against a barn door, so they took him down from there, at least, and they also took the head of my red-haired crofter from the fence spike and laid it beside its neck stump.

You know what the full-mortals call us? *The People of Peace.*

They flatter us. Why? Maybe it's fear. Maybe it's folk-memory.

I heard none of what Conal and his lieutenants said to me. They did bring away two bodies: Conal went with Righil down into the well and they carried up my father's sodden remains. Of course they took those and Niall MacIain's. When the bodies were roped to the other two horses, Conal picked me up and put me on his, then swung up behind me, and he brought me back to the dun like a living corpse. I could feel the warmth of his body behind mine, the pulse of his blood and the rise and fall of his chest, as if it was the only thing in the world that was real.

The clann waited for us at the dun. Leonora already knew, of course, that her bound lover was dead, but she stood in dignified silence in the courtyard and waited for her son to ride through the gates and halt before her. With Conal's arm around my waist, I looked into her blue grieving eyes and knew that in an instant she'd have me dead, and perhaps even Conal too, if there was a witchcraft that could bring Griogair back in our place.

She was all in the colour of grief: loose white silk trews and a long embroidered white coat, her beautiful tawny hair woven into a long white-ribboned braid. Her raven hunched on the wall behind her. A faint breeze stirred its glossy wingtips and the spiky feathers at its throat, but it was unnaturally still, watching the corpses with eyes that were sly and as black as marble.

Under the wordless gaze of the clann, Leonora took a knife from her belt, sliced the braided twist of hair from her head, and laid it across her lover's body. When Griogair was carried away to be given to the buzzards, I thought the raven would go too, but it didn't move.

Leonora put her hand on Conal's reins and looked up at him.

'Will you go with Griogair?' he asked her, very quietly.

'No,' she said. Her voice was even and steady. 'Not yet. I'm needed.'

I could sense his curiosity despite the circumstances. 'Who?'

'I don't know. Not born yet, whoever it is, but I have to stay.'

'You want the Captaincy?' he asked.

'No, I'll renounce that. The dun is yours.'

'All right.'

She looked at him very hard. 'That means you're no longer Kate's.'

'Of course. She knows that.'

'Yes,' said Leonora thoughtfully. 'She does. It's a pity she didn't foresee . . .'

Her eyes snapped to me, as if she had only just remembered I was there, and she swallowed whatever words were on her tongue. But I wasn't interested anyway. Through my daze of shock I knew only that Conal was returning, that he'd be Captain of the dun now, that I was getting him back. And even though I knew the birds were already eating my own father, and Sionnach and Eili's too, I couldn't help the welling happiness in my heart.

Told you I was an optimist.

8

For a few weeks, I was contented with life as I'd never been before, as happy as I could imagine being. With Conal their Captain now, only a very few of the clann still saw me as a living insult to him, though a few still mistrusted me as the spawn of a witch. Leonora continued to ignore me. Raineach gave up hope of ever making me a silversmith, but Righil found the time and inclination to teach me to play fiddle and mandolin. I was never going to be a musical prodigy but I picked up the basics fast, and that made me all the more welcome in the great hall of an evening.

I still had to put up with Eorna's scathing remarks and his very evident pleasure in giving me regular hidings, but I didn't mind, because there was a purpose to it and I was getting better all the time. He still hurt me more than I hurt him, but the fights grew less and less one-sided. One day he paused for breath—well, he would, with my blunt sword-tip at his throat—and chucked his old swathed sword down into the sand

and grinned at me, and suddenly I knew what he knew: that one day I was going to be better than him. Better than all of them. Maybe never better than Eili, though I'd at least be her match, but my most shameful ambition was the one I kept blocked from everyone. I wanted to be better than Conal. I loved him, but I still wanted to prove I was Griogair's son too, and not always the pointless one.

When I wasn't training, and I didn't manage to slip away and simply run wild on my own, we were set to hunting food, Sionnach and Eili, Orach and Feorag and me, and that was no chore. I was always good at fishing and catching rabbits and hares, and I'd got the hang of a bow quickly, so if we wandered far enough I shot the occasional buck. Sionnach had taught me how to trap gulls and guillemots; they didn't taste wonderful but their feathers were useful for arrows. Collecting shellfish had always been a game: mussels were easy and crabs were fun and we loved whacking limpets off rocks with an old sword, or digging manically after razor shells, racing to beat them as they tunnelled, and not always catching them. It was hard work but it was competitive, and we spent most of the time laughing and squabbling and shoving, and mostly we ended up stripping off and tumbling into the clear water of the bay. If we'd gathered enough food we'd build a small fire of driftwood, scraping dry fungus off scrawny birks and rocks for tinder, kindling it with dry bracken. Then we'd eat some of our catch ourselves, shivering over the flames and huddling together, telling our own fantasies and gently mocking one another's. Sometimes I could only stay silent and watch the rest

of them, afraid of my happiness, terrified that friendship might suddenly vanish in the dusk. I think Orach
knew what went through my head: she often did. If I
was silent too long, my heart and my tears in my throat,
she would sit close against me, insinuating herself under my arm and letting her warmth sink into my bones.

Conal was mostly absent for those weeks, keeping
vigil over our father on his bleak hilltop. I went up to
join him occasionally, but I did not like the business. It
was too easy to imagine the birds and the foxes tearing
at my own flesh, and my new acquaintance with mor-
tality still smarted too much for me to bear the smell
for long. When it was finally decent for Conal to leave,
when the bulk of Griogair's rites were completed and
the stripped bones were gathered, Conal left him with
two guards and came back to the dun.

And the day after that, we found out.

'What do you mean, hostages?'

Eili and I stared at Conal in disbelief, but he carried
on fletching arrows and didn't look at us. He seemed
different now that his hair was shorn close to his scalp:
not older, exactly, since a grown Sithe never looks
older till he's practically on his deathbed; but somehow he looked harder and wiser. I hoped it had done
the same for me, since I'd decided on balance that my
hair too had to be shaved, though mostly out of respect for Conal rather than Griogair. My skull felt
strange, bristly and cold. The arrow-feathers had been
dyed sky blue and Conal's fingers moved deftly and
fast; his work was so hypnotic we'd been watching in

silence for a while, and the whole time he must have been trying to choose his moment. I'd wondered why his block was up.

'What do you mean?' I said again, more aggressively.

'What I say. It's just like last time, Seth. It's not a request.'

'But . . .' I was completely bewildered. Politics were beyond me, and I couldn't begin to fathom Kate's reasoning.

Conal's two lieutenants exchanged glances behind him, raising their eyebrows. I knew what they were thinking; it was more than audible. Why did Kate have to choose the two stroppiest pains-in-the-arse in Conal's dun? Righil and Carraig knew they were in for a long afternoon. Carraig sighed, sat down and pulled out his blade to sharpen it, while Righil simply slumped against the steps, folded his arms and shut his eyes, sunbathing in the winter brightness.

'Is this something to do with my mother?' I asked acidly.

Conal shrugged. 'Maybe. Sounds like one of her ideas.'

'Kate doesn't need Seth,' put in Sionnach. 'She wants two. If Eili's going, I am too.'

Conal rolled his eyes fondly. 'Obviously. But then there will be three of you because she insists on having Seth. The people closest to me, of course. I'm sorry.' He glanced at me, and I knew he truly was. 'She doesn't trust me, Seth.'

'How can she not trust you?' I exploded. 'You've been one of her captains for, what . . .' I counted swiftly. 'Fifteen months!'

'And opened my mouth once too often. She knows

my opinions too well, and she doesn't trust them or me. Maybe she has cause.'

'What kind of a queen is that?' snapped Eili. 'What kind of a queen doesn't want her captains' opinions?'

Gently Conal placed his fingers over her lips. 'A powerful queen and a ruthless one. Don't think such things, Eili. You mustn't think them, or she'll hear, one way or another. How do you think she got to be queen? You've no idea what she's capable of.'

Eili was barely listening. She blinked at him, and I saw her swallow. As he withdrew his fingers from her mouth, she almost yearned back towards his touch. Even now, I felt a rage of jealousy constrict my chest and throat. Well, I was going away with Eili now, and Conal wasn't going to be in the way. That had to be good, didn't it?

Misery swamped me, made worse by my own treacherous train of thought. Trying and failing to hide his unease, Conal got to his feet and hugged my shorn head against him.

'I won't do anything to endanger any of you,' he said. 'I'll be an obedient bondsman. Good as gold.' There was acid in his tone, but then he smiled again. 'And it isn't for long.'

Bitterly I said, 'I've heard that one before.'

I slept that night, but only for minutes at a time. The night was cold but I couldn't feel it, could only kick off my blankets and roll over to lie spreadeagled on my stomach, staring out at the star-bleached landscape and the glittering sky. Funnily enough, I missed the stink of the tannery since Conal had given me new and better rooms. I missed the unintelligible muttering of the guards up on the dun wall, their coughing and spitting and their occasional raucous laughter as they shared bad jokes to ward off the boredom. My new rooms were too big and quiet, the rafters too high, the carved stone too elegant.

Orach was further away, too. I wanted her and I didn't want her. I missed her skin against my skin, I missed her slender arms loose in sleep around my neck. I missed the feel of her back: muscles shifting beneath my palms, her ribs expanding with her soft sleeping breaths, my fingertips idly mapping the contours of her spine and shoulder blades as I lay wakeful. Love was meant to send you to sleep, I'd heard. It didn't do it for me, but that didn't matter. What mattered was being wanted. It flattered me, it contented me. She contented me.

Still, tonight I did not want her, except with that common raw animal ache. I wanted to look at the stars while I could, and I wanted to look at them alone. For a moment I couldn't breathe, and my lips parted as I sucked in breath with a high sound. It was almost like a sob, so I was mortified when I heard a footfall on the floorboards. I rolled onto my back and saw the dark shape of my brother against my open door.

I sat up, shocked. 'You should knock.'

'I did.' He sat down on the end of the bed. 'I thought you spoke.'

'Must have been a dream. What's wrong?' I thought for a moment *Eili*, and I was afraid.

'Nothing's wrong.' He shrugged. 'Except for the

obvious. I'm sorry about it, Seth. I'm sorry about the whole business.'

'Nothing you can do,' I said coolly.

'There should be.'

'But there isn't.' In a way it was reassuring, I told myself. Even the perfect almighty Conal couldn't control everything. Involuntarily I tightened my arms around my knees, crushing them against my stomach, trying to crush the ache inside me. 'Can't have it all your own way.'

He grinned.

'You didn't wake me up just to go through all that again,' I said.

'I didn't wake you up at all, you wee fraud.'

This time I grinned.

'There's something we should have done long ago,' he said. 'Want to go up to the Dubh Loch?'

I tried not to whoop with delight; then cold reality kicked in. 'But I'm leaving, Cù Chaorach.'

'Doesn't matter. You have to do it now. The animal must be more than two years old by now. If you wait much longer it won't be masterable.'

'I won't be here. I . . .'

'Listen. Once he's yours he's yours, but you need to do it while he's young.' He gave me a wry look. 'And of course, when he's young he's got less chance of killing you.'

That went right over my head. I was too excited. 'Tonight!'

He smiled, a little sadly. 'When else?'

. . .

What a night it was, the sky so frosted with stars it hardly mattered there was no moon. I sat behind Conal on his black horse, holding onto his waist, and now that it was so close I was almost mad with the hunger for a horse like this one. Conal seemed in no hurry; I wanted to race at a gallop, but he kept his black to an easy canter. I craned my head back to look up into the Milky Way, dizzy with the distance and splendour of it. Night air is different; it tastes younger, newer, darker. Fill your lungs with it, and you fill your lungs with night. Riding to the Dubh Loch that night I felt my innards cold and keen and hungry for life, and I thought that perhaps after all a man could live forever.

The black slowed to a halt when we were still half a mile or so from the water's dark lapping edge, hooves squelching in marshy ground. I slid off before Conal did, and he had to send a brusque order into my head to stop me charging ahead of him.

I paused reluctantly, looked back at him, and then towards the loch that glimmered between slopes of bleached scree and scrappy heather. I could hear the soft slap of tiny waves on a pebbled shore, the hiss and suck of water between rocks. As I drew closer it was a breath of wind in the rattling reeds I heard. And the scrape of a hoof on wet stone, and the scatter of silver droplets as a mane was shaken dry, and the questioning snort of fierce breath in the stillness.

Don't know why Conal was so hesitant. The creature's hide glowed like a pearl in the starlight, and I knew before it raised its head from its lochside grazing that it had heard us coming, but it was entirely unafraid. It looked unthreatening, unthreatened. Its jaws crunched round tough grass from the lochside, and as its tongue came out to lick its lips I glimpsed its canines. Eyes watched us, black and featureless. The empty stare might have been unnerving, but for the way it lowered its head and whickered, flicked its tail and shook its black mane once more, playful and confident. Its face was black too, and its long still-coltish legs. You couldn't see its true colour in the night; its neck and shoulders and flanks were all starlight and phosphorescence. Beautiful. My horse was beautiful.

'Careful,' said Conal.

'Yes.' My fingers clutched the bridle so hard I didn't know if I'd ever be able to unfreeze them. ~ *What do I do?*

'You speak openly, for a start. It'll hear your thoughts anyway.'

'Not very straightforward, this, is it?'

'Where would the fun be otherwise? Now give me the bridle. It's no use to you yet. And don't let the horse go into the water, that's the main thing.'

'Don't let it go in the water,' I echoed, as he eased the bridle from my fingers.

'If you go into the water you're dead. Now, listen. You're not taming it, you're offering it an exchange. You're offering yourself and you're taking its freedom.'

'Like a binding,' I said.

Conal suppressed his laughter. 'Not unlike it. But different. It's a horse, for gods' sake.'

I glanced at him and grinned, but the horse can't have liked me turning away from it. It gave an exasperated snort, shook its head, so that I looked back. Gently it tilted its head. It looked a bit like an invitation.

'Find its mind, that's the thing,' said Conal. 'Find its mind, stay there, stay on.'

'Stay on?'

'You have to get on it, of course.'

I swallowed hard. 'I have to get on it.' I knew how flat my voice sounded, and I was ashamed of myself. What had I expected? To bridle a water-horse and lead it back tame to a stall in the dun? I found Conal's eyes again.

He smiled, swung the bridle lightly at his side. 'There's nothing like it,' he said.

Smooth skin under my palm. The opalescent shine of its hide as I drew my hand across its neck and the hairs flattened, then sprang back. Warm blowing breath on my neck, the tickle of its muzzle as it nipped gently at my cropped hair. The cry of a night bird.

Its heartbeat beneath my hand as I slid my hand down its shoulder to rest against its chest. The ripple of muscle, the quiver of flesh as I touched its withers. Its heartbeat, fast and strong. Another heartbeat echoing. Mine.

Its warmth, leaning into me. My weight shifting, the sudden light spring and scramble, and then, for a moment, my arms around its powerful neck, loving the sheer strength and beauty of it.

And then insanity.

Nothing else on earth could have moved so fast. Night air swamped my lungs as it bolted forward, and I looped my fingers tightly through its silky mane, holding on in the sheer fear of death. I made myself pant out my breath, breathe in again. Impossibly powerful beneath me, the horse pelted for the hillside on the dark north shore of the black loch. If my heart beat any harder my chest would explode. Find its mind? I could barely find my own.

The angle of the slope seemed to slow it hardly at all. Its strong forelegs ate up the hillside like a race-track, and I could feel the strength of its haunches driving us forward. Gods, even if I died tonight I wouldn't have missed this, not for anything.

When the creature reached the crest of the hill, I saw the whole moor and the hills spread out beneath me, the jagged broken curve of the earth at the horizon. I couldn't get off the horse. I didn't want to. Plunging, swerving, it swivelled its head to enjoy my awe and my terror. Its jaws opened in a knowing grin, and the canines flashed again. And then, impossibly, it sprang down the precipitous slope, straight for the dark water and its lair.

~ *Murlainn!*

Conal's cry came into my head, crystal clear as the night. An unfamiliar name, but I knew it, I'd always known it. The joy of recognition drove the panic straight from my head, and instead of fighting the horse I clamped my heels into its sides and drove it on.

I felt its utter surprise, its brief jolting hesitation. Then it was flying down the hill again and I was flying with it, both of us plummeting like a hawk towards oblivion. Its hooves scattered stones and earth and the scree rolled, but it kept its footing. For a wild moment I thought it had left the slithering, treacherous ground, that it was airborne. Tightening my grip on its mane I leaned forward to press my cheek to its muscled neck, and let my mind go. And in that instant I found the beast's.

I found it. I knew it. I recognised it. So much hunger, so much violence. Such inchoate longing. *I know you.*

Its hooves slammed into the solid lochside ground and it lunged towards the silver line of the water, but I pressed my mind into the horse's, turned it, slowly turned it. We swerved just as we reached the pebbled shore. It struck the stones like Raineach's hammer on raw iron, noisy with sparks. Then we were back on the moor, and its hooves were dull thunder. I loved it. Its heart was mine. I was on its back outracing the wind and we were one.

'I told you there was nothing like it.' Conal held out the bridle to me.

I slid off the roan's back, keeping my hand laced into its mane. I was shaking. Maybe that's why I couldn't let go of it. I didn't want to let go of it, ever.

Overhearing, Conal guffawed. 'You can't, believe me. Now give it its bridle.'

I held my breath as I fumbled the straps over its black head, but it only snorted fondly, accepting the bit like a child's well-schooled pony. I kept looking at it, taking my time buckling the throatlash, as I said, 'Conal. My name.'

'Yes.'

'Did you know it before?'

'Of course not. I'd have told you. Do you like it?'

I still didn't look at him, but I grinned.

'Me too,' he said, and laughed. 'I'm a bloody sheepdog. You're a small if deadly falcon. Ya wee bandit.'

I had my name. I had my horse. Life could be no better. If it wasn't for tomorrow . . .

Suddenly I needed to share it all. I needed Orach, I needed her to know my name, I was hungry for her and not just physically. I needed my friend, my lover, before we were separated for the gods knew how long. How long would Conal have to be Captain of his dun before Kate would trust him? How many years was I going to have to live underground like a worm?

Still, even that prospect couldn't squash my spirits tonight. When Conal and I finally tired of racing one another's horses along the lochside, I slipped the bridle off the roan and let it loose, and rode home at Conal's back again. I couldn't take the creature to Kate's fortress, after all; it wouldn't be fair on a wild thing. Besides, like all its kind it had the combination of savage loyalty, unpredictability and utter violence that would have got it shot within a week by any fighter of Kate's who combined a lack of superstition with a latent deathwish.

In the courtyard, outside the stables, I hesitated. Conal's footsteps faded, his door closed with a soft clunk, and I wondered if there was a woman waiting for him. Probably. I grinned to myself, thinking that if she'd waited up, she was going to be disappointed:

when he left me he looked like a man who wanted to sleep for a week.

I didn't, though. I felt high, as if I'd been drinking hard but it hadn't hit my stomach or my limbs yet, only my head. Doubling back, I headed for the southern section of the dun, my feet silent on the bare stone of the passageways. In a star-silvered corner I gently pushed open an oak door, followed the flickering light of burned-down torches and turned the iron latch of Orach's door without a thought.

'Seth?'

She was awake.

I stopped, immobilised by the dull inevitability of it. Well, why should I expect her to be free just because I suddenly had to scratch an itch?

Feorag propped himself up on his elbows, blinking. As he focused he gave me a sleepy, friendly smile. Orach pulled a plaid around her nakedness, perhaps just to keep the chill of the small hours at bay. Slipping off the bed, she came to me and kissed my cheek, then drew back, surprised.

'Murlainn,' she whispered.

'Yes,' I said.

'It's good. It's you.' She smiled, kissed me again, put arms round my neck that were floppy with sleepiness, and hugged me. Then her smile faded. 'What is it?'

'Nothing.'

'I thought you didn't want me tonight,' she said softly.

'I know,' I said. I tightened my fingers round her arm, then hesitated, glancing at the puzzled Feorag, and let her go. Detaching her arms, I kissed her back.

'I'll miss you,' I said.

'I hope so.' Her fingertips caressed my cheekbone, and tears glinted on her lower lids. 'Please come back.'

'Yes,' I said. 'Soon.'

'Seth,' she said. 'Just come back.'

9

Being a hostage wasn't intolerable. The three of us were left to our own devices; we were fed and treated well, and Sionnach's father's surviving men had come with us: Conal had insisted on that, and they were glad to do it, as loyal now to the twins as they'd been to Niall. So at least we had friends who knew and understood us, friends who could talk about the dun and the sea and the black cattle and the smell of the machair. We were even allowed to ride out or hunt with our escorts, so long as they included Kate's fighters too. That's what we did as often as we could, getting away from the dark beauty of the underground fortress, because the only thing I could not bear about my confinement was the absence of sky.

Well. The absence of sky, and the presence of my mother.

Lilith chose to ignore me, and I was happy with that. Had I ever loved her, I wondered? Had she ever given me the least opportunity or encouragement?

Sometimes I looked at her and thought that I must have loved her once, when I was very small, but I couldn't even recall an echo of a trace of a memory. I couldn't imagine how it would feel to love Lilith.

She was always with Kate, on the queen's right hand, and she commanded the captains with the easy grace of someone who expects to be obeyed. I knew they didn't respect her so much as fear her, but it certainly worked. Besides, her beauty was awe-inspiring; that had never struck me before. And I'd forgotten the loveliness of Kate NicNiven, but then I suppose it hadn't mattered to me when I was seven, and the last time I'd seen her I'd been preoccupied with things I didn't even want to understand. Now I had time to watch Kate, study her, absorb her. Be dazzled by her.

Our queen was the Daughter of the Snows, as beautiful and terrifying as her name, but there was no coldness about her. Her hair was a bolt of copper silk, her eyes warm amber, her skin under-earth-pale but luminous. The gods knew how old she was; no-one else did. Older than Lilith, even. Far older than any of us, except for Leonora. And don't go thinking that extreme old age makes you good and far-seeing and wise. It makes you neurotic and cruel.

That was something I learned about my own race, there in that black labyrinth.

Several times Eili caught me gazing at Kate from the shadows, and she would tease me about it. We teased one another a lot, the three of us: it helped kill the dreadful wearing boredom.

'You're bewitched,' she said one time. She'd caught me loitering behind the archway that led to Kate's great hall. It was loud and crowded that day (or it might have been night; it was always hard to be certain), but Kate was very visible, relaxing on a chaise on a raised step where her people could see her and love her. It was one of her court days, and the great hall seethed with visitors and courtiers and captains. Eili nudged me. 'She's got you spell-bound.'

'Don't be stupid.' I reddened. 'She's lovely to look at, that's all. Can't I look?'

'You're in love with her,' taunted Eili.

My throat tightened. 'I am not.' Though I can't say I wasn't affected. Perhaps I should have used it to try to make Eili jealous, but I was still young and a green-arse, and I didn't know about love and deception the way I do now. I didn't want to make her jealous, I never wanted to hurt her in the smallest degree, not even her undaunted pride. 'She's beautiful, that's all. So's my mother, and I'm not in love with *her*.'

'Lilith?' said Eili, dripping scorn. '*Lilith?* Beautiful?'

I stared at her. Her voice had grown suddenly loud and brash, and I was shocked at her defiance. The boredom, that's what I blame, with hindsight. We were bored, she was bored, that was what was so fatal.

'Well,' I blustered, trying to calm her down and bring the conversation back to a comfortable place. 'Don't get stroppy. You're beautiful too.'

'I'm not beautiful,' she said dismissively. 'Sionnach, now. Sionnach is beautiful.'

That was perfectly true. A sharp-boned physical attractiveness was characteristic of our race, but somehow Sionnach's looks were gentler and not so cold; beauty fitted him better than most. But I was uncomfortably aware that Eili had no block in her mind at that moment, and that voices around us were falling silent, that people were turning, homing in on her loud excited voice. She must have known it but she was bored, she was in a bloody mood, and she didn't lower it.

'Lilith abandoned you,' she said bluntly. 'Dumped you on your father, and she couldn't even keep hold of *him*. What kind of a mother is that? Of course she's pretty, I suppose. But my brother's beautiful. That's what I call beauty. And,' she added the triumphant clincher: '*he's* beautiful on the inside, too.'

There was silence now. The throng was parting, making a nervous corridor, and through it walked my mother, elegant as a viper. She was smiling, but no-one failed to get out of her way as she walked from Kate's side right down the centre of the hall. She stopped before Eili, who met her cool gaze with disinterest.

Into the terrible silence, Lilith said: 'Bring her brother.'

Eili gave a little gasp of shock. I really don't think it had occurred to her that Lilith might bring Sionnach into this. But Eili herself had done that, after all. I could see my mother's terrible cruel logic and already I was terrified for Sionnach.

He didn't look frightened, though, only mildly perplexed as one of his own father's men shepherded him to the small clearing where Lilith stood. Sionnach glanced at me and at Eili, raising one eyebrow as if to ask what was going on. Eili stood, stunned; I could see she was too confused and guilty to let her brother see in her mind. That was so rare as to be unheard of, and he frowned.

The fighter with him was watching Lilith warily, one

hand on Sionnach's shoulder, but two of Lilith's men came forward and took Sionnach from him. Our man looked at them mistrustfully, but he had no grounds for protest. He didn't know, after all. He didn't know what they'd be told to do.

'He is beautiful, isn't he?' Lilith tilted Sionnach's chin to gaze into his eyes. She was so tall she had to stoop a little. 'And beautiful on the inside too. Of course, we only have his sister's word for that.'

I found I couldn't breathe.

My mother nodded to her men. 'Let's see this inner beauty. Open him up.'

Eili screamed and lunged for the guard, and if she hadn't clung to the man's sword arm he would have gutted Sionnach before anyone could recover their breath. The fighter who had escorted Sionnach forward drew his own blade, but was surrounded instantly by Lilith's guards. I threw myself between Sionnach and his appointed killer, but it was my mother's eyes I fixed on as I begged her. 'Mother, no. Please. Please.'

I'd sworn never to ask her for anything again, and here I was begging her for mercy. It made me hate her more than ever, and she knew it, and laughed.

'They are hostages!' yelled one of Sionnach's father's men. 'They are hostages for Cù Chaorach and they're under protection!'

'*He* isn't,' smiled Lilith, nodding at Sionnach. 'He wasn't asked for.'

Sionnach had said nothing, but there was such shock and disbelief in his eyes he didn't even struggle against the men who gripped his arms. Eili was howling her rage and terror, but Lilith turned and struck her brutally across the face to silence her. Then, as casually as if I were a full-mortal servant boy, she did the same to me.

I was so shocked I stumbled, and one of her guards stepped forward and kicked me savagely in the belly. It knocked the breath out of me so that I couldn't even move. I was still desperately sucking for air I couldn't get when Lilith nodded once more to the guard with the drawn sword, and he stepped up to Sionnach. There was nothing on his face. Nothing at all, and I knew that Sionnach was lost.

'Stop,' said Kate NicNiven.

The whole scene seemed to freeze. Some in the hall were too shocked to move, some too afraid; some were too plain curious, avid for blood and a thrill, and I never forgot that. Sionnach's father's men were surrounded, and though their blades were drawn, they were encircled and held at spearpoint by royal guards. Slowly, painfully, I sucked air into my lungs and the mist across my vision began to clear. Eili was on all fours beside me, and as she tried to scrabble to her feet I lunged and grabbed her into my arms, holding her hard and pressing my mind into hers, the way Conal used to do it for me. She had to be calm, had to. If Sionnach had a chance at all, this was it, and I didn't want her to lose it for him. She fell still and silent, but she was as tense as a drawn bowstring in my arms.

Kate laid a gentle hand on Lilith's arm. 'Lilith,' she crooned. 'There is no need for this.'

Though I'd only just got my breath back, I found I was holding it.

'I have been grievously insulted, Kate.' My mother sounded sad and grave and dignified. How I hated her.

Kate glanced at Eili. 'Arrogant child,' she said coldly. 'But your brother does not deserve to die for your stupidity.'

As I watched my lovely queen, I knew she didn't care if Sionnach lived or died horribly. This was political. Her hall was in uproar and she needed to look just, and merciful, and stern, and generous. And most of all: in control.

Eili was trembling in my arms. 'That's true, Kate. Punish me, it was my insult, my stupidity. Do as you like to me. Lilith can revenge herself on me. Not Sionnach.'

'No!' cried Sionnach.

~ *No,* I echoed in my head.

'No,' agreed Kate, lifting a hand. 'No, Eili, that would be no punishment for you. You're too tough and too brave and too stubborn. I'm afraid Lilith is right. He doesn't deserve to die, but you need to be punished.' From her belt she drew a long, jewel-handled knife. 'This is the only way to do it.'

Before any of us could draw breath she'd turned and swung the blade once, twice, at Sionnach's face. Back, forth. Left, right. I saw blood spurt, saw his eyes widen, but he didn't make a sound. He stayed absolutely silent as Kate opened his face with the blade, splitting his flesh into four new scarlet mouths, two on each cheek. He said not a word, and neither could I or Eili, as Kate destroyed his beautiful face for Lilith.

Then Kate stepped up to Eili, who could only stare

at her disfigured brother, at the torrent of blood streaming down his face and dripping from his jaw onto the flagstones. Kate lifted Eili's hands, and wiped the bloody blade on them without leaving so much as a scratch. Then she polished the blade clean on Eili's white shirt, and sheathed it, and turned to walk back to her place at the head of the hall, the smirking Lilith at her heels.

10

'It was my fault.' Eili was inconsolable.

We clustered around Sionnach in an anteroom off the great hall, Eili and me and our furious men. We'd have been better to give him some air and some space, but we couldn't bear to leave him. The healer summoned by his father's lieutenant was struggling to seal the wounds, but they were deep and vicious, there was blood everywhere, and the point of the blade had gone through to the inside of his mouth. There was no way he'd be left unscarred. Kate had done my mother's work well.

'No.' Sionnach's voice was distorted and mumbling but it held only patience, and sympathy, and a terrible undercurrent of pain. 'Not your fault.'

'You did not do this to him,' said one of our fighters angrily.

'Hush,' said the healer, wiping sweat from his forehead. He pressed another linen cloth to Sionnach's cheek, and gestured for one of the fighters to hold it there. The healer had been working for most of the day and half a night, and he was getting next to nowhere with sealing the wounds. Sionnach had lost consciousness several times, and he'd lost a lot of blood before the healer staunched the flow, but he'd never cried out or cursed. He'd left that to Eili and me. He was his silent self, as if holding onto the part of him she couldn't change.

'Witch. *Witch.*' Eili could barely contain her rage and grief and remorse.

'That's enough,' I hissed, eyeing the strange healer, and afraid for her.

'No! I swear, Seth . . .'

'Stop.' Niall's lieutenant's head snapped up. 'Listen.'

'What?' said Eili irritably through her tears.

There was a silence of unease about the place. The idle murmuring talk out in the forecourt had stopped. Booted feet shifted; spear shafts dragged on stone, swords creaked loose in scabbards. A horse, unnerved, scraped its hoof and gave a shrill whinny. I thought I could even hear the sigh of wind in the trees far, far beyond the cavern mouth.

It was his mind we felt first: his cold enraged mind. You couldn't help gritting your teeth when you felt it grate on your own. Then I heard them, we all heard them: the hoofbeats of a devil horse.

'He's come,' I said. 'He's here.'

Thirteen hours after I'd called him, my brother rode his horse to a clattering, sweating halt in the forecourt. Conal didn't look at me as he strode in; he didn't look at anyone but Sionnach. Very gently, he took Sionnach's face between his fingers and gazed at it. Releasing him, he stroked Sionnach's hair. Then he turned and flung open the hall doors, and shoved past the stunned guards. His footsteps rang and echoed on stone as the great hall too fell silent, and he marched right up to Kate's dais.

'What have you done, Kate? Where was the need for that? Just to placate Lilith's vanity?'

'The twins have always been a little above themselves, Cù Chaorach.' Kate smiled up at him affectionately. 'Perhaps this was a necessary lesson. It will do them both good. Humility is a fine virtue.'

'You had no right. They were hostages for me! If their father was alive he'd be at war with you.'

A light dry laugh, a flutter of lashes. 'He isn't alive.'

He was ice and steel. 'But I am.'

Languidly draping yourself across a chaise is fine for flirting with your courtiers or your captains; it's fine for striking a pose so your people can admire you better. Kate had made a huge mistake staying there to receive Conal. He stood above her, and he looked a great deal stronger, and nobler, and more dignified. He looked a thousand times angrier. Not all the sympathy in the hall was with Kate, and not all the respect, either. Kate's flirtatiousness looked suddenly foolish, and I wasn't the only one who saw a tiny shiver go through her. Almost, for a second, there was fear in her eyes: a distinct focused fear, like a woman eyeing her own death and knowing it. You could have heard a feather fall to earth in that hall, and I've often played that scene over in my head and wondered if Conal could have put a stop to everything, then and there, if he'd demanded the kingship from her. But he'd given her his loyalty, and despite his growing distaste he hadn't yet been driven to betrayal.

The moment was gone, and Kate gathered herself.

'Are you questioning me, Conal MacGregor?'

My brother's fury turned to bewilderment. 'Since when has that been a crime among the Sithe?'

There was a long silence, then, and all they did was look into each other's eyes. I don't know what passed between them; no-one did and I think no-one ever will, even now. But at the end of it Kate blinked, and rose to her feet.

'Get out of my sight, Cù Chaorach. You may take the hostages back to your dun, but tell your lieutenant Righil he's in command of it. As for you: let's see if living with the full-mortals teaches you some self-control.'

I backed swiftly away from the archway, horrified. I couldn't believe I'd heard her say it, and yet where else could the confrontation have gone without an actual overthrow? I tried to make out the excited whispers and the muttering in the hall, to guess at what support he'd have if he resisted, but I couldn't distinguish shock from glee, indignation from sympathy. I was too numb with dread.

But Conal was smiling as he slammed the doors of the hall and walked over to join me.

'Well, Seth, that's me exiled. Across the Veil, no less.'

'I'm coming with you, then,' I said. It wasn't bravado; there was simply no question of him going alone. I'd heard too many of Eorna's terrible stories, I knew what the full-mortals thought of us and what they were capable of. It was probably fairy-stories, told to frighten children, but I wasn't taking any chances. Of course I wouldn't let him face them alone. Of course I was going with him.

He grinned at me. 'Of course you are.'

So I did. And many times I've wondered how things would have gone, for worse and for better, if I hadn't.

PART TWO

EXILE

11

'Time you learned to read, you wee barbarian.' Conal dropped a heavy leather bag onto the rough table and grinned at me.

I swore at him.

'Your vocabulary needs work, no question.'

I cursed again. 'You think I'm not miserable enough?'

He shrugged lightly. 'You can always go home, Seth. You don't have to stay.'

I swore at him yet again, the way I always did, because that was a conversation we'd had a hundred times over the last grim months. Once again I thought longingly of the watergate in the damp green woods, the one we'd come through to reach this otherworld. It was so close, maybe a day's fast ride away.

I didn't want to be here, but I wouldn't leave Conal. The full-mortals were everything Eorna had warned me about: louse-ridden, disease-ridden, priest-ridden. I trusted every one of them as far as I could reach with the point of a short sword. They lived in squalor and darkness, and if they were rich they lived in finer squalor. Wash? You'd think they'd never heard of water, unless it was to brew crude alcohol that they never knew when to stop drinking. It seemed they couldn't connect the filth they lived in with the filth and pain they frequently died in. No wonder they were fully mortal.

Conal, of course, said it wasn't their fault. Conal said it was the way they were built, the way their kind had developed, that they were vulnerable to disease and rot in a way we weren't. He said short lives meant desperation and panic, and little time for study or memory or thought. He said their lives would lengthen in the end.

My theory was different.

Here's what I thought: they couldn't be inside another mind. They couldn't know about pain or grief or death till it hit them personally, and even when it did they reckoned the pain and grief of others less than their own, and that's why they'd never done anything about it. And maybe that's why nature had given them so much less time. I thought my race vastly superior, and nature obviously agreed with me.

Conal did not approve of my course of thought, but he refused to get into an argument.

'Don't go getting too proud, Seth,' was how he usually left it. Or, 'We're all fully mortal on the point of a sword, Murlainn.'

I was hardly likely to die of pride in my exile. From fine rooms in our own father's dun we'd come to a hovel, earth-floored, turf-and-heather-thatched, walled with stone and mud and dung. Inside it was blackened, since the cold leaked in no matter what we did to plug the gaps around the door, but the smoke never, ever found an easy way out. We kept our blackhouse as clean as we could, but there were limits to our enthusiasm. Conal liked its position, a good two miles from the clustered homes and farms of the clachan, and half-hidden by rowan and birch trees. There was nothing I found to like. I hated that place.

Now Conal tugged a few dusty volumes out of the leather bag and flipped one of them open. It smelt of dust and worm, and candle smoke, and knowledge.

'I didn't say I was *that* bored,' I told him.

'What else have you got to do this evening?'

I backed away. 'I could go and clean mouse shit out of the larder.'

He laughed and grabbed my shoulder, shoving me into a chair beside him. 'Gods, how did this end up being my job?'

'I dunno. Lilith being so nurturing and all. Where did you get these?' I nodded at the books.

'The minister.'

'The priest?'

'I've told you, he's not a priest, not any more. He's a *minister*.'

Whatever he called himself, the priest was bearable. He was tall and thin, ascetic and often severe, but kind enough. And he had a pragmatism that appealed to me, since his religion seemed adaptable to his troubled times: even the full-mortals couldn't decide what their god wanted of them. Priests who called themselves ministers were driving out priests who called themselves priests, and the priests who called themselves priests were either caving in (like this one) or running away. They were fighting over things I couldn't understand, except that the new priests were keener on sexual continence and a lot less keen on dancing and drinking. As far as I was concerned the whole crowd of them could go to their hell in a handcart, where doubtless there'd be no dancing to bother anyone.

At least this one hadn't grown fat on the tithes of his flock, and I found his grey hair fascinating, when there was clearly so much life left in him. And when he remembered to notice Conal, he liked him. Anyone who liked my brother was fine with me, and the man never made the mistake of trying to evangelise me. If I came home to find him sharing a drink and his malleable philosophy with Conal, he would nod to me, and smile in his solemn way, but that was all. I would nod back, and occasionally smile, and get on with something useful. He thought I was brain-addled, but that didn't bother me.

'Did you tell him you were teaching me to read?'

'No.' He gave me a withering look. 'I don't tell anyone anything about you. That's what you want, isn't it?'

'Yes. What does that say?' I jabbed a finger at the curled hide cover of one volume, at embossed hieroglyphics I couldn't interpret yet.

This time it was Conal's expression that darkened.

'*Demonologie*,' he said, his voice cold. Somehow, though, I didn't think he was angry at me. 'That's a book you should read, not one you'd want to. Same with this one: *Malleus Maleficarum*. Let's not start with those.'

'Fine.' I shrugged.

He gave a huffing laugh, as if trying to cheer himself

up, and pulled forward a third book. 'Come on, then. You'll be glad you did.'

And I was. In the end I was grateful he taught me to read and write. It's come in more useful than I'd have liked to admit when I was fourteen and already knew everything about everything. Disappointingly for me, Conal couldn't leave it there. He tried to teach me politics, and philosophy; he tried to teach me about the modern world, and how the full-mortals had made it, and how and why the Sithe did things so differently.

So he had to teach me ancient history too: how the foremothers had been smart enough to see how things were going between us and the full-mortals; how they'd made the *Sgath*, the Veil, back when our race was strong and had magic, because we couldn't live in the same world as the full-mortals any more. How we were just too different from them. How we stayed more and more in our own dimension, till they didn't even know us any more.

And how, sometimes, some of us couldn't resist going back.

That I didn't understand. To go into exile when you had a choice in the matter? It was the kind of thing the Lammyr were said to do. The Sithe had cut off that sickly twisted branch of our family tree, so the Lammyr chose instead to wreak havoc on the full-mortals (and find their protégés among them). Constantly, doggedly, the Lammyr slipped between the worlds, till guards had to be placed on the watergates to stop them; and still they slipped through.

It did nothing for our reputation. They're warped, the Lammyr. A piece is missing. It's the way they're built:

they don't love life, only death and pain. Who knows why the gods thought of them? Maybe they didn't give them much thought at all. Perhaps they just happened, when the gods were looking the other way.

I had never seen one, and never wanted to. Even Conal hadn't, because Griogair and the other dun captains had driven them away long before he was born. But we heard stories, and shuddered, and were glad they were gone. They'd never returned: I don't think they feared Griogair's blade or any other, but he'd spoiled their fun and they must have found a more promising playground in the lawlessness and poverty of the otherworld.

Oh, the poverty. Since my first exile I've seen many things, I've seen them all over the world. I've seen degradation and hunger that was worse, but it's never shocked me to the bones the way that first experience did. The Sithe worked hard, and we fought hard, but we lived and loved and played hard too. The full-mortals were born with nothing but their dignity, and they died with less. Out of pity there were some I'd have helped from the world, but Conal wouldn't let me. It wasn't allowed, he said. They had different traditions, different rules. Their lives did not belong to them, but to their god and his priests.

Winter was more merciful than the priests: it killed off many of the old and sick, though it had a tendency to take the very young as well. Those dark months were hard, so hard. I experienced cold like I'd never known before, cold with no respite; and I knew real hunger for the first time in my life.

There were compensations to exile, though. Even

the otherworld's open air was better than Kate's sky-less halls, and the spring that followed our first winter was a lovely one, as if to make up for the months of relentless hardship. It brought a new snow, one of gean blossom and hawthorn, and a dazzle of yellow whin heaped on every verge and hillside.

By the time spring came I could appreciate that some of the girls were good-looking, too. Not with the delicate fierce loveliness of Sithe girls, but they had a blunt charm and an earthy outlook on life that appealed to me.

I was downright offended that none of them took the least notice of me.

When I'd come out of my furious sulk at Kate—I was far more indignant on Conal's behalf than he was himself—I tried to settle down and enjoy the other-world. That didn't seem possible without the company and friendship of women. Unfortunately, none of the women seemed to require mine.

I didn't understand it. I wasn't a troll, I looked like Conal. Conal was considered beautiful even among the Sithe—but then the full-mortal girls took no more interest in him than in me. Once or twice I saw a girl in the stinking clachan take a second look, and smile and edge towards him, but if her friends or her mother called out to her she'd be easily distracted and you could see that he'd drifted quickly out of her consciousness.

It didn't bother him. He seemed amused, and it was much the same with his work. Among the Sithe Conal wasn't regarded as much of a smith, but he could fash-ion basic weapons and tools, and he was clever and inventive when it came to mending things. Nor was he a true-born healer, but he knew as much about herbs and roots and the setting of bones as any of us, and so one way or another his services were in regular demand.

But none of his customers struck up a friendship. If we saw, say, a farmer in the inn of an evening, he'd never acknowledge Conal, even though he'd sung his praises earlier in the day for a cured horse or a soothed infant or a mended plough blade. You'd think Conal had simply slipped from memory, just as he did with the girls. Even the priest would arch his winged brows in surprise when Conal struck up a conversation with him.

My brother at last took pity, and broke the truth to me one frustrating day when I'd finally managed to catch the eye of a girl in the clachan. Some of them, washing plaids with their bare feet in the burn, had been laughing in their raucous way and flirting with the boys. My favourite was the quietest one, a girl with a long black braid and solemn green eyes and a slight sceptical smile. I'd noticed her before, and thought I could like her. Now here she was, courted by boys who were ruddy-faced and crude-boned and fatuous, and I couldn't bear the wound to my vanity. Sidling into the group, I grinned at my black-haired girl and dragged her sodden plaid from the water. Skirts still hitched up, slim bare legs red with cold, she rewarded me with her half-amused smile, and I felt a jolt of lust.

'Well, hello!' said one of the others. 'And aren't you the handsome one? Where did you spring from?'

A red-haired boy gave me a filthy look.

'Ach, you ken him,' said another girl. 'He's aye up at the smith's.'

'Oh aye, I do.' Critically the first girl examined me. 'The smith's brother.'

'The quiet one. You know what they say about quiet ones!'

I was still most interested in the cool black-haired girl, but I was enjoying the unaccustomed attention from all of them. 'So tell me what they say?'

'Seth.' Conal's hand was on my shoulder. 'A word.' Smiling at the girls, he tapped his finger lightly against his temple in a clear insult either to my sanity or to my intelligence.

He drew me away, and as I glanced back over my shoulder I saw that not one of them was watching us go. Their attention was back on the skinny red-haired lad and his short ugly sidekick. I lingered resentfully, but Conal pulled me on.

'They've forgotten you, and just as well. Drink?'

I was livid. 'I was getting somewhere with her, Cù Chaorach. What are we, monks?'

'Chaster than monks,' he grinned. 'If you know what's good for you.'

'The first girls who take any notice of me,' I said bitterly, 'and you drag me off them. It's not easy, you know. They've strange tastes. They like their men like the back end of a horse.'

Laughing, Conal shoved me towards the inn. 'It isn't that. It's not your fault. You're a smouldering ball of sex and good looks, all right? Now shut up and have a drink and forget your precious extremities.'

I laughed too, I couldn't help it. 'You're buying.'

'Course I am. Listen, I mean it. They can't see you, Seth. Not really *see* you.'

I gave him a dark look.

'It's true. It's because of the Veil.' He held up his hands mockingly.

'That's nothing but a skin between the worlds,' I said.

'It's that, but it's also your protection. On this side of it . . . well, the Veil doesn't hide us, but it's camouflage. We're easy to forget. We slip from their minds like a fistful of water.'

'Uh-huh?'

'They know we're there, but they won't take an interest.'

'I see.' I thought for a moment. 'That would explain a lot.'

The inn was dark and woodsmoky, like every other hut in the clachan. It was there, theoretically, for the drovers of the north, stopping for the night on their way further south. They drank and they passed on news; they rested their ponies and their cattle, whether honestly traded or thieved; and they moved on the next day to more promising markets. But the locals haunted the inn too, trading in gossip, and dreich fiddle tunes, and a few hours' respite from grim lives. A woman from the lowlands rented the place, and made some kind of business of it: who knew how she'd ended up here with wild Highlanders? They gathered here to buy or barter good ale, and bad whisky, and forgetfulness. The place stank of alcohol and exhausted hopes.

'Listen, Murlainn.' Setting a flask of whisky on the rough table, Conal dug me in the ribs. 'Don't get the wrong idea about the Veil. Don't go thinking you can get away with murder. You're inconspicuous, not invisible. Right?'

'You might have told me this earlier.'

'You found out, didn't you?' He shrugged. 'I didn't think you'd like it.'

'I'll live. So what am I supposed to do? Lie back and think of Orach?'

He smiled. 'You could do worse. We won't be here forever.'

I wished now I hadn't made the remark. It felt like a deception of Conal, and a betrayal of Orach. To change the subject I said, 'Couldn't we just . . .'

'What?'

I glanced around at peasants who were no better than slaves to their clan chief. There were worse lairds; I'm sure there were better. In the dimness of the inn, men sat and stared into their filthy cups, beaten down by work, and work, and more work, for no reward that I could see but survival. And their women worked harder, for less pleasure.

I loathed them and pitied them. Where was their wild-hearted music and their dancing and their joy in breathing the world's air?

'We could make it better for them,' I said. 'We could improve them. We could . . . we could change their minds.'

Conal took his time filling our dirty tumblers with whisky. At last he took a mouthful, and cuffed my cheek gently.

'That's beneath you, Murlainn.'

'Nothing is beneath me.' I regretted that too, as soon as it was out. He'd stuck a thorn in my pride, but I'd let myself be provoked, and my words reeked of self-pity.

'They have free will just like we do. Why shouldn't they keep it?'

'Much good it does them.' I snorted.

'Look, how strong do you think your mind would have to be? You can influence one or two, if you're clever. Twist a perception, adjust a memory. Whether you should or not . . .' He shrugged. 'Well, I don't think so.'

'Why not? When we're better than they are?'

I saw the temper flash in his eyes. 'Sometimes I despair of you. Better, you call yourself? Go ahead and fight people with your mind, if they can fight back. If they know what you're doing, why not? Otherwise it's as honourable as taking your sword to an unarmed man. You want to be like Kate, or your mother?' He nodded at the surly-mouthed drinkers. 'Kate wants to manipulate their minds. She wants to rule them, to own the otherworld.'

'Why doesn't she, then?' I muttered, 'Gets her own way with everything else.'

'Can't.' He grinned again, I was relieved to see. 'That's why she wants rid of the Veil. She's got the strength in her head to control a mob, even a nation. But not if they can't see her.'

'And she's no more conspicuous than the rest of us?' I said.

'Quite. She wants to be seen, she'd love to be loved by them, but she doesn't know how to destroy the Veil. That's beyond even her, thank the gods.'

I communed with the gods as little as I could. 'Why?'

'Remember what Leonora said, that night you came spying? It's true, we *need* the Veil. The full-mortals are easily whipped to fear, and from there it's only a step to hatred. Destroy the Veil, you destroy the Sithe. In the end you do.' He shook his head. 'I like to think Kate doesn't understand that. Hasn't thought it through, you know? Why would she do such a thing to her own people?'

'Cause she fancies some full-mortal boy?' I thought about the pretty girl in the marketplace, and my groin ached. 'I'm with Kate.'

It was supposed to be a joke. Partly. But his voice was frosty when he said, 'You're my brother, Murlainn. I want you on my side.'

I stared at him. I could barely believe he would even question it.

'Always,' I said. 'I will always be your bondsman, Cù Chaorach. I'll never let you down.'

He glanced up, searching my eyes, then gave me a troubled smile.

'I know that, Murlainn,' he said. 'I know that.'

12

'Ah, your brother. He's hard on you, isn't he? I think perhaps he has to be, my beautiful boy.'

I blinked at my filthy whisky, then raised my glass to eye the speaker through its murky filter.

So I'd finally been noticed. And she thought I was beautiful. Unfortunate, then, that my new admirer was the old crone who ran the place. She was leaning on the chair Conal had left five minutes ago to do some business with the miller. I'd stayed to sulk. It seemed ironic that I couldn't now get any peace to do it.

Her name was Sinclair. Her principal business was the brewing of ale, but she also paid men to turn bere-meal into whisky up in the hills. The laird turned a blind eye, or he simply didn't care, or the arrangement suited him as well as it did everyone else.

'Hello,' I said. 'What do you want?'

She sniffed and gave me a haughty look, but pulled out Conal's chair and slumped down anyway, leaning her bare sinewy arms on the table. 'Too old for you, am

I? And here was me thinking you wouldn't be that fussy, seeing as you never have a girl in your bed.'

I felt my jaw sag, so I shut it with a snap. 'Look, no offence, but . . .'

She gave a raucous howl that I decided was a laugh. 'Oh, don't panic, laddie. You're a youngster and I'm not after your body. Fine as it is.' Her wink was so suggestive I laughed.

'And how would you know?'

'I've seen it,' she said briskly, and poured herself a dram of the whisky I'd paid her good money for. 'I go up the hill by way of that linn under the waterfall. I've seen you and your brother swimming of a morning.'

'The cheek of you,' I said.

'The cheeks on *you*,' she said, and let out that barking howl of a laugh again. 'Fine pair of backsides you have, you and him. And more. If I was twenty years younger . . .'

'Aye, right,' I said. 'Forty maybe.'

She guffawed into her whisky, then downed it in one and wagged the glass at me. I was grinning, but her eyes glinted with seriousness.

'I know what you are,' she said. 'I've seen your kind before.'

Pushing my glass away, I got to my feet. 'I'll be going.'

'No.' Her claw of a hand was round my wrist, and surprisingly strong. 'I don't mean you harm.'

'Is that right? You tell me something, then.' I shook her off, but sat down again and glared at her, one hand possessively on my whisky bottle. 'Why are you talking to me?'

'I told you. I've seen your kind before. I know others

don't see you so well.' There was a note of pride in her voice. 'They say I've a bit of the blood myself. I have the sight.'

'The *sight* indeed.' But I stared at her. Behind the crumpled skin and veins and tiny sprouting hairs there were bones like a lovely rockface, high and prominent and well-defined. 'Aye, maybe, but a *bit* would be right. And don't believe everything you hear. Two sights! Prophecy! It's horseshit wherever you get your blood, lady.'

'And see? You're calling me a lady.' Her cheeks dimpled with her huge gold-toothed smile. 'That proves it, then.'

Exasperated, I rolled my eyes. 'Is there a point to this conversation? Seeing as you don't want my body?'

'I'm telling you to be careful.' Her sudden plummets into seriousness were unnerving.

I hesitated. 'We keep our heads down.'

'Aye, your brother's a wise man. You're less so, but then you're only a boy still.' Her gilded grin took the barb out of her remark. 'And I'm not the only one who sees you well.'

A little shiver in the nape of my neck. 'Is that so?'

'That's so. And you know who I mean and all.'

I did know. There was one otherworlder who never failed to notice us, one man who always acknowledged Conal with an unsmiling nod: the man who'd given us our sorry strip of land and the right to farm it. Our laird, our new chief, our landlord. The MacLeod.

Conal said we had to be grateful to him for a place to live and work. I wasn't, but luckily we didn't see him often. Occasionally he rode through the clachan with his men, collecting rents or judging disputes or sentencing thieves and cheats. He was an earl and a clan chief, one of the old Mormaers who had controlled these otherworld lands for centuries and had never bowed to interfering kings. It gave him an easy authority that I resented; I'd have liked to slap his complacent face, to let him know I was at least his equal, that I was the son of a dun captain, the scion of a powerful Sithe clann. But it would have meant nothing to him, and I'd have ended up flogged or branded or kicked out of our meagre home, so I kept my resentment to myself.

Anyway, Conal liked him. Conal liked most people, whether or not they noticed him.

I didn't want to encourage Ma Sinclair and her gossip, but the curiosity was killing me. 'The MacLeod.' I cleared my throat gruffly. 'What? He's got the blood too?'

'Him? Never!' A raw whoop of mirth, then she lowered her voice, all conspiratorial. 'But they say he's had *dealings*. With you. With the People of Peace, I mean.'

'If you knew that much about us,' I said, 'you wouldn't be using that expression.'

'Well.' For the first time she looked offended. 'He's had a lover among you. That will explain it, you see. The MacLeod knows how to see you. Be careful. That's all I'm saying.'

She stood up, whisking away my half-full bottle and shuffling back to her counter. I was so startled by her nerve I could only gape at her swishing grubby skirts, but all she did was dump the bottle on the dirt floor and rummage on a shelf for another. That one she brought back and clanked onto the table in front of me.

'There,' she whispered. 'It's better, that one. And I'll be giving you that, you and your brother, next time you come, and all the times after.'

I cocked a sceptical eyebrow. 'Why?'

She winked again; for her age she had a real way of looking lascivious. 'Because I'm superstitious, my beautiful lad? I'll be staying on your good side if I can.'

'Nice. So long as you know it won't do you any good. You won't be finding your chores done in the morning and your enemies' cows won't be running dry.'

'I have no enemies, laddie, and I've had all I wanted from your kind. You taste that second bottle and you'll see. And I know some healing ways. They were taught me by someone like your brother.' A lustful nostalgia misted her eyes. '*Thirty* years ago. So no more cheek from you.'

I laughed, and taking the whisky I rose to go after Conal, but she tugged on my sleeve again.

'You tell him to be careful, mind. With his healing.' Her eyes were pale and watery, but that wasn't all that made them so cold. 'It's all fine and well when it goes as it should. Wait till it doesn't, and you'll see less gratitude.'

I gave a short laugh, bewildered now and cross. 'Is that a threat?'

'It's a warning, my lad. You're too beautiful to burn.'

The silly crone had too much time on her hands. I'd seen this before with women in the marketplace: she was old, and lonely, and thirsty to make excitement out of thin air. It wasn't till I opened the whisky later that night that a chill set into my backbone.

It wasn't that the drink was bad. It was too good, and I could taste the truth of her words, and I realised she knew what she was talking about.

I tried to forget what Ma Sinclair had said. Conal was already too careful, too nervous for my taste; I almost yearned for a decent bar brawl to brighten up my life. There seemed no need to pass on any extra warnings, and besides, I could keep an eye on him. That was what I was here for, after all.

'I've wondered about the MacLeod,' I told Conal one cold and damp spring dawn.

'I know you have,' he said. 'Me too. But he's a born reiver, and I don't want to get involved in wars here. He's always away on raids. Taking cattle. Picking fights.'

That was kind of my point. 'He'd take us on as professional fighters. You know that.'

Like the other chiefs, he'd call up the men of his clan—only the men!—if he went to serious war with a neighbour, but for his regular raids and small quarrels the MacLeod kept around him a small band of well-paid men who were not even of his own family, but who were fiercely loyal and fought like demons with a grudge. The gods knew where they came from, those private mercenaries of his. They were his personal bodyguard, and they were the terror of the glen because they had no allegiance to any clan member but its chief. Why did he need them? The ordinary clansmen could fight, and very much liked to, dashing off at the drop of a whisky flask to snatch their weapons from the thatch of their hovels and fling themselves into battle for the head of their clan and its honour. But the MacLeod's guard lived better than any clansman, in their captain's castle; they were a privileged elite, and they existed only to fight. I liked the sound of the job.

'It would be a better life than grubbing in the dirt,' I said. 'Half what we grow we have to turn over to the laird anyway.'

'Don't exaggerate.'

I wasn't exaggerating much. 'We can fight. We're born fighters too. We'd be valuable to him, we'd be rewarded. And see that last scythe you made? It was crap.'

He gave a small amused gasp, his fingers flicking out lightning-fast to clip my ear.

'I'm not a farmer, Conal. I'm a hunter. I'm a fighter.' I was sick of tilling a pathetic rig of land with a borrowed horse and a community plough. I was meant to trade for grain and bread, trade for it with wild meat and the farmer's guarantee of my sword arm in his defence.

'Ach, you've a long life ahead of you, if you're lucky.' Conal gave my arm a mock punch that hurt quite a lot. 'You'll learn to do most things. Fighting all the time dulls your mind. Sometimes it's good to sit still and work at a trade.'

'You sound like Kate,' I said. 'As if it's good to be humbled. I never saw her humble herself.'

'I'll not argue with that,' he said with a roll of his eyes. 'But it's not about humbling. It's about learning patience.'

'Yes, and I've done that,' I snapped.

Conal laughed.

'What's so funny?'

'If you don't know, I can't tell you. Anyway, we hunt, don't we?' He tugged his bow out of the thatch, bringing down a light rain of mouse droppings. 'Speaking of which, I'll get breakfast.' With that he slouched out into the early morning darkness.

I had a job coaxing the smoored fire back to life, but I didn't think I'd lost all track of time, so I was shocked when I heard Conal curse foully enough to make me wince. Back already?

The door slammed open. He didn't have his bow in his hands, or indeed any breakfast, but a parcel of some kind.

'What am I supposed to do?' he barked. 'What am I supposed to do?'

With gentleness he laid the bundle on the table, and the filthy rags that bound it fell away, and I saw what it was. So I don't know why I said: 'What the *hell* is that?'

There were tears in his eyes, but still he gave me a dry look.

I took out my knife. 'We have to kill it.'

Violently he struck the knife out of my hand. 'It's a baby!'

'It's a dying baby! Have you gone mad? It's in pain, look at it!'

'It wouldn't be dying if some poverty-stricken cur hadn't left it out all night!'

'Well, they did! That won't survive.' I took a step back from it as if its inevitable death would be catching.

Conal took one look at me, a look I did not like, and took the creature into his arms. It didn't cry; I wondered when it had stopped crying. Some time last night, I thought. If it ever had the strength to cry at all.

I think it breathed its last even as we watched. It was a rickle of bones anyway, and probably diseased, because it stank. Conal didn't put it down even when it was dead. He stroked its hollowed cheeks, and brushed its thin eyelids down over sunken eyeballs, and then he shut his own eyes and pressed its fragile dead face into the hollow of his throat. As if it could feel anything now, as if he could make up with a little belated affection for its brief hideous life.

'Jesus, Seth. Jesus.' He'd taken to barking their god's name when he was angry or upset. 'This isn't ancient Greece, it's the back end of the sixteenth century.' He opened his red eyes to glare at me. 'Who are these people?'

'Just what I keep asking you.' I shrugged. 'We need to, ah . . . what is it they do?' I took as little notice of their rites as I could, but I was pretty sure they didn't give their dead to the raptors and the wild beasts.

'I don't know,' he said, and then, 'They bury them.'

'In the ground?' I tried not to raise my eyebrows. Different people, different cultures. 'So what do we do? You'd better put it in fast, or it'll rot.'

'But it needs . . . it would want . . .'

I gave him a droll look. ~ *It isn't capable of wanting*.

'I know, but . . .' Carefully he laid it back on the table and unfolded the remaining rags, gave the tiny naked corpse a brief glance, then covered it again. 'It's a girl.'

'So?'

'I didn't want to go on calling her *it*. Listen, we can't just . . . put her in the ground. We need to get the minister.'

'Are you *mad*?'

He had that stubborn look I'd grown to dislike. 'It's not just the rites. It's . . . I don't want to do this without his knowledge. It might be trouble. I need to ask his advice.'

'You ask me, the most trouble we'll get is if anyone else knows about this.'

'Somebody already does,' he pointed out. 'Whoever left her. Gods, did they expect me to find her sooner? She was quite close. On the edge of the clearing. Shit, shit, shit.'

I hated Kate more and more for this exile. I'd never before known Conal to be insecure and indecisive, so uncertain of himself. It was my first experience of being the one to do the reassuring, the one to take decisions. I wasn't sure I liked it after all. Besides, me taking decisions was pointless when Conal wouldn't accept them.

'Let's put it in the ground,' I said.

'Her.' He shook his head. 'Her. I'll get the minister.'

I sat with it—with her—while Conal was gone. If it had been a dog or a horse I might have left it and got on with my chores, or forced myself to look at the book Conal had ordered me to read, but for some reason I didn't like to turn my back on the creature. It lay there like an accusation.

There was no point pitying it, so I tried—without much success—to pity whoever had left it on the cold ground to die. Or perhaps not to die. Perhaps they had indeed left it for Conal. Perhaps he was their last hope. Suddenly I understood the panic in his eyes, and his despair. *What am I supposed to do?*

There was nothing he could have done, nothing, you could tell just by looking at it. How did full-mortals react, I wondered, when their last hope failed them?

'Trouble,' I said aloud. 'Trouble.'

I stood above the pathetic cadaver, unfolded its wrapping of rags. I used to see stretched hides hung in the tannery: that's what this looked like. Dry taut dead skin hung on a framework of bone. Glancing at its eyelids, I half-expected movement beneath them, for its eyeballs to shift as if it was dreaming, dreaming of daylight. Instead a fly buzzed onto the frail lashes. Even then I expected the infant to blink and stir and cry, but of course it didn't. Angrily I batted the fly away, but it was quick to return.

I felt an urge to pick the infant up as Conal had done, to cradle it against my neck and warm it back to life. Stupid impulse. I shook my head, and rubbed my red and tired eyes. The otherworld god could bring people back to life, I knew that, so if he wanted to do it he would. It was his job, not mine.

My gods didn't make crazy promises. They kept themselves to themselves, and my life was no business of theirs. I liked it that way, I liked that they weren't interested in my personal development, that they didn't try to make me feel guilty just for being born. I'd had enough of that. Martyrs didn't impress me, judges didn't frighten me, and even those petulant Greek and Roman warrior-gods left me cold. They couldn't let a battle go the way it should but took sides and chose favourites; they interfered and destroyed fine fighters on a whim. Gods! It was fantasy to brighten grey lives and greyer deaths.

I waited and watched, but this little one's god wasn't interested in her either. The fly settled on the table by the tiny corpse, and I took my chance, slamming my palm onto it. It clung to my hand, sticky and vile. Furiously I rubbed my palm against my trews, then washed my hands in the bucket of cold water in the corner. With wet chilled hands I wrapped the infant once again in its swaddling, tugging the cloth carefully over its face before more flies could come.

When the priest arrived, the first thing he did was uncover it again. I wanted to slap his hand away.

'Unbaptised,' he said, and shook his head.

So that explained the god's indifference. I kept my face stony and uninterested.

'What does it matter?' asked Conal. I knew from the way the priest looked at him in surprise, from the way Conal's gaze shifted and he bit his lip, that he'd made a mistake.

'To me? It doesn't,' said the priest. Fumbling in a small leather bag, he drew out a vial of oil. 'To others it will.'

'Um,' said Conal. 'Can you, er . . . bury her, then?'

The priest blinked at him. 'Of course she has to be buried. But we can't put her in the graveyard. She can't go in consecrated ground. Now, if you'll give me a moment?'

Glancing at me, Conal shrugged slightly, looking bewildered, and I made a wry face.

~ *Different cultures*, I said.

~ *Bloody incomprehensible cultures*, he retorted.

~ *What's consecrated ground, when it's at home?*

~ *No idea. Same as holy ground?*

~ *So how do they define that, then? Not like ours?*

~ *Dunno*. He went back to watching the murmuring priest, who was making crossing motions with his fingers on the baby's face. When he'd finished whatever bizarre rites he was conducting, he stepped back and smiled sadly at Conal.

'There are those,' he said, 'who would say the child is trapped in Limbo, barred from Heaven. I want you to know I don't think that.'

'No,' said Conal, trying to look as if he understood what the man was on about.

'So can we dig a hole for her now?' I asked.

I knew, from the way the priest looked at me, that I'd put my foot in it. So I gave him my simplest smile, and after a moment he returned it, with a kind look of understanding that made me want to punch him.

Conal's mouth was twisted; I could tell that even in these evil circumstances he was trying not to grin.

'I'll take her,' said the priest. 'Best if you're not involved.'

Conal stared at him for a moment.

'I promise I'll bury her,' said the priest gently. 'In the birchwood. It's a lovely place. I've done it . . .' He cleared his throat. 'I've put them there before.'

Conal nodded, his arms tightly folded.

'I think you understand,' said the priest, and he

glanced at me, and said again, 'Best if you're not involved. Neither of you.'

'I understand. Thank you,' said Conal.

The priest folded the scraps of cloth back around the infant, and lifted her into his arms. 'Thank you for calling on me, my child.'

I opened my mouth to point out that Conal was the son of Griogair, not the priest; Conal gave me a mental cuffing in the nick of time. It must be an expression they used, I thought, rubbing my forehead crossly.

'You should have left her where you found her,' I said, when the priest had gone and Conal had shut the ill-fitting door behind him. Outside the breeze had risen. A breath of cold snaked in, and my skin prickled.

'You know I couldn't do that.'

'Sentimentalist. There'll be trouble.'

He shrugged, looking tired. 'Maybe.'

'The child was exposed, Conal. The woman left her near you to salve her own conscience, that's all. The creature was one hungry mouth too many and it was sick. If she thought it could survive she'd have *brought it to you.*'

'Maybe,' he said. He was about to lose his temper but at least he'd also lost that miserable defeatist look. 'What did you want me to do, Seth? Pretend I hadn't seen the child?'

'And you're the one that wants us to keep our heads down,' I spat. 'Well, I'd rather have the MacLeod's protection and a weapon and a fighting chance. You know what Ma Sinclair told me? You put a foot wrong with all your damn healing and you'll *burn.*'

'I could *not leave that baby!*' he yelled.

I'd caught him in a weak moment. 'What's *Malleus Maleficarum?*'

Wrong-footed, momentarily silenced, he kicked out a stool and sat down. He didn't meet my eyes. '*The Hammer of Witches.*'

'Yup, I worked that out. Did that priest give it to you?'

'*Minister*. Yes. But not because he believes it.'

'It was written by priests.' Impatiently I slung the cover open. 'Here. On the authority of Innocent the Eighth. *Innocent*, if you please!'

'It's just a name.'

'His true name?'

'No, not like that. I think they choose their names themselves.'

'What's the point of that?' I shook my head in disgust. 'Who was he?'

'Some high priest of theirs,' said Conal. 'Popes, they call them.'

'See? They don't have *high priests* any more, but your *ministers* go on reading their filthy books. They're all the same.'

'That one isn't.'

'He's a hypocrite! He's supposed to be of the new church, but even I know oils and crosses isn't Covenant business.'

'He's a realist! And he's a good man.' Conal sighed and rubbed his temple. 'He gave me that book as a warning. Innocent made witchcraft a heresy, and yes, heretics are for burning.'

'We're not witches,' I pointed out.

Leaning across, he pulled the book to himself, turning

the thick pages till he found what he was looking for and shoved it back to me. 'There you go. Read it to me.'

I growled, but I began to read.

'*Many persons of both sexes . . . by incantations, spells, superstitions and horrid charms . . . blast and eradicate the fruits of the earth, the grapes of the vine and the fruits of trees . . .* I read all this.' I gave a barking laugh. 'We can't do any of that. Even our witches can't do that! Why would we want to?'

'Go on,' he said. 'It gets better.'

'I know, I know. *These wretches afflict and torment men and women . . . with pain and disease . . .* oh, it's bollocks, Conal, come on. Witchcraft's mind manipulation, that's all.'

'Not quite all,' he said patiently. 'It's misuse of your abilities. It's taking advantage of your . . . advantages. But go on.'

'*They do not shrink from committing and perpetrating the foulest . . .*' I was stumbling over the words now, out of distaste more than ineptitude ' . . . *the foulest abominations and excesses, whereby they offend the divine majesty and are a cause of scandal . . .* for crying out loud, Conal. Presumably it was the divine majesty who gave me a pr . . .'

'Whoa, enough!' he interrupted with a snort of laughter. 'It's not personal, Seth. This is all folk memory and hysteria, and filthy minds, and fear of nature, and fear of their own natures.'

'So it doesn't matter what we do?'

'Hell, no. If I'd cured the damn baby they'd have thought me even more of a witch. It's not so bad just now. All we need to do is keep quiet, keep our heads below the parapet, but this witch-fever comes and goes. Like a tide or a disease. If it rises here, staying out of sight won't be enough. We'll have to run.'

I tapped the book. 'You said it yourself. Even the priest—*minister*—doesn't believe this stuff. These are extremists.'

'Did you get to part three?'

'No, I got all caught up in part two and what we get up to. All that shape changing and sexual deviance. What have you been getting up to behind my back, you selfish bugger?'

'Heh! I know it's a riot, but you really should have got to part three. It makes torture and death *compulsory*. In a witch-hunt any witness can testify, and their motives don't matter. The religious inquisitors are in charge, no questions asked. Here. The MacLeod's a law unto himself, of course, but look at this bit.'

I took the book again. '*The inquisitors be empowered to proceed to the correction, imprisonment and punishment of any persons for the said abominations, without let or hindrance, in every way . . .*'

I swallowed hard.

'Now do you want the girls to notice you?' he asked dryly.

'I want to go home,' I said.

'So let's keep our noses clean. Kate will recall us one day, and we'll have to kiss her hand and swear loyalty on our knees, and you, Murlainn, will have to do it without a sarcastic sneer on your face, just as I will. Until then, let's just survive, shall we?'

'Yes,' I said.

'And let's be grateful for the Veil,' he added, 'even if it means scratching our own itch.'

I managed to laugh.

13

I needed some air. We both did. Conal didn't want to think about the dead infant; I didn't want to think about how homesick and afraid I was. So we did what we always did when we were miserable. We went hunting.

Or, as the MacLeod might put it: we went poaching.

There was more forest even in those days, beautiful, dark, breathing with life. A hunt was easy enough, if you were discreet. Game, to many of the full-mortal clansmen, was fair game, and there was plenty of it: coneys, birds, hares. If we could get away with it Conal and I liked venison: we liked the stalk and the chase as much as the smell and the smoke of it choking us in our blackhouse and the warm fat feeling in our bellies. In the wake of the winter just past, we liked knowing that our hidden meat store was full.

We had little luck that day, but it was good to be out there, a long way from the clachan and death and sickness. When we were far enough from what passed for civilisation, and the deer seemed regrettably far from us, we usually found a clearing and went through our paces with staffs in place of swords, or we practised with longbows or crossbows or throwing knives. Because one day, we kept telling each other, we'd go home, and we'd better not forget all that we knew. And we'd better be able to fight, we'd better be able to defend ourselves and our dun. That was the part we never said aloud.

If we wandered far enough on our hunts, there were places I could make out the contours of home: an escarpment here, a rivermouth there, a sea loch eating into the land. This world was so like ours: only the towns and the farms and the people were so terribly different.

Funny: I questioned the gods but I never questioned the Veil. I never questioned why I couldn't simply reach out my hand and touch home, how it was so completely separated and hidden from me, and yet I could see its outline like a ghost in the otherworld. That was only a taunting mirage, but I knew that if I walked for enough days I'd come to our watergate, and I'd only have to step into it to be at home again, back in the real world.

Yet I wouldn't do it. Not while Conal couldn't. Sometimes it made me laugh, that I could love another human being more than I loved my home, the home that had nursed me when no human being would touch me. Yet I did: I would give up my home forever for him. It ran quite counter to my self-image. All I could do about it was laugh.

'What's funny?' Stretched out in the grass below a

rock outcrop, Conal sounded too sleepy to be genu-
inely interested. The stone slabs crowned a high bare
hill; around and below us stretched the forest, striped
with gold, the pine-tops lit with sunlight. Our weapons
lay where we'd dropped them in favour of basking in
the late afternoon sun. I was propped against the
smooth grey rock, liking its coolness at my back con-
trasting with the warmth of the sun on my chest and
face. We were barefoot as we always were when we
hunted, and I felt a spider run delicately across my
toes. I wiggled them and it fled into the coarse hilltop
grass.

'Nothing's funny,' I said at last. 'I'm happy, that's
all.'

He gave me a dry sidelong glance. 'Finally? Good.'

I laughed again. 'I'll be happier when we're out of
here.'

'Me too.' He sat up very suddenly. 'Sh. Did you hear
that?'

I stilled. There wasn't much breeze, only an idle stirring of the pine-tops. I heard small animals about their
business in the forest litter, the distant susurration and
slap of the calm sea. There was a faint sad whimpering . . .

Whimpering.

Conal's eyes met mine, then slewed over my shoulder.
'The rock,' he said.

It wasn't just one rock, it was a jumble of them,
propped against one another like drunks enjoying the
view. One of them had been split by time and weather
as if by a giant sword; you could still see the matching
veins of glistening white on either side of the shadowed

cut. Rolling onto my belly I wriggled between the halves, pausing to listen.

~ *It's stopped*, I told Conal, twisting to look up at him.

~ *Heard you, whatever it was.* He was crouched above me, one foot on either side of the crack. Staring down, he said, ~ *Go a bit further in.*

I did, like a snake on my belly. There were advantages to being smaller than Conal; he'd have been stuck like a cork in a bottle before now.

~ *By your left hand, look.*

I could see what he meant. Rather, I could feel what he meant. There was a slit of a gap beneath the rock, half hidden by stunted grass and earth. I slipped my fingers in. There was only cold silence, but I could sense something in there, trembling in the stone darkness. Tentatively I reached out my mind, and the something growled.

I wriggled awkwardly out, shivering with the shadow-cold. Conal, back on my level, hauled me the last few feet by my ankles.

'Ow,' I said, rubbing my scraped elbow. 'Something's there, but there must be another way in. A lizard couldn't get through that hole.'

It took us a long time of searching; the slash of an entrance was well-concealed among the rocks and even I had to bend almost double to get round the crook of the short tunnel. Conal couldn't get in at all. Once inside, I could almost stand upright. The cavern was substantial and there was a little dim light leaking through cracks. My eyes dilated swiftly and I could see.

Four pinpoints of light glared back at me. Their owners had jammed themselves as far as they could under a shelf of rock, and one of them had begun to snarl again. There was a smell of death, and I quickly saw the scraps of fur and inert flesh scattered around the bare floor. Surprisingly little damage had been done to the tiny corpses; I think the surviving two had mouthed and chewed on their siblings, out of desperation, but they weren't old enough to make much impression. What they needed was their mother's milk, and clearly they wouldn't be getting that again.

~ *What is it?* asked Conal.

~ *Wolf young.*

~ *Thought so.*

I lay on my belly and gazed at one of them. ~ *Little earth-son*, I coaxed. ~ *Mac tire.*

Snarl.

~ *Little earth-daughter. Sorry, my love.*

She pulled back her lips to reveal her baby teeth as I crawled slowly forward.

Snarl.

Sighing, I rolled onto my back, tipped back my head and gave her my best smile. Which was a lot like a wolf's. So I'd been told.

Crawling forward, she snuffled at my face. I could see now she was very pale-coated. Her eyes were sunken with hunger and when I slipped my hand beneath her body I could feel all her ribs.

~ *Earth-daughter,* I said grimly, ~ *I've seen one die today already. Come.*

She let me close my fingers around her skeletal body. Getting to my knees, I held her in two hands. Her heart thrashed hard and she shivered, but she didn't struggle, even when I crawled to the cavern mouth and manhandled her round the tunnel. When I felt her safe in Conal's hands, I turned back for the other survivor.

I was expecting another pale shape, so it took me longer than I expected to find him in the murk. The eyes that glared hopelessly at me were set in a black-furred face. I went down on my knees, sliding my hand under him and drawing him gently out from his hiding-place. No need to seduce this one. It couldn't run or fight.

~ *Do you have the other?* asked Conal.

~ *It won't live. Give me a minute.*

I set the cub on my lap. He tried to stand but flopped onto his side.

'Sh,' I said, rubbing his bony forehead with my thumb. Quietly I slipped my hunting knife from its sheath. 'Sh, now, earth-son.'

His dull eyes followed the knife as I tested the edge of it on my other thumb, and he cringed away. A sliver of light caught the blade, flashing into his eyes and turning them briefly alive.

Which is when he sank his baby teeth deep into the base of my thumb.

'Ah ya wee . . .' I dropped the knife abruptly, for fear I'd be provoked into using it.

'What's up?' called Conal.

I didn't answer, just reached for my knife and slipped it back into its sheath. The little black demon was shivering at my knees where I'd dropped it, all its last effort spent, but it still glared up at me, daring me to kill it. Daring me even to touch it.

'I'll call you on that,' I murmured, and gathered it into both hands. One hand I slipped gently around its throat to hold its head away from my flesh, then I held it against my body and ducked down to worm back out of the death-cave. Conal's hand reached down, but I said 'It's all right,' and I slithered out myself, the little wolf clutched against me.

'That the lot?' he said.

'The rest are dead,' I said. 'No dam.'

'Dead too, then.' He had the white wolf-cub cradled in one arm against his chest, and he offered me a hand. Gratefully I took it, blinking in the bright light, and he hauled me to my feet.

When he released my hand, his own was sticky with my blood. He raised his eyebrows.

'It'll live,' I said dryly, 'the wee bastard.'

He laughed.

'I'd like to find the dam,' he said.

'Why?'

'She wasn't an otherworld wolf. Look.' He turned the scrawny pale cub towards me. It blinked, its eyes squeezed narrow, but deep in their dullness shone a spark of silver light.

I never thought about that light. It was in Conal's eyes, and mine, and every other Sithe's, and I knew the full-mortals didn't have it. Sometimes you'd look twice at a full-mortal, thinking you'd seen something, and then you'd realise it was only a reflected light. A Sithe had eyelight when there was none to reflect.

'The miller brought in a dog wolf's-head last week for the bounty,' I told him. 'He probably went looking for the mate.'

'Found her, then,' he said. 'But couldn't find the den.'

'I'm not going to say the f-word,' I told him wryly, 'but these aren't going to help our image, are they?'

The scrap of pale wolf managed to lick his nose, and he grinned.

'So let's keep very quiet,' he suggested, 'about our *pets*.'

He called his wolf Liath, for the greyness of her coat. I called mine every name under the sun, especially when it bit me, which was often.

'Bloody little runt.' I swore at it. 'Runt of the litter.'

But so was I. And I'd learned to bite, too.

In the end the name that stuck was Branndair, because he was hard like iron. He wouldn't have survived otherwise, and for a while I was afraid he wouldn't. But the two cubs grew accustomed to cow's-milk and pigeon-meat, and eventually they fattened and were fully weaned, and Branndair at last stopped being such an aggressive little bastard and crawled onto my cramped box-bed at night and slept in my arms, grunting and whimpering in happy dreams.

I grew to love him. And with every new thing I found to love, I grew more afraid.

14

'Agnes Sampson,' said Conal. 'Agnes Sampson and James the Sixth.'

Branndair tumbled over my foot, so I swept him up in one hand and set him down where he wanted to go. When we were at home it was safe enough for the cubs to be with us; when we were away we always hid them in an old badger sett halfway up the hill. They knew to stay there and stay silent—they were Sithe wolves and they'd learned that before they even learned not to piss in the blackhouse—but still, we hid the entrance of the sett with rocks and branches to be on the safe side.

In a shadowy corner of the room, a darker shadow himself, Branndair began to stalk a knotted piece of old rope I'd given him for a toy. Far more regal and superior, Liath sprawled on her back in Conal's lap, pretending to be asleep. Rubbing her belly, he went on doggedly educating me against my will.

'James the Sixth, Murlainn. Whose mother was?'

'Mary Queen of Scots,' I said in a bored voice.

'Mary Queen of Scots,' he agreed, 'who introduced a statute banning witchcraft in 1563.'

'Who provoked rebellion by her captains, was betrayed to a neighbouring state and decapitated after due judicial process,' I said, only half under my breath, 'thus setting an intriguing precedent.'

Conal didn't say anything. I thought he was angry with me, because absolute silence was often a sure sign of his fury. I used to mistake it for disinterest, till his fist would lash out unexpectedly.

These days I preferred to see it coming, so nervously I raised my eyes. He was looking at me, but he seemed deep in thought, biting the edge of his forefinger.

At last he said, 'Be careful, Seth. Be careful what you think.'

'I could say the same to you.'

'Yes.' His mouth twisted. 'Remember, Seth: on your knees. Abasing yourself. Kissing her hand in front of her entire court. Nothing in your eyes but humility. Get used to the idea.'

'Did Kilrevin have to do that after his exiles?'

'Every single time. I've watched him do it.'

'Did he sacrifice his pride?'

Conal hesitated. 'No,' he said. 'No, somehow he never did.'

'Then I never will either,' I said. 'Even on my knees.'

He gave a meaningful sigh. 'Agnes Sampson,' he said again. 'Denounced by Gilly Duncan under torture, a few years ago. Gilly Duncan was arrested for using herbal cures.'

'The moral being, we should keep our noses out of full-mortal business and stop doing them so many sodding favours.'

'The moral being,' he said darkly, 'we need the Veil. There is no other defence. Never take it for granted.'

'I thought you said Kate couldn't affect it anyway.'

'She'll keep trying. You and I are going to talk her out of it.'

'Oh,' I said. Hell's teeth. What was I, some kind of diplomat? Sometimes I thought my brother wasn't a very good judge of character. 'Agnes whatshername,' I reminded him with a sigh.

'Agnes Sampson. Educated, respectable, but it never did her any good. The king was in on her torture.'

'Then he should rot in a hell of his own imagining,' I said, tapping his *Demonologie*. 'Only a halfwit believes a tortured witness.'

'Yes, but unfortunately it went so far with Agnes Sampson, she went crazy and told the king she knew what he said to his bride on his wedding night. And she told him, word for word.'

I sucked my teeth. 'That's not difficult.'

'It is if you're not part-Sithe, you eejit. She never knew she was, wouldn't have known she was reading his mind. So James started out a sceptic and ended up writing that bloody *Demonologie*.'

'What happened to her?'

'Strangled and burnt. Lucky woman.'

I raised my eyebrows.

'Lucky to be strangled first, I mean.' Abruptly Conal got to his feet. 'That's it for today. Sorry, Seth. I've had enough.'

'Don't apologise to me,' I said, swallowing my glee.

'I've business in the clachan. Meet you in the inn?' He lifted Liath.

'Yep,' I said.

Branndair had his piece of rope cornered. Watching his stillness, the tension of his muscles, his sudden swift mock-kill, I thought: he's going to be a fine hunter. If he lives.

I opened my arms, he scrambled happily into them, and I kicked open the back door and carried him out, Liath trotting at my heels. 'Into your hole, my loves. Just like the rest of us.'

'Withered it, I'm telling you. Withered it! And on the man's wedding night!'

The men in the corner must have been sousing their heads in Ma Sinclair's worst whisky for hours. The speaker couldn't keep his saliva behind his brown teeth, but was spraying his drinking companions as he thumped the table with a fist. They were so far gone they didn't even mind. At least the one with the fiddle had stopped torturing it.

I watched, fascinated, leaning on the counter while Ma Sinclair smuggled me a bottle of the good stuff. Her gold grin glinted at me, and I made a face of exaggerated disbelief. No point getting involved. Half of them were going to be senseless on the floor before long.

Ma Sinclair couldn't resist a contribution, though. 'Is that right, William Beag?' she called across. 'The way I hear it, there wasn't much to wither.'

That earned her a glare from Brown Teeth. 'You mind your tongue, woman.'

I was about to snap at him when someone else did: a crofter from further down the glen. He was on his own in a dark nook, nursing an ale, but he raised his head to glare at the rowdy table. 'And you mind your manners, William Beag. Roderick Mor drank like a fool the day of his wedding. It's no wonder it wouldna work by nightfall.'

Brown Teeth's nose and cheeks were suffused with blood. 'Roderick Mor was cursed by witchcraft!'

'There's no such thing, you credulous numpty.'

Roars of fury, and William Beag got unsteadily to his feet. 'Is that so, MacKinnon? And will you call me that to my face?'

'He just did,' snapped Ma Sinclair. 'Now sit yourself down, William, or you'll not be coming in here again.'

Grumbling, he subsided before he could fall. 'It's only servants of the devil that say there's no witch-craft,' he muttered.

It was MacKinnon's turn to rise threateningly. 'Will you say that again in a man's voice?'

A few of the other men were glancing uneasily at one another; I doubt they fancied William Beag's chances of staying on his feet long enough to get hit. I didn't like the atmosphere in the place, and glancing at Ma Sinclair's anxious face I'd lost the appetite for a scrap too. Nervously the fiddle-tormentor lifted his instrument and drew a funereal note out of its poor strings, and that was when I could bear it no longer. I slapped down my tumbler and went to him, holding out my hand. Startled, he lowered his bow.

'Ach, don't give it to him! That one's feel. Stupid in the head. The smith's brother, ken?'

'*Feel* disnae mean he canna play,' said another.

Ma Sinclair was eyeing me with misgiving, but I kept my inane smile on my face as I winked at her. She shrugged, as if to say *On your own feel-head be it*.

'Aye, give it to him, Calum,' she called. 'I don't want more of your dirges. He can't do worse.'

Reluctantly, resentfully, Calum passed me the fiddle and the bow. I drew an experimental and scratchy note from it, making William Beag guffaw and shower more spittle on his pals. Another dodgy note, then a better one, and it started to speak to me. Poor fiddle, it wasn't its fault. I tightened a peg, tried another long note, and smiled. It liked my fingers on it. I turned on my heel, tucked it safely beneath my chin, and let rip.

I don't think they'd heard the like of it before. They had their jigs and reels, lively enough, but their music hadn't the thrashing wild beat of ours, the song that got inside your ribcage, made your heart hammer and your blood leap. I had my eyes open, grinning, and I saw their mouths hanging agape. But I saw their feet beat the floor, too, and their fingers drum the table whether they liked it or not. I wasn't the best fiddler in my clann, not by a long way, and when the drunkest of them rose and lurched into a clumsy jig, I laughed, thinking how Righil could have made them dance till their feet bled.

Ma Sinclair was staring at me with a mixture of gratitude and awe; MacKinnon was soberly hypno-tised and had forgotten all notion of a fight. I was get-ting into my stride, now, playing like a devil, like *their*

Devil, their Anti-God. The full-mortals said he was the father and lord of all the Sithe: that's what they really thought of us. We weren't the People of Peace, we were the fallen ones; Hell's angels, irredeemably evil. Turning my back on them, a sudden rage swept through my body and into the fiddle till it howled like a demon. Then I laughed out loud, and spun again to face my clumsy dancers. William Beag stepped back so fast he fell on his backside.

We were all laughing now, even William. A chill swept my body, but I didn't realise the inn door had opened till something colder lanced my mind.

~ *Stop it.*

The fiddle shrieked into silence, leaving an absence of music like a frozen shroud. As Conal took the instrument from me, I gave him a surly triumphant smile.

'Drawing attention to yourself?' he murmured, and passed it into the hands of Calum the Crap Fiddler.

'The lad's good,' muttered Calum, afraid to look at me.

'Huh! The lad's got skills he shouldna have.' That was William Beag, but when Conal turned his stare on him, he looked away, shuffling.

MacKinnon couldn't let it go, now. 'You're a foul-minded creature, William Beag, you and your ugly talk. There was you happy to move your fat backside just a moment ago—'

It might have got worse, but right then a woman barged into the inn, skirts swishing in the dirt with her self-important urgency. Morag MacLeod, the clachan gossip: a sour frizzy woman who liked to be first with the news. It must be good news, or worthwhile at any rate. She'd never set foot in the inn otherwise; I'd overheard her views on those of us who did, and she disapproved noisily of the Sinclair woman and her whisky stills.

As she hissed excited words to her bald husband, I watched his sullen eyes widen in shock. Words were passed round, men rose to their feet and drew crosses on themselves with their fingers, forgetting they weren't meant to. They snatched their hands away and glanced guiltily at one another. A muttering became a murmur that became a rowdy, disbelieving rout.

Conal had a hold of my arm. 'Let's go.'

'What's happening?' I snatched up the whisky bottle. Hell, we needed our consolations.

'Nothing good.' Gripping my arm, he kept me beside him as he came out of the inn, slouching well back in the wake of the gathering crowd that swarmed towards the marketplace.

I call it a marketplace but there was never a real market there, just a desultory bartering of meal and ale and tools and skills, and the annual negotiations for the best and sunniest rigs. It was no more than a beaten-earth space in front of the squat church, between a few mud-walled cottages and the mill. Still holding my arm, Conal stiffened and jerked me back.

The priest lay sprawled on his back with his head against the rough dyke that encircled the church. He was still twitching and jerking as the crowd gathered round him. Moments after we arrived, the spasms stopped and he lay rigid and still.

Conal swore under his breath. 'Something's wrong,' he muttered. 'Seth, this isn't right. It's like . . .'

He was abruptly cut off as someone shoved him forward, and I was dragged with him. Conal glanced over his shoulder in shock, but there was no way of telling who had pushed us. A voice I didn't recognise shouted, 'Here's the smith! He's a healer.'

'Aye, so he is! Let him through!'

Conal let me go, pushing me back into the press of people so that he was alone beside the priest's corpse.

Morag MacLeod was somewhere near me; I could hear her. 'Fell right over on his back, so he did. Like a tree. I never saw the like of it. Not even a moment to cry out, poor man. Put his hands to his face like he'd been struck, and over he went.'

She was loving this, the auld bitch.

'Something not natural about it,' growled a voice behind me.

'That's no' the first unnatural thing I've seen the day.' William Beag slanted his eyes in my direction, a nasty little smirk on his face.

'A seizure,' someone suggested. 'A fit.'

The priest's eyes were wide open, but they were empty of light, empty of everything. I saw Conal's fingers shake slightly as he drew the man's eyelids down, but it took him a couple of attempts; they wouldn't close, as if the priest still couldn't believe what had happened to him. The crowd behind me fell silent as they watched Conal. At last he held the lids down with his fingers, and they stayed shut. Hesitantly, he took his hands away.

'Was there nothing you could do, then?' That was the miller. Wolf-killer.

Somebody was muttering on the far side of the crowd.

I couldn't hear what was said, but a voice agreed grimly, 'Aye. Damn right.'

'He's dead,' said Conal redundantly, standing up. For a moment he hesitated, as if he thought he was missing something, then stepped back and pressed back into the first line of gawpers. Morag MacLeod had pushed her way through for a better view, and now she made that ostentatious crossing motion with her fingers against her breastbone. Others glanced at one another, then followed her example.

Under his breath, Conal swore at himself.

'Seizure?' I asked him, as he hustled me away.

Conal was silent for a second, glancing over his shoulder. Once again, no-one was watching us. Back to normal. I thought.

'It could have been. Come on.'

That wasn't all it was, I could tell. I knew Conal better than that. 'What is it?'

'It's trouble,' said Conal, and spat. 'Let's go.'

15

It's all very well saying *Let's keep our heads down.*
There's still business to be done, and bread and ale to
be bought, and lots to be drawn. We couldn't stay
away from the clachan forever, but we spent as little
time there as we could. I worried vaguely about Ma
Sinclair, but I didn't go near the inn for a while.

It seemed the clachan couldn't do without a god-
botherer, so a new priest arrived when the old one was
barely cold in the ground. We'd see this new one around
the place: preaching his joyless gospel, frowning on the
flirting girls, wringing his bony hands in prayer, but he
didn't go to the inn as the old priest had. He was a lot
younger, though you'd think from the way he stood on
his dignity and his moral high ground that he'd lived
longer than a Sithe, and had loved nothing.

We never went to the services in the small grim
church, never had done and weren't about to start.
Besides, the priest's arrival coincided with an epidemic

of sickness in the clachan. When it first broke out, even Conal and I found ourselves nauseous and feverish, as if a miasma of disease lay over the whole glen and couldn't be escaped. It wasn't that we were vulnerable to plague, if plague it was; it's just that we were unaccustomed to sickness and Conal seemed ever more unnerved. He muttered about the people of the glen thinking he was a healer, that he didn't know what was wrong or what to do about it so there wasn't any point sticking his neck out. And then under his breath I heard him say something about blame, and the laying of it, and that we'd better keep our mouths shut and *keep our heads down.*

It wasn't plague. After a few weeks the sickness ebbed, and glen life grew normal again. We swallowed our misgivings, and frequented the clachan, and did our best to ignore the priest proselytising in the muddy marketplace. We kept ourselves as much as we could to ourselves, and we trusted to the Veil. And I'd almost forgotten the priest, had almost learned not to worry about him preaching his god's wrath and his own hate, when he walked up the glen and through the mossy birchwood one night and rapped his staff on our door.

Conal was shocked, and suspicious, but he could hardly turn the man away. The priest sidled into the blackhouse with a look of contempt he couldn't hide, his nostrils flaring in distaste. He was the boniest creature I'd ever seen, short of actual cadavers (of which I'd now seen plenty), so at least he seemed to follow his own strictures of thrift and frugality. His pale eyes had a yellowish tinge, his skin a papery cast, his hair was lank and sparse. Gods knew—well, his god would—why he cast such a spell over the clachan and the glen.

'Good evening, my brothers.' He smiled. I could taste bile in my throat; I didn't smile back, but Conal gripped his proffered hand, glanced down at it, then let it go like a viper.

'I'm not your brother,' I pointed out.

He looked at me, silent just long enough to make me fidget with discomfort. His voice, when he wasn't braying his hatred, was like the rustle of air through dead leaves. 'You're the simple one, aren't you?' He gave me a conspiratorial smile. 'Well. Perhaps not, hm?'

Conal had backed slightly against a wooden chair, and I knew why, but perhaps it was that movement that gave us away; perhaps it was just that Branndair could not repress his tiny growl of distrust. He got a nip for it from Liath, but it was too late. I glanced up at the priest, alarmed, but he only looked thoughtful as he stooped to look at the cubs beneath the chair, then straightened again.

'What a quaint choice of . . .' he hesitated, licking his upper lip '. . . pets.'

I knew he'd been on the point of using another word. But he was choosing his words very, very carefully.

'It's kind of you to visit, Father,' said Conal mechanically.

'Please,' he smiled. 'Don't call me Father. I am Pastor of my flock. I have no idolatrous pretensions.'

'No.' Conal flushed and glanced at me. I rolled my eyes. I'd known all along he was making a mistake:

trying to understand these people and their mutating theologies, that god of theirs who couldn't make up his mind. I told him so, silently, but he didn't even snap back at me. He just looked miserable.

'You haven't been in church,' said the priest. 'You know attendance is compulsory?'

'Yes, Fath ... your gr ... Pastor,' Conal managed, lamely.

'You are strangers here, of course, so we have to make allowances.' Taking his time, he looked us up and down, examining our clothes. I'd refused to wear the coarse shirt and plaid of the peasants; I found them ugly and uncomfortable, though the peasants seemed to find them practical enough. Conal had given in too, in the end, and like me he'd gone back to his own shirt and trews made of leather or decent wool. He was worried we'd stick out like bogles, but the astonished stares hadn't lasted more than a week. They'd got used to us. And I'd got used to the Veil. In fact I was getting to like it very much.

This man had taken notice of us, though. This man didn't look as if he was going to let it drop. I felt my upper lip curling, so quickly I made my face expressionless again.

'The kirk session has decreed,' he told us with a tight little smile, 'that those who fail to worship on Sundays should be punished in the stocks.'

We both just gaped at him.

He looked keenly at Conal. 'I believe you often kept company with my ... predecessor.'

'Yes,' said Conal.

The priest made a little sound with his tongue and

teeth. 'Reverend Douglas was not strict in his application of God's will. I have had much work to do since I arrived.'

'That's too bad,' I said. 'You should relax. Come to Ma Sinclair's place.'

His gaze on me was suddenly unshielded, and I saw the loathing with crystal clarity. 'Whisky,' he hissed, 'is an abomination. The people of this glen see their error and sin, and their mortal peril.' His lips twitched. 'I hope I will soon be able to say the same of both of you.'

I must not spit. I made myself not spit on his feet. Conal nodded and muttered a few more niceties, and when he finally shut the door on the priest, he closed his eyes and exhaled as if he hadn't breathed since the man had put his foot over our threshold.

He turned to me. 'You ever seen that man in the sunlight?'

I frowned. 'I suppose. It's summer. And he's over the glen like a rash, all the time.'

'I mean, have you seen him in full sunlight?'

I thought about it. 'I don't know. What are you thinking?'

He shrugged. 'Oh, probably something stupid. I can't be sure. Don't worry.'

~ *Aye, right.*

He grinned at me suddenly. I liked that, I liked to see him looking himself again. It happened less and less often, but it reassured me when it did. Conal being afraid made me very, very afraid.

I didn't know how we were going to get out of the

interminable, mind-numbing church services, but Conal was going to have to find a way. I swore to him that if I had to sit through the man's brimstone-reeking opinions, I'd cut my own throat and put myself out of my misery. A long life was a long life, I told Conal, but it had to be worth living.

Conal thought we would have to submit. I had never submitted in my life, unless it was to Conal's damned educational ambitions. I loved him and I knew he had my best interests at heart but he didn't own my conscience.

I gnawed it over in my mind all week, till my head throbbed. I wanted the priest to forget we existed, I wanted us to slip from his mind the way we should, but it wasn't happening. His pale gaze found me whenever I slunk into the clachan, and he'd smile.

I was afraid of him.

I wouldn't submit to him, though. My life was not my own anymore but my soul was, and I wouldn't do this. I didn't want to go in the stocks, I didn't want a whipping, and more than anything I didn't want to fight Conal. He was my Captain and he had the right to order me to go, and he was capable of knocking me senseless and dragging me to church. But if I capitulated to this priest I'd lose something indefinably precious to me and I'd never get it back. Standing my ground was worth a beating, from the priest or from Conal. I just didn't know how far it would go, and yes, I was afraid.

My last morning in the clachan was a Saturday. I remember that because I had gritted my teeth and wound myself up to face my Captain either that evening or, failing that, at dawn on Sunday. I was there alone; I'd gone to draw lots for the best rigs next year, to negotiate our turn of the community plough, to fix a price for the shoeing of a horse. I'd gone to buy some ale and whisky, and with it some courage.

I was so anxious, wound so tight inside myself that I almost failed to hear the men. But one voice caught my attention, thank the gods: William Beag's grievance-ridden one.

'She's a bloody cheat. Waters her ale and overcharges for that shite whisky of hers.'

I stopped in my tracks, but they hadn't seen me, so I dodged into the shadows. It was obvious who they were verbally ripping to shreds, but what made me most uneasy was their dark huddle, their quiet grumbling voices, their quick over-the-shoulder glances. These were not the empty complaints of men who'd go straight to the inn and be cheerfully cheated again.

'Aye,' said another. 'And it is true what Roderick Mor told you, William. Such a woman is a peril to all good men. There are those who don't want to hear, who don't want to know the danger. That is all.'

'Aye, the fools! When their own bairns fall sick, when their own milk sours, when their own parts fall to disease: that's when they'll take notice. They don't care about other folks' misfortunes: no, not till it happens to them, and then they are sorry. Well, I will not sit by and see my neighbours ill-used.'

'You are a good man, William Beag. You're right, it's time for right-thinking men to take a stand. I am with you.' The burly redhead clasped William's fat arm.

'We'll go up and find the boys at Nether Baile. They will want in on this.'

'I'll watch the place.' William Beag nodded gravely. 'She must not have the chance to slink away, and she may have charms to warn her. There are other villages that would not thank us for letting her go to them, unshriven and unrepentant and *unpunished*.'

'Will you get the minister?'

'Later,' a small man growled. 'Let's find the Nether Baile boys first. They would not be wanting such business to go ahead without them.'

As I watched them go, bloated with bloodlust and self-importance, I leaned against a mud-and-wattle wall and made swift cold calculations. The three brothers at Nether Baile: the blackhouse they shared with their beasts lay not a mile further up the glen, but this crowd was in no hurry. They were basking in their moment and they'd want to stretch it out.

Conal had said the witch-terror came in waves, like a tide. He said that for years it would subside, and grow calm, and then it would roar to life again like an Atlantic storm. Conal had hoped we'd be lucky with the tides, lucky in the timing of our exile.

Always looking on the bright side, that was my brother.

Ma Sinclair kept her sullen old pony in a hollow beneath a small cliff, separate from the drovers' ponies, penned in only by steep slopes and grey rock and its own disinclination to make a bid for freedom. Through a ragged forelock it glared at me, jaws moving round a mouthful of tough grass, but it didn't shy away when I seized a handful of its coarse mane. It just swallowed its grass and bit me, so I bit it back, and so we came to an understanding, and I led it through the narrow gap in the rocks and round the back of the cliff.

Overlooking the clachan from the north, I stopped, rubbing the pony's warm neck. The little settlement backed onto the rocks here, sheltered and shadowed, with the bere-rigs on the farther side. No-one ever glanced this way, except by chance, and I could see the back of the inn quite clearly, and William Beag skulking at its rear.

I laughed, and the pony shook its neck and whickered in echo. Flicking one ear back, it gave me the evil pony-eye. Scratching between its ears, I shoved the grubby grey forelock out of its face. Deep down in the brown eyes I thought I saw a gleam of silver that wasn't weak reflected sun.

I pulled back its eyelid with my thumb to make sure, and then I laughed again, and let the forelock fall untidily back.

'Where did you come from?' I scratched its neck. 'The lover? Have you been thirty years with her? Or was it your dam or your sire he gave her?'

The pony ripped up more grass and ignored me.

'You, I think.'

Sagging as if worked to exhaustion, the beast sighed and rested a hind leg. I looked out across the rough ground to the walls and the yard behind the inn, and the fool William Beag who thought he was hiding.

'You're not daft,' I said to the pony. 'You know what needs doing.'

· · ·

'Ma,' I said, knocking on the counter. 'You're needed.'

Irritably she turned from a customer. 'Now, lad, what is it? I'm busy, can you not see?'

'You're needed,' I said again. 'You're needed to come now. It's the pony. The pony's needing you.'

A bearded wonder glowered at me. 'Ach, you wee feel, can you not leave her alone?' Impatiently he rapped his tumbler on the counter.

Ma Sinclair had turned to me. Her look was long and solemn, and broke at last into a smile. Her teeth glinted.

'There now, Donal, the lad's come to help. And you are to help yourself now, till I get back.'

'I am to help myself?' Bearded Wonder needed no further invitation, and he wasn't bothered with me any more. I slid a pewter jug off the counter and led the old woman out the back.

At the end of the dank passageway that led out to the yard, I stretched my arm across Ma Sinclair's way and she came to a halt. Lifting the bag of clothing and money and meal that I'd thrown together from the few possessions in her hovel, I thrust it into her arms.

'Do you have anything else you need to take?'

Briefly she peered into the bag. 'Nothing more than what's here. You're a good lad. Is it so bad?'

'It's so bad. Shush, there's one of them out the back.'

'Who?'

'William Beag.'

'Oh, laddie. Little William? Name or no name, he's a good bit bigger than you.'

'I've got help.' Putting my fingers to my lips, I eased open the plank door.

Bang on time, I heard the dull clop of hooves, and the pony turned into the yard and shook its mane. William Beag's shadow, pressed back out of sight just to my left, detached itself from the wall and he took a step forward.

It wasn't a water horse or anything like one, but maybe it had known one in a previous life. It certainly seemed to know the routine. Lifting its head, all shy and enticing, an uncertain whicker, the rap of a hoof on the stones when William Beag's attention seemed to wander back to the inn door. Raddled old nag that it was, it arched its thick neck and plumed its scraggy tail and was, for an instant, beautiful.

'Ah,' crooned William Beag, 'and where did you come from, my bonny boy?'

He stretched out a hand to the pony's bridle, his fingers closing on its cheekpiece as mine tightened on the pewter jug. He did not look at its eye, and he did not look at the tilt of its head. He played true to form and forced its mouth open to look at its yellow teeth; and the pony, not liking his impudence, clamped them savagely on his fingers.

I hadn't meant that to happen, and I hadn't meant the fool to scream like a girl, but I cut off his noise fast enough with one strong blow of the jug. He buckled and his face hit the mud. Catching the pony before it could shy and bolt, I strapped the meagre bag of belongings to its saddle.

No untimely modesty from Ma Sinclair: she hitched up her skirts, and I caught a flash of her voluminous underwear as I gave her a leg up. I passed her a flask of water and one of whisky, and she stuffed them into the folds of her skirts.

'Come on,' I said, and I grabbed the pony's bridle and dragged it into a shambling trot.

When I left her, the sun was low in the sky and we were high enough above the glen to see the curve of the ocean, shimmering silver at the horizon.

'Well,' she said, 'I'll never be seeing my whisky stores again, but I thank you. Will you be fine yourself?'

I turned to look back down the glen. 'He never saw me.'

'Donal did.'

'Well, but I'm a fool. They'll think you hit William yourself,' I said with a shrug.

'Aye. Well, it's true that I could and it's true that I would.'

'I'll be fine,' I said again. 'You'd best go. Go far away.'

She leaned down and I felt her dry lips kiss my cheek, her whisky breath on my skin. 'And you go further, you and your brother. It's time for you both to go, I'm thinking.'

'Aye.' I had a nasty feeling she was right. I squeezed her gnarled hand tighter on the pony's rein. 'Go, Ma.'

She turned once to look at me and smiled. 'I told you,' she called.

'Told me what?'

'I'd keep on your good side. I was right to be superstitious, aye?'

'Aye,' I muttered.

I watched her and her pony till they went over the brow of the hill, her skirts hitched up her raw bare legs, and the pony trudging stolidly down the whin-thick hillside, whisking midges with its ragged tail. She didn't turn back again.

That was the last I saw of Ma Sinclair. I never found her alive anywhere, but nor did I see her in any stinking jail and I never saw her squeal in a fire, so I like to think she found another place to be. I hope she found some village that liked her whisky and didn't mind her healing ways and her potions and her handsome crone-face. I like to think she survived that witch-terror, and all the others after, but I don't know and I never will.

I turned back to the clachan, smoky and faint with distance, and I began to run.

16

I did not want to go through the clachan again, and I'd planned to give it a wide bodyswerve and take the long path home, but I couldn't fail to see the knots of people hurrying towards it, surging into an already busy marketplace. Watching their urgency, hearing their voices high and drugged with the thrill of danger, I knew I had to take notice. I crept inside the low walls, slouched in the wake of the gossiping clusters, and kept my head down.

Like always.

The priest was there, standing on a straw bale. He wasn't waiting for the people to gather and fall silent, but berated them as they approached. His urgency made them hurry all the more, afraid to miss a word.

'What are you waiting for?' he cried, thumping his fist against his cracked old bible. 'Are you waiting for them to come for your children in the night?'

I halted uneasily, edging under ratty overhanging

heather-thatch. Just those few words had chilled my spine. Perhaps I knew what was coming.

'Are you waiting for them to feed your babies to their wolf-familiars?'

A gasp of horror went round the crowd. 'They have taken a baby already,' shouted someone. 'Isobel's bairn!'

'Aye! My poor sister! Her poor wean!' The sobbing voice was Morag MacLeod's. 'Reverend Douglas it was who found her. He brought her for burial but she could not go in the holy ground. The Lord have mercy on her.'

'Found her?' snapped the miller. 'It may be he was in league with the warlocks!'

I had to put my hand over my mouth to stop my gasp escaping. They'd all adored the old priest. But this was madness I could smell in the air.

A male voice interrupted. 'I heard she could not feed it. The last thing she needed was another wean. She only left it near the smith's because of her conscience.'

'That is a lie!' screamed Morag MacLeod.

'It was a cold night. The bairn was not well. You cannot blame the smith.'

'We can blame him for killing it!' shouted the miller. 'A sacrifice to his Master!'

The priest was holding out his hands, pleading for calm. 'If your old minister had allied himself with the Enemy, then he is answering for it before God, as we speak. Let us not concern ourselves with the dead.' He paused, the wrinkles deepening on his pallid brow. 'Though it's true that his death was an unnatural one.'

'Witchcraft,' hissed someone.

How did I just know that word was going to come up?

The priest shook his head sadly. 'If there is any truth in that accusation, Reverend Douglas must be exhumed and burned at the stake. It is prescribed.'

'He should not be in holy ground!' someone yelled. 'Struck down by the Devil his Master. Did you see his staring eyes?'

'Aye, and he wouldn't close them! Something scared the man to death and Hell.'

Silence fell. 'Aye, that's right,' muttered someone at last.

'He could not close his eyes on a servant of the Devil!'

Remembering Conal, standing out there alone and helpless with the priest's corpse, struggling to close those staring eyes, I wanted to be violently sick. But I couldn't make a sound. I drew back into the shadows, and that was when the priest looked up and straight into my eyes.

He smiled. I thought he would give me away, but he didn't.

I was close to yelling a protest; luckily someone got there before me. MacKinnon, the crofter, the stranger, the loner. 'The smith is a good man,' he shouted. 'And all of you know it!'

'Do you?' asked the priest solemnly. 'What do you all know of MacGregor?'

'Nothing!' yelled the miller, shooting a furious glare at MacKinnon.

'A good man!' he snapped. 'The smith has cured your children! Aye, and *yours*, William Beag!'

The priest closed his eyes, as if in distress. 'Ahhh . . .'

'Was it cures? Or was it witchcraft?' A shrill woman said it for him.

The priest turned to William Beag, who stood behind and a little to the right of him. There was an expression on the man's face that combined wounded propriety with vicious hate, though it was half obscured by a length of bloodstained cloth wound round his head. His hand was bandaged too.

Obviously I didn't hit him hard enough.

With one thin long-fingered hand, the priest gestured to him. 'Here is a fine and a well-respected man,' he said softly. 'What is your story, William?'

'We had determined to confront the witch who cast the charm on Roderick Mor,' he said sourly. 'Ale isn't all she brews. I stood guard—'

'You watched her while your mob assembled, you fat coward,' called MacKinnon.

William Beag glowered. 'You stay out of this, Malcolm MacKinnon. You are not from here. And you know nothing of witchcraft.'

'Indeed I do not. And even if you call him a witch, there is a court. The laird must hear the accusations!' MacKinnon was a persistent bastard. Poor devil.

The priest shook his head sadly, as if about to announce something that pained him. 'The kirk session has jurisdiction in matters of heresy and witchcraft. The civil courts are subject to the justice of God. Besides, the MacLeod is raiding and burning in the north with his pack of mercenaries. When will he return?' He paused for effect. 'In time to save your children?'

'No!' screamed a woman.

'He's been gone too long!' yelled another. 'Too much harm can be done before he returns! I am with the minister. Who else?'

There was a chorus of enthusiasm, and the priest had to call for calm again. 'We will have no mob justice. The judicial process will take its course,' he said gravely. 'I insist on it.'

There was much nodding of heads at that. 'A fair man,' called someone approvingly.

'MacGregor the smith is a fair man!' Malcolm MacKinnon was not giving up, bless him.

The priest gave a tiny shrug. 'He has found himself . . . unable to cross the threshold of the Lord's house. What does that tell us?'

'He could not make the sign of the cross when Reverend Douglas died! Did you see?'

'But none of us are supposed . . .' someone began, but he was drowned out.

'He brought the pestilence!' They were getting more hysterical by the minute, dragging up every misfortune of the past year and longer.

'He made the bere-crop fail on half the rigs.'

'His brother plays the fiddle like the very devil. Such music is not natural! It is bought with the soul.'

'They brought the plague!'

'That was no plague,' said MacKinnon in disgust. 'It was a sickness from the grain, more like. If you were not so hidebound about your plantings the bere-crop would have been fine.'

'Aye, and did he help any of us when the sickness struck us?'

You'd have included it in his witchcraft if he had, I

thought bitterly, but there was no point joining the argument. They'd stopped making sense now. They were losing all their reason, scrabbling for excuses to replace it with mindless hate.

'He is a good man, and no witch,' grumbled MacKinnon. 'And so was our minister! This witchcraft is nonsense. Childish superstition!'

The priest chilled visibly. His voice was like a glacier, grey and cold, when he said, 'Denial of witchcraft is heresy, and it would do you good to remember it.' His call grew louder, all strength and purity and determination. 'Evil is the more sinuous and deadly when it appears as an angel of light! Did you think they seemed good men?'

'Aye,' interrupted MacKinnon acidly. 'And no *seemed* about it.'

The priest ignored him. He could afford to; the crowd was with him. 'The Devil himself can recite a prayer! What do you think: that it would burn his forked tongue and shrivel his lips? No! Evil can masquerade as good, it can disguise itself; it is superstition to believe otherwise! God himself despised and rejected *Les Mauvais Anges*: Satan's evil angels: the fallen ones!'

I slipped from my dingy corner and ran. Educated, and worse, clever with it. I wanted to cry, I wanted to scream; mostly I wanted to turn round and go back to the clachan and cut the priest's throat. I couldn't do any of those things. I kept running, though there was no chase. Yet.

The judicial process will take its course. I insist on it.
Oh, gods.
The day was threatening, the sky heavy and pressing

above me. Grey and overcast with a monochrome layer of cloud. No sun. I tried to remember if there had been sunshine in the marketplace; I didn't think so. I should have remembered to take note, but then I didn't understand Conal's obsession. Besides, I could hardly think straight back there.

The judicial process will take its course.

'Conal!' I screamed.

I insist on it. The judicial process . . .

'Seth?' He hacked his axe into the chopping block and left it there, dusting his hands as he came towards me. 'Seth, what's wrong?'

I didn't waste time talking. I opened my mind and let him See it.

'They're right. The MacLeod has been away too long,' said Conal, breaking abruptly away from me. He'd been holding my head in one hand, staring into my mind, and when he let me go I almost stumbled, dizzy with the dislocated memory and all its horror. Remorseful, he seized my arm and steadied me. 'Oh, Seth. This is more trouble than we can handle.'

'We're always in trouble.' It was myself I was trying to reassure.

'No, this is different. We have to leave now, or we'll die. Witchcraft and lycanthropy? There's no defence.'

'I'm sorry. About the old woman.'

'Don't be stupid. You did right.' He gave me a fleeting grin that didn't hide his fear. 'They won't take chances again, they'll do it properly. They'll be coming for us.'

'What'll we do?'

He shrugged. 'We have to go back. I'll throw myself on Kate's mercy, but we can't stay here.'

I felt cold. 'But Kate . . .'

'Can't do us more harm than that minister. Let's get out of here.' He started throwing our few possessions into a hessian bag while I hauled our swords and dirks out of the thatch, scattering mouldy straw and heather and mouse droppings.

'Never mind that.' He snatched up the sacking I was using to wrap them and took over the job himself. There was sweat on his temples. 'Get Liath and Branndair. Make sure no one sees you, that's all.'

I flung open the rickety blackhouse door, catching his fear, but he stopped me.

~ *Block, Seth. From now till we get home.* His eyes met mine, his own block came down like an iron yett; then he was parcelling up the weapons again, and I turned and ran.

The slope was treacherously steep, all clinging birks and jutting stone, thick with bracken, but I knew every inch of it. My thighs ached and my lungs stung, but I made it up to the sett in record time. Hauling away the branches, flinging small stones aside, I called to them.

~ *Branndair. Lia . . .*

Block, Conal had said. Remembering, I was angry with myself. I raised my block and knelt by the hidden entrance as a doubtful snuffling nose met my hand.

'Branndair.' I scratched his throat. 'We have to leave, my love. Come.'

I wondered how the hell I was going to persuade them to travel in a knotted sack when I couldn't even

use my mind to reassure them. It was while I was pon-
dering the logistics that Branndair's hackles sprang erect,
and he snarled.

The back of my neck prickled.

Liath forced her way impatiently through, scrabbling with her paws at the earthen entrance and nipping Branndair to get him moving. I laid a hand on her
head.

'Sh, earth-daughter. Sh.'

I turned, still on one knee, and stared down through
the trees. I knew I'd heard sounds. The branches dipped
and moved, rustling in a cool summer breeze. Above
them the angular jigsaw of sky was murky with cloud,
but there was no rain, no mist. There was no birdsong.

I shuddered. 'Back in,' I told the wolves. 'Back in. Stay
here.'

Liath gave a whining growl of irritation.

~ *Stay here*, I told her, exasperated. ~ *You must.*

This time she did as she was told. My block was down
anyway, so I took my chance.

~ *Conal!*

No answer. Only his remorseless block.

~ *Cù Chaorach!*

Nothing. I shivered once, and then I was running
and leaping, jarring my knees on the impossible slope
but not slowing down. When the blackhouse came
into sight, I only just managed to brake my hurtling
run and slither onto my backside behind a great grey
rock. My heart choked me; it thrashed like a hammer
high in my chest, constricting my lungs.

They had Conal. Six of the brutes, and the priest
looking on with satisfaction. I don't know if he'd tried

to fight, but now he was on his back, wrists manacled, face bloodied as they hauled him towards a rough cart. He was conscious, but that block of his was immovable.

~ *Conal!* I screamed.

He winced as his head cracked against a stone, then tried to scramble to his feet, but it was impossible, they kept on pulling him backwards, six of them. They were afraid of him, I thought. At the cart they stopped, kicking him over onto his stomach, then one put his foot against his head and shoved his face into the mud. Cowards, bloody cowards. As he kicked and struggled for air they looped a chain round his manacles, fastened it to the cart, then backed swiftly away. One of them whacked the pony's rump, and it tossed its head and jerked the cart forward. Conal staggered to his feet before he could be dragged along the ground.

They were going to make him walk, I thought, and that was what finally lit the fuse of my incoherent rage. I knew one thing: they weren't taking my brother, not without a fight from me.

I ran faster than I've ever run, and that was fast. I kept low and silent, my teeth sunk into my upper lip; I was biting it so hard I could taste my own blood but I didn't care, I couldn't contain my fury any other way and I had to reach them before I released it. I knew I would catch up. I had no other choice. We'd die today, or they would. I was close, so close, coming at them through a forest of birks down the last stony slope of the hill.

They hadn't seen me. Or so I thought till I felt the most incredible bolt of pain in my head. From temple to temple it seared my brain like cold fire; it hurt too much even to scream.

I thought they'd killed me. I thought the priest had killed me. That's what I was certain of as the world swung on its axis, and darkened around me, and turned into a cold blackness and deafening silence, and then into nothing at all.

17

I'd expected death. When that didn't happen, when awareness and life and hard reality leaked back, I expected a dungeon. I remembered everything, instantly. I lay with my eyes shut, still unable to move for the pain that lanced my eyeballs. I did not want to open them and see utter darkness. I barely wanted to breathe, in case I would smell foulness and rot and fear.

There was cold dampness beneath my bruised cheek: that was what I'd expected, but not fresh air, and the rich scent of earth and leaf-rot. Instead of looming silence, birds were singing once again, and there was a whisper of what might have been a breeze. I felt its breath on the skin of my limp hand, and that made me curl my hand into a fist.

My fingers clutched damp leaves and scratchy bracken. Shocked, I let them go and opened my eyes. Daylight blinked and shimmered through the shifting branches above me. I closed my eyes briefly again as pain like a shower of sparks filled my brain. Then I forced my eyelids wide.

I lay where I'd fallen, beneath the birks. I didn't know how long I'd been unconscious, but a raging thirst and a biting hunger told me it had been a long time. Though it was summer, it was a Highland summer, and I'd lain on the cold ground too long. My bones were rigid with cold. As violent shivers erupted through my body, I realised that of course the priest hadn't struck me down. The priest hadn't shattered my block like some half-formed cobweb of thought. Conal had.

I was shaking uncontrollably as I clambered to my feet, and almost fell again. Clutching a branch, I steadied myself. It was impossible to walk properly. I fell to my hands and knees and began the long painful crawl back up the hill. I was crying, and I don't mind admitting it. The cold cut through my body like knives; moving was a torment. My brain felt swollen to twice its size, as if it were trying to burst free. I thought I would never be warm again. And none of that would have mattered, if they hadn't taken my brother.

I desperately wanted to be warm, but I was afraid of it. If I began to feel warm I would lie down in gratitude, and then I would die out here. I knew that, I'd learned it young. I kept reminding myself of that, repeating it over and over in my head as I put one hand and one foot in front of the other, again and again. I was almost in a trance when my scrabbling hand splashed into shallow cold water.

A feeble burn seeped down the rocks: I recognised it as the water that ran near to the sett. My throat was on fire, so despite the cold that racked my body I let myself collapse into what was barely more than steep bog, desperately gasping at the trickle of water, licking the wet rock, sucking on the moss that covered the rocks. I don't know how long that took, either, but when at last I wasn't thirsty any more, my body was shaking violently. I made myself crawl again.

When I reached the sett, a hundred yards or a hundred years later, I felt for the crumbling opening and pulled myself in by my fingertips. The cubs were still and trembling, but as I forced myself into the tiny space they crept around me, pressing their bodies against mine. I couldn't stand or even kneel, but there was space for breath, and the warmth of animal bodies filled the tiny den so fast that another century or two later, I began to feel warm again. And that was all right. It was all right, now. This much was all right.

I had time to tug the Veil around us all like a comforting blanket, and then I think I slept again, may whatever God exists forgive me.

I must have been unconscious or crawling on my belly for two days and nights. I don't want to imagine what happened to Conal in that time. It was what he intended, but that did not help me forgive myself. When I could feel anything other than physical pain and cold, all that seeped in to replace it was impotent anger and despair.

But that too passed, and far more quickly than the pain. The cubs had been surviving fine on grubs and beetles and small game, but it was time they had a decent feed. Nervously I dug my way out of the sett, wondering how desperate I must have been to dig myself in in the first place. My head had almost stopped hurting; my body still ached, but it was a healing ache.

There were signs of a desultory and belated hunt, and I blessed the Veil yet again. Bracken lay in broken swathes, earth had been disturbed, branches snapped. Clumsy brutes as well as cruel. It dawned on me that the priest had been no part of the hunt: I don't know why I was so sure of that. He would not have been clumsy, that was all, and I knew he would have found us.

My block was still in place. I did not move it.

At least the cubs seemed to understand, now. They stayed at the entrance to the sett when I told them to, and did not try to follow me down the hill to the blackhouse. I made my way down in silence, with far greater care than when I'd crawled up. I waited an age in the moving shadows of the birks, an unmoving shadow myself, but there was no sign of a watch, no stir of life, no stamp or spit from careless guards. Perhaps they were just not that interested in me. Perhaps they had what—or who—they wanted.

The place was a mess, but our remaining belongings tossed onto the floor did not amount to much. The worst blow was that our weapons were gone, but of course they would be. Some attempt had been made to torch the place, but the fire hadn't caught well, and they obviously couldn't be bothered to finish the job. The door and all the timbers had been stolen, the larder emptied of meal and bread. The heather thatch was charred to fragments—that must have solved the mouse problem—and they'd burned our alien-looking clothing rather than steal it, but otherwise there was only some blackening of the earth and an acrid smell of charring. Not a lot of difference there, since our own and our predecessors' cooking fires had darkened the whole place to a black hole anyway. Taking a sharp stick, I dug down in the earthen floor to the stone-lined pit we had excavated for a meat store. The butchered deer was starting to reek, but the wolves wouldn't care.

For that matter, neither did I.

To this day it remains the best-aged piece of game I've ever eaten, and I ate it raw, tearing at it with my teeth. I did not look to see if there was anything moving in it: there was no point. I needed something in my belly, and it wouldn't kill me. At least I hoped it wouldn't. It was probably better than anything Conal would be getting.

That thought killed even my ravening appetite. I pulled some pieces of deer together into a charred scrap of linen that had once been a shirt of Conal's, then made my way back up the hill. The cubs were waiting for me, no more than a yard from the mouth of the sett, though their muzzles were wet and they must have recently drunk from the burn. They were clever animals, and obedient.

I shoved the stinking bits of carcass into the sett, then picked the wolves up one by one and hugged them against me, tears leaking from my eyes into their fur. Warm tongues lashed my face and they whimpered.

'You stay here,' I whispered. I couldn't make myself speak out loud. 'You stay here till I . . . you stay here till we come for you.'

I didn't know where to start looking, and I knew

that Veil or no Veil, I couldn't go openly back to the clachan. At the edge of the forest I turned in the other direction and walked for as long as I could, dodging off the track to hide whenever I heard someone approach. Night fell, moonless but alive with stars and a meteor shower. I lay in a ditch and watched the sky, wrapping myself in a stolen plaid that I'd found drying over a bush outside another mud-walled hovel. I still disliked the things, scratchy and crude and utterly lacking in style, but I can't deny that it kept me warmer than I'd have believed possible. Even when it was wet with rain and ditchwater, it kept my body heat locked inside me, and I felt a first grudging admiration for the full-mortals' practicality with so few material goods.

By morning, which paled the sky perhaps four hours past midnight, I had a plan of sorts. I stripped off my trews, shivering, and wrapped them in a bundle with a few thieved bags of meal (I felt bad about that, but hunger beat my conscience by a long mile). My good shirt was by now worn and stained and muddy enough to pass for a peasant's clothing, and after a few failed attempts I managed to wrap the plaid around myself much the way the clansmen did. I was barefoot, which was fine: a lot of the men wore shoes, but certainly not good boots like mine, and plenty of them—including all the women—wore none. I hitched my bundle onto my shoulder, left the stony track behind, and took to the heather.

I made my way over the hill, to the neighbouring glen and its bailes and farms. There no-one knew me, and I could mingle freely with the full-mortals, playing the simpleton and begging for food and ale. They gave it to me. I marvelled at their capacity to combine such kindness and hospitality with such cold savagery, but perhaps, in that one respect, they were not so very different from us.

It took me half a day's travelling, and then a day of lurking and eavesdropping. You hear a lot, and you hear it quickly, when people think you're too stupid to understand. Besides, they were a naturally gossipy race, and the witch trials had brought excitement and scandal into their lives.

Conal had not been taken anywhere in this glen; he was in a keep at the desolate place where the two glens merged, farther inland. He'd been taken there four days ago, along with the witches they'd managed to scrape up from this clachan and the neighbouring ones. People were full of the spells that had been cast on their cattle and their crops and their genitals. It would have made me laugh, if I hadn't wanted to cry. The excuses a man will find! But I quickly grew sick of their fantasising, and I'd heard enough. I went back to the heather, and made my own road inland, but I left no tracks.

Before the MacLeod's father had built his new stronghold, the MacLeod ancestors had had this meaner castle keep. It had fallen into dilapidation, being a relatively unimposing square tower in a less than defensible position and too far from the sea to suit the MacLeod. The great hall and courtyard had been colonised by small brown sheep and black cattle, the rafters by crows. But its walls and roof and its cramped chambers were intact, and so were its dungeons.

Running straight in there, defiant and weaponless,

would have been beyond stupid, no matter how angry and desperate I was. I skulked in the woods close to the keep, and found a tall pine that was far enough from the keep to be relatively safe, but gave me a vantage point to see right into the courtyard. Then I made myself comfortable, and watched for another day.

The courtyard had been cleared of its livestock. I watched the guards, and I timed them, and learned their positions. I saw brushwood piled high in the centre of the courtyard—they wouldn't waste good timber—and in the afternoon I saw it lit with human fuel.

I don't know how to describe that first sight I had of a burning. For the best part of it I was numb. I felt for a long time as if I was watching some bizarre piece of theatre. The audience, boisterous and over-excited, had trickled in through the morning, and by afternoon they were a heaving mass of enthusiasm. It *was* theatre. And the actors, two of them, played their part. Unwilling; begging, screaming, burning; but they played it till they were dead, and the crowd ate their picnics and teased their children and set off home in the dusk.

Last of all, so did the priest. Smiling, his bible clasped against his breast, he nodded to the guards, mounted his fat pony and set off on the rough track to the clachan five miles away.

I followed, paralleling his route for a short distance, silent among the trees. It was stupid, and risky, but above me the blanket of cloud was fraying, thinning, glowing with a last sickly sunlight. The bright paleness broke feebly through latticed cloud cover just as the pony came out of a rowan thicket. The priest had been humming to himself, but now he stopped. A little guiltily, he glanced around and behind him; then he visibly relaxed, and smiled, and rode on.

Something bothered me, but I couldn't place it. Maybe the sun was too late or too weak, but I had no idea what Conal was on about. If he trusted me, I thought bitterly, he might have given me something to go on.

Well, I did not know what the priest was, but Conal's orders about blocking were all to do with him, I was sure. Only when I'd made it back to the grim keep, and I could be sure the priest was far away and in the clachan again, did I let down my block.

I searched the keep for Conal, but he was far too clever and determined for me. I was reduced to picking the minds of the guards, and the other prisoners, and the things I found in them as I searched made me dizzy and nauseous in a way that even the burning hadn't. I tried not to linger in the prisoners' pain and indignity and terror, or in the sub-human brutality of the guards. When I had Conal's location narrowed down to one corner of the keep, I went as far as I dared from the evil place, slunk into the heather and waited for nightfall. I'd learned a lot.

There was a burn. I stripped off the plaid and my shirt, washed myself as well as I could, and scraped a hole to bury the plaid, glad to see the back of the filthy thing. I was even more glad to be back in my own soft leather trews, battered and dirty as they were. I'd have liked to wash the shirt, but the muddier the better; I needed camouflage. I mixed some oatmeal with cold water from the burn, left it to soften, then made myself eat it. Just as well I had no meat and could light no fire. I couldn't have stomached roasted flesh, not that evening.

I know how to be silent, I know how to be as close as possible to invisible. And what were the men posted outside the keep guarding against? They were barely watching at all, and it was almost time for the evening guards to relieve their daytime colleagues. I waited at a distance, then as the new guard settled himself for the night, and the other pissed against the wall, I darted across a small patch of rough ground and into the black evening shadows beneath the keep.

The priest had brought men from the distant town, hard-eyed professionals, strangers. These weren't them. They were local clansmen roped in to help, and enjoying the change of scene and the excitement. They resented the arrival of the newcomers, but not enough to complain to the priest. Complaining about anything to the priest resulted in a dungeon, and inventive torments, and smoke too close to your nostrils. One of the men in the keep, waiting for his turn on the brushwood, was that solemn-eyed crofter who liked his own company. When had they decided he was a witch? He was there for saying the baby was exposed, for saying witchcraft was nonsense. That his name was Malcolm Bhan MacKinnon is all I know about him, that and the fact that he died on a slow fire two days later.

The clan guards took their time exchanging places, bored and in the mood for talk. The new one brought out a flask of whisky, and the other took an appreciative swig.

'They eat babies,' growled the off-duty one. 'It's true. The minister told us.'

'Aye, I heard. Sacrifice them to the Devil'—the second guard crossed himself quickly—'and then they feast on them. And they want us all enslaved to their godless ways.'

'This one here'—the first jerked his head at the wall —'there's no doubt about it. Witches have unnatural strength, they say. Well, this one does. He's a warlock and no question. How else do you explain it? It's four days since that little man came from town with his . . . equipment.' It was this guard's turn to cross himself.

His colleague nodded, and took another mouthful of whisky. 'They tried everything. I never would believe anyone could last so long. He wouldn't, not without supernatural help. Know what broke him?'

My heart turned over and I almost fell. They'd broken him? My brother was not breakable. I forced back my tears and tried not to listen.

'It was the boots,' the man went on. 'The Spanish boots, that's what they call them. They make pulp of your feet, so I've heard. Well, he took one look at them, and shook his head, and said he wouldn't be dragged to his own burning, he'd walk.'

'Is that so?' The first guard laughed gruffly.

'Aye. He gave them a fine confession, and he laughed as he gave it, the black-hearted devil. I think the minister was a bit put out that he'd given in. The man from town certainly was. The longer they last, the more he earns.'

'Still, the pay is good for a burning, too. And he'll be well paid in the next few days.'

'The strong one, he's one of the last, I hear. It will be three days of waiting for him, so he'll have plenty of time to repent of his arrogance. The others did not last so long anyway. Did you hear the Balchattan witch squeal?'

'Aye, and serve her right. She was up to the same as the Sinclair crone: spoiled a man's wedding night. Cast a spell on the ale, can you credit such wickedness? She tried to claim the groom had taken a dram too many and his bride was ugly enough to shrivel iron, never mind a male member.' He laughed. 'She'd a tongue like a knife, that woman, before they interrogated her. She wasn't laughing after they'd finished. She confessed, like they all do.'

Thinking of Ma Sinclair, I felt sick, and not just with relief.

'The devil's-whore howled this afternoon when they lit the fire under her. She won't like it too well in the other fire, and that goes on forever, the minister says.' The other man gave a delicious shudder. 'The warlock is not to be strangled first?'

'None of them are. The priest says an example must be set. Besides, the people come from the clachans and the bailes. It's a fine entertainment for them.'

'And a fine warning. There won't be many taking the Devil's mark from now on.'

'Ah!' exclaimed the other, and sniggered at a memory. 'Did you hear? They found one of those on that pretty girl from Balchattan.'

'The younger one?'

'Aye. It took them a while, but then she was awful pretty. You'll never guess where they found her mark. All I'll say is this: they had to shave every inch of her.'

They collapsed into raucous, whisky-fuelled laughter.

I watched them from only a few yards, and knew that I could have the dirk off one of them and he'd never know it. At least, he'd never know it till he was staring in shock at the blood gushing from his own throat.

I made myself think of Conal. I couldn't take the risk, not just to indulge myself.

Later, maybe. Later.

18

Inside the keep I wouldn't have got near Conal, I know that now. Even the Veil has its limits, with ruthless and professional guards who know what they're doing. That was why I liked these two fools on the outside wall—at least, I liked their carelessness and their over-confidence and their taste for rough whisky. There were things I'd seen as I sat silent and watched the keep, and one of them was that both guards always made sure to empty their bladders in the same spot.

After the first guard had finally wandered off to his bed or his woman, I lay within yards of his replacement for an age without being seen. Partly it was down to my own fieldcraft; mostly it was the Veil. Kate must be mad wanting rid of it.

I waited till he'd taken his own long piss, chuckling to himself and calling out an obscenity, and then had sat down again with his back to the wall. The whisky was weighting his eyelids, and he'd rid himself of his bladder discomfort, and his head sagged from time to time, but he must have been more afraid of the priest and his mercenaries than I'd guessed. He forced himself to stay wakeful, getting up now and again to walk around and stamp his feet.

I knew he'd sleep in the end, but I'd been patient and canny long enough. Silent, I crawled towards him on my belly. One touch was all I needed, but close to his spine or his brain. I thought of taking his dirk, but it would still have been a self-indulgence, and the alarm would have been raised when he was found. Instead I took him with laughable ease, with the childhood strategy of a stone tossed to the far side of him. When he glanced aside at the noise, I sprang the last yard and caught hold of his neck, and held it till the sleep swamped him. It took less than two seconds, and he didn't have time to object. He didn't even know about me: when he woke he'd blame the long hours they made him work. He was a lucky bastard, I thought bitterly, that he was going to wake at all.

I didn't even have to pull aside the coarse overgrown grass, since the guards had done that. The smallest and narrowest of gratings was set into the very bottom of the wall, and as I lay down and put my face close to it I smelt first the sharp reek of their urine, both stale and fresh, and then the fouler stench that lay behind it. My vision is like a cat's, always has been, but even I could see nothing of the subterranean hole beneath.

He was there. I shut my eyes, feeling my heart clench with a mixture of emotions. Relief, pity, pain. His mind remained as closed to me as this dungeon. I tried to say something, but my throat was constricted and thick with tears, and I couldn't. I pressed my forehead to the rusty grille of cold iron, and then I heard him.

He spoke very softly, but my hearing is as good as my eyesight. I knew right away he wasn't speaking to me, because he didn't know I was there. I cursed in my head over and over, the worst curses I could think of. He wasn't alone.

'Listen to me.' His voice sounded dull and dry. He needed water. 'You must confess.'

'I won't!'

My blood stilled in my veins. The voice was a girl's, but it was high-pitched with fear and pain more than with her gender.

'You have to.'

'You're one of them!' She spat it at him, but I could hear her terror. 'You're with the guards. You're with the minister!'

'No,' he said.

'I won't confess! I'm innocent!'

'It doesn't matter. So am I.' There was a long pause in the blackness. 'I'm as innocent as you are, and I've confessed. So will you. Make it quick.'

For a moment I could hear only her rasping, terrified breathing as she thought about it. Then she hissed, 'You're an agent of theirs. I know what they do. I know the tricks!'

'In the morning,' he said, and the dryness in his voice was now the amused kind, 'a sliver of light will come in up there, along with the morning piss from the guard. Then you'll be able to see me, just a very little, and you'll know that isn't true.'

'I don't believe you. Where did you come from? I didn't know you were here. *I don't believe you.*' She was on the verge of terrible tears, and I was afraid she'd turn hysterical. Shut up, I thought viciously. Don't you dare cry and bring the guards. Don't you dare, you silly bitch.

'Listen,' said Conal. 'Quiet, now.'

There was silence again, and I heard her breathing slowly ease, and quieten.

'Do you trust me?' he said.

'Why would I?' There was an edge to her bitter words, but it was no longer hysterical.

'No reason. But do you?'

'Are you a witch?'

'No.'

There was a tiny hesitation, then her small voice. 'Am I?'

'You're no witch, lady, any more than I am. You're guilty of nothing. I'm guilty of having the wrong ancestors, being the wrong person. I'm different to you but we'll both die the same death. You can't avoid it now. Even if you denounce me.'

There was a smile in the way he said it, and her wave of shame was palpable. The idea must have occurred to her.

'Make up a story,' he said into the silence. 'Make something up for your confession. It'll pass the time anyway.'

'Why?' Her aggression had faded; she sounded bewildered. 'Why would I do such a thing? I've done nothing.'

'You must. Give them what they want. Tell them you've been to Black Masses, flown in the air, kissed the Devil's backside. You must make something up. Tell them some perverted rubbish. Come on, I'll give you some ideas. It's for your own good.'

Tears threatened again. 'I could never even say such things, let alone do them!'

'Doesn't matter. You have to say it. Please.'

'Why?' she cried.

'Because if you keep them happy with a good story, and renounce the Devil, and show you're penitent . . .' he hesitated.

'What?' I could hear her renewed hope, and I felt sorry for the stupid child.

'Then they might strangle you first,' he said. 'Before they burn you.'

She started to cry in earnest, but softly, and in despair.

'It's worth it,' he added.

He didn't know, I realised. He didn't know his death would be merciless. Somehow the priest had kept it from him. There was no sound for a while but the quiet aching sobs of the girl, but sooner than I expected she got a hold of herself.

'You're not chained, are you?' he said after a while.

'No.' She sniffed.

'I stink,' he said, 'and I'm no help to you, but I'm manacled myself. I can't hurt you.'

She scrambled across to him, fast and noisy, stumbling and falling. I heard the rattle of his chains as he put his arms round her as best he could. Love for him lanced under my breastbone. It hurt so much I had to hold my breath. ~ *Look after yourself*, I thought. ~ *You sentimental idiot. Never mind her.*

But he still wasn't listening to me.

'When you hear them coming,' he told her softly, 'get away from me. They put you in here hoping I'd terrify you. If they find us like this they'll put fetters on you too.'

Her tear-choked voice was muffled by his chest. 'So I can't stop them killing me.'

'No,' he said kindly. 'But you can try to die less badly. And with luck we'll be together.'

With better luck, I thought grimly, you won't.

'I don't know,' she whimpered. 'I don't know. About confessing.'

'What have they done to you so far?'

Her words, when they came, seemed half-stuck in her throat. 'A . . . a needle or something. The pricker. They looked for a mark where I couldn't feel it.' Her voice went higher. 'In the end they said they'd found a spot. I don't know. Maybe they did.'

'No, they didn't. Poor girl.'

'And there was . . . they . . . tied my arms behind me and hung me up by them. I thought,' she swallowed hard, 'I thought I couldn't bear even a second of it.'

'Next time they'll hoist you up and weight your legs and drop you. I survived it, but you might not. You think they can only dislocate your limbs once? That man from town puts them back. Every time. Confess, lady.'

She was silent again, but this time when she spoke her voice was calm and steady. 'They'll want me to name others. They'll want me to denounce people I know and I can't do that.'

'Listen, that much I think I can help with. Tell them

you were my acolyte. My *only* acolyte. I sent you to Balchattan to work my spells for me. I'll tell them the same, I'll volunteer the information because I want you in Hell with me. I can convince them of that, at least. And the minister is only interested in me.'

'Why?'

He paused, then said wryly, 'It's personal.'

I'd heard enough. Actually I'd heard too much. Quietly, under my breath, I said, 'Conal.'

There was no sound, only stillness for a very long time, perhaps as long as ten minutes. I waited. I didn't speak again; I knew he'd heard me. Then, in the silence, I heard the deep, intermittent breathing of a sleeping girl. I doubt they'd let her have any sleep for days, and now she was dead to the world. And to me. He shifted, moving the slight weight of her in his arms; I heard a small dull clank of chain. Moving must have hurt him: I heard him grind his teeth.

'Seth,' he said softly, a reluctant smile in his voice. 'Did I not hurt you enough?'

'Aye, you did. I'm thinking of leaving you here.' I gritted my teeth and swallowed tears, but my voice broke anyway. 'Speak to me, Conal, properly. Please.'

'No.'

'Please,' I said. 'Don't block me. Not now.'

He was silent again, for an age. 'I'll talk to you. But only talk. Try to get inside my head and I'll block you again, and this time it'll be for good. Understand?'

I knew the reason, and my heart shrivelled in my ribcage. I knew then I'd kill them for his pain. All of them. But I only said, 'Yes.'

~ *Murlainn*.

The gentle way he spoke my name brought fresh tears to my eyes. ~ *I'll get you out of here, Cù Chaorach. I swear I'll do it.*

~ *Don't swear anything, because you won't. It's too difficult.*

~ *I have to try.*

~ *Do that, and they'll have you too. It will be a hundred times worse for me if they get you. It'll kill my soul. I thought you'd gone home.*

~ *How could you think it?* I was furious with him.

~ *Well. I don't suppose I did, really. You wee bandit.*

~ *We could use the Veil . . .*

He laughed softly. ~ *I told you before, you're inconspicuous, not invisible. You think they can't see me when they do what they do?*

~ *I'll kill them,* I said. ~ *I'll kill the priest last. I'll make him beg to die.*

~ *It's not a priest. And don't, Seth. Just go home.*

~ *I could wait till the guards are at their lowest point. Before dawn. I could pretend I'm . . .*

~ *Put it out of your head, greenarse,* he said gently. ~ *Besides, there's her.*

I clenched my jaw to stop myself saying what I wanted to say. ~ *We could . . . I don't know. Draw the Veil over her too. Keep her right beside us.*

~ *Can't be done. If we were caught we'd all be in this together, and they'd break my heart as well as my body. No, Seth. I won't leave her, and I won't risk you.*

I could only despair, frustrated beyond reason. 'Then there's nothing I can do for you,' I said aloud, dully.

'Yes. One thing.' His mind touched mine gently once more. 'Bring me a dirk.'

I knew what he meant. 'No!'

'Bring me a dirk. Please. I don't want to burn, Seth.'
His voice shook. 'I heard the last ones.'

Heard them? I'd seen them. Have you ever seen skin
bubble and melt, eyeballs explode, fat sizzle and pop?
Have you smelt live flesh roasting? Have you heard
them? Do you know how long it takes them to die?

A thousand years. A hundred thousand. Forever.

'Yes,' I said. 'All right.'

'I'll cut her throat and then I'll cut my own. Don't
worry about me any more.'

'Aye,' I said. 'As long as you don't waste too much
time on her. See to yourself. And do it right, you clumsy
sod.'

I thought I glimpsed his grin in the darkness. 'I will,
if you bring it. I promise. Now go.'

'I don't want to leave you,' I said.

'I know.'

'What will they do now?'

'Don't worry,' he murmured.

'Don't make me laugh.'

He laughed, instead, a little hoarsely. 'The interroga-
tion's over, all right? They'll bring me food and water
to keep me alive for burning. Bring me a dirk, that's
all.'

'Shut up. You don't have to keep asking me.'

'How often do I have to ask you to *go*? If they catch
you they'll burn you, and they'll do it slowly. And they
won't even burn you till they've made you sorry, and
me sorrier. How much dignity do you think you'll have
left, Seth? How much of your precious pride?'

I pressed my face to the small grille as if I could

somehow melt through it and touch him. The stink of urine was unbearable. I thought, I'd know those guards anywhere by their smell. I could track them down now like a hound. And one day I would.

'Seth.' His voice was almost a whisper now. 'They're coming. Try to bring me what I want but don't risk capture. That's an *order*.' Then he was silent again, just for a moment.

~ *Don't let them catch you. Go home and live. That's what I want most. Go.*

The girl was stirring in his arms, I could hear her.

'Hey,' he said, and his chains clanked as he shook her. She must have woken at once, because she scrambled from his arms and across the cold stones, gasping with fear.

Backing away, I almost tripped over the unconscious guard. I swore. The man had a dirk, and if I'd had my wits about me I'd just have taken it off him and passed it through the bars to Conal. Now the bolts of his dungeon were being shot back with an echoing clang, and the guards were coming in. It was too late.

Besides, I don't know if I could have done it then; the shock of Conal's request was too new. And after all, this had been so easy. I could slink back and put the guard back to sleep any time. Next time, I'd slit his throat before I gave his dirk to Conal, and then I'd disappear, and Conal would be beyond their vengeance. I smiled. There would be a next time, after all.

I'd be back.

19

I'm an arrogant toad. Full of myself, always have been. But I have never again been so arrogant when the life of someone I love is at stake: literally at stake, in Conal's case. I know now that I have to think ahead and plan for the worst. Now I know I'm not the cleverest fighter who ever walked the earth. Now I know I can be out-thought and outsmarted and outfought. Now I know the value of contingency planning.

Not then, I didn't. But I learned.

It was the following evening when I made my way back to the keep. I stayed in the tree line for more than an hour, panic squeezing my skull and my chest till I could barely think or breathe. I put my hands in my hair and gripped fistfuls of it and tore it till it hurt, trying to make myself think clearly, but I couldn't. I couldn't even think in a straight line.

The guard at the outer keep wall had been trebled, and they were no longer local clansmen. Cold-eyed, unsmiling, they were the paid mercenaries of the priest and I knew that they would have the wits to keep their eyes open and to watch each other's backs. There would be no putting sleep on these grim fighters, and they'd be damn sure to hold onto their weapons.

I hunted in a wide circle around the keep, staying in the trees. Only at the wall outside Conal's dungeon had the guard been changed and strengthened. My brain and spine prickled with terror. How had they known?

Two days. Could I reach the watergate in that time? Yes, but the time might unbalance. It often did. No speed would matter if a month passed while I ran helpless to my clann. Or a year.

How long would he take to die? How long would it feel?

The courtyard gate swung wide and out came the priest, hands clasped piously before him. Close to me was the vertical base of an uprooted pine, blown down in a spring gale. The trunk and branches were gone, but the mud-choked tangle of roots was nearly twice my height, so I ducked behind it and watched through the trees.

The priest walked to the new guards, his robes flapping like batwings, and spoke to them for a minute or two. There was much nodding, many gestures up into the surrounding hills and trees, and at one point they all looked up simultaneously, almost directly at my hiding place.

The priest glanced down at his feet and stamped hard. I heard the clang of solid metal. He leaned down and tugged at something with his fingertips, quite hard, then straightened, nodding in approval. Sickness turned my stomach, and tears burned my eyes.

They'd covered up the little barred hole. They'd taken away his last light, and his last air, and his last chance of a death of his choosing.

When he left the guards, the priest did not go back towards his pony as he usually did. He walked out towards the trees, straight towards me. For a moment panic almost made me leap from my hole and run, and I felt for every hare and bird I'd ever hunted to its death.

But his pale gaze swept the low slopes and the trees, and I knew he hadn't seen me. I thought I was safe, I thought I could breathe again, but the next thing that happened almost knocked the air from my lungs.

~ *Where are you?*

His voice was clear in my head. I was scared for a fraction of a second that I'd left my block down, but no. At least I hadn't been quite that careless, but how was he doing that? How could the thoughts of a full-mortal echo through the forest like a hunting cry?

~ *Where are you, my little warlock?* He sniffed the air and smiled, a death grimace if ever I saw one. ~ *I smell you, little one. I smelt you in the grass by the keep and I smell you now.*

Do not panic, I told myself. Do not run. Do not run.

~ *We gave your brother an extra whipping, to cele-brate your visit. He's good, he's very good. He only screamed the once, when we hung him up by his poor sore arms.*

You're dead, I thought. My fingers flexed and clenched, wanting his throat. But not now. Not now. I had to live to kill him.

~ *There. You don't interest me, so forget your brother.*

*Run along home now, or I'll warm my chilly old fin-
gers on your burning bones.*

He snuffed the air again, and turned, and made his
unhurried way back to the courtyard and his pony.

It's not a priest. That's what Conal had said. I'd
thought he was correcting my vocabulary, like always.

I'd thought he was saying *It's a minister, you daft
greenarse.*

That wasn't what he'd been saying at all. A shudder
went through me, and wouldn't stop for more than a
minute.

It's not a priest. It. It.

No-one cared about the western wall of the keep. Obviously, whoever was rotting or screaming in the dungeon on that side had no brother who was trying to
get them out of it. That side was still protected, for
want of a better word, by clansmen who were by now
chafing at the contempt of the professional men, and
resentful enough of their presence to be careless. They
bitched and moaned to one another endlessly, and
shared drams from their flasks, and wandered off to relieve themselves less entertainingly now that their
amusing latrines had been sealed. They left their weapons lying while they did it, among them new and alien
weapons that I doubt they could even use. Some of
them I couldn't, either; I knew nothing of the slender
steel pistols and how they killed. Others, though, I
could use better than anyone here.

And one of the clansmen was so drunk, and so tired,
and in such a furious temper with the sneering profes-

sionals, I knew fine he wouldn't even miss the crossbow.

I whittled bolts from lengths of hazel. I rubbed them
smooth and honed their tips to a needlepoint that
would have pleased a witch-pricker. I took my time
with the job; what else was there to think about? One
day. Two days. I had a store of bolts, far more than I
needed: every one perfect and deadly. When I was finished, I looked into the blue dawn and blinked. The
cloud cover had dissipated at last. The day was going
to be blazing. He would not die today. The priest
would not stand in the courtyard.

Not till the shadows were long.

My woodland lair was beautiful: a clearing that was
green with life. It smelt of summer and rain and new-
ness. It was patterned with shifting light and shade,
alive with the trill and whistle of flirtatious birdsong.
Oh, this was too lovely a day to die, too lovely to kill.

But the shadows would, in the end, grow long.

I walked with my crossbow to the middle of the forest clearing. The grass was cool beneath my bare feet,
still damp with dew despite the warmth. Sitting down
cross-legged, I let the birdsong distract me from reality,
and in my head I went to the courtyard. I walked it in
my mind, counted stones, timed my paces. I had watched
guards and clansmen and doomed prisoners walk it;
in my memory I watched them again, and walked with
them, and measured my paces to theirs. And when
I'd sat there and walked it over and over again in my
mind, I stood up and opened my eyes and paced the

length of the courtyard in the clearing, my stolen cross-bow clutched against my breast.

When I had the distance I scrambled into the branches of a high pine with the bow slung across my back. I saw the clearing and replaced it in my head with the courtyard.

And when I'd done all I could do I shinned down the tree, and hung my last small bag of meal on a branch at the far side of the clearing, then climbed once more into the pine. I fired bolts at the dangling target till oatmeal lay wasted and scattered through the grass, and the hessian bag hung in shreds, and as far as I could possibly estimate the distance, my stolen bow was sighted for death.

You would never have thought the keep walls were scaleable. But then, no-one I knew had thought the dun's northern wall was scaleable, till I made a habit of scaling it. One of my father's fighters had spotted me once, clambering down hand over hand to avoid my chores. He'd yelled for his companions and they'd stood there, leaning over the parapet and chucking things at me, anything that came to hand, and laughing their heads off. When I made it safely to the bottom, and brushed bits of oatcake and horse manure from my hair and clothes, I stepped back and made them an elegant bow, then gave them two insulting fingers. That had made them laugh even more as they clapped and cheered. I was smaller than most of them, and lighter, and from then on whenever anyone needed a climber they called for me. I could find handholds and footholds where any Sithe would have sworn there were none. There were always handholds, always. And—so far—I was living proof that I'd never fallen.

I tried to remember all of that as I looked up at the sheer keep wall that evening. One of the clansmen snored at my feet; the guard was light again. It was all over. The prisoner who was going to die was the one they all wanted to see, and there was no hope of rescue for him now. Even the professional fighters had gone inside the keep walls to help tend the fires and enjoy the entertainment. I'd made mistakes. Well, so could the priest. He'd underestimated me.

I wouldn't do the same for him, not a second time. I swore that day I'd never again make the same mistake twice. I kept all my senses fixed on the priest, all but the one he could track. I knew where he was all the time, and I stayed downwind.

I made sure my crossbow was slung tightly on my back. Running my palms across the wall, I found a first small uneven ridge. For a second I paused, and leaned my forehead against the cool rough stone, and breathed hard, and got a hold of myself. Then I curled my fingertips round the invisible handhold, and found and gripped another, and began to climb.

20

Why have they bothered to put them in a cart for a journey of a hundred yards? So he can be seen and spat at and pelted with shit and sent to Hell with their curses ringing in his ears?

Yes. I suppose so.

The crowd is not under the priest's control. I do wonder for a moment if they are. I want them to be, but I only have to look at them once to know their sacred free will is intact. No one is bending these minds, though bent they are. I certainly can't twist so many, though gods know I want to. Even the priest, whatever he is, couldn't do that.

He's shown Conal to them, and he's told them what they didn't even know they wanted to hear. The rest is their own instinct, their own foul cravings. The priest has nothing more to do, only watch and smile. There among the mob is my quiet black-haired girl with the sceptical green eyes. She's not so quiet now: she's howling her hate.

The priest stays in the long shadow of the courtyard wall. I notice that. I'm trying to remember something I was taught, a long time ago, when it was all fairy stories to me. I'm trying to remember, but instead I remember the pale sun coming out as he rode from the rowan copse not three days ago. I remember his nervous glance, and his ironic smile. And now I do remember what I saw: I see it again, clear in my head. I saw the sun cast a shadow on the track, but it was the shadow of a saddled pony, no more. The priest threw none.

It threw none.

Conal is a dead man limping to his death-fire, and I know it.

I can't do this alone. And the priest isn't watching for my mind. Either he doesn't care any more, or he's so in thrall to the coming spectacle that he wants to concentrate on nothing else. He can't. He's in a trance of ecstasy. *It's* in ecstasy, I mean. It's loving it. It's what it was born for. You can't blame it.

It isn't watching, and that's why I can talk to my brother one last time. I can let him know I haven't let him down, that I haven't failed after all, that his black despair when they sealed the dungeon vent wasn't the end of everything. Finally, at the end of his life and possibly the end of mine, I've done something right and I've done it for him. I've returned the favour he's been doing me since I was eight years old.

I squeeze my eyes hard shut and open them again. Damn the blurring of my eyes: I have to see straight. Maybe that's why I change my mind. I'm sorry for the girl, but it has to be Conal first. I can't risk my eyesight failing through sentiment and weakness. It has to be now, and it has to be Conal before the girl. I'm sorry, whatever your name is. Catriona. I'll get to you later. It has to be my brother first. He's dead already, after all. He's dead already.

And my mind is as cold as my heart as I tighten my finger on the trigger.

'WHAT IN THE NAME OF GOD IS GOING ON?'

PART THREE

FIREBRAND

21

So many years. There have been so many years between then and now, and still I'll dream that my finger was a fraction of an instant faster on that crossbow, and I'll wake shaking and screaming. Still.

So in the darkness I'll reach for the woman beside me, for that other half of my soul and my self, and she'll put her arms around me and soothe me back to sleep, thinking I'm dreaming of another time, of terrible things that were still in my future. Sometimes—often—that's what it is. Sometimes it isn't.

She knows, of course, that I almost killed a man she loved. There have been so many women we both loved, but she was different. She still is. I waited too long for her. Too long. Fate's cruel.

No, it was kind that day. It was kind the day I didn't kill my brother. It's just that I so nearly did, and Fate likes to remind me. In the small hours.

But I don't tell her when I dream his death. It doesn't matter. I have plenty of night terrors to choose from now. She doesn't always need to know which. She only needs to know she's my firewall against them. That's all. And she knows that fine.

Hooves clattered into the courtyard, horses neighed, swords rasped out of scabbards. The man on the grey stallion looked familiar, but for a moment I couldn't place him. He was well-dressed, tall and elegant, but he had the dirt of a long journey on him, and the hard ruthless fitness of a man just done with battle. The twenty-three men on horseback behind him had a similar look, and they all had naked swords in their hands.

Utter silence had fallen, broken only by the muffled aching sobs of the girl at the stake.

'If you put those flames to that wood,' said the newcomer in a voice rimmed with ice, 'my men will cut every one of you down where you stand. Men, women and children.'

The men holding the firebrands exchanged glances and stepped very slightly back, but the priest barged forward, brandishing his bible. 'You have no authority in this matter, lord! *Thou shalt not suffer a witch to live!*'

'And nor shalt thou kill,' said the horseman calmly. 'But I suspect you have as much respect for that as I do.'

The MacLeod. Back from his hobby-wars and alive. I forgave him every disdainful glance, every patronising smile. I forgave him my lowly otherworld life and I forgave him our hovel. Never in my life did I meet a man with better timing.

The clansmen had shrunk back, shifty and terrified, but not the priest's professionals. Their fingers twitched by scabbards and on pistol hilts, waiting for a word.

For interminable silent ages the priest and the earl stared at one another. The skin was stretched even tauter across the priest's cheekbones—cheated of his prey, I thought he might launch himself at the earl's throat—but I couldn't speak or move. I could barely breathe.

Snatching the firebrand from the closer of the two clansmen, the priest raised it high, a smiling snarl on those thin yellow lips. Almost simultaneously the Mac-Leod raised his own hand and snapped his fingers.

A blade flew from the hand of one of the riders behind him, straight and true, impaling the priest. Someone in the crowd screamed once; there was a collective intake of breath. The mercenaries stared, swords and pistols half-drawn but far too late.

The priest sank to his knees, robes billowing around him like black smoke, the snarl—and the smile—still on his lips. He tried to utter some anathema, but only a horrible rattling sigh came out. He did not fall, but remained kneeling before the earl. It took me long heartstopping moments to be sure that he was dead.

That *it* was dead.

'Conal MacGregor is no witch, you fools, and even if he was he'd be better than any ten of you. Bring him down,' said the MacLeod calmly. 'The girl too. The rest of you go home, and be aware that I will hang each and every one of you, and evict your families to starve, if it even crosses your mind to behave in this manner again.'

The priest's men simply melted away, silent. I watched

them go. I knew their faces, every one, and I promised myself I'd see them again one day from a different angle. From the crowd, beginning to disperse, there was very little mutinous muttering. With the priest dead, there was only one man to fear, and they knew who buttered their bread, and on which side. Some had already begun to look ashamed of themselves.

Two of the earl's fighters were cutting Conal's bonds, and his hands trembled as he rubbed life back into them. He swayed, but righted himself, teeth gritted, and he refused their help. And he had the nerve to complain about my insufferable pride?

The girl was incapable of standing, only sank down weeping onto the pile of firewood as they freed her. She cringed away from the fighters, but Conal crouched down and lifted her into his arms. I saw him stagger again, and almost drop her, but he recovered. I saw all that, though I was running down the steps from the parapet to the courtyard. I trusted to my mind to sense the steps and my feet to find them, because I couldn't take my eyes off my brother.

He scrambled unsteadily down from the pyre, the girl's face pressed fiercely into his neck, her arms almost choking him. A fighter tried to take her from him, only to help him, but he froze and jerked away, giving the man a wary look.

The man only smiled an intent smile. There was a silvery glow in his eyes. As I leaped impatiently from one flight of steps to the bottom of the next, I heard him quite clearly.

~ *Get out of here, Cù Chaorach.*

Conal stared at him. Then, as he stumbled back, he

turned and almost fell, but he was still upright when he stopped in front of the MacLeod's horse.

His arms tightened round the girl. 'Thank you, *Morair*.'

The MacLeod gave him a long searching look.

'I suggest you leave here, MacGregor, you and your brother. I'll be sorry to see the back of you but it would be safer for you both.'

'You'll have trouble over this, lord. I'm sorry for that too.'

'Oh, not as much as I should.' The earl shrugged and gave the dead priest a look of contempt. 'That is the privilege of wealth and power. But things will get worse before they get better, and my protection will not be limitless. So go.'

'Yes, *Morair*.'

'Give up the obsequies, MacGregor. They don't suit you.'

I reached them running, the crossbow still in my hands. Several fighters turned to me with weapons raised, and I'd happily have taken them on barehanded to get to Conal, but the MacLeod lifted a hand, and they lowered their swords.

'Ah. A contingency plan, MacGregor.' He smiled. 'You are lucky to have such a brother.'

'I know that, lo . . . I know that.'

He couldn't put his arms round me because he was holding the girl, and I resented her bitterly for it, but he pressed his face against my head as I embraced him, tears soaking my cheeks.

'What about her?' The MacLeod nodded at the whimpering creature.

'Her mother died five months ago. She has no other family. It was her stepfather who denounced her to the . . . to the minister,' said Conal bitterly. 'She can't go back to Balchattan. She'll have to come with us.'

The MacLeod waved a hand dismissively. 'Of course, of course.' He clicked his gloved fingers again. 'Give them horses,' he told his men, 'and escort them to the borders of my land. Beyond that their fate is their own. You should go far from here, MacGregor. You know *exactly* what I mean, don't you?'

Looking dumbfounded, Conal bowed his head.

'I wish you wouldn't do that,' sighed the MacLeod.

I caught the flash of Conal's old grin as he straightened.

Horses were brought, we mounted, and it was over. I could barely believe it. I thought I would start to shake, but I made myself keep control: we were still surrounded by full-mortals and I still trusted none of them. As far as I knew this could be a sick joke to torment us with before they killed us.

Not all of them were full-mortals, of course. The silver-eyed fighter gave the girl up into Conal's arms, and as he stepped back he winked. Something undoubtedly passed between his mind and my brother's before Conal turned to the MacLeod.

'Thank you. *Morair*. Your God go with you.'

'Goodbye, MacGregor, and let's hope against hope he's with all of us. And in future?' The earl sighed. 'Do be more careful who sees that light in your mind's eye.'

22

We detoured, of course, to retrieve Branndair and Liath, and we stopped once so that we could eat. We didn't have anything, but the earl's fighters were Highlanders enough to share what they had. They didn't speak much, and I wondered where they were from, but I didn't care quite enough to ask. I was desperately tired, and desperately worried.

Conal sat hunched and silent, his body curled up, and though he was thin and hollow-eyed he could barely force down the oatcakes and dried meat they gave him. I made him drink a little water. Liath lay with her head against him, watchful. Branndair tried to curl in my lap, though he was too big to fit there now and his haunches sprawled on the ground. I'd been afraid the earl's fighters might try to kill the pair of them, but when I coaxed Branndair and Liath out of the sett, the men had only raised their eyebrows and shared glances, and then took no more notice than if they had been hunting dogs.

The girl crouched a little apart, cramming down food like a ravenous animal but never taking her wary eyes off us all. She didn't say a word. She hadn't spoken since they dragged her to the stake, and she'd even stopped crying, thank the gods. When it was time to move on, and I'd given Conal a boost into his saddle, she went straight to his horse without asking, put her bare foot in its stirrup beside Conal's, and mounted behind him, hitching up her thin shift. She rested her hands on his waist but she didn't grip him too tightly, I was glad to see—it would have been a pity to kill her now—and he didn't seem to mind her being there. He seemed to find it comforting.

I knew things were bad with him because he rode with stirrups. If he hadn't, I think he'd simply have slipped from the horse's back. I'd crossed my own across my horse's withers: a saddle felt strange enough. But Conal had his feet jammed into the stirrups, and he clutched the pommel like a drowning man clinging to life. Anxiety ate at my guts.

The men left us in a small clearing that lay on the edge of the MacLeod's lands. All but one turned their horses and rode off without a word, but their captain waited beside us.

'It isn't far from here, is it?'

Conal's head hung so low in exhaustion I knew he couldn't even speak, so I answered for him. 'No. Not far.'

'Keep the horses. They are a gift from the MacLeod. Do you know the way?'

I glanced at Conal, saw his head nod slightly. The girl's wide anxious eyes were locked on him.

'Yes,' I said. 'We'll be fine.' At least I hoped we would. All of us.

'Don't come back here, any of you, if you know what's good for you.'

'I wouldn't dream of it,' I said bitterly.

'But if you do, and you're in trouble,' he said, 'ask for me. I am Iain Ruadh MacLeod. And if I am not here,' a smile twitched his mouth, 'ask for my descendants.'

A muttered *thank you* was all I could manage as he put his heels to his horse and cantered after his men. When I looked again at Conal, he had already ridden on in silence. I rode after him, the wolves at our heels.

These were pretty lands, wooded and wild but lush, and sheltered by hills. The climate was damp and warm in the low-lying forests; there were flowers and deep green grass and springs soaking through the earth. Midges hovered in a cloud around us, but none of us minded much. I recognised it all, though it had been almost two years, and my heart lightened the further we rode. If I could get him home, we'd be fine.

The little loch lay quiet among the trees, and we were silent as we halted and stared at it. My heart was in my throat and my eyes burned. Beyond the reedy edges its surface was absolutely still, sticky-glossed with the intense reflected colours of bank and tree and sky. If you dipped in your hand, you might think you'd draw it out dripping with raw pigment.

'Girl,' I said. 'Get off the horse.'

The girl slid off the horse's back and stood there, looking at me and then at Conal and then at the loch. Conal half-turned to give me a withering glare that was a ghost of what he used to inflict on me. I tried to smile.

Dismounting, Conal gripped his horse's stirrup leather tightly, and leaned against the animal's flank for a moment, and so kept his footing. Gathering himself, he walked forward to the reedy bank. He turned to the girl.

'*Catriona*,' he said pointedly, with a glance at me. 'This is where we go.'

She shook her head, took a step back, and shook her head again.

'Do you want to stay here and die,' he asked her, 'or will you trust me?'

Staring at the still water, she swallowed, her pale throat jerking. She took a step towards the loch, then another, but then she stopped and seemed unable to move.

'You have to be with me,' he said, and in front of my disbelieving eyes he went to her and picked her up in his arms again.

She was a wisp of a creature, but I wanted to drag her off him and fling her away. I jumped down off my own horse, but something held me back. She was shaking her head violently, touching Conal's face, stroking his cheek.

'It's all right,' he said. 'I'm all right.' And he carried her into the water.

He stopped when he was up to his thighs, and waited for me. Whistling a low note to Liath and Branndair, I slipped a hand under the cheekpiece of each horse's bridle so that the backs of my hands were pressed to their bony heads. Then I led them forward. They were obedient beasts. They followed me and the wolves without shying or balking. Hell, they must have got a shock when the watergate opened.

So must the girl. She must have been petrified, but she never showed it. I was fighting terrified horses by the time I surfaced and shook water from my eyes. They were tossing their heads, jerking away from me, going back on their hind legs, bucking and plunging and dancing sideways. Grimly I held onto them, though one was snapping frantically at my hand. We needed horses and I couldn't lose them, so although I was desperate to get to Conal, first I had to tether the beasts to a bleached stump of dead tree. Liath and Branndair shook their fur dry, and sat down, and stared at the moorland, looking a little bewildered but not unhappy.

The girl was still clutched in Conal's arms, her arms now tight around his neck, her face buried in his throat. He sank down to his knees and I heard him say something to her, a note of desperation in it. Squirming from his arms at last, she crawled back on all fours and clambered to her feet, staring at him. He forced another smile, and tried to stand up, but instead he pitched sideways onto the heather and lay still.

I screamed at her, though I don't know what. Just to get away from him, I think, and at first she did, tugging up her dirty rag of dress and backing away, her eyes wide with terror. Shoving her aside I fell to my knees beside him, and that's when I heard a snap and crack, and an abrupt thunder of hooves. Out of the side of my vision I saw one of the horses break free and run, galloping in a full-blown panic towards the far hills. In my rush I hadn't tethered it properly. I swore, but we still had one horse, and right now I only cared about Conal.

The girl hung back, trembling. I just wanted her to go away, go away and let me help him in peace, but I was cold, and hungry, and more exhausted than I'd realised. My arms trembled, aching from the vertical climb that I tried not to remember, the climb that chilled my guts when I remembered clinging to life and the fortress wall like a pathetic insect. I blinked away the memory, but still my arms wouldn't take Conal's weight. I wasn't big enough. I wasn't strong enough. He was going to die here.

'Help me!' I screamed.

And to give her credit she did, rushing to my side and helping me half-carry, half-drag him to the horse. It was hell, and it was even worse trying to lift him onto its back. In desperation I tugged off the animal's saddle roll and unwound the cloth and looped it under Conal's arms, and between us we dragged and shoved him up; then Catriona sprang up behind him and held him, balancing him, while I unfastened the stirrup leathers and the reins. I buckled the stirrup leathers together and used them to tie his feet under the horse, and then we used the reins to strap his body as best we could to the horse's neck. Catriona slid off again.

'Don't you want to ride too?' I asked, because I felt I should.

She shook her head.

'It's a long way,' I warned her.

She shrugged.

I looked around for landmarks, and glanced up at a sun that was barely risen, a pale and clear early-morning sky. *My* sky. Then with me leading Conal's horse by the cheekpiece of its bridle, and Catriona walking at its other side, we set off on the long walk home.

We must have been within a few miles of the dun by the time I blinked and pulled together my scattered thoughts and my exhausted brain. I knew I should call for help. We must be in range by now and help would come, if I could only think who to call. I struggled to make my mind work, knowing the girl at my side was staring at me in fright as I flailed my temples with my fist, fiercely enough to bruise them. I scratched the skin, drawing beads of blood. I couldn't remember when I'd last slept. I could remember no-one in the dun.

Raineach. The name came to me very suddenly. I stopped, clenched my teeth, and called Raineach.

It was perhaps another mile or more before I was answered, but her answer came in the flesh. I almost wept when I saw familiar fighters riding towards us, but I didn't. I kept walking till I couldn't walk any more, and then I stopped, and Catriona stopped too, and suddenly we were surrounded by people I knew. I just stood there, silent, while they unbuckled the tack straps and lifted Conal with infinite care from the horse, and laid him on a hide stretcher beneath a soft plaid. Riders jostled me aside, threw questions at me, but I couldn't answer, could barely speak. I tried to say he'd been hurt. I tried to say what had happened. I tried to say that I'd tried to stop it, but really, none of my words came out right, and not many of them were listening. I was so tired. Dully I watched them. I couldn't hear them properly, and the scene was jerky.

Eili was in front of me. I stared at her in shock.

'Why didn't you come for us?' she cried. 'Why didn't you come?'

I felt as if I'd been jerked awake, and my words stuck in my throat. 'I couldn't . . . you know I . . . the time. It might have slipped. I couldn't leave him. The time, Eili . . .'

She was already gone, running to Conal's side, and helping to slide his stretcher gently onto a cart.

And then the cart was gone, and the horses, and their riders, and Conal with them, and Liath was running at their heels. I'd brought him home, I thought, and I could let him out of my sight and know there was nothing more I could do. They'd do their best, they didn't need me. Relief and fatigue swamped me like a spring tide, and I halted on the track, hoping my legs weren't about to go from under me. Branndair tilted his head at me and whined.

The girl halted too. She was still beside me, I realised with mild shock.

'Go on,' I said. 'Go on. They'll look after you.'

She didn't move, only turned towards the riders as they shrunk in the distance. Her eyes darkened and she frowned. I followed her gaze.

They were so worried about Conal. So was I. Almighty gods, he was the one who was at death's door. I was fine. I was just tired, that was all. There was no other reason for the crushing ache in my ribcage and the stinging pain in my eyes. I raised my arm to rub them, or tried to, but my arm felt too heavy. It was too much effort.

She touched my arm. I looked down at her hand. It looked frail against the lean hard muscles of my forearm, her skin dungeon-pale and blue-veined. Her nails were torn, and a little displaced, and there were deep wicked lines running towards the base of them, red turning purple and black. I wondered what had been stuck beneath them. The pricker's needle?

Seeing me look, she snatched her hand back, but when I looked up her gaze held mine. Defiant, so she was. I eyed her with disdain. She was scrawny after her imprisonment, but she can't ever have had much muscle on her. Her eyes were huge in a delicate pointed face, but maybe they just looked that way because of her shorn head, scabby and scarred and louse-bitten. Pity twinged in my chest, but it was swiftly overwhelmed by disgust. I hated the way she was looking at me: half sympathetic, half scared. She was too fragile, too snappable for my taste.

Too full-mortal.

I turned on my heel and headed straight west, Branndair trotting at my side. What I needed right now was sky and sea, clear salt water over my head. I knew the girl was following, and it irritated me, so I stripped naked as I walked. That made her stop and sit down on the fringe of the machair, so I kept walking, plunging down the sandbank and breaking into a sprint when I reached hard sand. I leaped and somersaulted, flinging myself into the waves.

Once I was under, just for a second or two, I never wanted to surface again. I wondered if this was what they called a deathwish. Conal said we all came from the sea, even the full-mortals, and that was why so many of us went back there.

Shutting my eyes I swam down, then drifted weightless, tugged and turned by the force of the water as it roiled towards the shore, feeling nothing but cold silky water on my skin, the light caress of seaweed, tangle coiling round my ankle. All I could hear was the sea and the pulse of my blood, roaring in my ears, and I didn't know which was which. My feet touched the seabed, wet sand shifting between my toes, so I pushed back up and broke the surface, sucking in sky.

So deathwishes didn't last. With luck they didn't come true.

I wiped my hair out of my eyes, kicked onto my back and floated, rocked in the swell. I could see Branndair, anxiously pacing the shoreline, whimpering his concern. While my attention was distracted, a bigger wave tumbled me into shore. I surfaced again, choking water. Damn, but it tasted good. The air tasted good. So did the whole world.

I should go to the dun now. Soon. No. Maybe later.

The girl hugged her knees, watching me. Grinding my teeth, I stood up and walked out of the sea, and that made her look hurriedly aside. I picked up my scattered clothing and tugged it back on, the sand scratching my skin in painful places, then went deliberately to the southern end of the bay and scrambled out to the rock headland. This time she didn't follow, but she didn't move either. I forgot her. I sat and stared out at the water, hypnotised by the waves, happy to be home.

But I didn't want to go back to the dun yet. The notion twisted my stomach. I didn't want to see anyone. I wanted to see my home, that was all. This was more than enough. I'd wanted it for two years. Till Conal recovered, I didn't need anything or anyone else.

'Hello.' There was a footstep on rock behind me. 'You sorry son of a wolf-bitch.'

I sprang to my feet, shocked. The voice was deeper than I remembered: almost a man's. It was a beautiful voice, the more so because he used it sparingly. That part of him was still beautiful, at least. He smiled at me.

'Hello,' I said, 'you ugly bastard.'

'Ugliest bastard in the dun,' said Sionnach cheerfully. '*Only* ugly bastard in the dun.' He put out his arms and I embraced him fiercely.

'I missed you,' he said, 'you insufferable wee savage.'

'I missed you too.' I hesitated. 'How are you?'

'Grand. The women like this look.'

He'd managed to grow a goatee beard, neat and trimmed though he hadn't bothered cutting his wild hair. Scruffy tinker. Maybe he thought the beard drew the eye from the scars. They didn't look too bad, to be honest. Well, all right, they were bloody awful, but they gave him a rakish look.

'I'm telling you. Women like a face with character. They don't go for pretty boys like you.'

'Nah,' I said. 'They're just being kind. They feel sorry for you.'

'Could be my personality, I grant you that much.'

'Aye. Wit, repartee and natural eloquence.'

He laughed, and I laughed too, I couldn't help it. He hugged me again.

'So,' he said. 'Want to go back to the dun yet?'

'Seeing as you mention it.' I grinned. 'Yes, I do.'

23

The girl trailed us to the dun but she stayed well back in our wake. Sionnach glanced at her, curious, but he seemed more interested in Branndair, who I noticed fell instantly in love with him without going through a bad-tempered biting phase. I was amused and miffed.

When we got closer to the dun gate Sionnach stopped. Branndair put his paws up on his chest and Sionnach pretended to be preoccupied with rubbing his neck, but I knew he was giving the girl a moment to catch up. Sure enough, she'd quickened her pace, suddenly afraid of being left outside the gates. When she got within touching distance, he gave her a brief smile, and we all walked past the guards together. One of them shouted out a greeting to me, and I glanced up, surprised. Eorna.

'Lost your weapons, greenarse,' he shouted, and winked.

I grinned up at him. 'Lucky for you.'

'The arena tomorrow morning, you lazy out-of-practice wee bastard.'

The girl sidled between him and me, walking protectively at my side and giving Eorna a defiant glare. Oh, hell's teeth: I didn't need her protection. She was making a fool of me, and I was furious, but remonstrating would have made me a bigger fool, and I couldn't help admiring her nerve. I tried to ignore her.

'Lost your weapons, but you picked up a couple of useful hounds!' Eorna pointed at Branndair and the girl, hooting with laughter as the other guards joined in.

'Ignore them.' Sionnach grabbed my arm and steered me towards the smithy.

It took a moment for my eyes to adjust to the hot darkness. In the glare of the forge Raineach straightened, eyeing me. Her red-brown hair was braided behind her and her lovely pointed face was flushed with heat. Yanking a strip of steel from the forge she laid it down, but she only stared at it, and laid her hammer beside it.

'I hear you lost your swords.'

Clearly I was never going to live this one down. 'Conal never took his sword.'

'I'm aware of that, shortarse. I gave him a damn good one to take in its place.'

My lip curled. Her response to my desperate call had been beyond swift, but gratitude had its limits. I was never going to be as tall as Conal, I knew that now, but I'd put on height and muscle in two years. I wasn't so short. I was nearly as tall as Sionnach and if she tried to say I couldn't fight I'd take that glowing strip and brand her backside with it.

Watching my eyes, she gave a wry laugh. 'Aye. You've grown.' She dusted her hands on her leather apron and said, 'You'll be needing a weapon of your own, then.'

'Yes,' I said.

'Then I'll make you one. Show me your hand.'

I held out my sword hand. She turned it in her own, splaying the fingers wide and holding her left hand up against it. She looked me up and down. 'Have you finished growing?'

I shrugged.

'You'll be Sionnach's height, I think, or near enough.' She took the fingers of her left hand away, but still held my sword hand in hers. I felt the smallest squeeze before she let it drop.

'You did well,' she said.

I muttered something incoherent, too surprised to be gracious.

She examined one of her ragged fingernails, and tore it off with her teeth. 'Your brother was conscious an hour ago. He wanted to see you. Murlainn.' The name sounded awkward on her tongue, but she gave me a sudden grin. Then she straightened and stiffened.

I turned to look at the doorway. The girl sidled close against me, and for a moment I had an urge to clasp her hand to reassure her. Fortunately I got my wits together in time to restrain myself. Beside me even Sionnach stood straighter.

Leonora stepped just inside the workshop, her eyes on me. She looked thin and tense from the effort of staying in the world, yet she didn't look as if she was going to leave it any time soon. In her beautiful face her eyes were haggard, but still hard. Her hair had grown

back past her shoulders, and was drawn back in elaborate silver clasps. The raven sat on her shoulder, basalt
eyes locked on mine.

'Murlainn,' she said.

'Leonora.'

She stepped sideways, examining me. I didn't move
but my eyes followed her.

'A little faster on the trigger, Murlainn,' she said,
'and you'd be Captain of this dun and the heir of
Griogair.'

'I know that,' I said. I could feel Sionnach's cool anger, and the girl at my side pressed her body closer
against me, touching my fist with her thin hand. I was
grateful to him, but I shook the girl off. I didn't need
her support. She was getting embarrassing.

The raven crooned hoarsely, tilting its head, and
Branndair snarled back at it, his hackles up. Leonora
half-smiled.

'Thank you,' she said coolly, 'for being slow.'

She turned on her heel and stalked outside, and the
raven took off into the sky, soaring and turning till it
was a scrap of black on the wind. Raineach released a
breath, and a shiver rippled through Sionnach. He
shook himself in annoyance.

'That's as good as you'll get from her,' he muttered.

'Better than he might have expected,' said Raineach
crisply. 'Go to your brother.'

The girl followed me, again, but this time I turned
on the stone steps that led to Conal's rooms and told
her to stay where she was. I told her it in the same
voice I told Branndair, only harsher. Giving me a dry
look, Sionnach stayed with her, murmuring reassurance

as she watched me go. I wondered, idly, if he wanted her. It would be a strange sort of wanting if he did.

There were guards on Conal's door, but I didn't even have to speak to them; they stood aside and one of them jerked his head to tell me to go on. Inside, Conal lay on his side, his fingers clutching the pillow and his hollow eyes closed, but he opened them as soon as I closed the door. He stared at the wall.

'Seth,' he said, still not looking at me.

'You should sleep,' I said.

'I will. I wouldn't let them give me sleep till I'd seen you.'

'The gods know why you're even awake.'

He turned his head at last, shaven and hacked and bruised, and dragged himself up to look at me, propping his weight on one trembling arm. I swallowed.

'Lie down,' I said, 'for gods' sake.'

'Get your disobedient arse over here.'

I did. I sat down on the edge of the bed. He gripped my head in one hand and hugged me against him. It was too much of an effort for him, I could feel it, so I put my arms round him and held him fiercely.

'I wanted to check,' he muttered. 'I wanted to make sure. I thought I might have imagined you. I don't remember coming home.'

'Aye. Your mind's going. That's why.'

'They told me they'd got you. They said they were going to kill you. But not for a while.' His arms tightened around me; his stubbly beard scratched my cheek and I could feel his warm tears trickling into my hair. 'I thought you were worse than dead.'

'They lied,' I said.

'I know,' he said. 'Now.'

We held one another in silence. I was remembering. He was trying not to.

'Catriona,' he said. 'Did she make it over? Is she all right?'

I drew away. I was still angry with him about that. 'I could have taken you out of there that night, if you'd left her.'

'Uh-huh. Like you left Ma Sinclair.'

I couldn't think of a retort, so I made a face.

'You couldn't have got me out, Seth. And you know I couldn't leave Catriona.'

'She wasn't even worth the risk,' I grumbled. 'She won't live much longer anyway. Twenty years at most? That's if she's lucky.'

'Their lives are short,' said Conal. 'It means a lot to her.'

'And she means nothing to us.'

He sighed, and rubbed his eyes.

'Sleep,' I said. 'You haven't got the strength to hit me.'

He gave me one of his old looks, and smiled. I put my hand against his scarred head and pressed it gently back onto the pillow. He was asleep in seconds.

I left my hand against his face, stroking his sunken temple and the beard growth that was longer than his hair. For a second, I shut my eyes and saw the might-have-been.

You could be Captain of this dun, Leonora had said. *Captain of this dun, and the heir of Griogair.*

Witch.

24

'So who's your shadow?'

I squinted up into the evening sunlight. As Eili sat down beside me we both glanced at Catriona. She was sitting twenty yards away, her arms locked tightly round her knees, watching the life of the dun go on around her.

'That's the girl,' I said shortly. 'She was with Conal.'

'She doesn't say much.'

'She doesn't say anything.'

'Strange,' said Eili.

'Not really. They tortured her and then they tried to burn her. What do you want?' I couldn't help sounding bitter.

Eili looked at the ground. 'I'm sorry, Seth. I'm sorry I was horrible to you this morning.'

I hesitated, a little too long. 'That's all right.'

'I know you couldn't have come, the time might have slipped. We could have gone to him right then, and found he'd been dead for months.'

'Years,' I said.

'Yes. I know that, and I didn't mean to be so short with you. I was worried about Conal, that's all.'

'So was I.'

She flushed a colour that clashed with her hair. 'Yes. I know. We treated you badly.'

I opened my mouth to say *No, you didn't*. Instead I said, 'Don't worry about it.'

'I know what you did for him. Everyone knows.'

'Including Leonora.' I gave a short laugh. 'I wonder what it is, precisely, that she'll never forgive me for?'

Eili shrugged. 'Being born.'

There was no answer to that.

'It's pretty ironic,' she added. 'I mean, her own daughter wasn't Griogair's. That never bothered Griogair. Why would it?'

I blinked. 'Leonora has a daughter?'

'Reultan. Didn't you know?' I couldn't miss the way her eyes lit up with stars.

'Anything like her mother?' I said scornfully.

'She's nicer. She's beautiful. She's very brave. And she's a fantastic fighter.'

'You could say all that about Leonora.'

Eili wrinkled her nose. 'Yes, but Reultan isn't a witch.'

'It runs in the family.'

'No, it doesn't,' she said crossly. 'It's a choice.'

'All right. The potential runs in the family.' I hesitated. 'Does Leonora scare you?'

'Of course she does. Doesn't she scare you too?'

'No.' That was a lie. The truth was she terrified me,

and that made me angry. 'Where is this Reultan then? I've never met her.'

'You probably have. She's in Kate's court.'

I wondered which of the beautiful cold-eyed hard-faced courtiers she was. 'That figures.'

'Stop it, Murlainn. Conal's very fond of her. He saw a lot of her when he was one of Kate's captains.'

'Aye, and where was she when he was exiled?'

Eili took out a dirk and a whetstone, and intently began to sharpen the blade. 'Do you like it?' She held the dirk out for my admiration. It was light and slender, the hilt elaborately carved but comfortable in her grip. 'I'm apprenticed to Raineach. She says I'm good.'

'It's beautiful.' It was. 'Why didn't Reultan object when her brother was exiled?'

'Look, she was away fighting. She's not like Lilith, she doesn't just give her precious opinions. She fights too.'

'How do you know what she was doing?'

Eili sighed. 'I asked about her. I'd wondered the same.' She added belligerently, 'And she's my friend. I like her.'

All right. I bit my lip to stop myself making any more cattish remarks, but I couldn't let it go. 'So what did she think about the exile?'

'She was very upset. That's what I heard. But she can't be disloyal to Kate.'

'Seems nobody can,' I muttered.

'Murlainn . . .'

'What did she think of the *reason* for the exile?'

Eili scraped the whetstone too hard along the knife edge, her fingers trembling.

I was growing angry too, so I pushed it. 'You blame my mother, don't you? It was Kate who cut him, Eili. Not Lilith. *Kate*.'

'Lilith would have gutted him!'

'So would Kate, if she thought she could get away with it!'

'Seth, don't you . . .'

'She knew she couldn't do it but she wanted to. She'd have had him gralloched if . . .'

'Shut up!' She snapped her head round to glare at me, and the knife slipped off the whetstone, slicing open the base of her thumb. Blood spurted.

'Eili!' Swearing, I grabbed her hand, pressing my fingers against the cut. 'I'm sorry, I . . .'

'I'm all right. I'm all right!' She wrenched her hand from my grasp. 'Don't make a fuss.'

She scrabbled backwards and turned away from me but I saw her quite distinctly. I saw her touch the gash with tentative fingertips, then grasp the ugly lips of the wound and squeeze them hard together. When she'd done it she turned back, her palm clasped over the wound. Her hands were wet with blood but it had stopped flowing. I reached for her hand and yanked it away, taking her so much by surprise that she didn't resist.

'Eili,' I said.

'What? Get away! I told you, don't fuss.'

'Who's fussing?' I was as angry as she was. 'No need to fuss, is there? You're not going to bleed to death when you're a healer. A *true-born* healer.'

Her pale skin reddened again. 'Don't tell anyone, Seth. I swear, if you do . . .'

'Why wouldn't I tell anyone?' My eyes widened. 'You're not saying nobody knows?'

'That's exactly what I'm saying. Keep your mouth shut.'

'But Sionnach must know . . .'

'*Sionnach* knows how to keep his mouth shut.'

'Sionnach has trouble doing anything else,' I snapped. 'What's your problem?'

'Just don't tell!' She jumped to her feet and stormed off towards the stables. I wasn't letting her get away with it, so I followed. For once the maddening full-mortal girl stayed where she was, though she watched from her quiet corner.

In the coolness of the stable I grabbed Eili's shoulder, and she flung me off, but not before I'd seen the tears in her eyes. I backed off as she slumped down onto a haybale, ducking her head.

'Eili,' I said more gently. 'What are you ashamed of? You'll be the toast of every detachment. It's a wonderful talent.'

'No, it isn't.'

'When did you find out?'

'Too late,' she said.

And I realised that of course she was thinking about Sionnach. I sat down beside her, risking an arm around her, and my heart floated when she leaned miserably into the hollow of my shoulder.

'There's nothing you could have done,' I said.

'How do you know? Maybe there was. Maybe it was there all the time and I wasn't paying attention.

Maybe my head was too full of swords and horses and . . .' She clamped her lips tightly together.

And Conal, I thought, but I wasn't angry enough now to let her hear it. 'Don't be daft,' I said. 'It comes when it comes. Grian didn't know till he was ninety years old, I heard him say so, and he's the best healer in the dun.'

'Not any more,' she said.

I didn't know what to say to that kind of certainty. 'Well. That healer of Kate's couldn't do much for Sionnach.'

'I'm better than him,' she said, and despite her misery there was an undercurrent of pride in her voice. 'I'm a hundred times better. It's so strong in me, Seth. If it had happened today I could have healed Sionnach and he'd barely have a scar.'

I doubted that, but I didn't say so. 'It didn't happen today. It happened two years ago.'

'I could have helped my brother,' she insisted stubbornly. 'If I'd known.'

'Eili. He's not that bothered, you know.'

'I am.' To my horror she started to weep.

I didn't know what to do. I stroked her hair, first lightly and then more strongly, and she pressed her face to my chest, mortified by her own tears. I felt her body convulse as she fought to get a hold of herself and master her rage. At last she calmed and stilled, and she sighed and pulled away a little. She managed to glance up at me. 'Thanks, Seth. Don't tell anyone.'

About the healing? I wondered. Or about the crying?

'About either,' she said.

Her face was tilted towards me, her eyes still misty from unfamiliar tears, so I kissed her.

I couldn't not kiss her. I sensed her shock, but that I could understand. When she drew back I twisted my fingers into her chopped hair and held her, desperately keeping her close and kissing her again. My hand brushed her breast, though I swear that was accidental. Then she jerked back and cuffed my cheekbone, knocking me away.

It was a light blow, the kind you might give an annoying puppy, but it hurt me more than many a blow since. I can still feel it, sometimes. My fingers were still caught in her hair and though I tried to free them, she wrenched away with such ferocity it tore free at the roots. There were red strands still tangled in my fingers when she shoved me away, and staggered to her feet.

She didn't run, and I couldn't stand. She stood there in disbelief, and I just sat and stared back at her like the fool I was.

'I thought . . .' I stammered. 'I thought you . . . that I . . .'

'How could you?' She shook her head, calm and steely. 'How could you think anything of the sort?'

'I don't know . . . I . . .'

'I love your brother, Seth. I love Conal. I will always love only Conal. How could you imagine I'd ever . . .'

She managed to stop herself, but the unspoken words hung in the musty stable air, all but audible.

Settle for you? That's what she didn't say. *How could you imagine I'd settle for you?*

Shaking her head, she skewed her gaze away. 'I'll go

to him. When I'm twenty I'll go to him, and he'll accept me. I know it.'

'He considers you a child!'

'For now he does.' She shrugged, still avoiding my eyes. 'But he's already in love with the woman I'll be. He may not know that yet, but it's true.'

Staring at her, I knew it was. She turned then, embarrassed more than angry, and walked away, pulling the stable door quietly shut behind her. I sat on, mired in shame and loss, aware of what I'd destroyed, and felt my heart disintegrate.

There is nothing like shattering a heart to make it stronger. I knew better now how to armour it, that's what I told myself as I sat there, terrified to go back out into the evening light in case the whole dun would be standing there laughing at me. I knew we'd get over it in the end: the Sithe live too long for it to be any other way. Between Eili and me it would never be quite the same again, but we'd get over it.

That's what happened, of course. Since we were children she'd always tried to be kind to me: now she tried too hard. Her kindness was fenced about with a deliberate distance, and I was humiliated by that more than anything. I'd never make the same mistake again, that wasn't my way, and it offended me that she thought I might. I knew my place in her heart: a good bit above Orach and Feorag and somewhere beneath her dead father and her horse; a thousand fathoms below Conal. I'd been taught my lesson and I'd never needed teaching twice.

All that, though, was in the future. For now I stood up and opened the stable door with a trembling hand.

My clann was not waiting in thick ranks to mock me,
of course, and at last I breathed out a shaky sigh.
There was only a last rider nodding to me as he led his
mount towards the stables, and my shadow. My *shadows*. Hell's teeth. The priest had had none: I'd managed to accumulate two.

Catriona had busied herself with a small sharp knife
and a little piece of ash wood, but I knew she was
watching me from the corner of her eye. I thought of
walking away, and letting her follow as usual, but
there was something comforting about her silent stillness. I went across and sat down beside her. She looked
at me keenly, then went back to her whittling.

I leaned back against the wall, and stared at the armoury on the other side of the courtyard. Branndair
laid his muzzle on my thigh, and I stroked his head. A
sentry coughed and spat on the wall above us, a horse
whinnied to its returning friend, and someone shouted
an order. The sun was low and the shadows were long,
the air clear and sweet. It felt peaceful sitting here.
Damn, but I was glad to be back. Even though . . .

'I just made a fool of myself,' I blurted.

Catriona glanced at me, smiling very little. The setting sun gave her pale bruised face some colour, and
you could see she might have been pretty before the
priest got to her.

'What are you making?'

Shyly she held it out to me. It was a little wolf, I decided after a moment. It wasn't very good, but I don't
think that was because she didn't know what she was
doing. It was like the writing of someone with a broken hand: crude and stilted, but you could see a skill

had been learned and was still huddled somewhere, licking its wounds and healing itself.

I took the hand that held the wolf. This afternoon Sionnach had looked at her, and glanced at me with a wry smile, and said *She's a strong one*. I'd been taken aback. To me she was the shivering pathetic creature who'd thwarted my only chance of saving my brother.

Now I looked at her fingers again, and this time she didn't jerk them away. I separated them and laid them flat against my own hand. They were still swollen, the nails distorted and horribly discoloured. I realised why she irritated me so much: she made me ashamed. She had suffered with my brother and I hadn't. She had comforted him in the darkness when I couldn't.

'The little man,' I asked her, 'the one they all talked about? Was it him?'

She nodded, then shook her head.

'Him and others?'

She nodded.

'One day,' I told her, 'you'll show me what they looked like.'

She raised an eyebrow.

'It's easy, I promise. One day you'll show me, so that some other day I can find them. Do you understand what I'm telling you?'

She looked first into one of my eyes, and then the other. It was a strange sensation, as if she was seeing right inside my brain though I couldn't quite meet her gaze. Then, slowly, she nodded.

'That girl,' I said, nodding towards the stable. 'Just now. I love her and I thought she might love me back, but she doesn't. What an arse I am.'

She looked down at her pale hand against mine.

'You know what I like about you? You're not going to tell anybody. About me being such a fool.'

Her wounded fingers curled round my hand. She drew it to her lips and kissed it, then put her arms round me and hugged me. Getting to her feet, she pressed her crude little wolf into my grip, and walked away.

25

I was taken aback when I stood up at last, and the girl
was nowhere to be seen. Maybe she'd stop haunting
me now. Or maybe not. Glancing down at the crude
little wooden wolf, I wondered if she really was a
witch. Maybe she'd cast a spell on the thing to make it
keep an eye on me, so that she didn't have to. I smiled
and held it out to Branndair.

'What do you think?'

He eyed it mistrustfully.

'No,' I said, 'it's not very good, is it?'

Deep in his throat he gave a soft whine, then
stretched, claws scrabbling on the stone. The dun was
all in shadow now, and the sun had vanished entirely.
Shivering, I remembered how long it was since I'd
slept, and how tired I was. I wondered where Orach
was, and at the same time I was glad she wasn't
around. My emotions were hopelessly tangled, and after two years I didn't know how she'd react to me
anyway. For all I knew she'd be bound to Feorag by

now, or someone else. For all I knew she could be
bound to a woman.

In my rooms I looked around. They were unchanged,
veiled in a thin layer of dust, and my bed smelt musty.
It was a thousand times better than anywhere I'd slept
in the last two years: too good, and I knew I couldn't
sleep here, not yet. Picking up a blanket I shook the
dust out of it, then took my bridle down from its hook
by the door. I ran it between my fingers, then hitched it
over my shoulder and backed out of the room, closing
the door softly. Branndair glanced up at me, waiting in
silence. I thought of my old room beside the tannery,
but I changed my mind.

The guards in the corridor outside Conal's room
still didn't speak to me, but they stopped their murmuring talk and watched me as I went past. Ignoring
them, I settled myself against the wall right outside
Conal's room, rolling myself in the blanket and curling
up on the floor. That felt better. There was rush mat-
ting between me and the cold stone, and that was all I
needed. Inside the blanket I clutched the bridle against
my chest, and Branndair slumped down alongside me.
I could feel the warmth of his body radiating into my
bones, the rhythmic beat of his heart and the rise and
fall of his ribcage. I could smell his wolf-breath close
to my face. Then I couldn't feel or hear or smell anything, and there was only the black oblivion of the best
sleep I'd had in two years.

If I expected anything, I'd expected to feel a lot colder
when I woke, especially since Branndair was no longer

beside me. Sleepily I reached out my mind: he was fine. He was out in the dun, being fed with the hounds: Sionnach had come and taken him. My body felt limp and immobile. The last time I'd slept this long unmoving, I'd woken to pain and cold, still exhausted, knocked senseless by my own brother. Now, though the floor was hard beneath me, I felt warm and drowsy, as if I'd slept away all pain and cold and misery. A couple of skins and another blanket had been tucked around me, and my head lay on a soft folded plaid. I was surprised they'd bothered, but I was grateful anyway.

Pushing myself up on one arm, I blinked. The guard had been changed. A man and a woman now efficiently blocked the access both to me and to Conal's room: Carraig and Geanais. I could sense the flinty shield of their minds, their sharp questioning defences. Beyond them, barred from Conal and from me, a small figure crouched against a corner of the wall, wrapped in a blanket as I was. She was awake, and someone had given her a cup of something warm that she held in both her thin wounded hands, but the guards ignored her.

I shoved off my wrapping of hides and blankets, and got to my feet, shaking off sleep as I hooked my bridle back over my shoulder. My body was stiff and I ached, but it was a good ache. Carraig glanced at me and nodded.

'Let her through,' I said.

Carraig looked at Geanais, and she shrugged, then jerked her head at the girl. Catriona stumbled to her feet, still clutching the cup though a little of her drink spilled, and edged warily between them.

'You couldn't let her near his door, or what?' I said.

'Don't be an idiot,' said Geanais. 'Of course we couldn't.'

'We let her through to give you blankets,' added Carraig, as if that was some great concession.

'And there was me about to thank you for them,' I said.

'I doubt you'd strain yourself,' said Carraig.

I called him something filthy, straight into his head. He gave me two fingers and went back to his conversation with Geanais.

Catriona was hovering uncertainly, staring at Conal's door.

'Here,' I said. Beckoning her, I opened his door silently. As it swung wide I stood back and let her look in at him. He lay absolutely still, his face hollowed out by the thin light filtering through the shutters, but his breathing was slow and deep and regular. His fingertips twitched, that was all. I drew her back out and closed the door.

'See?' I said. 'He's all right now.'

She nodded.

'And you are too,' I added. 'You can stay here with us if you want. It's fine.'

She smiled briefly, then studied my face. Lifting a finger, she touched my cheek questioningly.

'Yes,' I said. 'Yes. I'm all right now too.'

I thought about Eili, and realised it was the first time she'd crossed my mind since I'd woken. That was reassuring. I wondered where Orach was. I wanted to see her now.

'You must be hungry,' I said, taking the cup from

Catriona. It was milk warmed with whisky, I could smell it, but it was drained to the dregs. 'I'm starving too. He's fine, you know. We can leave him.' I raised my voice. 'Even with this pair of arses, we can leave him.'

This time it was Geanais who gave me two fingers.

I took Catriona's hand in mine and pushed past them. 'I'm due in the arena anyway. I want something to eat first.'

Carraig gave a bark of laughter. 'Eorna said to let you know he considers it a moral victory, greenarse. Seeing as you never showed up.'

Turning on my heel I snatched a fistful of his hair, and shoved my face close to his. I heard Catriona's small frightened gasp, and the light rasp of Geanais's dirk coming half out of its sheath, but I didn't look round. The dirk was still half-sheathed and that was how it would stay. Her movement had been instinctive but I knew she wouldn't dare. None of them would. Ever again.

I stared right into Carraig's eyes. 'What did you call me?'

He didn't speak.

I tightened my fingers in his hair till he winced. 'What's my name?' I hissed.

He was silent for only a moment more. Then he said, 'Murlainn.'

I let him go and left him to exhale. I didn't have to look back to know that Catriona was following at my heels. At the bottom of the stone steps I stopped and turned to her, and she came to a sudden halt, almost banging into me.

'What time is it?' I asked her sheepishly. 'Isn't it morning?'

Her gaunt face was lit by a huge smile as she shook her head. As her hand went to her mouth her breath came out in a little soundless snort that should have been a giggle.

I returned her grin. 'Did I overplay that a bit?'

Her hand was still stifling her silent laughter as she shook her head again.

'Come on, then.'

There would be no breakfast. As soon as I stepped outside I realised it was early evening and that I must have slept for nearly twenty-four hours. The late summer sun was still bright in the sky, and there were people in the great hall already starting to drink. In the kitchens I scavenged cold venison and bread and oat-cakes for us both, then took her up to the parapet. We sat and ate in companionable silence, looking out at the long shadows on the sunlit machair, and I thought that life could get no better.

Taking my bridle off my shoulder, I started to rub oil into it with a cloth I'd picked up as we passed the stables. The bridle was dull and stiff with disuse, but I was happy to have the work to do, and pleased with the way it softened and shone for me. Catriona wrapped her arms round her legs and watched, occasionally lifting her gaze to the machair and the sea and the far hills.

'Why won't you speak?' I asked her.

Looking away, she shrugged. Then she gave me a rueful smile.

'Fair enough,' I said. 'Fair enough.' I liked it anyway.

She was peaceful to be around. Like Sionnach, only more so.

Behind us there was the click of Branndair's claws as he padded up the stone steps to join us. I gave him the scraps of my venison, and scratched his ears where he liked it, and he settled himself down, head in my lap.

I was relaxed enough almost to fall back to sleep again, but she was fidgety and restless at my side, and eventually I opened my eyes and rolled my head to look at her. 'What's wrong?'

She looked back towards the dun, then, beseechingly, at me. To be honest I was growing impatient, and it came quite naturally to slip inside her mind. It was only when she jerked back with a scared gasp that I realised it wouldn't seem all that natural to her.

'Sorry,' I said, not very sincerely. 'Don't look like a scared rabbit, for gods' sake.'

I could see her pulse beating in her throat, and she was still eyeing me like a coney eyeing a stoat. I rolled my eyes.

'You want to go and take care of him. How else was I meant to find out?'

She swallowed, uneasy, and nodded once.

'So why didn't you . . . well. Obviously you wouldn't say so.' Sighing, I got to my feet. 'Don't try getting past those twats in the corridor. They'll never let you through. Come on, I'll take you to Grian.'

The healer Grian was perfectly happy to have a dogsbody, and I was relieved not to have Catriona dogging my every step. It was nice not to have to worry about her, either. My moment inside her mind had been something of a shock. I'd discovered she was still in pain (you'd think I might have guessed), that she was still very afraid, but despite our instant of coexistence I still knew little about what had happened to her. Much of it she had stuffed behind a block that would grace the mind of a Sithe. She needed a distraction, I reckoned, and I knew nothing could suit her better than looking after her hero. Grian found her helpful, and he liked her, and he was good at healing minds and bodies even when a patient didn't notice she was a patient. He and Catriona were good for each other, and I was pleased with myself for thinking of the pairing.

'She's a strong one.' A couple of days later Grian said exactly the same as Sionnach. 'Works hard. Dotes on your brother. Doesn't speak but Conal likes having her around.' He guffawed. 'Not sure Eili does.'

My grin was gleeful.

26

It dawned on me with excruciating slowness that only half the people in the dun thought I had been saved from a terrible obligation by the MacLeod's intervention at Conal's burning. The other half thought I had been thwarted.

It started with a nagging suspicion and a few gazes that refused to meet mine. It ended with a brawl in the great hall, and I could have happily taken on the three of them myself—it wouldn't have been the first time, since they'd had it in for me since I was eight—but Sionnach joined in with a cheerful heart. Eili looked on with rolling eyes and many pointed sighs, but when she eventually pitched in too, they finally yielded. My knee was on the throat of one of them, and it did occur to me simply to leave it there, to crush his windpipe for the benefit of anyone else who harboured the same poisonous idea. But it wasn't worth it. If they wanted to think badly of me they would, and hell mend them.

Besides, my brother, when he recovered, would have killed me.

Catriona watched the bloody fight with her eyes wide, her face horrified. Leonora looked on, smiling slightly, taking no sides.

Orach, of course, would no sooner think badly of me than she would of Conal. She returned to the dun a week after Conal and Catriona and I did, from patrolling the dun lands and collecting our payments in grain and meat. (The tolls were a great deal more reasonable than the payments Conal and I had had to make to the MacLeod, but I no longer resented the man even for hungry winters.) Orach, popular with the captains as much for her easygoing nature as for her shooting skills, had been escorting a cart laden with grain sacks, but she abandoned it half a mile out, ignoring the sharp shouts of her captain, and galloped into the dun gates. She threw herself off her horse and onto me, and I laughed and birled her in huge circles.

'I heard the story,' she said to me a little later. 'I want to hear everything, all the details. Not just now, later. How's Conal?'

'He's getting there,' I said. 'They used a knife to prick him; he lost a lot of blood. And they beat him and it damaged him where you can't see, and that's hard for the healers. You know there was a Lammyr?'

'I heard.' She shuddered. 'How long did it have him?'

I shrugged. 'A week.'

'Gods. How's he alive?'

'Luck,' I said grimly. 'And the L . . . the Lammyr was enjoying itself too much to ki . . .'

'I'm sorry.' Stopping, she squeezed my hand, and I stared at the corner where the stable met the armoury wall, where there was no-one to see my tears of rage. 'Sorry,' she said again. 'I shouldn't ask, not just now. What about the . . . good gods, is *that* the full-mortal girl?'

I glanced round, glad of a change of subject. Catriona had come down from Conal's rooms and was standing in the courtyard breathing the open air. Still too shy to go near human beings, she'd spotted a chestnut horse tethered by the stable, and wandered across to stroke its nose and rub its cheeks and ears. Whickering with adoration, it rubbed its face on her stubbly scalp. She was good with horses.

She looked terrible, though. She was spending too much time in Conal's sickroom now, watching Grian mend his broken and brutalised body, when her own had so recently been broken too. She'd had enough, I thought. She needed the sky above her and an empty mind and the north wind slicing into her skin. She needed the sun to take that dungeon pallor off her. It wasn't her fault she looked the way she did.

I opened my mouth to defend her, but I didn't get a chance to say a word.

'What the hell are you all thinking of?' said Orach indignantly.

Never having been snapped at by Orach in my life, I could hardly move my gaping jaw.

'Hasn't anyone thought to give the girl some proper clothes?'

I stared at Orach, and then at Catriona. Sure enough the girl was still in the thin grey shift she'd worn to her cancelled execution. She must have been washing it out each night, because it looked clean enough. That was all you could say for it. Shame washed over me in a hot tide.

'You crowd of thoughtless idiots,' said Orach, and marched across towards Catriona.

She was halfway to the girl when I remembered to shout, 'She doesn't talk.' Then Orach had caught the shocked girl by the arm, and was hauling her off in the direction of her own rooms, murmuring in her ear.

'Doesn't talk.' Orach was contemptuous. 'Doesn't talk, indeed. You don't listen, more like.'

'When did you get that attitude?' I laced my fingers hungrily into her hair and pulled her face down to kiss her. 'You used to be so quiet.'

She propped her hands on my chest and pushed herself up, making me grunt. 'Arrogant sod. I wasn't that quiet. It's just I couldn't get a word in edgeways.'

The sky was blue enough to hurt your eyes. Beneath me the seagrass was scratchy against my naked back and the blown sand got everywhere, but I didn't care. A breeze rustled the clumps of pink thrift, tangled her pale unbound hair. I could smell the sea, and the machair, and Orach's sun-warmed skin. I blinked against the brilliance of the sun, trying to focus on her intent face.

'How's Feorag?' I asked.

'Feorag's fine.' Straddling me, she gazed down, expressionless.

Laying my palms on her thighs, I raised an eyebrow. 'I take it you're not bound to him.'

'How astute. I'm no more bound to him than I am to you.'

I gave her the very slow grin that always broke her down, and sure enough she gave an exclamation of disgust and slapped my ribcage.

'Ouch,' I said.

'I never said I'd wait around for you, Seth.'

'I never asked you to.'

'Even if you had, I wouldn't have.'

'That's why I never asked. You break my heart, woman.'

'Liar.' She slapped me again.

'I love you, I'm telling you.'

'I'm sure you do.' Her eyes softened and she flopped down beside me into the dry salty grass. She stroked my cheek. 'But I'll never be enough for you.'

'Right. Of course.' I rolled to face her. 'And I'll never be enough for you.'

Her fingers drifted across my lips, making me shiver.

'If you say so, Murlainn.'

I curled an arm round her body and kissed her forehead, suddenly sad. Which wasn't how I wanted to feel. I changed the subject as always.

'Did she speak to you? Catriona?'

Orach gave me a long look. It made me uncomfortable.

'Well, did she?' I prompted.

'No, but she can and she will.' Orach glanced aside. 'It only takes someone to listen.'

'I listen,' I said, miffed.

'Aye. Only to your own echo.'

We lay in silence for a while, my arm around her,

Orach's lying lightly across my chest. The unseen sea moved, whispering and rushing, beyond the close horizon of our dune. When I closed my eyes, I saw red veins behind my eyelids, and I felt her kiss my skin.

'What will Kate do?' she murmured.

I opened my eyes again to the dazzle of sky. 'I don't know.'

'She must know you're back.'

'Yes. She'll wait till he's recovered. Politics.'

'Strictly you're still exiles,' she said, and there was a tremor of anxiety in her voice.

'I'll tell you something.' My fingers tightened unintentionally on her arm. 'I am never going back to the otherworld. Never, and neither is Conal, and I don't care what that witch says.'

Which was bravado, and pissing in the wind, and conclusive proof that telepathy is not the same thing as foresight.

Orach left the dun again two days later, having volunteered for another week of patrolling the borders. I could hardly believe it. I'd been gone for two years, damn it.

~ *No promises*, she told me, kissing me goodbye. ~ *That's what you say.*

~ *I know*, I said, ~ *but I'll miss you.*

~ *I missed you for two years. Know what? It's difficult, you being back.*

~ *Why?*

She slanted her gaze at me, rueful. ~ *Because of the way you look at her.*

~ *That's over. There's nothing between Eili and me and there never was. I've . . .*

~ *Sometimes you are just the stupidest man I know.* She turned to her horse. ~ *I'm not talking about Eili. I'm talking about the full-mortal girl.*

She might as well have hit me in the face with a fish. I was speechless as she gathered her reins into one hand. Reaching out, I gripped her blond braid, not wanting to let her get on her horse. 'I don't know what you're on about. Listen. I can't bind.'

'You mean you won't bind.'

'True. Are you dumping me, Orach?'

'No.' She kissed me again. 'Let go. We're leaving. I need to go.'

'You'll be back, though.'

'Oh, yes.' She gave me a droll smile. ~ *That's the trouble with you and me. I'll always come back and you know it.*

And that's why I love you, I thought, but I was scowling and in a bad mood by then and I didn't feel like telling her.

I'd have liked Orach back the next morning so I could give her a piece of my mind. Poor Catriona looked mortified to be wearing proper trews and boots and a decent linen shirt. All Orach's, of course, as was the leather jerkin that she'd fastened tightly almost to her neck. She kept tugging down the hem of it, as if there was a hope of it covering her scrawny hips, and she kept her face focused on the ground and her arms folded across her chest. I'd never imagined Orach's

clothes could look big on anyone. With her patchy
crop of hair, barely more than a stubble of regrowth,
you could have mistaken Catriona for a boy. I almost
told her so, partly to reassure her and partly to stop
her acting so damn silly. She was hardly about to be
ravished.

I was offended on behalf of our own women. What
was wrong with the way they dressed? They didn't like
to trip on skirts. They wouldn't swathe their bodies in
dingy fabric out of some bizarre sense of modesty. So
what? Sithe men had self-control, even if full-mortal
men didn't. Catriona's attitude was an insult to Orach
and every other Sithe woman—not to mention us
men—and I was so indignant I ignored her even when
she cast me a nervous glance of supplication. If she
wanted my support she could stop acting like a self-
conscious child.

She couldn't even hole herself up in Conal's room,
because Grian had kicked her out of it. Not because he
was fed up with her, but because he thought the same as
me: she was spending far too much time there. She was
trying to hide, now. She needed some air, and some
colour in her thin-stretched flesh. So he sent her out on
errands, to take this message or fetch that herb.

I was about to go hunting with Sionnach and Feorag
that morning—these days Eili was wholly absorbed in
learning weapons-smithing from Raineach—when Catriona darted out of the doorway like a terrified mouse.
We watched her scuttle across the courtyard, ducking
her face away from us and hunching her shoulders.
Sionnach and Feorag must have been as stunned as I
was by her transformation, because they didn't come up

with any immediate smart remarks. When I'd got over my own shock, I hissed in exasperation and flicked my reins to turn the roan. He was far better company, and I'd been smitten by him all over again when he answered my first call and came to me. I wanted to spend time getting to know him, letting him know me. The last thing I needed was the full-mortal girl attaching herself to me again.

'Tell her to come hunting with us,' suggested Sionnach.

'Get lost,' I spat. 'She'd be a pain in the backside.'

Feorag whistled through his teeth, and his hunting bitch stopped sniffing at Branndair's rear end and came to him. Branndair gave a low lustful growl, and when I called his name and caught his golden eyes, I swear he almost grinned at me.

'Ach, your wolf's as bad as you are,' said Feorag cheerfully. 'Tell him Breagh won't be in heat for a month. As for you, the gods alone know when *she'll* be in heat.' He jerked his head towards the corner where Catriona had disappeared. 'If ever.'

'The hell you . . .' I ran out of words to express my scorn. 'Don't you start as well. What would I want with her? Look at her!'

'What, like you do?' Critically he gazed after her. 'Might do. One of these days.'

I can't say why I wanted to smack that thoughtful smirk off his face. All I could do was stare silently at him while I rearranged my thoughts, and after a while he felt my stare and met it.

'Leave her alone,' I said, and then, because I'd sounded

unexpectedly ferocious, I added: 'For now, right? The girl's troubled. That's all.'

Sionnach gave me a look that made me want to scratch my scalp. I growled at the roan, and it went into a smooth canter from a standing start, and we rode out of the dun gates as they swung wide for us.

I was looking forward to a hunt. It was a long time since I'd felt quite so much like killing something.

27

'What are you frigging well laughing at?' Eorna glowered up at me.

'What?'

'You can wipe that smile off your face, shortarse.' At least he'd stopped calling me greenarse, and I wasn't about to fall out with him over a name-calling, since—unlike Carraig—he was a friend and we liked one another. The liking was buried deep, it's true, but it was there.

You wouldn't think it to look at his furious face now. 'Did I ever gloat at you?' he roared.

Fair enough. I made myself stop grinning. Truthfully I hadn't been aware I was wearing such a satisfied smirk till he'd mentioned it. Taking my blunt sword from his throat, I let him scramble to his feet.

The sky was a glassy blue dome above us and we were both dripping with sweat, but I was now beating him by six bouts to one and I'd wondered when he was going to explode. It didn't help that the warmth of the sun had brought out a few spectators, some of whom had begun to cat-call Eorna. That was largely his own fault, since he'd trained a good few of them and they'd all felt the flat of his sword on their backsides and, if they were male, the whack of his staff between their legs. It wasn't going to happen to me again.

Damn, I was good. I grinned again, couldn't help it.

'It's her, isn't it?' He jerked his head. 'Is that why you're showing off?'

I looked round. Sure enough Catriona was standing by the fence, watching, almost smiling. Of course, I'd known she was there. I'd just forgotten. Sort of. It wasn't as if I cared. The smile left my face.

She'd got used to her change of image. Nobody pinched her rear-end, nobody wolf-whistled her, nobody mocked. Nobody flung her to the stable floor and raped her. So she'd at last stopped hurrying from shadow to shadow, staring at the ground, her cheeks vermilion and her hands clasped in front of her crotch. I grinned, remembering her discomfort, and found her looking at me again, the shy smile back in place. Yes: still shy, still skinny-racked, but she had a nice backside. Her legs could use some muscle, though. Realising I was staring at them, I spat and turned back to Eorna, bringing my sword to my face in salute and invitation.

'Forget it.' Brushing sand off his practice sword, he stomped off. 'So frigging pleased with yourself,' he muttered. 'Smug little shit.'

The gathered knots of watchers dispersed, some of them taking no more notice of me, one or two shouting a compliment. Actually *smug little shit* was a compliment too, coming from Eorna. I was smiling again, and worse, I was looking straight at Catriona. Again.

'Doesn't Grian need you?' I gave her my coolest glare.

She shrugged, then shook her head.

'Threw you out?'

Glancing down at the disturbed sand of the arena, she kicked it with the heel of her boot.

I laughed, couldn't help it. 'Did my *brother* tell you where to go?'

Her eyes met mine, slewed away, and she laughed her funny soundless laugh.

'Don't worry,' I told her. 'Don't take it personally. He wants you to rest, that's all. It's not that he doesn't like having you around.'

Hesitantly she nodded.

'Really,' I said. 'I'm serious. He likes you. He worries about you.'

She gave me a very direct smile that made me turn my gaze away towards the dun wall. I didn't know what to say after that; I only wished she'd go away. I had things to do and friends to meet. I wanted to take the blue roan out onto the moor to meet Sionnach coming in, so I could tell him how I'd humiliated Eorna. He'd love it.

Puzzled, cross, ill at ease, I frowned at Catriona. Her serious gaze was turned on the sea horizon.

'Want to go riding?' I said.

· · ·

Cloud shadows chased patches of golden light across the machair and the moor beyond. Catriona sat close behind me on the roan, alive with nerves, unable to cling to me too tightly because of the small leather bag I had slung across my back. I'd put a thin blanket on the roan, since the girl was used to a saddle, but it didn't seem to make her any more comfortable.

I smiled. I liked her thin hands clutching each other around my waist, linked so tightly together her knuckles were white. I felt her weight shift slightly as she leaned back and tilted her face to the sun. I was glad she was starting to enjoy herself, but for some bizarre reason I wanted her to lean against me.

'Hey,' I said.

Her scanty weight came forward again, the drag of her arms on my waist slackening. When I glanced over my shoulder her look was questioning, a little apprehensive, as if she was afraid she'd done something wrong.

Half-turning, I slipped an arm round her and pulled her off the roan's back. As I swung her forward, her legs kicked wildly and the roan gave an angry snort. I heard her intake of scared breath, felt her fingers snatch at my arms, but before she had time to panic properly I had her astride the roan in front of me. I kept an arm round her waist, and one hand on the reins.

Through her ribs I could feel the hard beat of her heart. For a minute or more she was taut with fear, but when I said nothing, and did not move, her body relaxed a little. Her hands folded over mine, our fingers linking. At last she leaned her head back into the hollow of my shoulder.

I liked that. Her body fitted well against mine.

I thought I should say something but it didn't seem too important at that moment. It wasn't as if she could complain about anyone else's silence. And not long after that, I realised she wouldn't care if I spoke or not, because she was fast asleep in my arms.

I rode on because I wasn't sure what else to do and I didn't want to wake her. The fact that she was safe with us didn't mean she'd be sleeping. I knew that fine, I knew it from my own nights. Conal was the only one of us who slept, and that was because his body would let him do little else. His screaming nightmares would come later.

I didn't want to take the roan up to the high moor, to the Dubh Loch where his home was. That might be too much of a temptation, with a strange girl on his back, so I rode till I reached the still green pinewood at the Loch of the Cailleach. In the striped golden shadows the air was cooler, the filtered sun less fierce, and the loch glinted with diamonds between the trees. There was only the faintest stir in the air, barely even a breeze, and I let the roan come to a halt and strain his muscled neck towards the water. Tossing his head up and down, he struck the root-tangled earth with a hoof, danced his haunches sideways and gave a screeching whinny.

Catriona jerked awake, taking a high breath of fear. My arm tightened round her waist, and her fingers gripped my arm till it hurt.

'It's all right,' I said, and then, to the horse, 'A drink. That's all.'

It gave its whickering laugh as I loosed the reins to let it pace forward and drop its muzzle to the clear brown loch. It drank, then raised its dripping muzzle, took a few splashing steps into the water.

~ *Don't even think about it.*

Innocently it whickered again, and pawed the water, a hollow wet echo of hoof on stones.

Catriona's fingers loosened at last, so I squeezed my hands into fists to get the circulation back into my arms.

'You're strong,' I said dryly. 'It's all right. You're safe.'

I felt I had to keep telling her that.

'Do you know what he is?' I asked her.

She nodded her head, fast, frightened.

'It's all right,' I said yet again. 'But you have to get off first. Otherwise he'll take you when I dismount.'

She let go of me, then, and I helped her swing her leg over the creature's neck. It glanced back with a wicked look as that happened, but I took no notice. My hand tingled where it had touched her thigh, as if my circulation had stopped again. I shook myself, annoyed, and lowered her to the forest floor. Taking a step back, she watched me dismount, and then she watched the horse's black malevolent eye.

'Go on, my love,' I told it as I pulled the blanket off its back and slipped the bridle over its ears. 'Beat it.'

Tossing its black mane once more, it trotted off and merged swiftly into the tree shadows.

'He'll hunt,' I said. 'He's hungry. You?'

She nodded, not frightened now, just eager. I put the horse's blanket on a fallen pine trunk and we sat and shared the apples and the meat and oatcakes from the leather bag. She ate hungrily, almost violently, all her concentration on filling her stomach. Amused, I watched her. Her cheekbones seemed less hollow. The rack of her ribs had more flesh over it. There was more curve to her arse and her thighs, but she was never going to be what you'd call well-built.

Feeling my gaze, she hesitated and glanced at me. A huge self-conscious grin spread across her face along with a flush of colour. She's pretty, I thought. Pretty when she smiled.

The embarrassed smile stayed on her face as she sighed and threw her last apple core into the loch. It splashed in silver droplets that glittered in the sun, then bobbed on the surface. I scraped up some stones from the lochside and threw them at the apple core to see if I could hit it, and Catriona joined in. She was a rotten shot. I laughed and tried to teach her, but she stayed a rotten shot for a full quarter of an hour.

'You're crap at this,' I said.

She nodded, put her face dramatically into her hands.

I prised her fingers away, one at a time and very gently. The mutilated nails looked better now: some had fallen away and they were regrowing. Playfully she snapped her fingers back into place as soon as I let them go and I laughed, but her eye, when I pulled aside a forefinger to reveal it, was gazing at me quite solemnly.

'You're good with horses though,' I said. 'And you bring out the decent human being in Grian.' I hesitated, something catching in my throat. 'You're a dead good nurse for a clann Captain.'

Taking her hands away from her face entirely, she rested them on her knees, and smiled at the silver loch. She looked so happy I envied her.

I said, 'I think you could get used to this place, couldn't you? I think you could get used to us.'

Catriona tilted her head to look at me, and bit her lip, and said, 'Yes.'

28

'It's not that I couldn't speak,' she told me, when I'd stopped being stupefied.

Her voice still sounded awkward. Uncertain, and a bit hoarse, and she kept sucking her lower lip into her mouth and biting it.

'What was it, then?'

Her brow furrowed, as if she was trying hard to understand it herself. 'Well. Maybe I couldn't. But I knew I could if I . . . it was there if . . . if I had to.'

I said, 'What a lot you know about us all.'

A flush stained her neck and her cheekbones. 'It's not that . . . I wasn't . . .'

I threw another stone at the loch. 'Isn't it amazing what you'll say to a mute.'

The hot dappled darkness and light of the forest seemed unnaturally still. As the sun moved, the loch's sparkle had calmed, and now the water was a dark mirror, the sky above us solid with heat.

'I'm sorry. I wasn't trying to trick you. I swear.' She

leaned down to pick out good round stones, selecting them very carefully, putting them into my hand like an offering. 'If I know about you it's not . . . it's not because you spoke.'

I threw a pebble viciously at the bobbing apple core, making a direct hit.

'It's all so strange,' she said. 'You're all so strange.'

'Not us,' I said bitterly. 'You.'

'See? That's part of it. I've been afraid I'll put my foot in it like that. Give some terrible offence. Make myself look a fool. And as soon as I speak, that's what I do. I'm sorry.'

There was silence between us for long minutes. I thought she was sulking; it took me that long to realise I was the sulker. When I tuned in to her mood again I realised she was scared.

'Don't,' I said, annoyed with myself. 'Don't worry. We won't send you away, for gods' sake.'

She gave me a grateful look. 'It was easier not speaking. I had some peace.'

She passed me another stone, a good flat one. Drawing back my hand, I skimmed it across the loch surface.

'I could think it over,' she said. 'You know? Think about what happened.'

'Think it over, and over, and over?' I said. 'That's not good.'

'No.' She contradicted me for the first time; I was surprised and pleased. 'It *was* good. I had to think about what he did. I had to go over and over it until I believed it.'

I remembered. 'Your stepfather?'

'My mother's husband.'

'Why did he denounce you? What did you do?'

'Do?' Bitterness tinged her regained voice. 'It's what I wouldn't do. After my mother died. Do you see?'

Astonishing, the power of the bolt of rage that went through my guts. For an instant I couldn't breathe.

'I see,' I said. My fingers were trembling as I touched her lips. They weren't so pale any more, the ride and the fresh air had coloured her face with life. Yes, she was pretty. *That pretty girl from Balchattan.*

I let my finger drift to the corner of her mouth, and as her lips parted I felt rather than heard her small intake of breath. I kissed her.

For seconds her mouth was soft, and she was answering my kiss, and then her hands came up and pushed me away.

We stared at one another. Her throat convulsed as she swallowed, and she bit her lip hard again. Resentment coursed through me.

'Seth, I . . .'

'Please don't bother to explain,' I said icily. 'You're in love with my brother. It happens.' In a savage undertone I added, 'A lot.'

She stood up so fast she almost fell. I'd never imagined my unwanted protector could look so utterly furious, not with my enemies but with me.

She managed not to shout, though I knew she wanted to. She had to hiss her indignation through clenched teeth.

'Why would I be in love with your brother?'

'Well, I . . .'

'A woman can admire a man without being in love

with him,' she told me acidly. 'A woman can be grateful to a man, and think he's a good and brave and decent human being, without being in *love* with him.'

'Oh,' I said, lamely.

'And you know the trouble? Say there's a much less perfect man, bitter and angry and resentful. Say he's not a very good human being because he's so full of hate. Well, the sad thing is, she can still be in love with *him*.'

I didn't know what to say. It was hardly a declaration of undying admiration. But I was pleased that at least she was calling me a man.

'Haven't you got anything to say to me?' Her thin clenched fists were on her hips.

'Um,' I said. I could feel how wide my eyes were. 'I'm sorry?'

That shut her up. She sat back down beside me and stared fixedly at the loch, as if embarrassed by her outburst.

'Conal said,' she cleared her throat, 'he said he was going to cut my throat.'

'Yes,' I said, 'he was. You wouldn't have known. Or barely.'

'And he said when he couldn't, you were going to shoot me.'

'Yes.'

'Well,' she said after a moment's thought. 'Thank you.'

'What you said before.' I couldn't look at her. 'Did you mean that?'

'I'm like you,' she said. 'I don't say things I don't mean.'

'You do know a lot about me, don't you?'

'That's your own fault.' Her lips twitched. 'You came into my head that time, remember? It was such a shock. I never felt anything like it.'

I blinked, speechless.

'You must have known,' she said, trying not to laugh at my discomfort. 'You must have known I'd see as much of you as you did of me. I take it you just forgot. Or did you think a full-mortal wouldn't have it in her to see you?'

Rolling my eyes, I laughed. I reached out to touch her face again, but she flinched.

'Catriona,' I said. 'What is it? I thought you . . .'

'I don't want to sin,' she muttered swiftly.

'You don't want to *what?*'

'I don't want to sin!' she snapped, and her eyes glittered. 'Not again!'

'What?' I froze.

'See?' Folding her arms, she hugged herself, rocking slightly back and forth. 'You see? I thought it might matter to you and I was right. I'm not pure. Men do mind that, don't they? I don't want you to be angry but I can't lie to you. I'm not a vir . . .'

'*Who took it?*' I barked.

Swiftly she drew away, tightening her arms around her body. She wore her dignity like battered armour. 'I'm sorry, but you see now? I tried to stop it, that's the truth. I tried but I . . .'

'Your stepfather?' I said. 'Or the guards?'

Her teeth gnawed at her lip again.

The pretty girl from Balchattan. She was awful pretty . . .

'The guards,' I guessed.

'Yes.'

'So how,' I hissed, 'was it your sin?'

She stared at me with such incomprehension I wanted to slap her. Instead I found myself touching her cheek with my palm, slipping my fingers into her rough crop of hair to stroke it gently. She was as tense as a deer ready to flee, but she didn't pull away.

'Love isn't sin.' I was almost choking on my anger but I thought, if I show it she'll run and she'll never come back. I stroked her hair rhythmically. '*Sin?* Love is what's holy! Being mortal and knowing we're going to die and loving in the face of it anyway. I wish there was a hell for that priest who tried to burn you but there isn't, Catriona, and the only hell for you and me is letting his kind scare us out of loving. He's rotting in the ground and so will we. The worms are eating him and one day they'll eat us, if some kind soul doesn't give us to the raptors. The worms will inherit us, and they'll inherit the earth as well. Love while you can.'

I fell silent. I don't think I've ever got so many words out at once, and blood warmed my neck and cheeks. She must have thought I was insane.

Apparently not, though. She unwrapped her arms from her body and leaned towards me, touching my lips with her own fingers. I made an involuntary sound in my throat, helpless to stop myself taking her fingers gently into my mouth and tasting her skin. Then she kissed me.

When we drew apart I linked her fingers with mine. 'Is it too soon?'

She shook her head.

I said, 'I won't hurt you.'

'I know.'

We spread the thin blanket where the blaeberry scrub was dense and soft, and the sun could warm our naked skin, and I did my best to show her the difference between violence and love.

29

My brother was back in the great hall the next evening, gaunt and still haunted, but well enough to have a go at me. I avoided him for a couple of hours: easy enough, since he was surrounded by his captains, by adoring women (and some men), and one particular smitten girl.

Girl. He had noticed Eili was almost a woman: that was obvious to me. He flushed now when her eyes lingered too long on his, but on the rare occasions she looked away, his own gaze was drawn helplessly to her. I knew I was over her because it made me laugh. Poor Conal: I knew he'd fight it, because he wasn't used to thinking of her as a grown Sithe, but I knew that in the end he'd lose. And poor Eili: he wouldn't touch her till she was twenty, and probably not for a long time after. She had at least three years of frustrated, infatuated chastity ahead of her.

Not a problem for me, I thought smugly.

Catriona stayed close to me, which I didn't mind

now, but I grew tired of Sionnach giving me meaning-ful looks, Eili an occasional disbelieving one, and Feorag making lewd whisky-fuelled jokes about full-mortals and What They Say About Quiet Ones. Orach was cool with me and I with her; she had returned from her patrol to find me sleeping with the full-mortal girl, and we were both pretending we didn't care. I drank a bit too much and grew silent, after a spell of being a little too loud, so I sat on a bench with my arm round Catriona's shoulders and focused only on the music. The drums were loud and racing, the pipes and whistles wild, and Righil's beautiful raw voice drowned out the snide remarks around me.

I was tired of them all, and I felt suddenly protective of Catriona, and I knew I had it coming from Conal anyway. So it was almost a relief when I felt his cold call in my head and I turned to lock eyes with him at the far end of the hall.

A light hand touched my shoulder. 'Your brother wants you, doesn't he?' Orach's voice was low in my ear.

I didn't look at her, but at Catriona, still mesmerised by the music. ~ *Yes.*

~ *Go on then. I'll stay with her. Don't worry.*

Craning my head to look up at Orach, I touched her cheek with my free hand.

~ *Thank you.*

When I rose to leave Catriona jerked up, alarmed, but Orach immediately sat down in my place and said something that made her smile. It would be all right.

As soon as I was within twenty feet of him Conal excused himself from Geanais's ongoing rant about the failures of the stablehands. He didn't look at me but got to his feet, walked out through the anteroom and into the courtyard. It was very late by then but it still wasn't truly dark, and the coolness of the night air was a relief. The music faded to background noise, the voices and shouts to a murmur. His boots rang clearly on the grey stones till he stopped and turned on his heel outside the armoury, and stared at me in silence.

'You're your old self,' I said. I stayed warily back out of reach of his fist.

'Leave that girl alone.'

'Don't be shy, Cù Chaorach. Don't beat around the bush. Say what you think.'

'I'm serious.'

So was I, and I think for once I was angrier than him. 'What do you think, I'm not good enough for her? Think I'm going to rape the little scrap and dump her? Think I'm going to use her like her own kind did?'

'That's enough.' He spoke through gritted teeth.

'The hell it is. What do you think I am? A little less than human or a good bit less than Sithe? Well, I reckon the girl hasn't been hurt enough. I told you before. I'm better than any full-mortal and I'll do the job properly.'

'Stop this, Murlainn. Stop making yourself into what you aren't.'

'What does that mean?'

He paused for long seconds. 'You know very well what.'

'Her lover.'

'No, an all-round hater.'

My hackles rose, and now I'd had enough of this.

'She won't be hurt. I will not hurt her more than she's been hurt already. I doubt it's possible. Now piss off, Cù Chaorach. You're my Captain, not my priest.'

He raised his hands and I thought he'd strike me, but as if to stop himself he linked them tightly behind his neck. I knew I was pushing him, but by now I wanted a fight, even if I lost.

'It isn't her that worries me!' he barked. 'It's you!'

That shut me up for a moment.

'You're Sithe, Murlainn!'

'Gods help me,' I said with bitterness.

'Gods help us all, but think about it! You are what you are, and she'll live for what? Thirty more years, if she's lucky? If *you're* lucky. Snap your fingers and she'll be gone.'

'So.' I folded my arms. 'It's the binding. You don't want me to bind.'

'Look, they don't understand us, they can't. They can't *know* us.'

'Full-mortals.'

'Yes.'

'I thought you were the great equaliser,' I sneered. 'I thought they were humans too. I thought they were as good as us.'

Even in the blue half-darkness I could see the colour rush to his cheeks. I knew I had him. 'It's not that. It's not anything like that.'

'What, then?'

'You know what binding is, don't you?'

'Of course,' I snapped.

'So don't do it, that's all. Please. It's only once and

it's for life and death. It knots your souls. There's not many survive the separation.'

'It happens. And you're overreacting. Who said I was going to bind?' I felt a chill on the nape of my neck, like a warning from fate, but I was too angry to stop. 'I don't want anyone to know me. *Anyone*. I don't want my soul understood. The idea's vile. I don't want to be *known*.'

'I know you enough, Seth. You're too impulsive. Even if you don't bind, you . . .'

'I what?'

He turned away, embarrassed again. 'You'll get a taste for them, Seth. Full-mortals. What can they give you? They can't understand you, can't see your insides.'

'Yes,' I said. 'Oh, yes, she can.'

He was gritting his teeth so hard I thought he'd draw blood from them. 'Not the way Orach could. If you let her.'

'Who said I would ever let her?' I wanted to spit on the ground at his feet but I didn't. It would have been insulting to Orach and that wasn't what I meant. 'Is that what this is about?'

'You'll get too used to it, Seth. Love that doesn't last. Fooling in the shallows. One short life, one short love after another.'

'Don't patronise me.' I turned my head so that I could spit without too great an insult to him. 'And don't worry. I won't bind to her and I won't bind to Orach. I doubt I'll ever bind to anyone. Now you can damn well get me a drink for the insult to my intelligence.'

His grin was a little uneasy but he stepped forward and hugged me. I gripped him tightly against me, clenching my teeth because my eyes were hot with tears.

'I love you,' I said, 'but piss off out of my private life.'

'And I love you and your filthy disrespectful tongue and all. I should slap you but I'll get you that drink.' As he released me we each averted our eyes. 'I need one more than you do.'

And so I did the right thing. I did the right thing then, and it hurt so much that later, much later in my life, it helped convince me to do the wrong thing.

No. Even now I can't call it wrong. My conscience made me fight it, but when my conscience hollered too loudly, I'd make myself remember Leonora. I'd remember how long she survived Griogair, in the end, and I told myself it could be the same for another woman. That another, so like Leonora in so many ways, could outlive for centuries the death of her bound lover. I told myself *she* would survive me, and live, and be happy again. That's how I convinced myself.

But all that was far, too far in the future. For now, for Catriona, I did what was right.

That night we lay together, her back against my chest, my arms around her. Her body fitted mine in every way. Though she was turned away from me I sensed her smile as she reached out to the table beside my bed and picked up the crude wooden wolf.

'My fingers are better now,' she said. 'I could make this better.'

'Don't,' I said. 'I like it.'

'Oh! Good.' She set it carefully back on the table. 'Can I ask you something?'

'Uh-huh.'

'Do you mind if I keep my hair like this?'

I couldn't answer that. Behind her back I frowned, kissing her between her shoulder blades to buy myself time. Full-mortals bewildered me altogether.

'What's it got to do with me?' I asked eventually.

Wriggling round to face me, she drew a forefinger down my brow to smooth the frown. 'I thought you'd have an opinion. I thought you might like me to grow it.'

'I do have an opinion.'

'Which is?'

'That it's up to you how you wear your hair,' I told her patiently.

'Then you don't mind if I keep it short?'

'Why would I mind?' I was exasperated. 'It would be beautiful long. I'm sure I'd love it. I love it the way it is. It's beautiful short. What do you want me to say? It's your hair.'

'All right.' She made a face and gave me one of her funny smiles. 'You're still strange.'

'Look who's talking.' I put my forefinger against her lower lip and she kissed it. 'This isn't about your hair, that's what I think.'

My hair was a lot longer than hers. She stroked it

behind my ear, not quite meeting my eyes. 'No. But them shaving it. It hurt, they pulled half of it out by the roots. And it was terrible, it was humiliating. It was just before they . . . it was almost as terrible as . . .' She gulped. 'I never want that to happen again. If it's short no-one can . . . it wouldn't be so . . .'

'Stop,' I said. 'Stop. It will never happen again. Understand? Nobody will touch you again if you don't want them to. Including me.'

'Really?' Her eyes grew sceptical. 'You wouldn't touch me now? If I said not to?'

'Of course I wouldn't. Where do you people get your strange ideas?'

'You know, I keep thinking.' She gave a small and effortful smile, and when she spoke her words were jerky. 'Fighting off my stepfather. Waste of effort, wasn't it? If I'd just given in. He'd never have. Done it. Denounced me. And then the guards wouldn't have. Done *that*. I wouldn't have. Been there. Maybe it would have been better for me if I'd just . . .'

'That's what the bastard would want you to think. So don't.'

'And if none of it had happened,' she said after a moment, 'I wouldn't be here with you.'

'These are the thoughts,' I said, 'that can drive you mad.'

'No. That last one is the thought that makes it better.'

I caressed her thigh, felt her flesh tremble under my touch. She was a joy to love.

'Listen, Catriona,' I said. 'There can't be any binding. My brother won't let me.'

'Your brother won't *let* you?'

There was such gentle mockery in the question I felt heat flood my face. 'Well, I wouldn't just do what he . . . I wouldn't just *obey* him.' I looked at her ear, but that was so cowardly I made myself meet her eyes again. 'He's right.'

Laughing, she kissed me. 'I know. It's all right. I know about binding, I know what it is.'

'Do you?'

'Of course. I heard Griosach went into the sea. After her man Broc was killed. They were bound, weren't they?'

'See, you're a full-mortal, and . . .'

'And I won't be around for long.' She put her fingers over my lips. 'Not in your terms. But long enough for me.'

'And don't worry if I'm not faithful,' I said. 'It doesn't matter. We're not like that.'

That, it seemed, was pushing my luck. Almost as hard as she pushed my chest. I grunted with shock as I was thrown back onto the mattress.

She sat up, tugging the sheet across her breasts and slapping my supplicant hand aside.

'You may not be like that,' she said icily, 'but I am. It's not much to ask, Seth. It's not for long, after all. Not in your terms.'

Lost for words, I blinked. We faced each other across a sea of crumpled linen. Tentatively I reached out my mind, but she glared back, her dark eyes like flint, so that I had to back off. She looked so fierce, so determined, all I could do was grin.

'Then I'll be faithful,' I said. 'You've no respect for a foreign culture, have you?'

'None,' she said crisply, though this time she let me take her hand. Her gaunt pretty face twisted as she fought her own laughter, and then she gave in to it.

'And if that's your promise, Seth,' she said, 'go ahead and always touch me.'

30

Her dark brown hair would have been lovely tumbling down her back. It probably was, once. But I wasn't lying when I said I loved it anyway. I thought that again as I rode at her back to the forest a month later, my arms encircling her to hold the reins, the first frost of autumn singeing the air. I liked the brown crop that was like a seal's pelt. The stubble had grown enough to camouflage the still-raw scars where the razor had hacked off her hair, but it was short enough to show every angle and curve of her beautiful skull.

I don't make the seal comparison lightly. I'd swum with her in the rolling breakers of the north bay, and she was lithe and graceful as a selkie in its skin, her eyes as dark and deep; and when she broke the surface, laughing, her damp dark pelt of hair was beaded with silver. She was no longer shy of her nakedness, not when she swam with me. And not when she lay beside me in the echoing stone silence of my room that was no longer too big and graceful for me.

The October day felt keen and fresh in my nostrils; I was both sad and relieved to see the end of summer. It had been my first summer back at home and yet an unnamed dread had hung over it with the heat, an oppressive promise. We were still exiles, my brother and me. We had come home. The two were not compatible.

I knew Kate was only waiting.

It should have been too cold for us to fall asleep in the woods that day, but cheating the cold was no longer difficult for me, and Catriona was kept warm by my body. I never felt the cold as much as I used to; after two harsh winters in the blackhouse I had sworn I'd never be so cold again. Not only did the cold of home affect my bones less than the otherworld cold, I worked at feeling warmer and I did it with nothing but my mind. Instead of wrapping myself in skins and blankets and woollen cloaks, I found the place in my brain that controlled my body heat and I used it. Teaching myself the skill, though it bordered dangerously on witchcraft, had a double advantage: it added to my reputation. It did not make me better liked but it certainly made me better respected. To be seen stripped to the waist in bitter winds and snow made people think twice before taking me on, even if they hadn't seen me at swordplay. And most of them had.

But on that day, the snow was yet to come. Catriona and I both slept badly at night, and we had got into the summer habit of riding out in the dawn to our forest, exhausting ourselves with love, and falling asleep for an hour or two there on the soft peaty ground. That early morning, something in the atmosphere must have woken me. Something in the atmosphere *did* wake me, but I didn't realise it straight away.

Catriona was not in my arms. She must have gone to empty her bladder, because she wouldn't wander off otherwise. I was instantly awake as always, and I stayed quite still, propped up on one elbow and listening.

She screamed.

I was up and running straight away. It went through my mind that the roan had fatally disobeyed me, but instantly I knew that wasn't true. I called him and knew he was coming, but for now I was on my own.

A bank of sand, knotted together with pine roots, fell away ten or more feet to the grainy beach of the loch. She was there, forced onto her knees, her head yanked back by the jaw, and she was fighting. Smart girl, to keep her seal-skin crop. The thing could not get as good a grip on her chin as it would on a hank of hair. She thrashed and struggled in its hold despite the curved blade in its hand, she tore desperately at its scrawny arms. Cadaverous face, lank yellow hair, papery skin. Thin enough to be translucent. No shadow.

It straddled her, grinning, waiting for her to tire and settle down so she'd feel the cut better when it happened.

That's how they are, the Lammyr.

I took a running leap off the sand-cliff, not breaking stride, and it dropped her just in time to parry the slash of my dirk.

Fast, it was so much faster than any Sithe I'd fought.

I was fast too, but it took all my concentration, all my swiftness, every move I ever learned to keep me out of the path of its swinging blade.

Catriona did her best to help me, wrenching a dead branch from a twisted pine and swinging at the thing, but it was far too fast for her. All the same it was a small distraction for the Lammyr, splitting its focus enough to irritate it. At last, exasperated, it swung its skinny torso and loosed a blade in her direction. I heard her cry out but I didn't have time to think, could only spring for its neck and seize its lank hair to twist its head aside. It caught my disgusted eyes, grinning up at me as I slashed its throat.

I fell awkwardly as it did, rolling against the rough stones at the edge of the beach and grunting as the air was knocked out of me. Frantically I kicked away from it as it jerked and jolted, its colourless blood spilling into the sand. It was looking at Catriona as its eyes went dead, and it was still grinning.

I staggered over to her. She was clutching her side, and blood soaked her fingers, but she didn't cry out, only looked into my eyes, terrified.

I peeled her fingers away as the roan thundered to my side, skidding and backing and snorting when it caught sight of the Lammyr's corpse.

She flinched as I touched the wound. 'It's all right,' I said. 'I mean it. I'm not lying. It's all right but you'll need Grian. Can you get on the horse?'

She nodded, and I boosted her onto its back, not letting go of its mane. It didn't try anything. I was up and behind her in a second, and besides, it was a mischievous creature but not entirely evil. And it was mine.

I kept the roan to a smooth swift canter, talking to her all the way to keep her mind off the pain that lanced with every stride. Now I had time to curse myself for my complacency and my arrogance. For leaving my sword in my room, just because we were at peace and had been all summer. For leaving Branndair with Liath and the other hounds, because I felt self-conscious when he rested his amber eyes on me as I made love to Catriona. For forgetting I was a Sithe, and a fighter, not a lovestruck full-mortal boy from the clachan.

My lover was pale but quiet, and I admired her all over again.

'Did it remind you of anyone?' I said lightly.

'The minister. The priest.' She said it straight away.

'My clever one. It was a female, though.'

'Was it?' There was such dry humour in her voice I couldn't help kissing her neck.

'Believe it or not, yes. We're nearly home, Catriona.'

'I'm fine.'

'There aren't any more. We're all right.'

Actually I wasn't sure that was true. I was almost too afraid to roam the moor with my mind. There was a malevolence in the air that I couldn't pin down, and I reminded myself never to be so stupid and careless again.

'I'm sorry I wandered off.' She gasped as the roan thudded down a sharp three-foot drop, then recovered her breath. 'I felt sick.'

'Next time you feel sick,' I told her, 'don't for gods' sake wander off.'

She gave another small gasp that might have been a laugh. I tightened my arm round her.

The shock was beginning to wear off, the adrenaline leaking away, and a chill of suspicion was creeping into my bones. How long had it been since Lammyr were seen around here? Not since Griogair had cleared the place of them, centuries ago. It made no sense that they would return now, unless something was changing that I didn't recognise and couldn't understand.

Catriona's leaking blood was warm and wet against my arm, and I felt young and ignorant and helpless again. And my thoughts were drifting in horrible directions when the roan skidded to a startled halt for the second time that morning. I blinked, and shuddered.

Kate had come.

31

The gates of the dun were thrown wide, and five detachments of her troops were milling outside the walls, eating our food and drinking our ale. I rode straight through them. It wasn't a problem: our path cleared before us. The blue roan's ears were back against its skull, its teeth bared in a hideous grin, and the horses of Kate's fighters backed and trembled and skittered in terror, fighting their riders or jerking at their tethers. The fighters watched me, I knew it. But I did not look at them.

In the central courtyard Kate stood on the highest point of stone, where Conal should stand. Lilith was at her side, and five more detachments of her fighters waited around her, along with her personal guard. Their swords were sheathed but their eyes were cold. An absolute silence lay across the whole dun.

'Murlainn,' said Kate, her voice clear and lovely in the frosted air. 'We've been waiting for you.'

'Then you can wait one more minute,' I said.

There was a hiss of anger from Kate's guard captain, but someone was shoving through the ranks: Grian. He caught Catriona as I lowered her from the roan's back. Good old Grian, I thought as I dismounted. He was intimidated—who wouldn't be?—but his work came before his fear. Lifting her into his arms, he looked at Kate.

'Kate,' shouted my brother. 'The girl's hurt. Let Grian take her.'

He stood ten yards from me, weaponless, expressionless. Everyone looked at Kate, except for Lilith, who looked at me.

Kate waited a dramatic second, and another, then gave a gracious nod. Quietly Grian turned and carried Catriona away. Clutching his neck, she looked imploringly back at me, but I closed my eyes and let myself breathe again.

I walked over to stand with Conal. I knew he was furious with my insolence, but glad of it too. The faintest smile twitched the corner of his mouth before we both turned back to Kate.

~ *Are you ready for this, Murlainn?*

~ *If you are,* I told him. ~ *Cù Chaorach.*

'Come here,' said Kate.

It was the longest walk of my life to that moment, crossing that wide empty space in the centre of the courtyard. I knew what I had to do when we reached her, and there was sourness in my mouth. Gods knew what Conal was thinking; he wouldn't let me hear, though he was seething. That iron yett of a block was across his mind again.

Every eye in the place was on us. I amused myself thinking of what was going through all those Sithe heads. From our own clann, rage and resentment at Conal's humiliation and delight at mine. From Kate's, there would be smug satisfaction, and contempt for us both. Mostly. But there wasn't an opinion in the place that mattered to me, besides Conal's, and I knew what he wanted of me. I also knew I would not let him be first to kneel. At Kate's feet I dropped to my knees.

I did not look at my brother but I sensed his surprise and his gratitude as he knelt at my side.

She let us kneel there on the cold rock till I thought my knees would buckle, and my head would split open with my contained fury. Neither of us moved a muscle till she stepped forward and extended her hand.

I watched Conal. All that betrayed him was a vein at his temple that throbbed as he took her hand and pressed it to his forehead, then kissed it.

Kate smiled and turned to me. I felt Conal's gaze burning into me, felt him pleading with me not to be stupid. I took her hand. I pressed it to my forehead: her slender delicate bones and soft flesh against my skull. Pain throbbed at the front of my brain. I brought her hand to my lips and kissed it. Her skin was like cool silk. I released her hand and she took a small step back.

She slapped me. Hard. Then she turned, taking her time, and slapped Conal.

I said nothing; neither did he. I did not let my eyes drop from hers, and I know he didn't either. To lose our tempers would be to lose face, and quite possibly our lives. I hoped he knew it, because despite his seniority and his dignity and his quiet acceptance, I knew Conal was far, far angrier than I was.

She let us kneel there longer still. I thought the rock would grate right through to my kneecaps, and still we were surrounded by mocking silence. Oh, she was revelling in this. And then, quite unexpectedly, she laughed, all benevolence again. She had a lovely laugh.

'Look, Lilith. Your boy has become a man.'

My mother smirked. I looked at her, and then back at Kate, and I felt a shocking surge of fierce desire. Kate laughed again with delight.

'A man!' she murmured. 'And a fine fighter, I hear. Submission doesn't suit you, Murlainn.'

'No,' I said. 'It doesn't.'

Conal shot me a dark look, but if I had to stay on my knees much longer I was going to kill someone. I could still taste Kate's skin on my lips. It was as if all my own skin had been peeled off; I had never felt so naked and vulnerable and it made me ache to blind every man watching.

'I think you boys could be trouble,' smiled Kate. 'Trouble-makers, too.'

'No, Kate,' said Conal.

'Come, come. I'm not angry. After all I *like* trouble. It can be . . . fun. Well, now.' Lightly she clapped her hands. 'You broke your exile, Cù Chaorach, and since your brother chose to share it, he has broken exile too. What shall I do with you?'

We didn't answer. I think it was a rhetorical question.

'You both broke your exile, but I think you learned a lot. I like you both, and I need good fighters, and I do not want to have to exile you again. Do you think you learned humility, Cù Chaorach? Did the full-mortals teach it to you?'

'Yes, Kate.' He said it clear and without shame, and he kept his eyes on hers.

'That's what I heard.' Placing a finger thoughtfully against her cheek, she watched his face, and I watched hers. She did not look as cool and in control as she'd have liked, and she knew it. So did I, so did we all. Kate did not know quite what to make of his attitude. I was afraid for him, then.

'I heard all that they did to you,' she said, failing to use his name as she addressed him. It was a calculated insult. 'I've no doubt you learned to do without your dignity.'

'Yes, Kate.'

'You screamed, I dare say? You begged? You confessed to lies to make them stop?'

'Yes, Kate.' His face didn't flicker.

She'd have liked to be there. You could tell. 'Your pride was worth nothing. Am I right?'

'Yes, Kate.'

'And only luck and a full-mortal let you escape with your life,' she said derisively.

'Yes, Kate.'

She smiled. Gods, she was livid. I loved him more than ever.

'Here's my offer, Cù Chaorach. Serve me for a year.'

I took a breath. He didn't react: not so much as a twitch of his eyelid.

'Be my captain for a year. That's not long, is it? I want you, and your brother, and ten of your best fighters. That will prove your loyalty. I will invalidate your exile and this unpleasantness will be forgotten.'

It was too good a deal. We both knew it.

'And who captains my dun?'

Kate looked winsome. 'Is it your dun? Certainly it will be again, if you do as I ask.'

He ignored that; she had no right to say it. 'Who takes care of my dun in my absence?'

'Calman Ruadh.'

Utter silence. Even I was dumbstruck. Let me put it this way: his name was a great joke of nature. They called him the Red Dove to qualify it, because he'd been bathed in blood so often it must have soaked into his skin.

'Your sense of humour does you credit, Kate,' said Conal through his teeth. 'Calman Ruadh is Alasdair Kilrevin's lieutenant.'

'Was,' she corrected him sweetly. 'Alasdair Kilrevin is dead.'

I felt astonishment along with a gut-wrenching disappointment. That work had been Conal's, and mine, and someone had taken it from us without formal claim. Pure bad manners.

Kate's gaze and her smile slanted towards me. 'Don't worry, Murlainn. His death appears to have been somewhat . . . supernatural. He and his men were burned to a crisp. They were found in a field, after a night's drinking and gambling. It seems something, ah . . . overtook them. There's talk of the Devil. There's talk of an ill-advised bet with . . . let's say, extraordinarily high stakes.' She examined a polished fingernail, frowning as she pushed back a cuticle. 'Calman Ruadh, by great good fortune, was not with them.'

Conal muttered something inaudible.

'He has been on his knees, Cù Chaorach, just like you, and just as you will be, he is forgiven.'

'Kilrevin was on his knees to you more than once,' said Conal savagely. 'It never stopped him picking up his sword again.'

'Now is really not a good time to make that point.' Her smile was quick and catlike. 'Calman Ruadh is my trusted ally and your dun will be secure in his hands. No living person would protect it as well as Calman will. You notice I say *will*, not *would*. I am not offering you options, Cù Chaorach. This, or I return you to the care of the full-mortals where they will no doubt finish what they started. And,' she raised a finger to stop his interruption, 'I burn your dun and hang its inhabitants.' Tutting, she wagged the finger in his face. 'I've really been *very* cross with you. Now, what do you say?'

Elegantly twisting her hand, she presented the back of it to him a second time.

He looked to his left, and his right, meeting the eyes of his clann. They knew as well as he did: it was no choice at all. After perhaps a minute, he took her hand again as if he was taking hold of a snake. He pressed it once more to his forehead, and kissed it.

'How I wish,' she said softly, 'your mother could see this moment. It's not like her to run, is it? But perhaps she couldn't bear the shame.'

She jerked her hand away before Conal could fling it.

This time she didn't even bother to slap him. One of her captains brought forward her horse and helped her mount, and she rode away without a backward glance. The creature was milk-white, but for its soft black muzzle and its dove-grey tail. Bells and ribbons and crystals were woven into its silky mane, its hooves were embellished with silver, and its bridle was braided green silk. The tinkling of the elaborate harness was the only sound as she rode out; it was all that broke the silence of dread and awe, and her guard captain gave Conal the most contemptuous stare I'd ever seen anyone dare to give him. I didn't want to see him look at my Captain like that, so I glanced towards the sky, and that's when I saw the raven sitting silent and still on the grey north parapet, watching us all.

Swiftly I looked back at my queen on her jewelled horse, until the gates swung shut behind her.

'Jesus, Mary and Joseph,' I barked. 'See that poor pony? Does the woman believe her own frigging myth?'

Conal exploded with muffled laughter at my side, and that was the cue for nervous hilarity from our own clann and shocked stares from what remained of Kate's. The silence and the awe were shattered. I was pleased with myself as I heard first grumblings and then ever more indignant raised voices of anti-monarchist complaint.

'So where did you pick that up?' said Conal, throwing an arm round my shoulder.

'Ah, some old weaver who came through the clachan last year. It's got a ring to it, you think?'

'And then some.' He was grinning. 'I hope to gods she didn't hear it, but I doubt you're that lucky.'

His laughter faded and he gaped past me, but the smile that split his face was one of adoration. 'Reultan!'

I turned with a sinking heart; I don't know why. The

woman striding towards him was one of the most beautiful I've ever seen, and she wore embroidered linen, silk trews, fine black leather boots and an elaborate silk coat like the ones Leonora favoured. Her hair was raven-black and straight as a fall of water. Her eyes were blue like sheet-ice on a cloudless day and they brimmed with tears that made them glitter.

'Cù Chaorach, you fool.' The woman put her arms around him and pressed her face to his, closing her eyes as he embraced her. 'Why did you have to antagonise her?'

He shrugged and smiled, tightening his arms round her.

'You forced her into it. You nearly died! Conal, you're an idiot. Please, please don't make her do it again.'

I gasped with fury. '*Make her?* She did it because she wanted to. He didn't exile himself!'

Her eyes opened, focusing on me, hardening and cooling like molten metal thrust into water.

'So. This is the brother, is it?'

Conal released her, but he kept an affectionate arm around her. 'This is Seth, yes.'

I could feel the contempt coming off her like an ice-mist. She was the archetypal courtier: arrogant, dismissive, frighteningly certain of her place in the world. I think I did remember her, from my childhood days in Kate's caverns, but to be honest I could have been mistaken. She and all her kind were interchangeable. 'Tell me she's not my sister.'

'I'll tell you myself,' said Reultan. 'I'm not your sister, thank the gods.'

'There.' Conal rolled his eyes. 'You're not related;

you don't have to like each other. Just get on, won't you?'

Some chance. Reultan and I loathed one another on sight and for our entire lives, but gods, we always understood one another. Perhaps that was the problem.

Still, that first time we met, she fascinated me and I fascinated her, on a purely scientific level. In some ways we were alike, but still it felt like the collision of alien species. Her upper lip curled. I took a deliberate, insulting step away from her. So I was confused when her eyes lit up, warmed with joy.

I was knocked off balance as Eili flung herself past me into Reultan's arms and the two women embraced. 'Reultan!' whooped Eili.

I could tell I was going to grow sick of that name.

'*Eilid!*' Her eyes widened with delight. 'Little Eilid! Is that you?'

'Yes, believe it or not she grew up,' I muttered, and Conal kicked my ankle.

'They all call me Eili,' said Eili. 'For short.'

'I like it. Conal, where is our mother?'

I admired the way she said *our*, subtle, but stressed just enough to exclude me.

'Gone to the soothsayer. Asking an idiot charlatan how to find some bloody talisman that doesn't exist. A *Stone*, if you please. She's been gone for a month.'

'Don't be so disrespectful, Conal. The *prophet* is an oracle and a reliable one.'

'The prophet is fooling herself,' laughed Conal. 'And everyone else.'

'So,' said Reultan dryly. 'You're saying Leonora can be fooled? I'd like to see you say it to her face.'

Conal shrugged, defeated but grinning.

'She left Faramach.' Reultan nodded at the parapet. 'To keep an eye on you?'

'Who knows what that bird's for?' He made a dismissive gesture. Behind his back, I gave it the finger, but it didn't react. Something struck me as I gazed into its still obsidian eyes.

I said, 'Kate didn't dare turn up till Leonora was off the scene.'

The raven flapped down to the inner wall of the tannery, stretched its massive wings and gave a harsh laugh.

'Seth's right,' said Eili.

'I know he is.' Conal looked thoughtful.

Reultan looked as if she wanted to slap me. I could see from the tension in her jaw that her teeth were tightly clenched. Conal winked at me and squeezed her arm.

'It'll be good to see more of you, Reultan. Even in the circumstances. You won't ignore me, will you? Pretend you don't know me?'

'Don't be a bigger fool than you already are,' she said crisply. 'Who will you take with you? Ten, isn't it?'

'Eight,' said Eili. 'Obviously Sionnach and I are going with him.'

'With *us*,' I said resentfully.

'Yes, yes.'

'So who?' said Reultan.

32

The answer was: ten of his best fighters. That was what Kate had asked for, and that was what she had to be given. Carraig and Righil, his lieutenants. Sionnach and Eili. Orach. Feorag. He managed to negotiate to keep Raineach in the dun, but one of her sons had to come with us. Eorna was left behind; his lover Caolas rode out with us with unashamed tears flowing down her face. The skilled bowmen Luthais and Raonall were bound lovers, and inseparable, and they were the last two.

Kate had to wait for me, and she was not pleased, but I would not give in, and she had to be a little careful now. She had pushed her humiliation of us far enough, and if she went too much further she would be in danger of losing sympathy even among her own clann. Kate was not a tyrant, or if she was, she was a very clever one and she knew the power of consent. Her legitimacy sprang from consent and she ruled by it; it was just that she knew how to gain consent for the cruellest actions by sweet reasonableness in others. And subjects who love will excuse a great deal, and a great many of Kate's subjects loved her to the point of irrationality.

I would not leave the dun till Grian said Catriona could travel. Her wound was not life-threatening, but it was a serious one, and she was already weakened when she took it, and full-mortals are prone to infection. Nor would I leave her alone; my clann might feed and water and shelter her but they would not befriend her, and I wouldn't inflict twelve months of solitary misery on her. I gave her the choice and she chose to come with me, as I knew she would.

So we rode to Kate's fortress together a month after the others, taking Branndair, but letting the blue roan loose at the gates of the underground fortress. Kate ignored Catriona, but she summoned me to stand in front of her—she did not risk asking me to kneel—and in front of her smirking courtiers and her dead-eyed captains and my own friends, she told me I would stay an extra month to serve her when my brother and my comrades had gone home. I shrugged, then bowed my head, to signal that I was at her command, but I didn't have to care about it.

She worked us hard. Conal was one of her captains and he had his own detachment, of course, and he kept Carraig and Righil as his lieutenants. The rest of us were split among her other captains. Some were pigs and loved having Conal's clann to order about. Some were decent human beings. Luthais, Raonall and Feorag were under the command of Cluaran, monosyllabic and shaven-headed and a hard taskmaster but fundamentally a good man. Sionnach and Eili had the misfortune of being in Fearchar's detachment, as did Raineach's son Eachann: Fearchar was a spiteful bastard who delighted in giving them the worst jobs and treating them as second-class fighters. Orach and I were split up, Orach to be commanded by a woman named Alainn. Probably just as well, given that I was sometimes separated from Catriona for days at a time.

My captain, and Caolas's, was a man called Aonghas. I liked him and admired him, and deep down he liked me too, but he couldn't show it too much, because his lover wouldn't like it.

His lover was Reultan.

They became bound lovers about a month after I arrived, which was bad news for me because after that Aonghas was less inclined to be friendly to me, though he was fine with Caolas. He would occasionally give me an apologetic look when Reultan treated me with contempt, but rarely spoke up for me. He was besotted with her.

To be fair, the besotting was mutual, though they seemed very unalike. He had cropped dark hair and moss-green eyes and a face that smiled a lot, and one of the kindest natures of all the captains. Gods knew what he saw in her, but there it was, he was bound to her and there was no going back and clearly he didn't want to go back. He even brought a softness to Reultan's eyes, though not when she turned them on me.

Aonghas was very like Conal, in many ways, and the pair of them were the closest of friends. As soon as Conal had returned to the caverns, I heard, Aonghas had walked forward to embrace him, right in front of

Kate and Lilith and all the courtiers. You had to admire him for that kind of cheek, and for that kind of loyalty.

I say Conal and Aonghas were the closest of friends; that's a little dishonest of me. The fact is, they loved one another like brothers. I tried not to be jealous and resentful, but sometimes it leaked out and I disobeyed one of Aonghas's orders, or gave him cheek, and then he'd have to punish me with solitary confinement or a beating whether he liked it or not. Conal gave me no sympathy on these occasions, saying I'd driven Aonghas to it. I still liked the man.

I don't know if Kate thought she was knocking the rebellion out of us. Sometimes now I wonder if she was actually playing some elaborate game, provoking us to worse rebellion for some purpose of her own. That didn't occur to me at the time, of course. What a greenarse I was.

I watched Sionnach being beaten, once, for some minor offence he'd given to Fearchar. He stood gripping the post he was tied to, and his eyes were locked on mine, his jaw clenched, his knuckles white. I could do nothing for my gentle friend. All I could do was watch, and hate, but he made not a sound, and in the middle of it he smiled at me through the cold sweat on his face, and I knew that rebellion was being thrashed into his bones, not out of them.

A year, I kept thinking. It's only a year.

No-one had a worse time than Conal, despite his captaincy. Kate tested him with the foulest jobs: executions, punishment beatings, croft burnings and confiscations. He had kissed her hand and sworn loyalty. He had to do it. But his eyes grew empty and his face set hard.

I was sleepless as ever one night when I heard his footfall in the corridor. They happened a lot, these night-time pacings. I hadn't dared follow him before but each time, a fresh line was slashed into his arm by morning: one for every crofter he'd hung. With Conal she was trying to beat all the goodness out of him: that much I knew. That night I lay beside the sleeping Catriona and had the first terrible sense of being made into something against my will.

Carefully I eased out of bed, determined not to wake my lover. She'd been sick every morning for a week, and there wasn't a Lammyr in sight, and I had a terrible foreboding. To take my mind off it, I followed Conal again.

Down a long torch-lit tunnel and through two antechambers the caverns opened out into a huge wet-walled space where a silver fall of water filled a clear pool. The noise of the water was a constant sibilant rush, and the underground waterfall was as cold as water can only be when it's never seen the sun. By the time I stepped into the echoing space Conal was stripped and standing beneath the waterfall, arms propped against the stone wall and his head bowed into the full force of the water.

There was someone else in the cave. Aonghas sat against the rock wall, arms resting on his knees, a silver flask in one hand. He turned his head and looked at me, but he didn't smile.

~ *Murlainn.*

I nodded to him, wondering if I was in trouble again,

and not much caring. After a moment he held out the flask to me, so I sat down against the wall beside him and took it. The whisky was peaty and sharp; it burned the back of my throat and made me feel slightly sick, but I drank a good dram of it anyway. Too late at night. I passed the flask back to him and he took it without a word. In silence we watched Conal.

When he stood up straight and took his arms away from the wall and the waterfall, I saw the dirk in his right hand. I didn't dare say a word as he carved two methodical neat lines on his forearm, parallel to the rest. Blood flowed from his split flesh, and he thrust his arm back under the water till the wounds were washed clean.

'Does he want a healer?' I asked, my throat dry.

'Never does,' said Aonghas. And sure enough Conal stepped out of the water and wrapped a cloth round his arm, expertly, as he must have done it many times before, tightening it in a slipknot. He pulled his clothes back on over his soaking skin and sat down beside us.

'Today,' he said, 'I was ordered to kill a child.'

I thought his voice would echo. Instead it seemed to be swallowed up in the darkness and the damp stone. Aonghas held the flask towards him, but he shook his head.

'He was the age you were, Seth, when I first laid eyes on you.'

Reflexively I swallowed.

'You didn't do it,' said Aonghas.

Conal gave him a sidelong look. 'No.'

'Didn't think so.'

'I hanged his father and his uncle,' said Conal, 'and I

turned him and his mother out on the moor where they might very well starve, but no, I did not kill him.'

'For which disobedience,' remarked Aonghas, 'Kate may very well kill you.'

'If you report him,' I said. My voice was swallowed by the cave just as Conal's had been, so I said it again. 'If you report him I'll kill you.'

Aonghas did not react at first. Carefully he set down the flask, then sat back against the wall and stared at the roof, unseen in shadow.

'Murlainn,' he sighed. 'Be insolent here and now, if you like. The rest of the time, keep your tongue in order. I do not like having you whipped. I did not like Fearchar setting his thugs on Sionnach. But it's what must happen if you're stupid. I have my own life to think about.'

True. I fidgeted uncomfortably, remembering. My back didn't hurt any more but the scabs itched. Just as well it was dark in that place; I wouldn't have liked Aonghas to see my flush of shame. Conal wouldn't have noticed anyway. He was silent, his head bowed onto his arms, his arms resting on his knees.

At last he said, 'My mother hasn't returned to the dun.'

'She had business with the soothsayer,' said Aonghas.

'Half a year ago.' Conal gave a dry miserable laugh. 'No-one's business could take so long, even with that old charlatan.'

'But you must know where she is?'

'No. Only that she isn't at the dun. Last time I felt her she was very far away. She's been blocking me for months now.'

'Well.' Aonghas shrugged lightly. 'If Leonora was dead you'd know it. So would Reultan.'

'Maybe. But she found it hard not to go with Griogair.' He laughed again, high-pitched and desperate. 'That's an understatement, isn't it? *Hard*. Could be she's stopped fighting it. Could be she's going to go to him after all. She's the only person since Griogair died who could stand up to Kate, and she's leaving us. *Leaving us*.'

Aonghas put an arm round his slumped shoulders.

'One day this'll be over,' he said.

'So I tell myself,' said Conal bitterly.

'No,' I said, 'it won't.'

They both turned their heads and stared at me. I was shocked too. I don't know what had brought it on, but I knew it was true.

'She'll never let us be,' I said. 'We may as well walk out now.'

'You better have your block up, you stupid little shit,' said Aonghas.

I gave him the filthiest look I could get away with. 'Indeed. I'm not stupid.'

'You could have fooled me.'

'I obviously did.'

'Quiet,' said Conal. 'Both of you.'

He linked his hands behind his neck, digging his fingernails into his skin. I thought he was thinking over what I'd said, but after a while he just put his face in his hands.

'Won't stop you seeing it,' I said. 'Won't stop the dreams. Won't stop the screams.'

Aonghas growled in exasperation. Conal ignored me. I stood up.

'You hear me? You're craven. Both of you.' I shouldn't
have had that whisky. I'd come here to comfort him;
instead I could hear myself losing my temper and I
couldn't hold on to it. 'She has you dancing on a string,
Cù Chaorach. What are you afraid of?' I spat. 'Your
sister?'

Aonghas half-rose at that, a snarl forming on his
lips, but Conal seized his arm and he sank back to the
ground, glaring at me. Conal would not meet my eye.
Rage burned my throat as if I was going to throw that
whisky back up.

'She'll go on making you dance to her tune, Cù Chaorach, till you forget what it's like to sit still. Tell her
where to stick her fiddle. What can she do? If Leonora
won't stand against her someone else has to. No-one's
better qualified than you are.'

'Careful, Murlainn.' Aonghas's tone was surprisingly
gentle, and he very nearly smiled. 'He doesn't want to
lose his dun and his clann. And he doesn't want to lose
his brother.'

I said. 'Neither do I.'

And like a foot-stamping toddler, I stalked out.

33

Why was I so angry with him? I danced to Kate's tune too, I kept her beat. My captain too killed for her, killed people who did not deserve to die, and I watched in acquiescent silence as he did it. I told myself I was angry because I would walk out myself if I could, but that I couldn't, because I wouldn't leave him. That was not true. It was only an excuse. The fact is, I was angry because it didn't matter so much what I became. There was not so much in me to change. For Conal to let himself become her golem, though: that seemed like a blasphemy.

Yet what Aonghas said was true. Through Calman Ruadh Kate held our dun and our clann in the palm of her hand, and she had it in her to destroy them both. When Conal could drag his mind out of the black pit it lived in he would yell it at me. Once, he thrashed it into me. He didn't have to. I understood fine. But he thrashed it into me anyway.

I'd answered Aonghas back, again. Oh, I should be

honest. I had muttered a curse at him, under my breath but loud enough for his men to hear, and him. It was more than a curse, it was an accusation—another one on the theme of his cravenness—and I threw in a thoroughgoing insult to Reultan, just to make sure of my fate. There were days, you see, when I welcomed a beating. Usually the days that followed a croft-burning or a hanging.

Branndair had been chained up in the kennels like he always was on these occasions: everyone liked their throat intact. Aonghas's lieutenant was tightening the rope that bound my wrists to the post when Conal shoved through the press of watchers. Even Reultan had to get out of his way.

'Leave him!' he barked.

Aonghas's lieutenant looked at Aonghas, and jerked the rope tighter as he did so, but Aonghas shook his head. He knew what Conal was about, and so did I. I wasn't stupid enough to think he was coming to my rescue.

My brother unsheathed his dirk, and sawed through the rope, then cut the bonds round my wrists too.

'Get your circulation back,' he snapped. Turning away, he stripped off his shirt.

I rubbed my wrists and hands, but only because they hurt. 'I won't need to,' I said.

Turning back, Conal gave me a deadly look. 'You'll fight me.'

I gave him one back. ~ *I don't take orders.*

~ *You will after I've finished with you.*

~ *Not from you, I won't.* I linked my fingers tightly behind my back. ~ *You're not my Captain any more.*

His first blow snapped my head back and I was flung to the ground. I couldn't keep my hands behind my back after that, they came forward in reflexive self-defence, but I did not return a single blow. When he ordered me to my feet I got to my feet, and each time he struck me he gave me every opportunity to hit back. I didn't. Didn't he know what a stubborn bastard I was? How long had he known me? It almost made me laugh, except that it hurt so much I couldn't.

I just kept getting to my feet, or as close to it as I could after ten minutes of this. If anything he hit me harder. I thought my head was going to come off. My face was sticky with blood, I could taste it in my mouth and nose, and my ribs would barely let my lungs draw breath for the pain. In the end I couldn't get up again.

The watchers were silent. Their hoots and yells of encouragement had faded long ago, and even Reultan looked on stony-faced. Sionnach had his arm round Orach, who was weeping, but she wasn't making a sound. I lay in the gritty sand, staring up at the arching stone roof above me and the shadows that flickered with the torchlight. I felt almost peaceful and I'd have liked to smile, but my swollen face wouldn't seem to let me. It felt out of shape somehow, and I had to blink away blood to see anything.

Conal crouched above me, his hands gripping his head.

'Murlainn,' he whispered. 'You stupid, stupid, stupid bastard.'

Somehow I managed to move my head to meet his eyes. I think I even managed an approximation of a smile.

~ *Do I still look like you?*

. . .

'Well,' I mumbled. 'Do I?'

Almost silently he closed the door of my room. He took his time about it. I don't think it was me he couldn't face. Catriona gave him one cold look of anger before she knelt at my head again and went back to cleaning me up. What a gentle touch she had, and the damp cloth was cool, but the bowl of water was stained scarlet with my blood. I just wanted to lie here on the pile of skins and blankets with my aching head in her lap. For once I couldn't be bothered with Conal. I'd made my point; now I only wanted him to go away and leave me alone.

Fat chance.

He knelt beside me but he didn't touch me. At least he had the grace to look me in the eye, though mine were swollen almost shut.

'You look,' he began, and cleared his throat. 'You look more like me than I do.'

Slowly I let myself examine his face. Moving my eyeballs hurt.

'You have no idea,' I said, 'how true that is.'

He clasped his hands behind his neck. He was weeping, I noticed. 'I'm sorry, Murlainn. I'm so sorry.'

I spat blood, and Catriona cleaned the corner of my mouth. 'Why? Saved me a flogging.'

'You're not funny.'

'Neither are you.'

I let my gaze drift to his forearm, where a new cut leaked blood through a white rag. I managed another smile.

'I'm not dead yet,' I said.

He looked at it, silent for a long moment.

'That's not for you,' he said. 'That's for myself.'

'Make you feel better?'

He gave a dry harsh laugh. 'No. So I'll stop being so dramatic, shall I?'

I raised myself up on one elbow, and Catriona drew back.

'Conal,' I said.

'Yes? Call me another name. Or can't you find it? Because I can't. I'm losing my name, Seth. I'm losing my soul.'

'Fight her,' I hissed.

'I'd rather lose my name than lose my people.'

'You lose one, you lose them both.' I stared at him. 'Cold iron instead of a soul. That what you want?'

'Please, Murlainn. I didn't come here to fight.'

'Then why did you?' Catriona glared at him, white-faced. 'It's all that's left to you. You might as well fight. But best if you fight the right pers . . .'

We both stared as Catriona stumbled to her feet and ran to the bowl in the corner of the room. I watched her fall to her knees, retching till her stomach was empty. Conal sprang to his feet, but she shot him such a ferocious look he took a step back, and turned to me.

'What's wrong with her?' he whispered. 'Gods, Seth, is she ill?'

I looked at her. My insides ached, and not with my beating.

'There's a child in her belly,' I said flatly.

He crouched beside me, laid his hand very gently on my arm.

'I'm sorry. Gods, Seth. I'm so sorry.'

'Stop being bloody sorry,' I said. I'd bitten my lip before I remembered how swollen and tender it was, and made myself wince. 'What can you do?' Bitterly I added, 'About anything.'

'It might be okay. Sometimes it is. Look at Ma Sinclair! You've good blood, you've—'

'A living child's as common as hobbyhorse shit, and you know it. I'm not that lucky.' I took a breath. 'Nor's she.'

He opened his mouth to argue; changed his mind; rubbed his forehead. 'Have you told her? Have you explained?'

'Tried.'

It was all I could say. After that my throat didn't work.

What could I tell her, after all? It was the first of two pregnancies, and she was too happy. I hadn't thought a pregnancy was even possible. I warned her not to hope, but she wouldn't listen, and a few weeks later her heart broke when it died inside her. Then it broke once more. They were in the future, my dead children and Catriona's, but I'd never had the pain of hope.

Each one I buried for her. For the first I took a day's leave, given to me by Aonghas without argument, to ride far enough from Kate's caverns. I didn't want any soul it might have to linger near there. I put the corpse in the ground in spite of my beliefs, few as they were, because Catriona's beliefs were stronger and a good deal more numerous.

There was a ring of ancient stones a day's ride towards home. High on a plateau, the stones had lost their rigid geometry long ago: some had fallen, some had been split by lightning-strikes, some still stood tall. The place had a good atmosphere. I put my first son there and deprived the raptors of his tiny half-formed corpse for the sake of his grieving mother. I'd known he would die, as I knew they all would, so I tried not to weep for him too.

34

There were only half-heard snippets of news from our dun. We heard rumours and counter-rumours, but most news passed between Calman Ruadh and Kate, with little but gossip to pad it out, so none of it was reliable. Conal's clann were obedient, we heard, and dutiful, and loyal. I knew they were all that and more to Conal, but applied to Calman Ruadh it didn't sound like the clann I knew and didn't love. Conal fell on every scrap of rumour, while dreading it.

Eachann of course had a blood relative in the dun, in Raineach. Conal nagged him incessantly for news of her, but Eachann had grown evasive and haunted. When Conal at last lost his temper and yelled at the boy, Eachann confessed miserably that he knew almost as little of his mother as we did. She seemed fine. She seemed withdrawn. She was keeping something from him, that was what he thought.

Conal was haunted, and twitchy, and bad-tempered

(though he didn't lose it with me again), but he seemed more determined than ever to stick it out. He would last his year, and prove his loyalty, and regain complete authority over his own dun. He'd do it, he said, if it killed him.

Some figure of speech. Sometimes I wondered.

'When did this happen?' Aonghas asked him in a low voice one evening.

Kate had summoned the three of us from our sword practice to her great hall, and I had a feeling we were late. Not our fault. It seemed we were last to be told; every room and passage was deserted. Conal and Aonghas walked ahead; I hung back, teasing the wolves, but my ears pricked up when I heard the tone of Aonghas's voice. He was too easygoing to sound so bitter.

'When did what happen?' asked Conal.

'When did we lose so much autonomy? When did dun captains turn into henchmen?'

'Careful,' said Conal, but there was low laughter in his voice for the first time in I don't know how long. It cheered me up. He'd been sunk in darkness after that beating of me. But the bruises had faded weeks ago and the cuts had healed and my ribs fused and I looked more or less normal again. If any of us looked normal. Fact is, we all had an edgy suspicious hostility that seemed permanently etched into our faces.

Maybe, given what we saw when we turned the corner to the great hall, we had reason.

'What the *fuck* . . .'

I was still tickling Branndair's ear when Aonghas gave his exclamation of disgust. Branndair was twisting

his head and nipping at my fingers, and I wasn't paying attention, so I banged into Aonghas and we both
stumbled.

Recovering my footing, I drew my sword as Conal
and Aonghas did. The sound echoed in the silent hall. I
felt Branndair's hackles rise under my hand, I heard
Liath's low snarl, but the wolves did not move forward.
Indeed, Branndair took a pace back, growling his
furious fear. Kate rose to her feet on her dais, walked
down a step, arms extended towards us. The thing at
her side smiled as broadly as Kate did. It stood far too
close to my mother, its arm brushing hers, but Lilith
looked more charmed than revolted. It was barefoot,
bare-chested, skinny to the point of translucency. Its
coat flapped almost to its ankles, its trews were cinched
tight round a waist that was hollow scrawny muscle.
Lank hair, papery skin stretched over a concave skull,
a satisfied rictus grin.

'Gentlemen!' cried Kate. 'Swords in scabbards, please!'

Conal and Aonghas seemed dumbstruck. I saw
Conal's blade tremble in his hand, then he tightened
his grip again.

'It's a *Lammyr*.' There was utter disbelief in his
voice.

'It's my *guest*.'

I'd learned to be very suspicious of Kate's innocent
sweetness. 'Conal,' I whispered.

'There's a whole—frigging—*detachment*.' Aonghas
was so incredulous he could hardly speak.

It was true. Down the left side of the hall they stood,
their skin given a sickly cast by the torchlight. Even the

vilest of Kate's fighters hung back, keeping their distance as much as the cavern walls would let them. I could see Fearchar, his eyes wide, his spine pressed so hard against the stone wall it must have hurt. I was glad.

I looked for my friends. Sionnach stood far back, with Eili and Orach and Luthais. Sionnach's eyes were locked, expressionless, on mine; the other three couldn't take their eyes off the Lammyr. Caolas, Raonall and Feorag were near them, and Carraig and Righil stood together too. All our fighters had gathered close to one another, on the left hand side. Except for Eachann: I wondered where Eachann was. Perhaps he alone had got trapped among the crowd of Kate's fighters clustered tightly on the other side of the hall.

'Swords!' snapped Kate, the sweetness gone.

Reluctantly, slowly, we returned them to the scabbards on our backs.

'Guests,' Conal repeated, as if he'd never heard the word before.

'Yes,' said Kate. She was within ten feet of him when she stopped.

'They're *Lammyr.*'

'That line is becoming tedious, Cù Chaorach.'

'All right.' His lip curled. 'They're filth.'

Sighing, she tutted. 'Coming from you, Cù Chaorach, that shocks me. The Conal MacGregor whose tolerance for other cultures knows no limits?'

'Their culture is *death!*' He glowered at Kate, before remembering to make his features expressionless. 'Nothing else. Nothing but death.'

'They are our cousins.' Kate's gaze swivelled towards me, glittering. 'We have more in common with them than we have with, say . . . *full-mortals.*'

I didn't react. She smirked.

'I'm pleased you've tamed your firebrand of a brother, Cù Chaorach. You seem to have beaten some manners into him, and we're all grateful for that. Where was I?' Her fingertip tapped gently at her jaw. 'The Lammyr, yes. They are closer to us, and far more like us, than the full-mortals. Come, now. They can be very entertaining. A little less contempt, if you please. It's rude.'

Conal was lost for words. Slowly he walked into the hall, Aonghas at his side, me at his heels and the wolves at mine. Branndair and Liath pressed close to me.

Satisfied, Kate spun on her elegant heel and walked back to her chair, flipping out her silk dress as she sat. If cobwebs rustled, that's what it would have sounded like.

'This is Skinshanks,' she said. 'It and its fighters have pledged allegiance to me.'

As if on cue, my mother slipped her slender hand into the crook of the Lammyr's arm. It smiled down at her, a skull-smile devoid of every emotion but smugness.

'And what I admire about the pledge of a Lammyr,' Kate went on, 'is its constancy. The word of a Lammyr is binding. Its loyalty, once given, is given for the duration of its oath.'

'And why not,' hissed Conal, 'if it's offered death and prey?'

'Does it matter why?' Kate's eyes were frosted with suppressed fury. 'All I know, Cù Chaorach, is that a kept oath is better than a broken one.'

He lost it, then. 'I have kept every oath I made you!' he screamed.

'Did I say you hadn't?' The sweet smile was back. 'I admire the way you controlled your brother's excesses. I admire your intolerance of rebellion and mutiny. How he must have been humiliated, and yet you were willing to inflict it on him! That's admirable. What a pity you have so much less authority over your clann.'

'What?'

There was a horrible quality to the silence that returned to the hall. I felt my spine tense and chill, and I swallowed bile.

All world-weariness, Kate lifted an arm that might have been made of lead. Tilting her head to the side, closing her eyes as if exhausted by sadness, she languidly snapped her fingers.

The close-packed ranks of fighters on the right side of the hall parted, shuffling swiftly aside to reveal a long platform some five feet high, four nooses dangling empty in a row above it. Conal sucked in a sharp breath. Before the platform knelt four manacled prisoners.

So there was Eachann. And his brother, not more than fifteen years old, and Eachann barely any older. And there too was his mother, and his father Uilleann.

'Raineach,' I said, but not a sound came out of my mouth.

'Calman Ruadh sends me a sad tribute,' said Kate.

'What the *hell* is this?' roared Conal.

Kate shrugged lightly. At swordpoint the four captives were prodded to their feet, and at a further low-voiced order they stepped up onto a bench and then the higher platform. Eachann was still and calm; his brother was trembling but fierce-eyed and brave. I wanted to weep. The four captains who followed them slipped a noose around each neck.

'This gives me no pleasure, Cù Chaorach.' Kate pinched the bridge of her nose between her fingers, her eyes shut tight.

'Those are my people!'

'Those are rebels. Didn't you give instructions that Calman Ruadh was to be obeyed in your absence? Have you no control over your own clann?'

'Raineach?' Conal stared at his swordsmith, bewildered.

'It's true, Cù Chaorach.' Her whole slender body was tense with fear and fury. 'I'm guilty of all she says.'

'Raineach, *why?*'

'You don't live in the dun, Cù Chaorach.'

He raked his hands into his hair. 'This is not forever, Raineach.'

'But he's the man who killed my brother. I'm the one who felt my brother die.' She glared at Kate. 'If another chance was given me to kill Calman Ruadh? I'd take it. And this time I'd do it right.'

'We both would.' Dour Uilleann gave his first and last words on the subject.

Wearily, Kate shrugged.

'Conal,' I snarled, '*Eachann.*'

He seemed to get his mind back for a moment. 'Kate, not Eachann. Eachann has been under Fearchar's command since I brought him to the dun!'

'Even worse, Cù Chaorach. Snakes breed nothing

but snakes. You've kept a traitor under my roof for eight months.'

'You damn well know that's not true!' I yelled.

Instead of slamming his fist into the side of my face, Conal laid a hand on my arm. I was surprised at the gentleness of his touch. 'Have mercy, Kate. Please. I'll discipline them.'

Shutting one eye, Kate polished a fingernail with the pad of her thumb. 'No.'

Raineach's eyes met mine, and their hard defiance softened with something like affection. I'd have thrown myself at her and taken the rope off her lovely neck with my own hands, but Aonghas's arms were suddenly locked around my chest, holding me back.

'Murlainn,' he growled in my ear. 'No.'

'Cù Chaorach!' shouted Raineach, clear and proud. 'Both my sons are innocent!'

'Kate!' Conal swung towards his queen in desperation, but she only smiled, and nodded to the men behind the captives. A swift kick in the small of the back, and each of Raineach's boys jerked on the end of his rope. Then, her cold-eyed lover Uilleann.

Kate's captains were kind in those brutal kicks. She'd have preferred a gentle shove, then the swing and the struggle and the slow choke. Her brow creased in a tiny frown, but the captains were expressionless, and she had no grounds to scold them.

They might have been less merciful to Raineach, but they didn't get the chance. As soon as she saw her sons and her lover dangling by their broken necks, she leaped from the platform herself. A crack echoed, louder than

I'd have believed possible, as her neck snapped. And then there was only reverberating horror, and the quiet weeping of Eili, and the soft rhythmic creak of stretched rope.

35

I thought he would curse and weep and rage and cut his arm; I hadn't expected such ominous silence, such crushed-down fury. I had, though, expected him to come to my room, so I was still awake and dressed when he rapped on the door long past midnight, then walked in uninvited. I was sitting on the edge of the bed by the light of the fire's burned-down embers, whetting my sword blade. It was my own, my favourite sword: the one Raineach had made me.

Catriona sat cross-legged on the bed behind me. She didn't say anything, only watched me work, but her presence was endlessly comforting. We both looked up at Conal without a word as he paced our small stone room.

After a minute or more he came to stand right in front of me. Only when he was so close could I sense the trembling of his body. He took my head between his hands and forced me to look up into his eyes.

'Am I your Captain?' he whispered.

Resting my naked sword on my knees, I examined his gaze. Behind the despair and the self-hatred there was something else. Not necessarily what I'd want to see in him: that part of his soul was still lost to him. What I needed to see: that was something else.

'What I've been doing,' he said, 'it isn't loyalty. You're right. You've been right all along.'

And he was stone-cold sober, too. 'You're making me nervous.'

He didn't smile. 'You have been my conscience, Murlainn. I thank you for it. But it's time I got back my own.'

I dragged his hands down from my head. My gaze still locked on his, I pressed his right hand to my forehead. When I could bear to take it away, I brought it to my lips and kissed it.

He dropped to his knees. I only just managed to flip the sword away before he pulled me into his arms. A great time it would be to cut himself.

'I said I'd serve my year if it killed me.' Exactly one week later Conal leaned against the wall of the stabling cave, his arms folded, and looked every one of us in the eye. 'It didn't kill me. It killed Raineach.'

Nobody said a word.

'If I walk out of here I become outlaw, so I don't ask any of you to come with me.'

'If?' said Carraig, examining his dirk.

'When,' said Conal.

Carraig shrugged, sheathing his dirk. 'You needn't bother asking.'

'If you ask,' added Righil, 'we'll bloody well hit you.'

Conal let himself grin.

A horse stamped and whinnied. I glanced at it, hoping it wasn't calling to someone. It wasn't just Conal's nine surviving fighters who clustered in the flickering shadows of the stable; his whole detachment had opted for desertion. Besides them, there were some twenty more. If fighters of Kate's were here with us, their decision was already made.

There would have been fewer of them if Conal's decision had been taken a week earlier. Kate's alliance with the Lammyr had as much to do with it as any oath-severing loyalty to Conal. There were some things that even a hardened killer couldn't stomach. No doubt there were those among the Sithe who had the humanity and the soul of a Lammyr, and would enjoy their comradeship on a battlefield, but I hadn't met many. Maybe I was just lucky.

Kate had left the fortress straight after the murder of Raineach's family, accompanied by her detachment of Lammyr. No-one knew where she was going, and none of us asked. We didn't care, and she clearly didn't worry. That's how confident she was of her hold on us.

Or that's what I thought at the time.

'You want to join me, do it now.' Conal sounded emotionless. 'I can't and won't offer again. It will mean civil war, and if you want to cut me down instead, right here and now, you have every right.'

Carraig spat.

'You don't have to ask us, Cù Chaorach.' Eili leaned against the wall, her shoulder propped against Sionnach's, her gaze fierce with devotion. 'But you know that.'

Luthais and Raonall spoke together. 'Same here.'

Caolas just nodded; but then she was desperate to get back to Eorna and had only been waiting for Conal's word. Orach glanced once at me, then she nodded too.

Feorag looked utterly miserable.

'*Feorag?*' I said. 'Feorag, for gods' sake!'

'Murlainn, it's his choice. Let him make it.'

'As we all do,' said a newcomer.

There were murmurs of delight and some of disbelief as Aonghas stepped out of the shadowed doorway into the torchlight. He stretched out a hand as if for luck to touch the soft muzzle of his own horse, the one that had called to him.

Stiffening, Conal stood up straighter, pushing himself away from the wall. 'I'm not even going to ask you, Aonghas,' he said, 'so don't offer.'

'It's my choice,' mimicked Aonghas. 'Let me make it.'

Conal shook his head. 'Reultan won't come. You can't leave your bound lover.'

'Reultan will come.' Her voice was icy and unforgiving as she slipped from the darkness to Aonghas's side. Linking his fingers with hers, he kissed them. 'Though I don't want to.'

Delight lit Conal's face. 'Reultan.'

She did not smile. 'I think you're both fools,' she said, 'but you're fools I won't leave.'

She eyed Aonghas. Then, less forgivingly, Conal. They grinned at each other.

Conal led a horse from the stable; I took one for myself and boosted Catriona onto the back of another.

There were a few saddles in the tackroom, so I'd taken one for her: she wasn't the first full-mortal to be entangled with the Sithe and she wouldn't be the last.

I knew that, even then. I just didn't think hard enough about the others, and what had become of them.

We chose horses and mounted quickly enough, but we all seemed hesitant as we rode towards the exit passageway. The horses felt it, and shied and tossed their heads, catching our nervousness. What Conal had said was true: once over that threshold we were outlaw. We wanted it. But that didn't make it easy.

And no-one, it seemed, was going to make it any easier.

Three ranks of fighters on horseback faced us when we emerged into the dusk; at their head were Cluaran, Fearchar, and Cluaran's big, heavy-built, lethal lieutenant, Torc. Conal's only reaction was to take a breath and ride forward, halting his horse two sword-lengths from Cluaran's. Aonghas and Reultan rode to Conal's right side, and I rode to his left. Behind us, Conal's renegades fell into ranks. We all waited, wordless.

Conal ignored Fearchar. 'What do we do now, Cluaran? Kill one another?'

Cluaran didn't answer straight away. His eyes flickered over Conal's fighters, examining every face.

'We each have some fine fighters, Cù Chaorach. You seem to have seduced some of the finest.'

'A battle would be bloody,' said Conal, 'and destructive, and pointless.'

'Yes.' Cluaran sighed, and looked beyond Conal again. 'Anyone who wants to change their decision, change it now.'

Silence. I glanced over my shoulder at Feorag. He looked tormented.

'We do not fight today,' barked Cluaran. 'You will not be asked to kill one another tonight. Later, yes. Tonight there will be no requirement to kill your rebel friends, not even Cù Chaorach. Tomorrow they are legitimate prey for fighters of the queen, and we will hunt them down and kill them. Each of you, make your choice.'

He was looking straight at Feorag as he finished. Feorag was the only one who moved. Putting his heels to his horse, staring ahead, he rode into Cluaran's ranks and turned to face us.

Conal's face was impassive. 'It's all right, Feorag.'

~ *No. It isn't.* I looked right into my friend's eyes, and I saw them harden and chill as mine did. I knew then that one of us would kill the other.

Cluaran was his dour unconcerned self, and so was Torc. You'd think we were all standing here discussing a coney-hunt. But we could all sense the trembling rage of the other smaller man at Cluaran's side.

'This is not right,' hissed Fearchar. 'They are rebels and traitors and we should cut them down!'

'You and whose army?' I sneered. 'You couldn't fight a cat that wasn't tied to a whipping post.'

Aonghas gave a muffled snort of laughter.

His face white, Fearchar's fingers reached over his shoulder to touch his sword hilt.

'You draw that, I'll cut your fecking arm off,' I said.

Fearchar, I noticed smugly, couldn't look at me. He pretended it was contempt but every fighter there knew it was fear. He jabbed a finger at Aonghas instead.

'That one and his lover,' he snarled. 'They are the worst of the traitors. Reultan is an adviser to her queen!'

'Watch it,' said Aonghas, mildly.

'Tonight,' said Cluaran, an edge of impatience creeping into his voice, 'we let them go.'

'To what purpose?' shouted Fearchar.

'To the purpose,' said Cluaran, 'of avoiding a bloodbath. There are good fighters here. I would rather see them crawl back to Kate and beg forgiveness than spill their blood in the heather, and let them spill ours. You, Cù Chaorach,' he looked straight at Conal. 'You remain unforgiven to the end of your days. Your fighters have permission to give themselves up at any point. They will be subject to severe punishment but not execution. That goes even for your brother.'

What? There was something going on here that I did not like. I was about to spit in his face, but to my astonishment Reultan beat me to it.

Give the woman her due, she had good aim.

Keeping his temper—gods, but I liked the man— Cluaran wiped her spittle from his cheek. 'Now go. We'll call tonight a head start. After that, we'll hunt you down.'

'Not before I take my dun back from the murderer Calman Ruadh.'

Cluaran was absolutely expressionless. His face didn't flicker. 'That is your business.'

'Then we're agreed,' said Conal.

'So take my hand on it, Cù Chaorach.'

Conal didn't hesitate, but rode a few paces forward so that he was level with Cluaran, and their hard gazes locked. They had only just clasped one another's hand when Fearchar yanked his dirk from its sheath.

He did not get a chance to plunge it between Conal's shoulder blades. The big man Torc drew his sword and took his head off.

Not that I was immediately sure that was what had happened. Fearchar's head stayed balanced on his neck for all of three seconds before toppling to the ground and releasing a fountain of blood. Slowly the rest of him slid from his horse and thudded to the earth.

'Good blade,' I remarked.

Torc wiped it and sheathed it on his back, then spat on the ground. Cluaran shut his eyes and sighed through his nose. I got the feeling his patience was wearing thin.

Torc's brutish face flushed slightly. 'Can't break a truce.' He had a funny accent. I knew he came from some other country, far to the south. 'I wasn't 'aving that.'

Cluaran opened his eyes. They were watching the sky. 'Don't worry about Torc, Cù Chaorach. I'll blame you for that.'

'Fine by me. Now let us through.'

The files divided for us with no more argument. When the last of us was clear of them, Conal broke into a gallop.

We can't have gone more than five miles before I pulled up my horse, and Branndair slunk alongside me, panting. Catriona and Conal halted too, and he gestured for the others to follow Aonghas.

'What?' he said.

'We're being followed.'

'Cluaran wouldn't do that.'

'No. There's just one.'

'Friend of Fearchar's?' he asked dryly.

'Probably. I'll take him. Go with Conal, Catriona.'

'Be careful,' she said.

'Do I look like an amateur?' Grinning, I unsheathed my sword. 'Piece of piss.'

'Better be. We need to get to the dun yesterday.' With a withering look, Conal slapped the rump of Catriona's horse so that it leaped forward into a canter. As she glanced back over her shoulder, anxious, Conal rode on behind her.

I turned my horse. It was a handsome dark bay, darker now that it was sweating with nerves. A chilling thought occurred to me that our pursuer might be a Lammyr, and that I might not cope with it alone. So much for playing the alpha male and showing off to Catriona.

I drew my sword off my back and kissed its hilt for luck. 'What is it, Branndair?'

He tilted his head to look at me, grinning, tongue flopping from his mouth. Then he looked again towards the approaching rider. We could both hear the heavy hoofbeats. Disdainfully, the wolf wrinkled his muzzle, limbs stiffening, and growled.

I laughed. 'Piece of piss, eh?'

I shivered, though. No getting out of it now.

The horse that came over the darkening horizon was huge, feather-hoofed. Damn, but it looked familiar.

So did the thuggish shaven-headed fighter on its back. When he saw me he hauled the colossal horse to a halt and whipped his sword from its scabbard. The horse's head swung, its snarling mouth dripping foam, and for the first time I saw that its eyes were black and flat, the eyes of a water horse: the eyes of a killer.

Shutting my eyes, swallowing, I called the blue roan. I hadn't meant to call him till we were far closer to the dun. I hadn't thought I'd need to. I hoped he was going to get here in time.

'Oy, *shorty.*'

I raised my sword. Stupid bugger, getting me riled.

'Put it down,' yelled Torc.

'No.'

'Soddin' well put it down.'

'Aye. When you do.'

He was close enough now for me to see the thin membrane of his horse's third eyelid, flickering defensively across its black eye. Warily we circled one another, swords held to the side, Branndair snarling.

'I'm not gonna hurt you,' he barked.

I laughed in disbelief. 'Too right you're not. Any last words?'

'Not that you'll ever hear, you friggin' midget.'

'You're pissing me off now. Shall we get this over with?'

'Get what over with?' he roared. 'I'm trying to offer you my sword and all you can do is threaten me!'

'You're trying to *what?*'

'You 'eard me. Think I can go back with Cluaran after that?'

'Cluaran was just fine with what you did.' I narrowed my eyes.

'Yeah, but his boss won't be, will she? No way she

won't find out, mate. You might say I screwed up roy-
ally there.'

'That's your problem, *mate*.' I flipped my sword in
my hand and caught it.

He grinned at me, did the same flip-and-catch trick.
'I like your brother. Always did.'

I grinned back. 'That's different, then. Innit?'

Sheathing my sword, I held out my hand.

Sheathing his, he took it.

When we caught up with the others, camped for a
few hours' rest, I took him straight to Conal. Torc
looked at Aonghas, then at Reultan, then at my brother.

'Burnt my friggin' boats,' he said cheerfully. 'I'm
your bondsman now, Cù Chaorach. You idealistic—'

The word he used was blunt, and succinct, and as
Anglo-Saxon as he was. And the disgusted horror on
Reultan's face is a memory I treasure to this day.

36

They were expecting us.

What's more, the dun was impregnable. That was how it was meant to be. That was how Griogair had made it, and Conal after him, and the rest of us had pitched in. Knowing it was our own fine work didn't cheer us up.

Calman Ruadh came out with two of his lieutenants to stand on the parapet. He didn't jeer, only looked down at us with a smirk and limitless contempt.

'If he lets his block down for one second,' said Reultan coolly, 'I'll make his ears bleed.'

I gave Torc a sidelong glance, and he raised his eyebrows.

'Nice to see you entering into the spirit, Reultan,' I said.

'No point going along with this lunacy if I don't,' she retorted.

'Is it true she's a witch?' Torc muttered in my ear.

'Heavens, no,' I said loudly. 'We're not allowed to call her a *witch*.'

'Give it a rest,' said Conal, but his heart wasn't in it. He was too busy studying the walls and the defences, not to mention the three corpses dangling by their necks against the north wall. Two men and a woman. All ours.

'They weren't keen on defending the dun, Cù Chaorach,' shouted Calman Ruadh. 'Slackers. You're better off without them.'

'Don't answer him, Conal,' growled Aonghas. 'Don't give him the satisfaction.'

Conal ground his teeth but he said nothing.

I took a couple of paces forward to get a better look at the usurper. His pale red hair was cropped close to his skull. His eyes were pale too, and his eyelashes. He was a striking-looking bugger, I'll give him that.

'Calman Ruadh,' I yelled. 'When I cut off your balls should I feed them to my wolf or my horse? Or should I just feed them to you to stop your squealing?'

Reultan tutted, but Aonghas laughed. 'Murlainn, what are we going to do with you?' He dug me hard in the ribs. 'And what would we do without you?'

'Let's hope you never find out,' I said. I liked Aonghas better, now that he wasn't my captain anymore. I was never going to like Reultan, but there you go, you can't have everything.

'Be good little traitors,' shouted Calman Ruadh, 'and wait there till I decide what to do with you. Come any closer to the dun, this one joins her father.'

He yanked a small figure to the parapet beside him.

'Gods,' I said. Nobody else managed to speak.

Uilleann's nine-year-old daughter, the one he'd fathered on a wild night in the dun after a battle. She wasn't Raineach's, but Raineach had been fond enough of her to look after her when her mother was killed. I remembered her in the forge as a three-year-old, half-hiding behind Eili, daringly sticking out her tongue at me. The child's hands were tied in front of her. She was trying not to tremble. There was a thin rope around her neck.

'I let this one live.' Calman Ruadh was loving this. 'Thought she might come in handy.'

'I made up my mind,' I growled bitterly. 'He can eat his own.' But I'd lost my sense of humour now. No-one else laughed, either.

'I'll dangle her over the wall. Wouldn't want to break her pretty neck, it's awful fragile. Now, wait there like I told you. You leave, she dangles, but I need a while to plan some entertainments. Cù Chaorach, I'm looking forward to gelding your brother with a blunt knife.'

'Shit,' I muttered. 'Me and my big mouth.'

'Anybody wants to throw themselves on Kate's mercy, that's fine with me.' Conal looked like a black dog was biting his backside.

Some of them must have been thinking about it, but nobody said anything. Yet.

'Surprise attack?' said Righil. He was reciting a rule-book for the sake of it.

'You want to watch the child choke?' asked Conal bleakly. 'The last of Uilleann's offspring? I don't.'

'Somebody needs to open the dun gate,' said Raonall. 'Otherwise we're stuffed.'

'That's what they tried to do.' Carraig jerked his head at the dun wall, where the crows were squabbling and hacking at the three bodies. 'Nobody else will get near it.'

'Oh, yes. Yes, they will.' I rubbed my temples with my thumbs, wondering why I was opening my mouth again, after what happened last time. 'I'll do it.'

Conal said, 'You can't.'

'I've told you before, don't patronise me.' I wouldn't look at him. 'Of course I'll do it. I'll climb the wall and open the sodding gates, all right?'

They were all staring at me, none with more horror than Catriona.

'You want to die?' barked Conal.

'No.' I went on fiercely rubbing my temples, glaring at the ground. 'I don't want to be gelded, either. However sharp the knife is.'

Conal watched me for a long time. I didn't meet his gaze but I could feel it.

'All right,' he said at last.

'All right.' My heart sank.

'And since you're into miracles? Get the girl out first.'

Of all the people I might have expected at my shoulder that night, she was the last.

'You know the girl's as good as dead,' said Reultan crisply.

'That's what I like about you. You're so positive and so damn nurturing.' I stared at the dun wall as I rubbed wet earth across my naked chest and arms and belly. Behind me Catriona was dealing with my back and shoulders. 'Can you cast a spell on that moon, by any chance?'

It was like a great white lantern. Couldn't have been a worse night. I had doubts about getting across the stretch of empty machair that lay between me and the dun, let alone up the walls.

'No,' she said. Thoughtfully she eyed me. 'You missed a bit. There. You're as pale as a slug. He'll kill the girl whether Conal yields or not.'

'I'm aware of that.' I had to say it through gritted teeth.

Catriona rubbed mud down my spine, making me shiver. I loved the way she wasn't complaining or whining or trying to talk me out of it. Half of me wished she would. She was ignoring Reultan, and Reultan was pretending Catriona didn't exist.

Calman Ruadh had us besieged, despite appearances. There was nothing Conal could do, and in the morning his men would begin to drift away, either to go into the wilds, captainless, or to throw themselves on Kate's mercy as she had always known they would.

Or Conal could rally them and make his attack, and sacrifice the child. She was going to die anyway, everyone knew it. His fighters would think better of him for it, or at least they'd trust even more to his will and his strength. Conal, though, would never forgive himself.

He might do it. I didn't think he would but he might, and it would kill his soul. Cold iron within: what we dreaded most. I had to try this for him, and I had to do it for Raineach. Stupid. It wasn't as if Raineach or indeed Uilleann would ever care again.

'It'll be next to impossible to block and concentrate on climbing,' remarked Reultan.

Catriona's fingers stilled on my spine, trembling.

Damn the woman. I rolled my eyes. 'I'm also aware of *that*.'

'So don't even try,' she said coolly. 'I'll deal with it.'

Hesitating, I eyed her mistrustfully. 'You can do that?'

'It won't be easy, but I suggest you trust me. You haven't really got an option.'

'I don't care who your mother is, you can't break into the mind of every fighter on those battlements.'

'You're right: I can't affect them all. But I can do it to you. The only thing is for me to block your mind.'

'Let you,' I said slowly, 'block my mind?'

She shrugged. 'Take it or leave it.'

I did not like the idea of Reultan being anywhere near my mind, let alone messing about with it. Catriona's hand lay on my back like a warning, but Reultan was right: I didn't have a choice. 'All right. You get me killed, I swear I'll come back and haunt you.'

'I quite believe it, but you won't scare me. I shall throw wine goblets through your wailing insubstantial ghost. Now you'd better get started. You'll have to take your time. As far as their eyes are concerned, you're on your own.'

As she stalked off, Catriona slipped her arms round my waist. 'I hate her.'

'Know the feeling.'

'Is she telling the truth? Will she protect you?'

I put an arm round her shoulder. 'Don't know. I'd better get on with it anyway.'

'You're cold.'

'I'll soon warm up.' All the same I put my arms round her and let her body heat soak into me. Her face was pressed against my neck. Must be getting dirty. I didn't mind. She didn't seem to either. Still, even through the mud I could feel her face was wet.

'You'll make me streaky,' I said.

Her jerky laugh was that little silent gasp she used to make when she was mute. 'Please come back,' she mumbled.

'I love you,' I said. And then the moon slid behind a wisp of cloud, and I had to make myself pull away.

Conal and Reultan and Aonghas were watching me. As I turned towards the dun and took a breath, I felt something like sheet ice slam down across my brain. I winced. It felt so strange I curled my bare toes into the coarse damp grass, just to ground myself in reality again. And then, while the moon hid its face and dark shadow patterned the machair, I ran.

37

I'm under no illusions. I know what got me across the machair without twenty arrows in my ribcage. Undoubtedly I couldn't have done it without Reultan, but that would not have been enough. And my fieldcraft is good, but that wouldn't have been enough either. Not without the help of Calman Ruadh's men.

I ran low and fast, half-crouched, darting from shadow to shadow and flattening myself against the earth at any movement on the parapet. I wore only trews, mud, and a dirk at my waist. My head was already beginning to throb with Reultan's intrusion, but that was a pain I could ignore. At least I didn't have to worry about maintaining a block of my own against searching hostile minds. Adrenaline screamed through my veins, and I had that feeling again of being naked and flayed. Any of the guards on the parapet could turn at any moment, look my way, but they didn't. Some of it was luck. Most of it was arrogance. They knew they'd won.

Two of them turned and leaned over the parapet. I lay in a scrape of earth, still as a hare, watching them as they bellowed insults at Conal and his men. There was laughter behind them, and another figure was dragged up to the parapet wall, hands bound, a rope round his neck. I was glad that at least it was an adult figure, because they looped the rope round a buttress of stone, wrestled him to the edge, and lowered him slowly. The man kicked and struggled, choking on the end of the rope in the moonlight. It lasted a long time, and he died to the sound of their jeers, but it's a pity he couldn't appreciate how much his death helped me. I got to the base of the dun wall while the moon lit his death struggles and Calman Ruadh's fighters hooted their derision at Conal. Nobody looked at a shadow moving across the machair into the deeper shadow of the dun.

I sat with my back against the dun wall and looked at the moon for a while. I needed to get my breath back, and I needed to think. I was surprised at how afraid I was.

'Smaller one next time, Cù Chaorach!' I heard Calman Ruadh's voice echo across the machair. 'Keep your distance.'

I held my breath till it hurt, waiting for him to shout *The girl's as good as dead and so's your sneaking brother*, but there was only silence, apart from occasional laughter and a muffled weeping from within the dun. Conal must have tried a feinting move, or even an advance. The death of the prisoner had been nothing to do with me, unless he'd done it to distract them. They hadn't seen me. Don't be such a damn coward, I told myself.

This wasn't the keep wall. I'd climbed this a hundred times or more. No-one could see me. No-one could see me. What was I scared of? Not seeing Catriona again? Dying now and leaving her to live and die without me? Abandoning her to Calman Ruadh and his men? I hoped Conal would have the sense to cut her throat before she was taken. I hoped he'd have the time.

Now I needed to stop thinking.

I wiped my palms on my trews and ran them over cold remorseless stone. I knew this stone, it was hacked out of my land, the blood and sweat of my ancestors ran through it like veins of quartz. The stone was fine. It was mine. My fingertips found a crevice; my toes found another. I climbed.

I hadn't bargained on how much my head would hurt. Reultan's block was like ice against my brain. Halfway to the top I had to stop and hang there like a desperate spider, grinding my forehead into the wall to make the stinging stop. I wondered if she was doing it deliberately. For long moments I couldn't see for the pain, and I twisted my forehead against the stone till the skin broke. At least it took my mind off the terrible throbbing pain inside it, but now there was a trickle of blood running into my eyebrows, and in seconds I was having to blink it out of my eyes.

Voices above me. I could hear every word, not that any of it was any use. It was guard gossip, casual and cruel. Three fighters, I realised, pressing myself flat against the wall, pain screaming in the joints of my fingers and toes. The sound of them was so clear they must have been leaning over the wall. And then the voices faded, and footsteps rang above me, and the dreadful pain in my head eased.

Reultan. She must have seen the guards moving in my direction.

~ *Thanks*, I managed to tell her.

There was no answer.

The stone was better cut and dressed towards the top, and it was that much harder to find purchase. It was still a familiar climb, and if I hadn't been cold, and scared, and half-blind with blood and darkness, it would have been easy. It was the stone of my land but I did not want its harshness to be the last thing I felt beneath the palm of my hand. I tried not to think about Catriona's skin, the silky bristle of her hair, the bony beautiful shape of her skull. I tried so hard not to think about them that my right hand found the flat ridge of the parapet before I realised how high I was.

I didn't know what was above me, but there was no warning bolt of pain from Reultan. Taking the deepest breath I ever took in my life, I hauled myself up and over the edge of the parapet, and flopped to my belly in its shadow on the battlement.

Already I couldn't believe my luck in being up here and not being dead yet. I thought Reultan might leave me to my own block now, but she didn't. I suppose it helped Conal know where I was, and besides, the pain of her intrusion had dwindled again to a dull ache.

The gate itself was well-guarded, but not against me. The sentries around the perimeter walls were more sparsely placed, and certainly the nearest one to me was not expecting to be taken from behind.

I slit his throat and held him in an embrace like a

lover till his blood had leaked out of him, then lowered
him silently to the ground. No point clamping my hand
over his mouth: it wasn't as if he could speak, and if
you're quick the shock stops them calling with their
mind. As he slumped, I saw his face, and cold horror
flowed down my spine. He was barely older than me.

He fought for Calman Ruadh, I thought as blood
slammed in my ears. He fought and killed for Calman
Ruadh. I shut my eyes, opened them again, waiting
for the sickness to pass. This fighter was older than
the little girl, older than Raineach's stepchild. Older
than *her*.

Not quite twice as old.

He fought for Calman Ruadh. He was at war and so
was I. More conscience and I would fail. Swiftly I
turned from him, and ran.

At a flight of steps that led down to the first courtyard, I slithered down the ten-foot drop where the
steps joined the wall. That's where I got luckiest. There
was a small room just off the courtyard, no more than
a cramped space with a shelf and a cot where guards
could grab a brief sleep between spells of duty when
the dun was under siege. It was occupied now, though
not for its intended use.

Sorcha was a tough bitch who had joined in beating
me more than once when we were children. She had
hair the colour of a polished horse chestnut, and eyes
that seemed to hold every colour of the moor. Right
now they were more like a moor on fire, and she was
glaring such hate at her attacker I was surprised he
wasn't wincing. I dare say she'd have been breaking his
face if her hands weren't bound. Now I had my

conscience silenced. They were not young. They must know right from wrong. Yet they did not just kill for Calman Ruadh; they tormented for him.

I was glad Sorcha's attacker was preoccupied: it made it stupidly easy for me to kill his companion, who was waiting his turn in agitation. She watched me do it, and she never let on, never blinked, her face never altered its twisted mask of rage and pain and despair. What a girl. I liked her for the first time. I reckon she probably liked me for the first time too, especially when I laced my fingers into her surprised attacker's hair, pulled his head back, and dug my blade hard into his throat.

She spat out his blood and grinned. 'Never thought I'd be glad to see you, shortarse.'

I took her shoulder and pulled her up before she had time to refuse my help. 'Watch your mouth or I'll put you back.' Holding her against me, I sawed through the cords binding her wrists. She was tense as her bonds had been. I half expected her to bite my shoulder.

'Aye, right.' Sorcha flinched with pain, then, as if furious with herself, made herself stagger to her feet and drag her trews and shirt back into place. Her trembling hands were mottled and swollen, but she clenched and unclenched her fists till the circulation was back and the shaking stopped. I had to admire her; she must have been hurting. Her eyes glittered with furious tears and there was a blackening bruise down one side of her face. I was shocked: this was not a weapon of war with the Sithe and never had been, but Sorcha must have been a damn sight angrier than I was. Two now-ownerless swords were propped in their scabbards just inside the door, so she took one and drew it. Even I couldn't watch what she did next.

Wincing, I gave her a look out of one eye. 'Finished?'

'Aye. I wish they were still alive to feel that.'

'Sorry, I'm sure.'

'Don't apologise. Your timing's great. Though it could have been twenty minutes better. Who's with you?'

'You want the good news or the bad news?'

She swore.

'Hey, don't worry.' I winked at her. 'The good news is I'm a one-man army. Where are the other fighters?'

'Everyone who refused to fight Conal is locked in the store rooms. That's every one of us, by the way. Naturally,' she added dryly, 'the stores have been moved to the guard quarters.'

'What about the others?'

Strictly speaking everyone over the age of fifteen counted as a fighter. But apart from the children, there were some who simply were not fighters, either by inclination or profession.

Sorcha looked uneasy. 'I don't know. We were split up days ago. Something changed. There was a sickness. It passed, but they said some people were infected, and others were carriers, it was a plague. They were lying, of course. They split us fighters from non-fighters, no other reason.'

My stomach felt hollow. I was about to curse, but I changed my mind. 'Sorcha. I really, really need a diversion.'

'Murlainn, right this moment you could ask me to kiss you and I wouldn't poke out your eye. Don't ask tomorrow, though.' She winked. 'What do you want me to do?'

38

That great silver lantern of a moon was unforgiving, but no-one was watching for a single fighter strolling round the courtyard perimeter and ducking into a side alley. I could almost hear her whistling. From the shadow beneath the steps I watched Sorcha disappear towards the stores, two stolen swords slung across her back, and in my head I wished her luck. That would have to be good enough. At the very least, she'd enjoy dealing with the guards who held her comrades captive like so many cattle.

Calman Ruadh did not expect revolt from within, and though someone would miss those two fighters soon, they'd obviously been expected to take their time with Sorcha. The young guard on the parapet was more of a worry, but I'd dragged him as well as I could into hiding. I knew the crannies and shadows of my own dun; I wouldn't be much use if I didn't.

From my hiding place I couldn't see the gate, so I took a deep shaking breath and slithered back up to the battlement. When my fingertips were hooked over the edge, two more guards passed, but I hung there, unmoving, till they'd passed, then hauled myself up and scrambled behind a buttress. I was appropriately angry now, and it was overcoming my fear. I had no business crawling round my own father's dun like a worm, and Calman Ruadh would pay for making me do it. I'd have liked to feel the weight of a sword on my back instead of one small dirk at my waist, but what mattered for me now was speed and cunning. The dirk would have to do.

Now I could see the gradient of the battlement where it began to rise over the arch of the gate. It swarmed with Calman Ruadh's fighters, but that didn't matter. The important thing was the great wheel that lifted the gate. The pulleys that operated it were well-guarded too, but at least I could see my path to it, and I was hoping to manage without the pulleys. Piece of piss. A run, and a rope to sever, and a mad leap, and the hope that my weight would carry the wheel round. Piece of piss.

Gods. I shut my eyes. I must be insane.

I edged closer, and closer yet. I had to be in position when Sorcha returned, or she'd never let me hear the end of it in the afterlife. When I was as close as I thought I could manage without actually tapping the nearest guard's shoulder and introducing myself, I stopped. I pressed back, trying to make myself part of the wall. Pain lanced through my head from temple to temple. Reultan knew I had reached my endgame. Her block was ferocious and no doubt impenetrable, but it hurt like teeth round my brain.

The nape of my neck prickled. Block or no block, I'd been seen. I knew what a stare felt like, and this one could have cut me in two.

Looking to my left, I saw her. She sat against the wall, her bound hands hooked around her knees. Her face was bruised, her hair dishevelled, and her eyes were huge and hostile.

And my mind was blocked. Shit. I lifted my finger to my lips.

An assessing stare. Narrowing of her eyes. Then she stuck out her tongue.

The child was guarded, but they weren't taking any notice of her. I smiled at her. She didn't smile back.

Please, I thought, please don't let the guards turn in the next thirty seconds. As I slunk down beside her, she moved her wrists towards me, and I sawed carefully at the cords. Impatiently she shook her hands, and though the blade of my knife nicked her before I could pull it back, she didn't flinch or gasp, just glared at me meaningfully. Grinning, I worked my dirk under the cords and sawed hard this time. It took seconds, and I cut her, but her hands were free and she grinned back. Then she grew serious, and lifted her eyebrows.

I gave a tiny shake of my head, and looked towards the courtyard.

The whole place was still. A bored sentry yawned, kicked at a loose stone, turned on her heel towards us.

My heart practically choked me, and the child pressed against my side. Instinctively I wrapped an arm round her, but the guard didn't have time to catch sight of us. There were yells and cries of rage in the courtyard, and the ring of sword blades. The guards who didn't instantly leap down to the courtyard waited up on the battlement, swords drawn and watching. Sorcha's ban-Sithe shriek of defiance split the air, and the released fighters behind her gave a howl of fury, and then the two forces collided.

Sorcha's makeshift army was seriously outnumbered, but they were seriously angry too, and humiliated, and out for revenge. This was as good as it was going to get.

'Run,' I told the child, and grabbing her arm, I shoved her towards the steps. She only had to stay out of their grip for minutes, and the fighters in the court-yard weren't going to bother with her. For myself, I sprinted for the wheel that opened the gate.

The distracted guards saw me then, all right. One yelled, and brought up his sword too late, and my dirk was in his side. I yanked it out just as his friend came for me, and leaped and rolled, slashing at his ham-strings as he tried to turn. Then I was up on a buttress and taking a flying spring over the third as he ducked reflexively. And I was running, running for the wheel, and leaping into space.

I think I shut my eyes. Stupid, but true. I crashed into solid wood, found purchase more by luck than judgment, and dragged on a jutting spoke, legs flailing. The rope that held it jerked taut, and I slashed fero-ciously at it. The blade found purchase; grimly I sawed it back and forth.

It gave sooner than I expected and I swung wildly, not just trying to move the wheel but trying to make myself a moving target too, as arrows whined around me. Beyond the gate I could hear the roar and thunder of Conal's fighters storming across the machair. Oh, gods, the gate had to open. It had to open *now*.

Trouble was, up here on the wheel, the leverage wasn't the same. The chains we used to pull on it hung down fifteen feet and more; that was what turned the thing. My weight was dragging it, slowly and surely, but not fast enough. I kicked and swore, felt it give, grabbed for the next spoke, kicked again. It turned, inch by inch, and an arrow slashed across my thigh. It enraged me. I screamed at the wheel, kicked, grabbed another spoke. The thunder of horses was close. Too close. The gate had opened inches. Wide enough for a ferret, not a horse.

I wasn't going to do it.

Something slammed into me and I thought I was dead. Shock almost made me lose my grip on the spokes, but I fumbled, regained it. The thing hanging round my neck, arms almost choking me, was a nine-year-old child. I laughed, though it came out like a gasping cough.

See? I didn't need extra height. I didn't need extra weight. Not when there was another shortarse to help me. The wheel groaned, and swung round, and I managed to clamber up two, three more spokes. Grunting, I climbed again, the weight of the child almost killing me now. Her legs were locked round my waist, clinging on like a human grappling hook.

The arrows had stopped flying so thickly, and I saw the courtyard was filling. They could not concentrate on us any more, dangling like bowshot-practice, because Conal's troops were forcing the gate wide and slashing their way through Calman Ruadh's fighters.

Out of the corner of my eye, through blood and sweat, I could make out only the fast flash and glitter of blades, the agile twist and leap of bodies. I heard screams, and war-cries, and above it the agitated howl of Calman Ruadh.

'*Get the* CHILD. *THE CHILD*. HANG THAT FECKING GIRL . . .'

I smiled at her, and she smiled back, still locked round my neck. My arms were about to give way.

'Good girl,' I said. 'Thanks.'

Her smile faded. 'I think my father's dead.'

I thought about lying. 'Yes,' I said, 'he is. But he's proud of you.'

The smile came back, and then my sweating palms lost their grip and we fell together.

I managed to twist so that she fell on me, not that it did my lungs much good. If the fighters around me hadn't been so preoccupied, I'd have had it, because I couldn't breathe for a while. We lay there like corpses, the girl on top of me, and that's what they all must have thought we were. At last I sucked air into my lungs in a great whistling gasp. I took her arms.

'Run,' I said. 'Do as you're told this time.'

I caught the flash of her pixie-grin and then she was off, running and lost among the dun alleyways. I couldn't worry any longer. I snake-crawled to the nearest corpse and wrenched the sword out of its bloody fingers.

There comes a moment, luckily, when instinct takes over. Later that dawn I found that the arrow-wound in my thigh was quite bad, but I didn't feel it then, and it wasn't bad enough to bleed me to death. I just fought like I was fighting Eorna, like I wanted to thrash him, like my clann was watching and wanted to see me beaten, like I wanted to prove them wrong. My flying bare feet found bellies and throats and other points where flesh was soft; my blade whipped and snapped with a precision I couldn't have achieved if I was thinking about it. I was in a trance of ecstasy. Ecstasy.

Later I thought: is this how it feels for a Lammyr? But I didn't think it then. Just as well. It might have stopped me in my tracks.

I saw Sionnach and Eili, fighting like mirror images, catching one another's moves and echoing them with a deadly efficiency. I saw Aonghas, and Reultan, and Sorcha; Carraig, Righil, and Orach. No fast moves from Torc, who was simply hacking his blunt and brutal way through the fighters who came at him. Most of Conal's fighters were off their horses now; being mounted had given them an advantage but now they were hungry for close-quarters duelling. Nor did my horse, or Conal's, or Torc's, need a rider to encourage them to join a battle. The blue roan had one of Calman Ruadh's fighters by the throat, shaking him like a dog with a rat.

I needed to find Conal.

Reultan's block was gone now; she had abandoned me to my own efforts, and fair enough. At least my head had stopped hurting. The minds around me were a chaos of violence and fury, and I couldn't lock onto Conal at all. Furiously I rubbed my eyes. They were blurred once more with blood; the wound on my forehead had split open again.

There. I caught a brief glimpse of him as he leaped and turned in the air, then he was gone, and I had to fight my way through to him. Someone else was doing the same, hacking down Raonall to get closer to Conal. Raonall staggered back with Calman Ruadh's sword in his guts, cursing his killer in a spray of bloody spittle as he stumbled and went down, jerking.

Luthais's scream: I never heard anything like it. The man hurtled though the ranks, at the last minute springing up to run on heads and shoulders towards Calman Ruadh, who reached swiftly to whip his sword from Raonall's belly. The wide slash as he brought it round just missed Luthais's ankles. He was quick to recover his balance, though, and Luthais's rage was too wild with grief. He hacked violently, and missed, and Calman Ruadh's backswung blade half-severed his head from his neck.

The clash had brought Calman Ruadh closer to me than to Conal, though only just.

'Mine!' I screamed.

'No!' yelled Conal.

'*Mine! I claim him!*'

All right. That may have been impetuous. Conal stared at me, not just livid but horrified, but I had no time to endure a bollocking from him, and he had no time to give me one. I turned and raised my sword as Calman Ruadh, grinning, came towards me.

A space cleared around us. Partly it was that the battle was reaching its end, and only the last small deadly squabbles continued around us. Partly the survivors were intrigued that I'd been stupid enough to claim Calman Ruadh, and in front of so many witnesses, too. It was between him and me, now, till one of us was dead. No-one had the right to intervene on a claimant's behalf. True, accidents happened. But unless Calman Ruadh had an unforeseen heart attack right now, or a meteor fell on his head, it was up to me to kill him. A claimant laid his claim, and took the consequences.

I hate these ridiculous traditions.

I rubbed my eyes with my arm, not letting go of my double-handed grip on my looted sword as we circled each other. Damn it, I wasn't even carrying my own weapon.

That reminded me of Raineach. My heart chilled as I looked into her killer's pale eyes.

A child crouched by the steps, her eyes fixed on me. Of course: she still couldn't do as she was told and stay out of the way. My small comrade who'd been due to hang.

'And she will,' smiled Calman Ruadh, reading my thoughts. 'After I'm done with you.'

'After I put in all that effort?' I said. 'Not bloody likely.'

'Don't be scared, I'm not going to kill you. I still want the fun of gelding you.'

'What, like my friend Sorcha gelded your man in the guardhouse there?'

He can't have known. Calman Ruadh frowned, his gaze searching out Sorcha. She gave a yell to attract his attention, and grinned, and gave him two fingers.

'He was my cousin, Murlainn,' he snarled.

'Well, he wouldn't be adding to your family tree,' I told him. 'Even if he wasn't dead.'

'You kiss my sword,' he said, 'I use a sharp knife.'

'You kiss my backside,' I retorted, 'I won't let you suffer.'

He came at me. He was fast and flying. I ducked and rolled and was on my feet again, lashing out and spinning back out of his reach. I heard his blade cut the air just in time to bend out of reach of his strike, and when his backswing went at my hamstrings I jumped high. I could have had his head off then if I'd been fast enough, but I wasn't. The sword in my grip was heavier than my own, and it felt clumsy in my grip. I swung at him and he somersaulted backwards, landed like an elegant cat and eyed me.

I breathed hard. He smiled.

Hell, he was fast. He flew at me again, light and lithe. He knew I was having trouble with the sword. It was all I could do to parry his rain of strikes, and I didn't have a moment to riposte. He beat me back almost casually, and as I leaped to save my feet being severed at the ankles, I tumbled clumsily back and came to rest on one knee, unbalanced. Lightly he swung his sword across my ribs, smiling, then backed off.

I thought I was dead. When I felt the blood swell and trickle down my belly, I knew it was a flesh wound, a calculated insult. I was no good. He'd cut me to bits before he killed me.

I got to my feet, but panic was creeping in now, and with it pain. I could feel the slash across my chest, my own blood mingling with dried mud and sweat. Now I could feel the hole in my thigh, and even the irritating sting of the wound on my forehead. My head swam. There had been no need for me to die, no need for me to claim the man. Idiot that I was.

The watchers were wordless: the only sounds were rasping breath, and the moaning whimpers of the wounded. And then, the clean sibilant sigh of a blade sliding out of its scabbard.

I blinked blood out of my eyes and stared over Calman Ruadh's shoulder towards the sound. Idiot or not, I would rather die than face the shame of an intervention, and I was about to yell in fury at whoever had drawn his sword.

It was Conal, of course, but it wasn't his own sword he'd drawn. That was in his left hand. In his right was the blade he'd just taken from the second scabbard strapped on his back. Raising it, he smiled.

~ *He's yours. So kill him.*

I dropped the strange sword. And I sprinted empty-handed at Calman Ruadh.

I had enough time to see shock dawn in his eyes, and confusion, before his confidence reasserted itself. Then, as he raised his own sword to kill me, I saw the flash of a thrown blade spinning in the first murky dawn.

I reached for it as it passed me, snatched it from the air, flung myself skywards and came at him from above. He was looking up at me in disbelief as I drove Raineach's beautiful blade down into his throat, let go of the hilt, and twisted to make my own cat-landing.

Calman Ruadh fell awkwardly to his knees, clutched at the hilt beneath his jaw, then pitched forward and died.

39

There was no time for feeling pleased with myself. There was only a moment to plunge my head and shoulders into a water trough, scrub off the worst of the mud and blood, then strip the shirt off a corpse. My hands shook, so Conal took the shirt from my hands, helped me put it on, then pulled me into a brief fierce embrace.

'Where's Branndair?' I asked.

'With Catriona. Don't worry. I thought it was the best place for him. In case . . .'

He didn't finish. He didn't need to. Branndair was a Sithe wolf, and he was my wolf. He'd know to protect her, and he'd know, when he was no longer able to protect her, that it was time to kill her as he'd kill a deer.

'Thanks,' I said.

He laughed. 'You really don't need to mention it.' He hugged me again. 'I owe you.'

I felt terrible. Everything hurt, most of all my head, and I was furious, because this was not the moment.

No-one had seen the children or the non-fighters, and if they hadn't emerged when the battle-sounds died down, it meant they couldn't.

'Great hall,' said Righil sourly. He was kneeling by Raonall's corpse. Its open eyes were locked on the remains of Luthais, and Righil carefully drew the eyelids shut before he stood up.

'Yes,' said Conal.

Half of Calman Ruadh's fighters had withdrawn there. That's why it was over so fast. I couldn't help thinking—and I knew Conal was thinking it too—that they must have had a reason. Worse, they probably had a strategy.

So it was with naked blades in our hands that we approached the great hall of our own dun. It was quiet, even as Conal stepped over the threshold. I was at his shoulder so I saw it all at exactly the same time he did.

Kate sat in the chair that had been Griogair's for so many centuries. Even Conal hadn't chosen to sit in it yet. Her hands were steepled beneath her chin and she scrutinised each of Conal's fighters as they filed in behind him. Lilith stood at her side, the usual smirk fixed to her beautiful face. In three ranks on each side of Kate stood the remnants of Calman Ruadh's army, and in front of them were lined the Lammyr, thirty or more, and Skinshanks at their head.

Damn. I was afraid of that.

In front of the Lammyr, kneeling, chained together, were the children of Conal's dun and the remainder of his clann.

Kate sighed, frowned slightly, then looked up.

'Let's talk,' she said sweetly.

Conal walked forward, but when some of his fighters tried to follow he thrust his hand back in a vicious gesture to keep them back. I wasn't about to be put off so easily. Catching him up, I walked at his side.

'Now,' she said, clapping her hands lightly as he came to a halt in front of her. 'I don't want you dead, you fool. I still have hopes of you. Take a new exile and be glad of it.'

He stared at her, wordless. I could feel the hate coming off him.

'If you don't, I'll simply kill all of these here and now.' Her sweeping gesture encompassed all our chained clann. 'My loyal Lammyr will enjoy the sport, and you won't be fast enough to stop it. By the way,' she tossed her hair back, 'I'm glad Skinshanks's lieutenant didn't succeed in having you burned. I was disappointed at the time, but really, truly, I'm glad.'

'And at least it had fun,' Skinshanks said in its rattlebone voice, giving my brother a dry grin. 'All those dreary sermons, all that moralising. All that miserabilist lecturing. It enjoyed itself no end. And burnings to boot!'

Kate laughed. 'It certainly had fun with our humble dun captain. Now, do hurry up and decide, Cù Chaorach.' Her fingers fluttered in the direction of the captives.

'If I take exile, what guarantees do you give me?'

I couldn't believe it. I knew I couldn't bear it.

'Guarantees?' asked Kate in surprise.

'Guarantees of this dun's preservation.' Conal spoke through gritted teeth. 'Guarantees of the safety of my clann. Guarantees that they'll keep their autonomy.'

She looked at Lilith. 'Do you know anything about guarantees, Lilith?'

'None. There are none.'

I thought I'd heard venom in my mother's voice before. I realised I hadn't heard the half of it. 'You deserve no guarantees,' she hissed, 'you filthy damned traitor. You can ask for none. Take your exile and be glad you're alive. You won't fight us. You have too much to lose.' Lilith pointed a long fingernail at the captives. 'So do they. How dare you threaten your queen's life?'

I lost it. 'Not hers, bitch!'

I went for her and I think I might have killed her. I think it might even have been what she wanted, but Conal must have known what I was about to do. I didn't get within a sword's length of my mother before his arms were locked around me, wrestling me back.

'Have I taught you nothing?' he growled. 'Don't bring that curse on yourself. If anyone is to kill her it'll be me.'

'Such arrogance!' cried Kate angrily. 'Such presumption!' She rose to her feet.

'Lilith has no hold on Seth!' yelled Conal. 'He's no part of her!'

Kate glanced at Lilith, held out her hand, and Lilith stepped forward. She walked down one step, two steps towards me. I stared, confused.

Lilith unwound her elaborately braided hair. The ribbons fell away, and the strings of pearls, and the silky tumble of hair fell around her face, and she smiled.

Conal backed away. I just stared, feeling nothing at all. Lilith's hair was streaked and striped and glossed with silver. Her face was clear and unlined, alive with youth, but my mother was months from death.

'I have a message for your mother, Cù Chaorach.'

'Lilith,' he said, and put a hand on my rigid arm. 'Don't do this. Gods. Don't do this.'

'Your mother wants to die, Cù Chaorach, doesn't she?'

'Lilith.'

'But she doesn't have the devotion to die.' Lilith half-turned to smile back at Kate; the queen walked down the steps to stand behind her, never taking her eyes off Lilith. 'Bound or not, Leonora does not have the *need* to die. The courage. She does not have the *love*.'

'It's love keeping her here, Lilith!'

'Not for Griogair. For someone who doesn't exist yet! That's not *love*, it's self-importance. It's not good enough, Cù Chaorach; not good enough. I have the courage. I have the love. I'm going to him.'

'*Lilith!*'

'How much headstart will she give me, Conal?'

Lilith stepped back into Kate's arms, and Kate's fingers ran once through my mother's hair, then drew it aside. She kissed Lilith's neck, and pressed her cheek against hers, and then she kissed her greying hair.

'No,' said Conal.

'Tell her, Cù Chaorach.'

Kate's arm slid round Lilith, holding her in a close embrace. Smiling, Lilith closed her eyes, but not for long. She opened them again to look straight into mine, then tilted up her chin. The blade in Kate's hand flashed across her proudly raised throat.

Blood spat from it in a broad spray. There was no avoiding it. My mother's lifeblood was in my eyes, and my hair; it was in my mouth and some of it had run into my throat. I'd swallowed, convulsively, before I could even think about dodging it or wiping it off or spitting it out. Lilith's eyes were locked on me as they went dead, but she was still smiling, and she didn't fall. Kate cradled her in one blood-soaked arm as she looked up at me and Conal.

'You're mine,' she murmured. 'It'll be a long time coming, but your lives belong to me. Both of you.' Sweeping Lilith's body into her arms, she passed my mother as if she was a featherweight into the arms of Skinshanks. It shivered with pleasure at the touch of death. 'It will be worth the wait, Cù Chaorach, Murlainn. My patience is limitless.'

'You ask too much, Kate,' he hissed. 'For *nothing!*'

She came down the steps again to stand close to him, her voice soft and deadly. 'I don't object to a war here and now, Cù Chaorach. We shall fight, and I do not care if every fighter in the place dies. I will sacrifice every single one: yours and mine. I loved Lilith, you know that. You've seen now that I have no compunctions. You have far too many. Now take your exile, and don't ask me again for promises. You'll get none.' Her lovely lip curled in a snarl. 'You. Have. No. Choice.'

'No. But he does have me.'

At last, at last, a spark of true terror in Kate's eyes. It was gone in an instant, but I know I saw it. I saw that first, and then I saw the raven gliding in circles above Kate, I saw its black-marble eye and heard its cackling scornful laugh. It landed on Leonora's outstretched arm as she stopped between her son and me.

Well, well. It was a learning curve: all these detested enemies I was suddenly finding I liked. I'd certainly never been happier to see this witch. Though where she'd sprung from, the gods alone knew, because Conal looked as shocked as Kate did, and so did the fighters who thronged the door and the passageway beyond. Aonghas actually rubbed his eyes and made his mouth an O. Comedian.

'So,' said Kate, recovering her composure. 'We're going for death, and the destruction of this dun. Am I right?'

Leonora sighed, flicked specks of cobweb and earth from her coat, and tickled the raven's throat. 'You've never been right in your life.'

I rolled my eyes. I hoped this wasn't going to come down to a brief catty exchange of views, and a blood-bath to follow.

'I've just explained to your sainted son,' said Kate, 'that I have the advantage of complete ruthlessness. I'll sacrifice this dun and everyone in it.'

'No, you won't. Not if my son goes into exile, and I go with him.'

I actually couldn't breathe. I thought someone had kicked me in the gut. From the look of him, Conal felt exactly the same.

Leonora's sweetness was very like Kate's.

'Can we talk?'

Only four people ever knew what happened in those negotiations between Kate and Leonora. They spoke quietly, reasonably, like old friends discussing their childhood, and no-one else, I'm certain, overheard. That was an advantage for both sides. At the time it was. Later I wondered.

'I know what you're thinking, Leonora,' Kate told her.

'I should hope so. You wouldn't be much of a Sithe queen if you didn't.'

Kate gave a low laugh. 'That's disingenuous of you, Leonora, to say the very least. Now, I've been where you have been, and seen who you have seen, and I know all that you know.'

'Do you indeed?'

'She told me everything. She told me all she told you, Leonora.'

'That surprises me.' Leonora raised her left hand to the raven, and it rubbed its beak affectionately against her skin.

'It shouldn't. I had so much help from Skinshanks. It's very persuasive.'

'So the prophet's dead now?' Leonora sounded regretful, but not exactly devastated.

'Of course she is. And you won't find it.'

'The Stone?'

A chill crept down my spine, as if a Lammyr had walked on my grave.

'The Stone,' agreed Kate. 'The Bloodstone.'

'Oh, but I will. I'll have the heir of Griogair Dubh at my side, and that's the key, it seems. I can't imagine he'll ever be at yours.'

Conal grinned.

'So you find it.' Kate shrugged. 'Then I'll take it from you.'

'You can try,' I remarked.

Kate smiled at me. This time the chill in my spine made me shiver, visibly.

'The prophet had a few things to say about you too, my little bastard. Little cursed one. The one who would drink the blood of his own mother. One day I'll tell you what else she said, since she was obviously so reliable. Splinter-heart, winter-heart, lover-killer.'

There were a lot of dark night-things walking on my grave, now.

Kate tossed her head, dismissing me and my ill-starred future. 'Did you listen carefully to the old prophet, Leonora? She gave no word to say the Bloodstone will save the Veil. Nothing to indicate it will *preserve* it. It will decide the Veil's fate, that's all. Griogair's heir will find it, and the fate of the Veil will be determined. Not by the finder, you understand. By whoever holds it at the right time. So be my guest.' Kate wagged a playful finger. 'Take your son and find the Stone, and don't come back till you do.'

'The dun,' gritted Conal. 'If this is up to me, I want guarantees.'

'Oh, she won't destroy this dun,' said Leonora coolly. 'You see, it's the only thing on earth that matters to me more than the Veil. I don't want civil war, but I can be ruthless too. Kate will not destroy Griogair's dun or his people. If she dares to try in our absence, I'll come back here and destroy her. And she knows it. Don't you, Kate, dear?'

Kate's eyes glittered, her face frozen with fear and hate. 'So, Cù Chaorach. The survival of your dun and your clann depends entirely on your exile. For as long as it takes to bring me what I want.'

'And the autonomy and security of my dun is guaranteed?'

'Till your mother dies,' said Kate.

'Till I die,' agreed Leonora, smiling. 'Watch me live.'

'Must I?'

'Oh, yes. For a very long time.'

'Though you saw what Lilith did?' Kate's laugh was rippling and lovely, but brittle. 'You were here, weren't you, Leonora? You saw, you heard. You know what she has done to you.'

Leonora gave a shrug, though from where I stood, there seemed to be a weight of lead on her shoulders.

'Yes. It makes no difference. I live on, and so does the dun.'

'Only if your son and all his blood relatives leave for the otherworld.'

'Agreed. And while we're gone, you will not cross the border of the dun lands. You or any of your allies.'

Kate licked a fingertip, and held it high, shutting one eye as if testing the wind speed.

'What a dangerous woman you are, Leonora. You know what makes you so dangerous?'

Leonora only lifted an eyebrow. The raven tilted its head at Kate.

'You do want to die, that's the thing.' Kate's smile looked real this time. 'You'd actually prefer to die.'

Leonora smiled too.

'It gives you insane courage, a deathwish like that.' Kate tapped her fingertips against her cheek, then pointed first at Conal, then at me. 'But it makes you very dangerous to them too, doesn't it? How long will it be before you give in to the call?'

'Watch me live,' said Leonora.

40

'You can stay,' I told Catriona. 'You don't have to
come. You're happy here and you're safe in the dun.
You can stay.'

It was only words. She knew it and so did I.

'With you,' she said. 'That's where I'm happy.'

She ran her fingertip across the healed scar on my
chest. I kissed her. 'Good.'

If I'd known. If I'd known. Would I have left her
there?

I pitied Conal. Oh, when I think how I pitied him. He
had to leave his lover, and I did not.

He wouldn't take Eili, wouldn't let her come with
him, because he said the otherworld would kill her,
just the air of it. She was bound to her own world as
she was to a lover, and besides, she was already in pos-
session of another male soul. Her loss would destroy
Sionnach. His would ruin her. Both of them were tied

to one world by the only names they owned: taking them out of it would kill them both. Conal refused to bind to her.

'When I come back for good,' he said as she wept into his chest. 'Then.'

'What do you mean, *for good?*' I'd overheard him, and I had my misgivings.

'You think we won't come back?' He was almost savage. 'I won't stay away from here. Nor will you. We'll see it again, Seth. *Often.* One day we'll come back for good, but before then, oh gods, we'll see it again.'

'As long,' said Leonora dryly, 'as Kate never sees *you.*'

On the banks of the watergate, Reultan wept bitter tears, but she was bound to Aonghas, and of course she followed him. She'd have followed him to the gates of Hell; and in the end, I suppose she did.

I watched Leonora go into the little loch, and I watched my brother. Closing my eyes, I imagined them stepping out into the rain-soaked forested wetland, green and lovely, drenched in the colours of bank and tree and sky. I thought that perhaps life in the other-world would not be so bad. The watergate on that side was beautiful; there was no better place to arrive.

We'd go east, Conal said, where people did not know us. We'd settle on the shores of an eastern firth, and live quietly behind the dwindling Veil, and we'd hunt for Leonora's damned Stone, and when we couldn't bear our exile any more we'd creep home for a time like thieves.

Kate's patience was limitless. So, said Leonora, was hers.

Under the bluest Sithe sky, streaked with tattered cirrus and paling to infinity, I twined my fingers into Catriona's and smiled at her. She touched my lips with gentle fingers, and I kissed her. The day could not have been crueller in its loveliness, so I would not look at the stunning sky and the moor. I looked only at Catriona as I led her into that watergate, and she looked at me, and we went to our fate together. That at least we did together.

I wasn't looking at her by the time we surfaced and I shook the water from my hair like an otter. Her fingers were still wound into mine, tight and curled, but I was distracted, and shocked, staring at the woodland that was not a woodland. I was looking at bleak moor, and ancient stumps, and a grey sullen sky, and my feet sucked in boggy ground as I waded out of the watergate into our new life. It was changed, so changed. Catriona seemed loath to follow; she was slow, and stumbled at my side, and I tightened my hand on her curled fingers.

Ahead of me Conal had turned on the bank and was looking at me, and I thought there was horror in his eyes, and grief. Aonghas had much the same look. Leonora and Reultan? It was strange, and foreign: their faces held nothing but pity. I laughed.

'Come on,' I said. 'It's not so bad. New beginning and all that.'

Then Catriona stumbled again, and I had to turn to catch her as she almost fell to her knees in the sodden ground. Her fingers still felt strange, knotted and bony, and when she looked up at me, I knew that my mother must be laughing at me now, from wherever she was burning.

I lifted my lover into my arms and buried my face in her wrinkled neck and wept.

Epilogue

I don't know how often, in the so-many years since, I've tried to remember my lover's weary wicked grin and the touch of her dry wrinkleskin fingers on my cheek.

Thirty years, if she's lucky. I remembered Conal's brutal prediction. She hadn't been lucky, of course. She'd met her stepfather, and the priest-Lammyr, and Conal, and me.

I watched my tears dribble into her white seal-skin crop of hair, then pressed my cheek against it. It still felt the same: silky.

~ Don't cry, she said.

The weight of her was nothing. Lying against me she felt like a bird. As if her bones were hollow and I could fletch her with sky-blue wings and she could fly.

Her fingertips caressed my cheek, finding my tears.

~ That summer with you, my lennanshee. And a year with Kate. And two years here! It's more than I wished for, tied to a stake with your brother. It's been enough, my love.

~ *Not for me*, I said.

~ You knew, my love, she told me gently. ~ It was less than we thought but you knew. I'm glad. And I loved you. I'm glad I loved you.

Could she speak to my mind? I don't know. I didn't know any more if I was thinking or speaking, with her. It was all the same.

'Seth?'

'What?'

She hesitated. Perhaps she was catching her failing breath.

'Don't be angry.'

I couldn't answer.

'They're dead, all of them. Don't waste your heart on rage.'

How could I help it? I'd promised myself no end of revenge, on no end of men, but I had been cheated even of that.

'Please? I'm fond of that heart, my lennanshee. Don't waste it. Not for my sake. And they must be dead.'

'There are men like them, Catriona. There always are. Rage isn't wasted.'

'I didn't say, don't waste your rage.' She tilted her head, smiled a tired smile. 'It's your heart that'll waste. And I love it too much.'

I kissed her forehead. I didn't want to stop kissing her. I had to force my lips away from her skin, so I could say:

'I'll give it a try.'

'Good. Will you hold me?'

'Of course I'll hold you. I'm not letting you go.'

'Oh, you'll have to do that, my lover.'

'Call me by my name,' I said.

'Murlainn,' she said, and smiled. 'I'll see our sons.'

'Course you will.' I smiled back at her, then tucked her head close into my shoulder.

'Don't go, Murlainn,' she said. 'Not till I do.'

'You know I won't,' I said. I gritted my teeth. 'I love you.'

'I know that too.'

I had not moved for hours. I hadn't shaved for days, though it's not as if Catriona would care.

I heard his soft knock on the door, but I did not watch Conal come into the room. I stroked Catriona's dry lined cheek over and over. Her lips were a little upturned at the corners, but they seemed less creased than before, her face less lined and weary. I combed my fingers through her white crop, felt the angles of her skull with the palm of my hand. She was beautiful, still beautiful. While she aged with us beyond the Veil, aged in an eyeblink, she'd not had all the beauty beaten out of her by struggle and hunger. She'd aged well. She'd aged well.

Oh, gods, she'd aged. I pressed my wet face to her hair and clenched my teeth.

'Seth.'

I would not look at him, would not let him see my eyes. I blinked, very hard.

'Where will you go?' asked Conal.

I waited till I could speak. 'Up among the stones. It's like where . . . It's like where . . .'

'Where her children are,' he said gently. 'On the other side.'

I nodded. My whole body trembled. Grimly I tightened my arms on her frail body.

'But I mean,' he said, 'I mean, where will you go now?'

Slowly, slowly, I rocked her back and forth in my arms. I had to wait to speak again.

'Did you check for me, Conal? Did you find out?'

'Seth, they're dead. That's the truth. She outlived them all. The guards, the little man from town, her stepfather. All of them.'

'She didn't have so long.' *She had no time at all.*

'No. But she had more, didn't she?'

'I don't know. Did she?'

'Seth. You know it.' Crouching, he pushed my hair back from my eyes.

Furiously I wiped them. 'Go and look for your Stone, Conal. I'm going away for a while. A year or two. All right? I'll care about the Stone again, I'll care about the Veil. I swear I will. Just. Not right now.'

He didn't answer. Then I saw he was weeping too.

'I'll come back,' I said, and managed to smile. 'Don't worry. I'll come back.'

'Please,' he said. 'Please come back.'

He didn't say *soon* and I was glad.

'So you need your bastard brother?' I wiped my nose.

'I always did,' he said. 'I always did.'

'Yeah. I knew that,' I said. 'Call yourself a Captain. Where would you be without me?'

Gently he cuffed my cheekbone. 'Greenarse.'

I gave a desperate laugh.

'Here,' he said. 'I'll help. I loved her too.'

He took Catriona out of my resisting arms, and I stumbled to my feet, and pushed open the door. I filled my lungs with night air, alien but beautiful, and we took her out into the darkness to find her sons.

Turn the page for a preview of

BLOODSTONE

GILLIAN PHILIP

Available in November 2013 from
Tom Doherty Associates

TOR® A TOR BOOK

Seth

'We shouldn't be here,' said Aonghas.

There were so many replies to that one, I didn't know where to start. I kept my mouth shut, and my opinions to myself. My brother wouldn't thank me for starting a squabble. Conal wasn't looking at either me or Aonghas as he pressed his hand to the wet salt-crusted rock face, but I'd seen his shoulders tense with irritation, and I wasn't in a mood to push it.

The cliff face had unnerved him too: he never was good with heights. I'd found the way down and he'd climbed after me, but he hadn't liked it and his edgy temper lingered. I'd thought that being with Eili Mac-Neil last night would have softened his rough edges, but leaving her yet again had only made things worse.

So what? I missed Orach, as much as I was capable of missing anyone. It didn't mean I couldn't soak up the light and the landscape of home, storing it away in my cells for the next long exile. In my head I knew the silver sheen on the water was no different on this side of the Veil, or the shatter of waves on rock, or the clamour of gulls. My heart knew it was a different world: a whisper's breadth and a whole universe away. I'd never stopped missing it and I never would. I'd make the most of it on the chances I got.

Find me the Stone, Kate had said. *Don't come back till you have it.*

We shouldn't be here. But it had never been any other way. We'd stopped short of swearing that we'd never cross the Veil, would never come home till we found the Stone. We'd told Kate we'd stay away, but we'd given no oath.

So we lied. So what? As if we could live without breathing our own air once a decade.

Kate NicNiven must know that as well as we did. And she must suspect that we sneaked through the watergate like thieves now and again, as if we were skulking Lammyr and not the sons of Griogair Dubh. But if our queen wanted to kill us, she'd have to find us first.

It was a game, that was all. It had become our life's game. We risked death every time we played, but if we didn't play, we'd go mad. Anyway, what's life without an adrenaline kick?

I think I liked it better than Conal, though. And Aonghas liked it least of all, especially now.

'I'm serious,' he went on. 'We've been here too long this time.'

'I know that,' snapped Conal.

I gave Aonghas an I-told-you-so look, and he rolled his eyes. They struck me as even greener than usual because of the khaki green of his T-shirt. He also wore ripped jeans, and his sword in a scabbard on his back, and despite his claims to seriousness, a broad irrepressible grin.

He had that wistful look too, gods help us. I knew what was coming.

'You know,' he said, 'we could just stay over there. With the full-mortals. Settle in.'

'Gods' sake. You sound like Reultan.' And who'd have ever thought that proud bitch would become such a convert to the otherworld?

'She likes it over there. And know what? Maybe she's right. Maybe we should just—you know—adapt. It's all right. When's a full-mortal ever tried to harm us?'

I laughed in disbelief. 'Since May last year, you mean?'

'That was your own fault. I'd have got my mates to beat the shit out of you too, if she'd been my girlfriend.'

'So what are you saying? We should leave the Veil to Kate's mercies? Let it die?'

'Course not. But maybe . . . we could let things lie. Keep our heads down. Just for a bit.' He glanced out to sea, embarrassed. 'Till Finn's grown up?'

'Oh, right. It's your baby brain again. Wars don't wait for you to stop breeding, you know.'

'Shut it, you two.' Conal laid his head against the rock, as if he was listening to its voice. 'Sorry,' he muttered. 'But we've come this far. We might as well—Ah!'

Four hundred years on and his sudden smile could still catch me by surprise, could still turn my surliness to a matching grin.

'You found it,' I said, and laughed.
'I found it.'

'Knowledge is power, so it is,' I said as we rode east-wards. 'And Leonora wouldn't want me having that.'

'Ah, get over it. You know now.' Conal looked dis-tracted, but I was angry. The tunnel in the rock could have saved me a lot of hassle, a long time ago. It would have saved me a desperate run across the machair under a too-bright moon, and a climb that nearly killed me, and all to get Conal and me back into our own dun.

'She could have made it easier. It's not like anyone else knows about it.' The Veil had been woven tight, dense, thick as rope around the tunnel entrance, and that was a witch's work. No wonder it had been hard to find.

'And nobody ever should. You can both start working on a block right now. Put it to the back of your minds.'

'Why did you show us now?' Aonghas looked hap-pier, now we were on our way home, but that was un-derstandable.

'She's only just told me about it,' said Conal. 'Believe it or not.'

'And,' I interrupted. 'He's worried about the old bat. *Ow.*' I should have learned by now that if I was going to insult Conal's mother, I should make sure I was more than an arm's length away.

'But, Seth's right.' My brother's voice was all gloom. 'Kate keeps her hands off the dun only because she's scared of Leonora. If anything happens to her—'

'And there's no reason anything should,' pointed out Aonghas.

'Want to bet? She's got that look in her eye.'

Yeah. I'd seen it myself, and I had mixed feelings. Leonora's death was to be dreaded, and she'd already stayed in life three and a half centuries longer than anyone else I'd ever heard of, after the death of a bound lover. It was a hell of an achievement, what with her soul being dragged in Griogair's wake every minute of every day. Didn't make me like her any better, but it *was* an achievement.

All the same, if she gave in and went to her death, our exile would be over, and I wanted it to be over. How long since I'd stopped believing in the Stone? I'd lost count of the decades, if I'd ever believed in it at all. Prophecy, fate, talismans? Horseshit. Leonora and Kate might be the most powerful witches the Sithe had ever known, but they were both in thrall to some mad old soothsayer, and I expect the ancient loon was squawking even crazier nonsense by the time Kate's Lammyr finally killed her. I'd heard what she said about me—try forgetting it, when you live with a superstitious old Sithe-witch—and I shoved it to the back of my mind with the bad grief and the worse jokes and the old guilt, all the other detritus of life. No demented half-dead lunatic was dictating my life choices. Not any more. She'd sent me into a four-hundred-year exile in search of a nonexistent Stone, and that was more than enough.

No bit of rock was going to save the Veil, defeat the queen and return Conal and me to our dun and our people. I knew what was going to do that: fighters and good blades, and the sooner we abandoned the hocus-pocus and pitched into a proper fight, the better it would be.

I was glad to see Conal in a better mood as we rode back towards the watergate. Maybe he was thinking the same as me, at last. Or maybe he was just baby-headed, like his brother-by-binding. When Aonghas actually started to whistle, I couldn't take the surfeit of happiness anymore.

'Do shut up,' I said. 'That's bad luck. And wipe that stupid smile off your face.'

'Ah, leave him alone, Seth. He's soft in the head. It's his hormones.'

'Wasn't him that was pregnant.'

'You'd have thought it was. I swear to the gods, he threw up every morning.'

'And he put on a belly. Still got it, actually.'

'The pair of you can hide up your own arses,' said Aonghas cheerfully, patting his stomach, which to be honest was as thin and hard as mine. Well, maybe I was a little jealous. But he had a right to be happy. They'd waited long enough, him and Reultan.

It was one of those days of intense slanting sunshine and black rain. When the sudden spattering showers lifted, the light would come under the clouds like a torch-beam, bronzing the fields and making the sodden trees glitter. It was pretty. We were home, for now. None of us minded getting wet. We rode with the sun's rays, and I suppose that their dazzle was harsh looking the other way.

Which must have been why the child didn't see us.

It was under Conal's hooves before it realised its

danger, but its impetus carried it stumbling beneath the black horse and safely to the other side, where it tripped and crashed into the bracken. It was already scrambling to its feet, sobbing with terror, and I had to haul on the blue roan's bit to keep it from lunging for the boy. It *was* a boy, though in that state, to the blue roan, it was nothing but prey. Conal's black was showing a hungry interest now, and I could see a food fight coming.

'Don't run!' I shouted, furious. 'Don't run, you stupid little—'

I might as well have yelled at the rain not to fall. The boy—seven or eight, I'd guess—had bolted again; luckily for him, he ran straight towards Aonghas, who simply leaned down and scooped him off his feet and onto his rather more biddable horse, holding him tight in front of him.

'You're fine. Jaysus, child, you're fine, this is a horse, not a—'

Aonghas's words had no more effect than mine; already the boy was hammering him with his fists, biting at his bare arms, struggling and kicking. Aonghas swore and slapped him; the boy slapped him back and gave as good a mouthful of abuse, and Aonghas finally lost his temper and seized the child's forehead with one strong hand. 'Sleep, brat.'

The boy fought him for maybe two seconds, but he was too young to block well, and his body slumped, limp. Well, at least an unconscious child wasn't such a provocation to the black and the blue roan. As the two horses snorted and stamped and calmed a little, Conal stared at Aonghas, and the child, and me.

'What in the name of the gods? Doesn't he know a frigging kelpie when he sees one? Don't his parents–?'

I looked beyond him, and nodded. 'Wasn't us he was scared of.'

We fell silent as we watched the smoke curl beyond the brow of the hill. Now we could hear screams, the thwack and chunk of blades hitting flesh, the hungry crackle of building flame.

Conal lifted his thumb and forefinger, maybe an inch between them.

'This close,' he said through gritted teeth. 'We are *this close* to the dun lands.'

'But not within them.' Aonghas eyed him.

'Chancers,' hissed Conal. 'How feckin' *dare they*.'

Aonghas said, 'We can take the child. Get him away. More sensible.'

I stayed out of it. It was Aonghas's place to counsel him, not mine. But hell, I was hoping he'd lose the argument.

Actually, I think he was, too. A bit.

'Aonghas, listen to it.'

Aonghas cocked his head. 'Three of them. Four, maximum.'

'And they're not expecting us.' Conal was seething.

The roan was behaving now. It had forgotten the boy, and was yearning and tossing its head towards the sounds and smells of a fight. I patted its pearly neck.

'And famously,' I said, 'I'm a one-man army, me.'

Aonghas rolled his eyes. 'I had to try.'

Conal grinned, or rather he bared his teeth. 'Yes, you did. But you stay here with the child. Me and the one-man army'll do this.'

'Aw, come on—'

'An order.' Conal winked. 'I'm not half as scared of you as I am of my sister.'

Aonghas looked down at the unconscious boy in his arms, a smile tugging his mouth. Yup: baby-brained. 'Well, do it fast. I don't want to have to come in and save your arse, not with a child on board.'

They were not expecting us. They were expecting nothing but poorly armed farmers, who must have refused to give up tithes to Kate or one of her captains. The crofter was dead already, but the captain of the raiding party hadn't yet put his sword through an older boy; he was still gripping him by the neck while the youth kicked for air.

'Put him down,' barked Conal, and made him do it.

The leader's death left us only one each, and a spare, and Conal was in enough of a rage not to share nicely. He was flinging himself off the black and slamming the third one to the ground, his teeth grinding in the man's ear while I was still chasing down the last panicking horseman and trying not to harm the even smaller child screaming under his arm.

The fighter backed his horse into a corner by a burning shed, and as if that wasn't stupid enough, he dropped the child. I didn't bother with my blade after that, or only to strike his sword out of his hand. He was so scared of the roan, he was barely watching me, so I grabbed the neck of his shirt, pulled him to me and punched him as hard as I could. And again. And again.

I was still punching when Conal yanked my other sleeve. 'Wasting time,' he said, and spat out another bit of ear. 'Get that child. Its mother's alive.'

Its mother was half-blind with blood and grief and rage, but she was indeed alive and she had enough wits about her to know she shouldn't have been. And she didn't have a choice now, and anyway her croft was gone and her beasts slaughtered along with her lover. She took the smallest infant from my arms, and the middle boy from Aonghas's, and she and the older boy scraped up weapons from the raiders' bodies and limped in the direction Conal showed them. Our dun was two days' walk at most, and they wouldn't be safe outside it.

I was sucking on my bruised and skinned fist by now, and sulking at my own stupidity.

'Stings?' Conal winked. 'Eejit.'

'Don't listen to him,' Aonghas told me. 'You've got style.'

'I know I have. He's jealous.'

'You've got style, and he's stuck with morals. Course he's jealous.'

I laughed. 'You say morals, I say politics.'

'Cynic.'

I was still grinning at Aonghas as his laughter died. He wasn't looking at me any more; he'd raised his head to stare across the burning croft. I felt my heart shrink.

'Conal!' he yelled.

Conal rode to our side, staring with us at the distant riders. They were coming on fast; perhaps the remainder of this patrol. I'd wondered why there were so few of them. 'Damn. Let's go.'

'It's okay. They haven't seen us.'

'No, but they'll have to. We'll have to draw them off. *Shit.*'

Well, of course we would. We knew what would happen if this new patrol caught up with that woman and her children. I swore through my teeth, just to relieve my feelings, and then we put our heels to our horses' flanks and rode for it.

We crossed their line of sight in the full flare of that late sun and the burning buildings. They couldn't miss us, and we couldn't miss their shouts of shock and triumph.

'Cù Chaorach! Cù Chaorach, you rebel bastard!'

It wasn't a chance they'd pass up. Every one of them came after us, and I had time to be glad the crofting family were out of it, and to regret my brother's suicidal altruism for maybe the five hundredth time. Then there was only time to draw breath and ride.

There were trees ahead, and that made it easy for us. The roan leaped a fallen log and we plunged in among birks and thick undergrowth, Conal to my right and Aonghas to my left. I saw them only as blurred movement broken by silver trunks, and I could hear only my pounding blood, and the roan's hooves, and the yells and the thunder of pursuit.

It was fine. As I risked a glance over my shoulder, I knew it really was fine. Relief hurtled through me on a giddy high and I let myself whoop. We'd been far enough ahead and we'd taken them by surprise; we were going to outpace them with ease. I knew this land and I knew where Conal was heading as I swerved the roan around a slalom of birk trunks. He'd taken a wide arc round but we were almost on the northeast edge of the dun lands now, back on our own territory, and Kate's patrol would never follow there.

As we broke from the trees and galloped headlong onto the high moor, I almost laughed. Luck had held solid for Conal again. Beyond the saddleback hill I knew I would see the first boundary stone of the dun lands. Thank the gods for fast horses and stupid enemies.

Their frustrated yells were growing more distant, and as I saw the boundary stone flash past my left foot, I knew that one by one, the pursuing riders were drawing up. There was a strange note to their shouts, though; a funny mixture of disappointment and triumph. I didn't have time to think about it. I goaded the roan down a rocky slope and into the next belt of trees, Conal a neck ahead of me and Aonghas at my heels.

A few hundred yards on, Conal reined the black horse to a halt and spun to face me, laughing. The roan danced to a stop at his side and we turned to meet Aonghas, grinning.

He was upright on the horse's back, so for a moment I thought I was seeing things. He was playing some stupid joke. Typical, but a bit inappropriate in the circumstances. My grin froze, and I felt it die.

Aonghas was looking at Conal with regret and aching grief. A smile trembled at the corner of his mouth, and a bead of blood. His khaki T-shirt was stained wet, and the stain was spreading onto his jeans. Everything was so vivid in that slanting light, and I'll never forget the colours: the green of Aonghas's T-shirt and the brighter green of his eyes, the dark mud red of the spreading stain, and the inch of quivering silver that stuck out from his ribs.

'Aonghas,' I said.

He said nothing. His voice was already gone, and his life went as Conal hauled him off his horse and into his arms, weeping and screaming his name.

I wanted to say something: I wanted to tell Conal that the jutting point of the blade was hacking at his chest, mingling his blood with Aonghas's, but I don't think he'd have cared. I think, just then, he'd have taken the whole foul thing in his own heart, if it would only bring Aonghas back.

I had to hand it to Griogair's women: they were tough. Hard as permafrost. What were their souls made of, Reultan and Leonora? Steel in the genes.

It wasn't that Reultan didn't want to follow Aonghas. It was just like her mother when Griogair was killed: she made herself stay. And she did have a choice. Whatever any full-mortal thinks, she had a choice. We'd have taken the child and raised it; not my vocation, I grant you, but we'd have done it. I reckon we'd have made a better job of it.

Maybe if it had been Conal alone, she'd have left the child with him. But she had to factor me into the equation, and I knew that was what she did that day at Tornashee, in that drawing room flooded with summer sunlight.

Her eyes were bloodshot and she clutched the infant against her like some sort of lifeline. It was an ugly little thing, black-haired with startled eyes, but it was endearing when it wasn't squalling. It fascinated me. I could imagine growing to love it, the way you do with babies. The rest of the prediction was inconceivable, but Reultan must have feared it anyway. She couldn't look at me, but she was glaring at Conal with inextinguishable rage and grief.

'She'll stay here,' she hissed. 'Fionnuala stays here, where she's safe. Forever, Conal. Do you hear me?'

'I hear you, Reultan. I—'

'Don't call me that! *Ever again.*'

'Reul—Stella, don't make decisions now. Please. It's not the time.'

'Yes. It is. And you will never tell Finn about that—other place. Never. She's what's left of Aonghas, and she's staying with me. *Shut up, Seth!*'

I held up my hands. 'I never—'

'It's none of your business. Stay away from my child. She's nothing to do with you.'

'I know that. I—'

My block was down and it was a cheap shot, but she took it, knocking me physically backwards with the force of her contempt. I rubbed my temples, trying not to curse out loud, to make allowance for her grief. But I was afraid of her, now; afraid of what she might do.

'Get it through your stupid heads,' she hissed. 'Kate cannot be beaten. I was her friend and adviser for seven decades, and you *will not beat her*. And I? I've betrayed her for love, and my lover is dead. She has half her vengeance. If I go back there, she'll take the other half, and it isn't me she'll kill. I know her better than any of you. She's too cruel to kill me.'

'Stella, we'll protect the baby. You know it—'

'Damn right you will, and this is how. Listen to me, Conal,' she snarled. 'All of you. I swear on my life. You are my witnesses, and I *swear* I will never go back there.'

I stared at her. ~ *Don't. Please.*

Me, begging Reultan. For the first time, and the last.

Deliberately, coldly, she turned her back on me. 'I will never cross the Veil again. On my oath, Conal. On my *life.*'

In the silence, I heard the unaccustomed sound of Leonora weeping.

'Stella,' whispered Conal. 'What have you done?'

TOR

Voted

#1 Science Fiction Publisher
25 Years in a Row

by the *Locus* Readers' Poll

———•———

Please join us at the website below
for more information about this
author and other science fiction,
fantasy, and horror selections, and to
sign up for our monthly newsletter!

 TOR

www.tor-forge.com